The Forgotten Dead

Ferguson Shaw

Copyright © Ferguson Shaw 2013

All Rights Reserved

Cover photograph and design copyright
© Ferguson Shaw 2013

To Amy and to Cerys.

For changing everything.

And showing me what was missing.

Our dead are never dead to us until we have forgotten them.

- George Eliot

Chapter One

It started with the letter.
Just a letter.
A few words on a sheet of paper. A note, in effect.

Nothing more, and yet everything unravelled from there like a ball of twine spilled from lifeless fingers.

At least, that's where it began for me. I found out later that it had been building long before then; gathering strength in the dark parts of the mind. Creeping up on the ones involved – whether they realised their involvement or not – yet remaining hidden in that spot just outside their peripheral vision where they could feel... *something*.

So many acts of wickedness had been perpetrated by the time I saw the letter. Acts of premeditated cruelty, spontaneous violence, and casual brutality. And the victims would in turn scatter the remnants of those deeds in the wind like toxic ash.

And so it would continue.

But I knew nothing of this when she brought the note to me, and nothing more when I agreed to take the case. There were plenty of good reasons to decline, and what few there were to accept were ones I didn't care to examine too closely.

Even as I waited for the source of the letter to reveal himself, I tried not to think about my motivations, focusing instead on my surroundings.

He – assuming it was a he – probably thought he'd chosen a great venue for the payoff. George Square, bang in the heart of Glasgow's city centre, was usually busy, and at a little before one p.m. on a Tuesday afternoon in the hottest July for twenty years it was positively heaving.

With a mob of humanity basking in the sun – from office workers cramming in a precious sixty minutes of rays on their lunch break, to summer students deciding their next class wasn't all that important after all, to shoppers taking a well-earned break from the sweaty business of lugging plastic carrier bags between shops – there was plenty of cover. And if he was challenged, well, no-one needed a reason to be in George Square when the sun was splitting the sky, did they?

The square was mere moments from Queen Street railway station and the Buchanan Street subway station, either of which would have him far from here in a matter of minutes. Central Station was only a little further, bus stops were handy, as was the taxi rank at Queen Street. He could even have parked nearby if he was lucky, though the volume of traffic and the difficulty of a quick getaway by car made that unlikely.

But it was too busy. It might have given him cover, but it did exactly the same for me.

And I was better at this than he was.

I'd been sitting at a window of the Millennium Hotel, nursing a sandwich and a can of Irn-Bru, for ninety minutes before the scheduled time of the meeting, cunningly alleviating the suspicions of the staff by poring over the job section of one of the thicker broadsheets with a depressed look on my face. In all honesty, if I didn't start picking up more cases soon that might become more than just a cover.

I flicked to the classified section to check my advert was still being printed – the other reason, besides camouflage, that I'd bought the paper in the first place – and found it festering there in all its unimaginative glory: *Keir Harper Investigations*, with my office number printed below it in plain text.

The irony of a private investigator specialising in finding people yet being unable to find more paying clients was not lost on me.

But we were still hip-deep in a recession and the truth seemed to be one of those luxury items that most people had decided they could do without. That was my livelihood: non-essential.

It wasn't a comfortable spot, here in the window – not with

the sun blazing through the glass – but from my table I had a view across the entire square, and reducing the risk of being spotted by the blackmailer was worth feeling like a ready meal in a microwave. I'd already scrutinised the crowd around me in case he'd had the same idea, but the elderly couples and the knots of ladies-who-lunch didn't seem likely suspects.

Of course, the task would have been easier if I could have asked Nicole's dad for a description of the guy he paid off the last time. But since Gordon Dunbar had been missing for the best part of a week that wasn't an option. I didn't think he knew about this proposed meeting, but I kept an eye open for him all the same.

The letter had demanded the money be handed over beneath the statue of Sir Walter Scott, perched atop his eighty foot column in the centre of the square, but I doubted even the most foolish extortionist would stand waiting at the designated spot until the police slapped on the handcuffs. Giving the blackmailer more credit than he perhaps deserved, I relaxed into the almost Zen-like state that helps maintain my sanity when on surveillance. I let my eyes wander, waiting for them to register anything strange or suspicious. I wasn't sure exactly what I was looking for, but I'd know it when I saw it.

I saw it at exactly five to one.

He hadn't been there on my last visual lap, but now he was lurking at the back of the cenotaph. Hard to miss a guy dressed in a burgundy Adidas tracksuit top over a striped shirt with flared collar and chocolate brown cords. Add in the slicked back black hair, down to his collar, and the bandit moustache round his pointed chin, and he was pretty much the first person in the square who caught the eye.

Apparently I *had* been giving him too much credit.

He skulked around behind the cenotaph for a few minutes, occasionally glancing behind him in the direction of the City Chambers, sometimes flicking quick looks at the four corners of the square, sneaking peeks at his watch, but always – always – his eyes returned to the base of Sir Walter's column.

Subtle.

It was five past one by the time he ventured away from his post and began to make his way around the square, by which time I was certain that Nicole's father wasn't here. I dug in my pocket and dropped a few coins on the table as I hurried to the door. As I reached the street, I headed straight for a space that had opened up on a bench. I waited until I was seated and had my newspaper unfolded before I looked around for the bandit. I found him sauntering round the square, making an embarrassingly poor attempt at nonchalance. The sleeves of his trackie top were pushed up to the elbows, his narrow shoulders thrust back as though he hadn't a care in the world. But his hands gave him away: one was jammed deep into the pocket of his cords, fidgeting continuously with what I hoped was loose change; the other cupped desperately around a badly made roll-up as though he'd used the world's last match to light it and the slightest gust could have catastrophic repercussions.

I watched from behind my paper as he made a circuit of the square. I'm an ordinary guy – average height and build, short brown hair, a light stubble most days, jeans and a navy t-shirt with no logo today – and I knew how to blend into a crowd. But this guy was so oblivious to me that I could have hitched a lift by climbing on his back and he'd probably still have been none the wiser.

By the time he'd made it back to the cenotaph the cigarette was done and a look of simmering fury was stamped on his sharp features. Gone was the easygoing stride as he stomped off along the top of the square in the direction of Queen Street station. I got to my feet as he passed, tucked the newspaper under my arm and fell into step behind him. He crossed the street towards the station but didn't enter and continued instead towards Buchanan Street and its horde of shoppers and strollers. I hung back, following the greasy black hair as it wound its way through the throng and disappeared into the shadows of the subway.

I descended the stairs and found him at the ticket booth, counting out small change and sliding it under the window. I walked quickly to one of the automated ticket machines and pretended to fumble for coins.

The best thing about the Glasgow subway from my point of view was the flat fare regardless of how far round the circular route you travelled, or which of the fifteen stations you travelled to. Unlike trains and buses there was no need to awkwardly sidle up next to the target in an attempt to hear his destination. And since every train on the clockwork orange stopped at every station, all I had to do was faff around with the ticket machine until he'd chosen the outer or inner circle.

The blackmailer finally stepped away from the window and headed straight for the outer circle. He didn't stop to read the list of stations to check whether the clockwise or anti-clockwise line was quicker, suggesting he knew the route well. With any luck he was on his way home, and when I had his address I'd have his name. I got my ticket and headed in the same direction, noting from the station list that Ibrox was as far as he could go or the inner circle would have been quicker.

As I hit the escalator people started coming up the stairs from the platform and I broke into a jog to make sure I caught the train. I saw the bandit stepping into the second carriage and I slid through the nearest doors just before they closed, squashed between a middle-aged woman with a baby and a well-built guy with mirrored sunglasses and a shaved head who dived in behind me. The guy gave me a funny look and sat down halfway along the carriage, playing with his goatee and trying furiously to pretend he hadn't just been pressed up against me.

I walked along the carriage and took a seat beside the next set of doors, from where I could see through the window into the next carriage where my target was sitting. His face was pinched in annoyance. Mind you, if I'd just been stiffed for ten grand I'd be pretty hacked off too.

A few minutes later we pulled into St Enoch and the train, as usual, slammed to a halt. Glasgow subway drivers had yet to master the art of gently slowing to a stop. A few people got up and left the train, and several more got on, but my target didn't move.

The train started up again, equally smoothly, and sped to Bridge Street, where we repeated the same process: people alighted, others boarded, but the bandit and I stayed in our seats. More stops came and went – West Street, Shields Road, Kinning Park – then, as the train pulled into Cessnock, he glanced up to read the name of the station. He didn't get up, but he sat a little straighter, suggesting the next stop – Ibrox – must be his destination. Either that or the idiot had gone a long way for a shortcut.

Sure enough, he got to his feet as the train hurtled into Ibrox, swaying and grabbing the handrail as the driver stood on the brakes and the train leant forwards. I got up and stepped out after him. Several others got off too and I slowed to let a few fill the space between us as we ascended to ground level.

The brightness of the sun was startling after the fluorescent strip lighting in the subway, forcing us all to blink and screw up our eyes as we stepped into daylight. The blackmailer stopped in the doorway to the station, ignorant to the obstruction he was creating for his fellow passengers as he pulled a tobacco pouch from his pocket and slipped a ready made roll-up from beneath the band and between his lips. He flicked the lighter and touched the jittering flame to the cigarette with a pitiful desperation.

I busied myself at the kiosk while he got his fix, buying two bars of chocolate to supplement the sandwich I'd watched slowly bake. By the time I received my change he was on the move and shambling along the sun-drenched street. He looked more relaxed now. Maybe he was nearly home, or maybe the nicotine was easing his woes.

We passed a smattering of pedestrians strolling in the sun, a few kids kicking a ball around half-heartedly, until several minutes and a few turned corners later, he turned onto the path to a rundown tenement building. The weeds and overgrown grass beside the path snatched at his feet as he strolled over the cracked slabs and in through a close door that was missing its lock. I carried on along the street and turned at the next corner, stopping to lean against a buckled metal fence when I was far enough away not to arouse suspicion, but still within sight of the building.

I took out my phone and held it to my ear, helloing loudly as I carried on a one-sided conversation with myself: no-one pays any attention to a man pacing around while chatting on his mobile. I wandered in a semi-circle until I faced the building my target had entered. It was a down-trodden block, its appearance improved slightly by the sun bathing its outer walls with a brightness that masked the years of disrepair.

It was the onslaught of the sun I was banking on.

As I'd passed the building I'd noticed none of the windows were open. And with the sun beating down those front rooms must be sweltering. I was hoping he'd feel the need to let in some air.

Sure enough, before thirty seconds had passed a scrawny, burgundy-tracksuited arm pushed open a window on the first floor. A sharp face and droopy moustache followed it as both arms hung over the window frame, a can of beer in one hand, a fresh roll-up in the other, obviously very much at home.

Gotcha.

Chapter Two

The street I stood on was deserted, and, apart from a team of kids charging in and out of the blackmailer's building, so was the street he lived on – what I could see of it anyway – but that just made me more exposed. My target was no longer hanging out of his window, but I couldn't stay there long without attracting someone's attention. I perched on a low stone wall, dispensed with my imaginary phone call and placed a real one. The phone barely blipped at the other end before the call was connected.

'Brownstone,' said a voice I knew well.

'How's my favourite hacker?' I asked brightly.

'Not a hacker, Harper,' sighed the young female voice on the other end.

'Yeah, yeah, tell it to the cops.'

'Like they'd ever find me,' she scoffed. 'Anyway, I'm guessing this isn't a social call. What d'you need?'

'I've got an address and I need to know who lives there.'

'Fire away.'

I gave her the address and added, 'The flat's on the first floor, left-hand side.'

'No problem. How soon do you need it?'

'I'm kind of in an awkward position here…'

'You do surprise me,' she sighed. 'Give me a few minutes.'

She ended the call and disappeared into her own vast world of facts and databases, scouring the ether for the blackmailer's name.

This was information I could find myself, though not as easily while on the street, and certainly nowhere near as quickly as

Brownstone could. She was my trump card, my joker in the pack, whether it was intelligence I needed on the move like this, or simply something that no-one else could get. She'd acquired a powerful reputation in certain circles as the person who could get you anything you needed. For a price.

For me there was no price, no matter how many times I insisted on paying the going rate. Well, maybe not her normal rates – which would put her out of the range of several small countries – but something more my speed. As it was, she refused to accept any payment from me, and happily helped me at a moment's notice. And no matter how many times I told her she had repaid any perceived debt a hundredfold, she still felt she owed me.

Brownstone had run away from home at seventeen and her parents had hired me to find her. Which I did. In a Manchester crack den. They hadn't, however, hired me to hospitalise the worthless piece of trash who'd hooked her on heroin and was pimping her to anyone with loose change in their pocket. That had been a freebie.

Six years later and she was clean, and, though a dedicated agoraphobic who refused to meet people face to face, a renowned – and self-taught – expert in finding anything that had ever been in the vicinity of a computer, anywhere in the world. And I was one of the few people privileged enough to know her real name, though I never used it. She'd chosen Brownstone as a constant reminder of the drug that had almost destroyed her, and it was the only name she ever used.

And yet, for all I was glad of her help, this didn't require her specialist skills and I was saddened that I'd had to call her. Out on the street like this I should have phoned Jessica. But I'd been losing her these last few months. I didn't blame her – she'd been through something that would have left most people unable to get out of bed – but between her drinking and insomnia, and the days that oscillated between black despair and forced exuberance, I never knew what Jessica was going to turn up.

There had been a day when I was certain Jessica would become my partner in the business, given time. I had asked her to work with me and she had rejected the idea, convinced it was a charity offer. Now, there was an awkwardness between us, and I didn't know what could overcome it. We were too far along a path we hadn't known we were on until neither of us could risk our friendship by trying to save it.

My phone vibrated suddenly in my hand.

'Got him,' Brownstone said as I answered. 'Sean Reardon, sole occupant.'

'Brilliant. Any info on him?'

There was a pause. 'No. I never thought to actually find out anything about him. I thought we'd just guess.'

Whoops. 'Sorry. Carry on.'

'As I was saying. Sean Reardon, forty-two years old. Five foot seven, ten stone. Longish black hair, dodgy moustache, looks like he only just failed the audition for the 118 adverts.'

'That's him.'

'Okay, here's the good stuff. His record goes back twenty-odd years. All petty stuff, but he'll nick anything that isn't nailed down – cars, sat navs, mobiles, tills, wallets, purses, anything that looks easy pickings. Nothing violent though.'

'How long's he been out?'

'Two months. Lifted a charity box off a shop counter and done a runner. Of course, the lad in the shop ran marathons for cancer research, so Reardon didn't get far and ended up with three months in Greenock for his trouble.'

'Any word on what he's been up to since he got out?'

'Nothing. Either he's been behaving...'

'Or he hasn't been caught.'

'Seems more likely. Maybe he's getting smarter.'

'Doesn't look like it.'

I thanked Brownstone and hung up. It appeared straightforward: Reardon was a petty, lowlife thief who'd somehow got lucky and found out something about Nicole's father and had tried to blackmail him with it. The harder questions were what that information was, and why the victim had gone missing.

Of course, there was only one way to find out: ask nicely.

I walked back to Reardon's building where his window

remained open, allowing dance music to thump into the street. The missing lock on the close door worked in my favour but the stench of urine in the close was probably a more effective deterrent anyway.

A series of loud thuds came from the floor above and seconds later four young boys charged down the stairs and barrelled past me, their faces flushed with excitement and laughter. I waited till the last had cleared the stairs before climbing up and reaching the first floor just as a door was thrown open and a voice shouted, 'Bloody little bastards!'

A pair of angry eyes looked at me in surprise. I smiled at the elderly Asian man and his shoulders slumped. 'Bloody kids,' he mumbled.

'Giving you a hard time, eh?'

'Bloody parents should be locked up. Might as well be for all the time they're around.'

I made sympathetic noises as he turned and shuffled back into his flat and closed the door behind him with an air of defeat. I felt sorry for him, being victimised by youths too young for the police to deal with but old enough to know their own rights while conveniently ignoring everyone else's.

I turned to the flat opposite and pushed the little darlings from my mind as I knocked sharply on the door. There was no response for half a minute and I knocked again. Through the thin door I heard movements, then the music was switched off and feet came stomping towards the door. The door was thrown open and the man with the droopy moustache looked at me with barely concealed anger.

'Fuck you want?' he demanded.

'Sean Reardon?' I asked.

'What's it ab…' he paused, engaged his brain. 'Naw, he's not in.'

'Sure.' My expression told him how believable that was. 'Can I come in?'

'What? Naw. Piss off.'

'I'll take that as a yes.' I placed my hand in the centre of his chest and flexed my wrist. He stepped back embarrassingly easily and I followed him into the flat.

'Hey! What you doing?' he demanded as I closed the door behind me. 'Who the fuck are you?'

'My name is Keir Harper. I'm a private investigator.' I herded him backwards and he unconsciously turned left into his living room. 'Now take a seat.'

'Get the fuck out of my flat!' he shouted, hoping volume might overcome the tremble in his voice. It didn't.

I took a hold of his shoulder and pushed him into the armchair furthest from the door. I left the room and closed the door behind me before quickly checking the rest of the small flat to make sure he didn't have any friends visiting. The place was empty.

I'd just finished checking the last room when the living room door was yanked open and Reardon dashed into the hall. As he ran for the door I took two quick strides in the short hallway and pushed him between the shoulder blades. He lost his balance and thumped into the front door. I pulled him back towards the living room and propelled him across the room. That was four times I'd pushed him now and not once had he made any attempt to stop me.

'I told you to take a seat.'

'That's it,' he said, almost firmly. 'I'm calling the cops.'

'Go ahead.' I took a seat in the armchair beside the door.

It was a small room, and sparsely furnished. Other than the two armchairs at opposite ends of the room there was a huge flat-screen TV bolted to one wall and a state-of-the-art games console on the floor beneath it – both off the back of one lorry or another no doubt – and a small beer fridge in the far corner with a tall, glass-bowled uplighter beside it. The rest of the rooms had been similarly bare when I'd poked my head in.

Reardon was still looking from me to the phone where it sat on the floor beside the other chair, his eyes narrowed slightly as he tried to work out what I'd do if he picked it up. The answer was nothing. The man was a career criminal who'd graduated to extortion. He was no more likely to call the police than I was.

He lunged at the phone and picked it up. 'Last chance.'

I nodded in the direction of the beer fridge. 'You got any soft drinks in there?'

His brow creased in confusion.

'I've been at George Square all day waiting for you, and I've followed you all the way here. It's hot out there. A cold can would go down pretty well right now.'

He looked at me some more, but the hand holding the phone fell to his side.

'You're not going to call the police,' I told him.

He sighed and tossed the phone onto the armchair. 'Coke or Sprite.'

'Sprite, thanks.'

He opened the fridge and tossed me a can, then sat down with a beer, popped the top and took a long gulp. I did the same with the Sprite.

'So, tell me about Gordon Dunbar,' I said.

'Don't know him.'

'Maybe not, but you're blackmailing him.'

'Blackmail? Not my style.'

'No, I didn't think so either. Not after seeing your record. But,' I reached into my pocket and took out a folded piece of paper, handed it to him, 'there's this.'

He glanced at it and tried to muster up a look of surprise. After a long moment though, he gave up, shook his head and handed the copy of the blackmail letter back. 'Never seen it before.'

I took the paper and looked at it again, though the words were imprinted on my mind.

TUESDAY 10/07
GEORGE SQUARE. MIDDLE STATUE. 1PM
10K THIS TIME
OR I TELL EVERYONE

'You know,' I said, 'I was almost disappointed it wasn't made from letters cut out of magazines.'

'Never seen it before.' He shrugged, getting comfortable in the belief I had nothing concrete.

Comfort could be a fleeting thing though.

I jumped up, took two steps and knocked the can of beer from his hand. I grabbed him by the front of his tracksuit top and lifted him to his feet, bringing his face close to mine.

'What are you blackmailing him about?'

His eyes widened as it dawned on him that he wasn't dealing with the police and I might not be as bothered about evidence as they would. I let him go and he slid pathetically to the floor. 'What are you blackmailing him about?' I repeated.

'Why don't you ask him?'

'Because he's missing.'

'Missing?' he whispered. 'What's happened to him?'

'Worried about your ten grand?'

Reardon didn't answer. His eyes flitted around the flat, ignoring the now empty beer can and the foamy puddle beside it.

'How much did he pay you the first time?'

Again, no answer. Reardon began to look worried; he got to his feet, unconsciously nibbling at his fingernails. 'Missing?' he whispered to himself. 'Fuck.'

It wasn't exactly an admission, but it wasn't far off. There was genuine anger in Reardon's eyes and I wondered what he'd already spent that money on.

There was a sudden knock at the front door and Reardon's head whipped in that direction.

'You expecting anyone?' I asked.

'Yeah,' he lied. 'I better answer it, they know I'm in.'

I debated whether or not to let him answer the door. He'd almost certainly try to make a run for it...

'Coming!' he shouted at the top of his lungs.

Damn.

Reardon looked at me smugly. Now I had to let him answer the door or the person on the other side would become suspicious. I stood up and hauled him to his feet.

'Right, you wee prick. You go to the door and you tell them to piss off and come back later. I don't care who it is, you get rid of them. Tell them anything different I'll break your arms, alright? And don't even think about running. You make me run in this heat and I'll break your legs as well. Got it?'

He nodded, but his eyes were calculating. He didn't know what he was going to do yet – it would depend on who was at his door – but he was going to try something.

I stood in the doorway to the living room as Reardon went to the door. It was a short hallway; if he ran he'd only have a few yards head start and I knew I could catch him.

Reardon put his hand on the door handle and began to turn it. I tensed, prepared for him to run. The door opened and he looked out. I was on my toes, ready for a chase.

What I wasn't ready for was the boom of a gunshot.

Or the sight of Reardon's head being blown apart.

Chapter Three

The roar of the gunshot was still ringing in my ears as Reardon's body crumpled to the floor, the back of his head striking the laminate floor with a wet thud.

The door was thrown back against the inner wall and a gun barrel thrust toward me. I saw the shaved head and mirrored sunglasses behind it and recognised the well-built man from the subway. I kicked against the opposite wall, propelling myself backwards into the living room as two more bullets tore chunks from the doorframe. I landed hard on my back and swung my foot, kicking the door shut.

My breath came heavy and ragged. Adrenaline thundered round my body as I looked around the bare room for something to defend myself with. In a second or two a man with a gun was coming through that door and he was going to kill me unless I thought quickly.

But there was nothing in the room. I could hardly hit him with an armchair. I grabbed it though, shoving it against the door to buy a few more seconds, before moving to the side of the door and looking desperately at the objects within the room – TV, games console, fridge, uplighter…

Two more shots punched holes in the door. The handle turned and the door was pushed, stopping after an inch when it hit the armchair. I rammed the chair against the door, forcing it closed again. Another shot ripped through the door as I jumped to the side.

He'd be coming in again, and this time he knew there was something blocking the door. He'd hit it hard.

I had one chance, and I had to be quick.

I grabbed the armchair and pulled it away from the door. Then I reached behind me and grabbed the uplighter. It was a six-foot long piece of aluminium topped with a bowl-shaped glass shade. I stamped on the electrical cable and yanked the lamp, tearing the cable free. I held the lamp in both hands and pointed it towards the door like a lance. My shoulders were tense but my breathing was steady once more.

I heard two quick steps from the hallway and then the door burst open and the gunman came hurtling through it. There was a brief look of surprise as he found no resistance behind the door and he stumbled towards me, left shoulder first, raising the gun in his other hand.

I lunged with the uplighter, aiming for the gun. The glass connected with his gloved hands and forced the gun sideways as he pulled the trigger. The bullet smashed the glass and buried itself in the armchair at the far side of the room. I pulled the uplighter back and saw only a few jagged shards remained. I thrust again and he cried out as the glass caught him in the face. He stumbled backwards, his sunglasses falling to the floor amid red droplets, and I swept the lamp diagonally, slashing across the length of his body. The glass caught his left arm and his right hand, and the gun fell to the floor.

I dropped the lamp and charged forwards as he braced himself for a fight. He was expecting a punch – everyone does – but I drove my right knee into his left, the one carrying all his weight. He howled as his knee was forced backwards and I followed it with an elbow to the face, catching him heavily on the jaw. He toppled sideways and I helped him on his way with a left hook.

Then everything blurred as I battered him to the ground in a frenzy. It took some seconds before I realised he was offering no resistance. I stopped and looked at the blood smeared across my knuckles.

'Who are you?' I asked with ragged breath.

'Fuck you,' he moaned.

I hauled him into a sitting position and propped him against the wall, belted him hard on the ear and gestured towards the body in the hallway. 'Why did you shoot him?'

He said nothing as his head lolled onto his chest and one hand clutched his knee. His left eye was already beginning to close and his goatee was thick with blood.

'Is this about the blackmail?'

He still didn't speak, but there was a flicker in his eyes when I mentioned the blackmail.

'What was it about?'

I tried a few more times and got no answers. I wasn't sure if he was stubbornly refusing to co-operate, or if he was genuinely too banged up to think straight. I turned to look for the gun and saw it on the floor by the window. I crossed the room to pick it up and sensed movement as I did so. I turned back just in time as the gunman came at me with a combat knife. The bastard had been faking and I'd fallen for it.

The knife flashed towards my face and I leant back out of range. It slashed through the air twice more as I grabbed the seat cushion from the armchair and thrust it against the knife. The blade entered the padded cushion and I twisted it, trying to pull the weapon from his hand, kicking at his bad knee as I did so. I missed the kick and the knife was too sharp, cutting its way free with ease.

I threw the cushion at his face as the knife popped loose and hurled myself to the floor where the gun had fallen. I turned with the gun in my hand as he came at me with the knife. His eyes widened as the barrel lifted and he spun for the door.

I was on my back and he had a head start. I didn't hesitate. I fired as he disappeared round the corner of the doorframe and I saw a spurt of blood as the bullet caught him in the shoulder. There was a thud as he bounced off the wall but he made it to the door and I heard him on the stairs. I was up and after him, the gun still in my hand as I jumped over Reardon's body and raced down the stairs. As I cleared the stairs and charged out of the close into the sun, I squinted against the light, searching for him through narrowed eyes. Then I saw him, twenty yards away, grabbing the open passenger door of a silver Nissan X-Trail.

I lifted the gun and took aim, ready to fire. My finger was beginning to squeeze the trigger when I saw the group of kids ten yards behind him, their faces wide with shock. I've only fired a few shots in my life and I'm no kind of expert – I couldn't take the risk. I lowered the gun and sprinted for the car as the gunman dived inside and the driver floored the accelerator.

I came to a stop as the SUV rounded the corner and disappeared from sight. The kids stared at me, rooted to the spot, unable to take their eyes from the gun in my hand. I looked at it too, its weight suddenly increased tenfold as it tried to pull itself from my fingers. I looked at the kids and one of them – a girl of six or seven – began to cry. I walked away then, back to the flat.

The air in the flat was thick with the coppery tang of blood and the silence that only a dead body can bring. I stopped in the doorway and looked down at what had once been a petty criminal named Sean Reardon. After a few moments I stepped round the body, careful not to tread in anything that had formerly been inside his head, and entered the living room.

It was a mess. The uplighter lay against one wall, its broken glass scattered across the carpet, the shredded seat cushion occupied the middle of the floor, its innards spilling out, and there were spots of the gunman's blood scattered at various points throughout the room. I sighed heavily and sat down on the intact armchair, took my phone from my pocket and dialled a number I'd had to call all too often. As I waited for the phone to connect I drank the last of the now-warm Sprite.

The phone was answered with a brisk, businesslike tone. 'Andrea Jarvie.'

'It's Harper. I'm in a bit of a spot.'

'That's most unlike you. Who have you upset now?'

'I don't know, but he tried to shoot me.'

Her voice lost all trace of humour. 'Are you okay?'

'Better than the guy he did shoot.'

I gave Andrea the quick version. I knew I should have phoned the police first, but Andrea was a high-flier with Melrose McLean, one of the most respected law firms in the city, and I wasn't talking to the cops without getting her advice first. Besides, Reardon wasn't getting any more dead.

'Honestly, you're like a bloody magnet for lunatics,' she said when I finished. 'Right, first thing to do is call the police. I would imagine someone else has already, but it'll show you've nothing to hide if you do it too. Second, do not talk to them without me.'

'Andrea...' I began.

'Do NOT talk to them, Harper. They're going to find you at the scene of a murder, with your fingerprints on the weapon and evidence that you've fired it. I don't need you shooting your mouth off and inadvertently handing them any more ammunition.'

'Pardon the multiple puns.'

'Harper,' she warned. 'Just do as you're told.'

'And when you get here? What do we tell them then?'

'Everything.' Andrea was adamant. 'You're a private eye. You don't have any recourse to client confidentiality in the eyes of the law. Right now we need to focus on clearing you from the investigation and that means full disclosure.'

'What about my client?'

'I don't care about *your* client. You're *my* client and I expect you to do as I say if you want me to represent you. Is that understood?'

'Yes, ma'am.'

'Good. Now go and call them. And get them to tell me where you're being held.' She hung up and I looked at the phone.

There are instincts we all feel. Some we're born with, some we learn as we grow. Some we ignore, and some we heed beyond all reason. But our instincts are there for a reason: to protect us.

Right now my instinct was to get far away from this place before the police arrived. I'd been here before. Some years ago I called the police to report a murder and they almost destroyed my life.

I stared at the phone like it was a crystal ball, like it could tell me how this would play out. Would they do their jobs this time? Or would they focus entirely on the easy option again?

I closed my eyes and dialled *9*.

It didn't matter what my instinct said.

9.

I knew I had to do the right thing.

9.

My heart beat slowed.

The call was answered.

'There's been a murder,' I said.

Chapter Four

The police arrived in less than ten minutes. Sirens pulled up outside as I finished a cursory search of the flat, having found nothing that obviously related to the blackmail. I returned to the living room and lifted the gun, throwing it over Reardon's body into the doorway, in plain sight of any cops coming up the stairs. I hoped the old guy across the close didn't take it to use on the kids who'd been harassing him.

I knelt in the centre of the living room, as far from any of the furniture as possible, checked my watch and saw it was five past three, then raised my hands above my head. This day was rapidly going down the pan, but getting shot by some testosterone-fuelled macho cop with an itchy trigger finger would probably nudge it into my top ten worst days ever.

I heard movements on the ground floor, then coming up the stairs, until a deep voice shouted, 'Armed Police! Throw out your weapon!'

'It's at the door!' I shouted back.

There was a pause as they tried to decide whether my refusal to cooperate could be considered justification for storming the flat and shooting everyone inside. A few seconds later I heard footsteps at the flats front door and a creak as someone took a first step into the hallway. A moment later a figure with a gun appeared in the doorway, the gun sweeping the room from side to side. Behind him another bulky shape did the same with the small kitchen opposite. The guy facing me looked big and sweaty beneath a thick bulletproof vest. His face was stony as he kept the gun trained on me while more of his colleagues searched the rest of the flat.

'On the floor,' he told me. 'Face down, hands behind your head.'

I did as I was told.

The first guy kept the gun on me while another officer came round and pulled my arms behind my back and snapped on the cuffs. He lifted me to my feet and stood me against the wall, patted me down for any concealed weapons, then slipped my wallet from the pocket of my jeans. He flipped it open and glanced at my driving licence then stepped into the hall. I heard a crackle of static as he got on the radio. I couldn't make out every word, but I got the gist. The flat was secure but he was concerned about bringing me out, since I'd have to step over Reardon's body to do so. The guy was sharp: he knew a decent solicitor could try and use that enforced proximity to the corpse to explain away any forensic evidence. Had I been guilty and they'd walked me past the body I'd have accidentally taken a tumble on the corpse, rendering all the evidence tainted.

A few minutes later I was getting twitchy. So was the guy with the gun whose arms must have been aching from holding it trained on me for so long. A line of sweat had gathered around his hairline and was beginning to run at the temples.

'You can put it down,' I told him. 'I'm hardly going anywhere.'

'Be quiet.'

'Tell you what, why don't I take a seat here.' I nodded at the armchair. 'Then you'll know I'm not going to make a run for it.'

'I said, be quiet.'

'Oh, for Christ's sake. Fine, shoot me if you have to, but I'm sitting down.'

I flopped into the armchair, which had been far more comfortable when my arms weren't handcuffed behind my back. I was just getting used to the position when I heard the clip of high heels striding up the concrete stairs in the close. The cop did too and he grabbed my shoulder and hauled me face first onto the floor.

I was still trying to get my breath back when the heels appeared in the doorway. I glanced up and saw two legs that just kept going. A bit on the thin side perhaps, but they made up for that in length.

'Problems, officer?' the legs asked in a calm, authoritative voice.

'No, Ma'am.'

'Then why is he on the floor?'

'Wouldn't do as he was told, Ma'am. Couldn't take any chances.'

'So there are problems then?'

'Nothing I can't handle, Ma'am.'

'Of course, of course. Could you help him up, please?'

He did as he was told but he wasn't happy about it. His angry eyes told me how much he wanted to belt me. He wouldn't though, not in front of the female cop. And it was nothing to do with her sex and everything to do with the authority that radiated from her.

Now I was upright I could see the legs were just as long as they'd looked from the floor, and nicely in proportion to the rest of her. She was tall, maybe 5'9" – which put her only a couple of inches below me, and that was without the heels – and very slim, with deep red hair tied back in a loose ponytail. She had pale skin, and a long face that suited her height and was balanced by the narrow-framed glasses she wore. She looked in her early forties and was attractive, if, like the legs, a little too thin. Her skirt suit was navy and nicely cut, though I suspected she would be much more stylish when she wasn't on duty. And she was definitely on duty now. From the way the other cops deferred to her I knew this was a woman who took no nonsense and had earned their respect through hard graft, even if she wasn't going to be chasing anyone down the street in those shoes.

She glanced around the room, taking in the damage and casting an appraising eye over the bloodstains. After a few moments she turned to me, flipped open her warrant card and flashed it under my nose. 'Detective Inspector Claiborne, Police Scotland.' She pointed a neatly manicured finger in the direction of Reardon's decomposing form. 'Did you shoot him?'

'Nope.'

'Talking without your solicitor?' She seemed surprised, maybe suspicious.

'I have an irrepressible urge to tell the truth.' I had an idea what Andrea would tell me to do with my irrepressible urge to open my big mouth.

'Of course you do.' My wallet was in her other hand and she opened it and took out my driving licence. 'Your name's Keir Harper?'

I nodded as she found one of my business cards.

'And I see you work for Keir Harper Investigations.' She raised an immaculately plucked eyebrow. 'That must have taken a while.'

'My marketing guy was off sick that day.' Did Andrea's embargo extend to smart-arsed remarks?

'Ah,' she nodded to herself, as though that was somehow relevant. Then it was back to business. 'So you didn't shoot this man?'

I decided I'd pushed my luck far enough and settled for a shake of the head.

'Then you won't mind if we check your hands for gunshot residue.' She stuck her head into the hallway and gestured to someone. A moment later a Scene of Crime Officer in a white, hooded paper suit and face mask appeared in the room. Claiborne told the masked figure to swab my hands.

I said nothing while the figure behind me got to work.

'Shy, all of a sudden?' The eyebrow arched again. 'Shame. We were getting along like the proverbial torched maisonette.'

A moment later the tech plucked a few hairs from the top of my head and dropped them in a clear plastic bag. 'Don't you need a warrant for that?' I asked.

'Hair, saliva, fingernail clippings, we only need a senior officer's authority. An inspector or above.' She smiled and waved a hand in her own direction.

'Well, aren't we all glad you're here,' I said, before opening my mouth wide and letting the teach swab the inside of my cheek with a long cotton bud.

Claiborne flicked a finger in Reardon's direction. 'Tell me about him.'

I resumed my vow of silence.

'He looks a bit shifty. Steal something from you, did he?'

The tech was behind me again, trying to take clippings from my fingernails. He'd be lucky; I'd practically bitten them to the knuckle while I was waiting for Reardon to show up in George Square.

'If you didn't kill him who did?' Claiborne asked, as the tech left with the samples and another plain clothes cop came in. This one was male, about ten years older than Claiborne and thirty years nearer his grave. He was over six foot and a solid kind of fat, with a full black beard and bulbous, drinker's nose. His sports jacket and supposedly-dress trousers looked like he'd used them as a pillow and the tie round his neck looked as if it had been hung there for the sole purpose of hiding as many of the shirts stains as possible. He nodded at the armed officer who returned the gesture.

'This is Detective Sergeant Rowe,' Claiborne said. She handed my wallet to him and asked me again, 'So? Who shot him?'

I looked away from Rowe who was filling the doorway and scrutinising my drivers licence like some hobo bouncer. *A white male*, I wanted to tell her. *About six foot, maybe fifteen stone. Well built, probably late twenties. Shaved head, black goatee, sunglasses.*

The desire to talk was powerful. Some inbuilt need to explain, to tell the world I wasn't a killer, to be believed. Was it something instinctive, hardwired in my being since I had been born? Or something that had taken root inside me when the world had looked at Mack and I like it was a firing squad and hasty theories and a vindictive police force were their bullets.

I remained silent, staring down instead at where the gunman's sunglasses had fallen after I'd raked his face with the broken lamp.

'We're going nowhere till they move your dear departed pal there,' she persisted. 'So you might as well fill us in.'

'I think I'd rather speak to my solicitor first.'

Claiborne winced. 'Are you sure? No-one's been charged with

anything here. You could just tell us what happened and save yourself an unnecessary expense. You'd feel a bit daft if you spent a fortune getting some high-priced legal eagle to help you tell us how you got caught up in the middle of this, wouldn't you?'

'Thanks for your concern. Now, you can either continue trampling all over my rights or you can call my solicitor.'

'Fine. We shall call a solicitor for...'

'Not *a* solicitor. *My* solicitor. Andrea Jarvie of Melrose McLean, if it's not too much trouble.'

'No trouble at all.' Claiborne gave me the thinnest of smiles then turned to Rowe. 'Sergeant, please caution Mr Harper. I would loathe him to be unaware of his rights.'

The police doctor arrived as Rowe finished and Claiborne was called into the hallway. Rowe didn't say anything else while she was out of the room, just gave me cold, flat eyes. He was wasting his time. I'd been dead-eyed by far more intimidating men than him.

Claiborne came back quickly, since establishing death in Reardon's case was merely a procedural formality, required before the pathologist could have a look at the body. I was trying to see what else was happening in the hallway when DS Rowe returned to his previous position, blocking my view.

'Last chance,' Claiborne said. 'Save yourself a lot of hassle.'

'Has that ever actually worked?' I asked.

She waved a hand in a *suit yourself* gesture then beckoned Rowe into the hallway. Talking tactics no doubt. The armed officer and I stared at each other.

'So, busy day?' I asked.

'What do I look like? A taxi driver?''

'Well you wouldn't be getting a tip if you were. Not with that attitude.'

He gave me a look that said he'd gone from wanting to belt me to wanting to empty his magazine into me.

We bonded for a few more minutes until Rowe came back into the room. 'Time to go.' His voice was heavy and breathless. Must be hard work just moving that bulk from one room to another.

'Will you have me home by ten?' I asked. 'My parents worry.'

'They probably worried you'd find your way home,' he wheezed.

Rowe led me out of the flat past the curious gazes of the techs, most of whom had never seen a real live murderer outside of court. He took me outside where a small crowd of neighbours had gathered. The kids who had forced me to hold my fire as the gunman escaped were grouped at the front, faces flush with excitement. One of them pointed at me and shouted, 'That's him! He tried to shoot us!'

Ungrateful wee bastard.

Rowe handed me over to two uniforms who put me in the back of their car, closed the door and listened to the sergeant's instructions. They nodded several times then got in the car as he returned to the building.

'So, where we off to today, lads?' I asked cheerfully.

'Back to the station to get this car cleaned,' the driver replied.

'Last guy we lifted took a piss in the back,' the passenger added. 'Haven't had a chance to clean it out yet.'

I put my fingers to my temples and gave them a rub as the two cops snickered to themselves.

The way this day was going it might even crack the top five.

Chapter Five

They took me to the high security police station at nearby Helen Street. It was only a few minutes drive, for which I was grateful, since the clatty bastard who'd pissed in the backseat had obviously been drinking some foul concoction before he'd emptied his bladder. I took small comfort in the knowledge the aroma in the front of the car couldn't have been much better. And at least I wouldn't be the one cleaning it out.

After I was booked in they stuck me in an interview room and left me there. The room was small and bare with only four chairs and the table I was leaning my head on. I wondered if they would try to mess Andrea about in order to leave me stewing longer. Perhaps hoping I would be sitting there sweating, desperate to confess by the time they opened the door. They were going to be disappointed. I might have been perspiring, but that was purely down to the ineffective air-conditioning.

To my surprise, the door opened in less than twenty minutes and Claiborne stalked into the room with Rowe behind her trailing a fug of inhuman body odour in his wake. Andrea breezed in at their backs, a whirlwind of strawberry-blonde hair, blue-green eyes and a fierce determination to right wrongs and fight injustice. Batgirl in a £500 skirt suit.

I wondered if they'd decided not to be awkward or they'd tried and she'd chewed someone up and gargled with their remains.

Andrea placed her briefcase on the table and sat down opposite me. She turned to the two police officers and looked at them as though they were incompetent bellboys waiting for a tip that was never going to arrive. 'Thanks for the escort. I'll take it from here.'

Claiborne scowled then turned on her heel and left. Rowe lumbered after her and banged the door shut behind him.

'So,' Andrea began. 'Been up to much recently?'

'Oh, you know. Becoming the prime suspect in a murder. The usual.'

'It does seem to be a regular occurrence for you.' She gave me a sympathetic smile. 'Okay, let me check I've got things right here. Your client's father is being blackmailed and you went to the proposed payoff, identified the extortionist and followed him home. You were interviewing him when an unidentified man came to the door and shot him dead. Yes?'

'Bang on.'

'Okay, so tell me the long version. From your first meeting with your client.'

I did as I was told and Andrea walked me through my story, taking notes as she did so. Her eyebrows rose ominously and her pen stopped scratching momentarily when I told her my client's name but she carried on. It was only when I'd finished telling her the whole sorry tale that she came back to it. She put her pen down slowly and deliberately and said, 'Nicole Dunbar?'

'Yeah.'

'Even without the benefit of hindsight I wouldn't have said that was a good idea.'

I rubbed my hand across the stubble on my jaw, the rasping sound loud in the small room. 'Me neither.'

'Then why did you take the case?'

'What should I have done? Told her it was too bad that her dad was missing? Told her it was a shame that some low life was blackmailing him? Tough shit, away you go and take your problems to someone else?'

'Yes. That's exactly what you should have said.'

'I didn't know someone was going to get their face blown off in front of me, did I?' My voice had been loud in the confines of the room. Too loud.

Andrea looked at me coolly, allowing my outburst to pass.

'I'm not talking about that. I'm talking as your friend. This woman seriously messed you up for two years and dropped you like yesterdays newspaper. She was selfish, manipulative and deceitful. She can blame it on her background, her stupid parents, whatever, and you can let her if you want, but don't you sit there and try to tell me that she was anything other than bad news.'

I couldn't, of course. There was no denying it. Nicole Dunbar had been, and probably still was, trouble. She had torn me up and thrown me down and trampled all over me. And yet, stupid as it was, there was a part of me still cared for her.

'If you took this case purely to find a missing person, that's fine. But if you took it because it was her, well, you're a bigger fool than you look.'

I began to form some sort of pathetic denial. Andrea held up a finger to stop me and her blue-green eyes flashed. 'Don't even open your mouth unless you're going to tell me the absolute truth.'

I hesitated for far too long, then finally said, 'So what are we going to do about this whole murder thing, then?'

Andrea's eyes softened. Then she picked up her pen and it was back to business.

'I'll attack the evidence they have against you. And we focus on the real killer. If he bled at the scene…'

'He did.'

'… then it becomes obvious that a third person was there, casting doubt over you being the killer. Of course, we need to know who else might have wanted to kill Reardon. He must have rubbed someone up the wrong way.'

'The killer followed Reardon and I from George Square, which connects it to the blackmail.'

'Unless you were the target,' Andrea said quietly.

I had considered this and already dismissed it. 'I don't think so. He could have waited till I left on my own and shot me in the close or in the street. Or even before I went in. The fact he went for the flat suggests Reardon was the target.'

'But you didn't go in straight away. You were waiting for information on Reardon. So why did the killer wait till you were in the flat too? He could have gone in and killed Reardon while you were still outside.'

'Maybe he thought I knew something too.'

'Then he might try again.'

I shook my head. 'I'm sure this is linked to the blackmail. And I asked him about it. He knows I don't have a clue what's going on. He might try again, but if he does he's taking a big risk. As things stand he got away, and if he has any luck the cops will pin the whole thing on me. Even if they don't, they probably don't have any leads on him.'

'Apart from the car,' Andrea reminded me.

'Which will have been torched by now.'

'They might still find something. Claiborne's a good cop.'

'But is she an honest one? Or does she just want a closed case and a conviction?'

To anyone else this might have sounded paranoid. But Andrea and I had been here before.

'I only know what I've heard,' Andrea said. 'And most of that seems to be that she won't take any nonsense. She's apparently gone up against her bosses a few times, refusing to toe the line on some cases, asking hard questions of people that would rather not be asked them.'

'I'm surprised she gets away with it.'

'She gets results, and there's no arguing with that. I suspect she wouldn't go down quietly if they did try to get rid of her, and her bosses probably know that.'

'You mean she knows where the bodies are buried?'

'I don't know if that's necessarily true, but there have been rumours.'

'What sort of rumours?' I was intrigued now.

'Oh, you know, the usual thing. Bribery, corruption, falsifying evidence. It's only rumours, of course. Actually, she seems to have been a thorn in the side of Innes McKenzie for some time, so it wouldn't surprise me if he was the one behind these whispers, trying to undermine her.'

I was surprised to hear Andrea mention McKenzie. Not because he was all sweetness and light – I had personal experience of just how far that was from the truth – but as the most powerful *alleged* criminal in the city he seemed to be almost untouchable. Andrea must have seen the confusion in my face.

'No, no. She hasn't come even close to getting him near a jury. But she's taken down a number of people who work for McKenzie. Allegedly. If the numbers are right, I'm sure he'd be very keen to see her discredited.'

I was currently in McKenzie's good books, but not so long ago I had a terrifying glimpse into what it might be like to get on his bad side. If what Andrea said was accurate, I didn't envy Claiborne one bit.

I put McKenzie and the rumour mill out of my mind and came back to my own predicament. 'So what you're saying is, don't expect her to go easy on me?'

'Exactly. She's got a good closure rate and a good conviction rate. If you don't want to become another notch on her belt I suggest you listen to me and do precisely as I say.'

'When do I ever do anything else?'

Andrea didn't dignify that with a response. 'We need to get to the bottom of the blackmail. If we can do that we can cast doubt all over their case. I'll see what I can do.'

I smiled at her, grateful for the support. 'This is a wee bit out of your area of expertise, Andrea. I need to do this myself.'

Andrea looked more exasperated than surprised. 'Look, Harper. They probably will charge you with Reardon's murder. You need to accept that. I know I said I would attack their evidence, but what they have is enough to keep you at the top of the suspect list and in here for a while yet.'

'Then we find different evidence,' I said reasonably.

Andrea looked at me blankly. 'And who's going to find that?'

'Jessica.'

'Jessica? Really? I thought she was a mess these days.'

I winced inwardly at the description. Had I been the one who painted so cruel a picture of Jessica's current state?

'She's struggling. But she's still the best investigator I know.'

Andrea took a deep breath and looked as though she was

trying to figure out how to tell a child their puppy has died. 'That's a risk, Harper. As your solicitor and your friend, I'd advise you to get someone who's on the ball. You must know plenty of other investigators.'

I thought back to some of the investigators I had known, and the reasons I couldn't ask them. There were others, of course, ones who would do me a favour and tuck that card in their back pocket for a future date. But none that I trusted as implicitly as Jessica. And that was when I realised just how deep my faith in her ran. I was in trouble, no two ways about it, and the person I wanted at my side was Jessica, even if she was only operating at fifty percent.

'What about Mack?' Andrea was saying.

I looked at her as though she'd escaped from an asylum. 'I want to find evidence, not beat it into a coma.'

'Fair point,' she said, her face colouring. 'I don't know what I was thinking there.'

'Once I'm out and I know who I'm after, then yeah, Mack will help. But right now it has to be Jessica. She might be in a bad way, but this could be the reason she needs to pull herself up off the floor.'

'Do you think she can?'

'If this doesn't do it, then I don't know what will.'

Andrea nodded several times, trying to convince herself that this was the right course of action. She gathered her papers together and began putting them back in the briefcase. 'Then I'll get in touch with her.'

'Don't go easy on her. Pile on the pressure.'

'Are you sure?'

I thought of Jessica before she began to descend into depression. 'She thrives on pressure.'

Andrea shook her head sadly as she clicked the briefcase closed and got to her feet. 'What is it with you and troubled women?'

'Does that include you?'

She made a dismissive noise as she knocked on the door. 'My only trouble is keeping *you* out of trouble.'

Hard to argue with that.

Chapter Six

'Mr Harper. Would you please tell us, in your own words, the circumstances that led to you being present at the scene of a murder today?'

Claiborne and Rowe faced Andrea and I across the table, a folder on the table between them. Claiborne was as immaculate as she had been earlier, but Rowe, having added a bit of sandwich to his beard, managed to look even more dishevelled. Like Hagrid fallen on hard times.

'Certainly,' I said. Mr Cooperation. 'I was hired this morning by a woman named Nicole Dunbar to find her father, Gordon, who has been missing for several days. Ms Dunbar was concerned for the safety of her father, particularly as she had gone to his home and found among his mail a hand-delivered letter demanding money from him.'

'That would be this letter.' Claiborne held up a poly-pocket containing my copy of the blackmail letter.

'Yes.'

'Why was someone blackmailing Mr Dunbar?'

'No idea.'

'Some detective,' Rowe sneered.

'Maybe a genius like you can close a case in an hour, Rowe. The rest of us like to actually find the truth.'

'Can we move on?' Andrea said before Rowe could respond.

'Why did Ms Dunbar hire you?' Claiborne asked. 'Why not come to us?'

'She was concerned that bringing in the police might cause the blackmailer to carry out his threats.'

'Did she say why she chose you in particular?'

'We know each other.' I hoped they'd leave it at that. I was reluctant to dredge up my relationship with Nicole at the best of times, and this was far from the best of times.

Claiborne was too shrewd for that though. 'In what way do you know each other?'

'We were intimate.'

'Were?'

'We split up a year ago.'

'Amicably?'

'Reasonably.'

'And now,' Rowe added in a low breath, 'she comes to you when she needs help.'

I pointed at the crust in his beard. 'Keeping that for later?'

His skin flushed a deep purple as he picked the bread from his beard and flicked it under the table.

Andrea jumped in before things got nasty. 'I don't believe my client's relationship with Ms Dunbar is relevant.'

'I'll be the judge of that, Ms Jarvie,' Claiborne countered. She turned back to me. 'Now, after you were hired by Ms Dunbar, what did you do?'

'I went to George Square and waited till I identified the blackmailer…'

'What made you think Mr Reardon was the blackmailer?'

'He was the most suspicious looking man on the planet.'

'Not from where I'm sitting,' Rowe said.

I gave that one the cold shoulder and carried on. 'I identified Reardon as the blackmailer and followed him to his home. I knocked on his door and he let me in…'

'He let you in?' Claiborne was sceptical again. She must have been born that way. Probably sent her baby bottles off to forensics before she'd feed.

'… I was in the process of interviewing him about the blackmail when there was a knock at the door. Reardon answered it and was shot in the face. The killer came into the flat and tried to shoot me too. I fought him off and disarmed him. He was attacking me with a knife when I got a hold of the gun and fired at him. I think I hit him in the shoulder and he ran out of the flat.

I chased after him and saw him getting into a silver Nissan X-Trail.' I described Reardon's killer and gave them the number plate of the getaway car. 'Then I returned to the flat and called the police.'

'So who is this man? Why would he want to kill Mr Reardon?'

'If you didn't have me cooped up in here I might have found out by now.'

Rowe tried to clear his throat, though it sounded like he just rearranged whatever was rattling around in there. 'So this other man, this supposed killer, followed you from George Square to Buchanan Street, and then to Ibrox on the underground and you didn't notice him?'

I felt my face flush with equal parts anger and embarrassment. 'I was preoccupied with Reardon.'

'Sure.' Rowe leaned forward. 'Here's my problem. One of them at any rate. If he followed you to Reardon's flat, why didn't he just follow you straight in and shoot you both immediately? Why give you a chance to talk?'

I wasn't going to raise the possibility that the gunman thought I knew something about the blackmail. Who knows what they would do with that. Instead I looked at Rowe as though he was particularly slow. 'Because he had to wait for his getaway driver to catch up. I'd imagine it's a bit awkward to shoot two people dead then hang around waiting for a bus, wouldn't you?'

Rowe's mouth tightened so much it disappeared into his beard, leaving only an impenetrable wall of fur. 'You've got it all thought out, haven't you?' he seethed.

'One of us has to.'

Rowe's reaction was cut short by a little noise from Claiborne. He stopped at the sound and sat hunched forwards, glaring at me, like a bear wondering which arm to tear off first. Claiborne was silent too, her chin balanced on steepled fingers, studying me, though she did it more like a surgeon, deciding where to make her first incision.

'Okay, here's the way I see it, Mr Harper,' Claiborne finally said. 'By your own admission, you had a motive for killing Sean Reardon.'

'Excuse me?' Andrea said. 'When did he admit that?'

'He was, according to you, Mr Harper, blackmailing your former lover's father. Presumably you knew Mr Dunbar?' She carried on without waiting for acknowledgement. 'So perhaps you were willing to kill to protect him. Or perhaps you were willing to kill because his daughter asked you to. Of course, that's if we even believe this whole fanciful blackmail story. Perhaps you and your lover conspired to kill Reardon for reasons we've yet to uncover.'

'Or *perhaps* the man I've already described to you killed him.'

'But why? There's no motive. You and your lover – former, current, whatever – and her father are the ones with a motive. So we're back where we started.'

I rubbed my temples. My head was beginning to throb. Andrea put a calming hand on my arm and leant forward, her voice firm. 'Then explain this. Why did my client call the police? Why is the blood of a third party present at the scene of the crime? Why is my client not covered in Sean Reardon's blood from a point blank shot to the face? Why has the armchair cushion been shredded by a knife, yet none of the knives in the flat bear any trace of those fibres? Why does every single piece of forensic evidence at that crime scene support my client's version of events?'

Claiborne studied her for a time, then said, 'All very good questions, Ms Jarvie. Here's another one, Mr Harper – why do you keep turning up around dead bodies?'

I blew out a long breath. I knew where this was going and it wouldn't be pleasant.

Claiborne continued. 'At the start of the year there were bodies turning up all over the place and you seemed to be connected to most of them. Care to elaborate?'

I didn't want to elaborate at all. Something very dark had descended on my life and Jessica, among others, was still suffering the aftershocks.

'We have nothing to say on that matter,' Andrea told them. 'If you want to know more about it, talk to DI Greig Stewart.'

Stewart had been the officer in charge of the case, though Jessica, Mack and I were the reason he'd been able to close it.

Claiborne continued undeterred. 'What about Katie Jarvie?'

My blood chilled and slowed and I felt Andrea stiffen beside me. I looked at Claiborne with flat eyes.

'Lot of people thought you had something to do with that.' Her voice sounded reasonable, but every word struck me like a physical blow. 'You and your friend...' she checked the file, '... James Mackie. Lot of people seem to think you got away with murder there.'

The atmosphere in the room was thick and overpowering. It felt as though an unexploded bomb had been wheeled into the room and dumped on the table between us.

I could not trust myself to speak. I stared at Claiborne for thirty seconds, willing the redness to leave my vision. Rowe was no longer here, I had eyes only for the woman who had brought that pain back into my life. Into our lives, for I knew Andrea was similarly furious.

Claiborne and Rowe said nothing, seemingly content to let the pressure build. It was Andrea who finally broke the silence and when she did her voice was as flat and cold as a glacier.

'You might as well take that folder and leave. If you're going to bring my sister's murder into it we have nothing more to say. Charge my client if you like; you know this case will die with its legs in the air before it ever reaches court.'

Andrea sat back and folded her arms. I followed suit. For the first time I didn't feel the oppressive heat of the interview room. Claiborne's words had chilled me so thoroughly I felt I would have to walk on the sun to ever be warm again.

I glanced at the woman beside me and wondered if this was how Katie would look if she hadn't been murdered at the age of seventeen, or if the twins would have grown to look less alike as they aged. I believed they'd still be identical. So did Mack: that's why he had such a hard time around Andrea. To him she was a painful past, a non-existent present, and an impossible future all in one hauntingly familiar form.

Claiborne and Rowe persisted for some time. They laid

supposition on top of theory on top of speculation and tried to crack me. I remained silent, staring through them while Andrea batted back every question they threw at us.

At a little after nine o'clock they charged me with Sean Reardon's murder.

Chapter Seven

They took me down to the cells after Andrea left. The police surgeon came and took a blood sample for comparison against that found at the scene. Claiborne took great delight in pointing out that this time they had a warrant from the sheriff.

They took my watch, belt and shoelaces and pushed me inside the cramped, windowless room. I couldn't imagine how I would have been able to kill myself with my watch, but maybe they've had more creative criminals than me in these cells. Or they were just trying to be awkward.

I sat on the worn mattress of the bunk, reflecting that I'd had thicker sandwiches, and lay back to think about the case. I'd been puzzling over it for hours now, and I was no further forward. My mind began to stray to other things and when I closed my eyes the bodies appeared. There were enough of them for a lifetime of nightmares; some I felt responsible for – those who would still be alive if they'd never met me – and others whose fates had been decided long before I even learned their names. Yet they haunted me equally, as though they'd finally found someone whose soul would play cathedral to the fading requiem of their lives.

I fought to push them away, to keep my head clear and focus on my own predicament, but they returned, as always, like a relentless swarm. When, after an hour in the cell, I heard the key being turned in the lock I felt like running for the door. It opened and a tall thin man stepped in, his short grey hair dipped forward as he eased under the door frame. DI Stewart straightened up and looked at me with pensive eyes, his lived-in face full of conflicting emotions.

'I hoped you wouldn't end up like this, Harper.'

I sat upright and swung my legs to the floor. 'This wasn't in my top ten holiday destinations either.'

The door closed behind him and he leaned against the wall, a plastic cup of coffee in one hand, the other trying in vain to smooth out the wrinkles in his cheap suit. 'You want to tell me what happened?' he asked.

'Off the record?'

'Since I doubt you're about to offer me a confession, sure, why not?' He stepped away from the wall and took a can of Irn-Bru from his pocket and handed it to me. It was still cold from the vending machine.

'Bribing the prisoner?' I smiled. It wasn't only a drink, it was a symbol of something much deeper, something we'd been through together, and I appreciated the gesture.

'Of course.' He smiled too, though there wasn't much life in it. 'I slipped some truth serum in there.'

It might have been the fact I had nothing to hide, or maybe just that Stewart was the only cop I'd ever met who made me feel I might someday be able to trust them again. He'd been straight with me in the past and I thought he'd be straight again. So I popped the can, took a swallow, and told it to him.

By the time I'd finished he was sitting cross-legged on the floor with his back to the wall. He took a last sip of the coffee and placed the cup beside his knee.

'You shouldn't have clammed up,' he said. 'Makes you look like you're hiding something.'

I nodded slowly. 'I know. But once they mentioned Katie I didn't trust myself to keep my temper.'

'How long is it since she was murdered, Harper? Ten years? Twelve?'

'Thirteen.' I suspected he knew the details of the case almost as well as I did, having studied them when he'd once, briefly, thought I might be a murderer. Stewart was the kind of cop who didn't forget a victim.

'That's a long time,' he said.

'For a killer to be walking free? Yeah, it is.'

Stewart sighed. 'For you and Mack to let it run your lives.'

'We were accused of murder. They put Mack on trial for it. That's kind of hard to forget.'

There was a hardness in my voice and Stewart tried to defuse it. He spread his hands reasonably and said, 'Mack was her boyfriend. You know it's almost always the person closest to the victim. And you were with him when he found the body. It made sense to look at both of you. You know that.'

'We were seventeen!'

'Killers come much younger than that,' Stewart said softly, and I wondered if he was thinking of someone in particular.

'Look, Stewart, I can understand them looking at us. I get that, really. But they cleared me easily enough. They should have cleared Mack as well.'

'They made a mistake, Harper. They were under pressure and there were no other suspects.'

'Because Darroch never looked for any!' I took a deep breath and lowered my voice. 'Would you have taken Mack to court?'

He rubbed his hand over the top of his head and said quietly, 'No. But we make mistakes. Much as I hate it, we make mistakes. I'm just glad he wasn't convicted.'

I rubbed at my tired eyes. 'Not officially, maybe. But you know as well as I do that a Not Proven verdict is the jury saying, *Aye, we think you're guilty as sin, but we can't prove anything.* That follows you around. Meanwhile some arsehole who *is* guilty as sin is walking around with a fucking smirk on his face.'

'I know, Harper.' His voice was gentle, and I knew I was taking it out on the wrong cop.

'Where is Darroch, anyway? I'm surprised he's not down here to get the boot in.'

Before Darroch had somehow ascended to the rank of Detective Chief Inspector, he led the investigation into Katie Jarvie's death. He'd made the decision to persecute two seventeen-year-old boys and take one of them to trial. The last time I'd seen him he was holding a press conference wrongly naming another man as a killer. Not long after that I tracked down the real killer. He never did say thanks.

'He's on holiday,' Stewart said. 'He'll be disappointed he's missed this.'

'Saves him the hassle of trying to prove Mack was involved in this as well.' I folded my arms and leant back against the wall. My head was beginning to pound again.

Stewart watched me for a while, then said, 'You need to let go of her. Both of you.'

I studied him. 'Can you let go of the ones you don't solve? Can you let them go when you know you're the only one who still speaks for them?'

'Our dead are never dead to us until we have forgotten them.' He cleared his throat. 'George Eliot.'

'And yet you can't forget.'

His hands were in his lap and he looked down at them as though the answer to my question was hidden in the lines of his palms. Then he looked up and I saw ghosts in his eyes. 'No. That's why I'm telling you that you need to. I know what it does to you.'

I paused for a moment as I saw the pain deep in the blackness of his pupils. 'How long have you been doing this?' I finally asked.

He blew out a breath and a humourless laugh together. 'Twenty-five years I've been in the police. Fifteen in CID.'

'Who do you carry with you?'

It was a deeply personal question, and I wasn't sure he'd answer, but there was something almost confessional about the two of us sitting alone in this small cell.

'Margaret Devine. I'd only been on the force a year when I got the call. Got into her home and found her pinned to her kitchen table with a knife through her throat. I didn't have anything to do with that case once CID turned up, but they never got her killer.'

I nodded in understanding.

'Jack Cuthbert. Seventy-nine years old. One of my first cases after I got into CID. Found dead at his farmhouse, shotgun to the chest. Never found who did it. And no-one seemed to care. *Oh, he's had a good run, he wouldn't have lasted much longer anyway.* I don't give a damn what age he was.'

He blew out a frustrated breath. 'Oh, there's plenty more.

Those are just a couple of the early ones. I've had fifteen years of dead bodies to fill the wee quiet hours of the night, Harper. I'm never lonely.'

'How do you deal with it?' And that was the one question I really wanted the answer to.

'I go home and I hold my kids. I hold them like I'll never see them again and I hold my wife and thank God for what I've been allowed to keep when others have had theirs taken from them.'

'Ever think about walking away?'

'All the time.' He paused and inspected the coffee cup as though there might still be some caffeine skulking at the bottom. When he found none he looked up with sad acceptance rather than disappointment. 'You know what stops me?'

I shook my head, unable to guess what could make a man continue to torture himself.

'The next murder. Tomorrow, the day after, whenever – someone is going to die, and someone else needs to be punished. They'll haunt me too, I know that, and I've come to accept it. Every year I pick up one or two more that won't ever leave me. I can see their faces. I know the names of the ones they left behind. I know more about them than I do about my own family.'

'It's hard to let go, isn't it?'

Stewart nodded, short and shallow, like his head was chained to a rock. 'You've got to try. I'm too far down that road now. I can tell from the start now. I don't always know why – sometimes it's a kid, sometimes it's someone who left no-one to bury them, sometimes it's just the wall of grief they leave behind – but I know now, as soon as I see them, and it's like a voice says, *Aye, you'll be another one.*'

A small tremor ran through him, so small I don't think he noticed. 'Few days ago, we got called to a body found up the Campsies. Buried about a year, sniffed out by someone's dog. Took one look at the corpse and knew it would be one I wouldn't forget. Couldn't figure out why. Then I got the post mortem report back today – poor sod was buried alive. Can you imagine that?'

I shuddered at the thought. The cell we were in was already

feeling a little smaller. No wonder Stewart thought that one would haunt him.

'According to the report he had suffered serious brain injuries prior to being buried, so I've just got to hope he wasn't aware…'

I felt sick as I thought about the choice – buried alive or so seriously brain damaged you were no longer a functioning person.

' … And there were the two kids found at the council tip last week. Stuffed into a suitcase. Children, Harper… The children are the worst ones…' He looked up at me again, his eyes boring into mine. 'I mean it, Harper. Give her up. It starts off as remembrance, but it ends up as poison.'

Stewart stood suddenly and shook his head as though coming out of a trance. He banged his hand sharply on the door and looked at me with something like recognition. 'Right now, you feel like its driving you, that its fuel. But you can't control it. Sooner or later, it'll burn you up.'

The door opened and Stewart stepped through it. He paused on the other side and looked back at me, his eyes heavy with the weight of his memories. 'Look at Mack. He's been burning for years.'

The door was closed between us then, and shortly afterwards the light went out and I was alone.

I closed my eyes and I was alone no longer.

Chapter Eight

I slept badly, if at all, and I was wide awake long before they came for me the following morning. My mind was foggy and my eyes gritty with hours spent staring at the ceiling of a dark police cell. The lights came on and I assumed it was morning, and that I would soon be subjected to the next step in the legal process. I tried to gather my thoughts from the four corners of the room where they had sought refuge from the phantoms parading endlessly through my head.

Several hours passed, as best I could tell, and still no-one approached my cell. There was movement back and forth in the corridor but my door remained resolutely closed. Something was wrong. They should have been here first thing. Perhaps Claiborne had found something else that could be twisted to prove my guilt. I wondered what it could be, but my brain was tired and uncooperative.

Eventually two bulky officers opened my door and brought me from the cell. I didn't bother asking them questions. They would be unlikely to know anything useful, and even less likely to let it slip. We walked in silence until we wound up at the same interview room I had spent so many fun hours in last night. They opened the door and I saw Andrea and DI Claiborne facing each other over the table like old adversaries.

The taller, more primate-like of my escorts removed my handcuffs and the two of them left the room. Claiborne gestured to the chair beside Andrea and I sat down.

'Decided to let me go yet?' I asked her.

'Yes,' she replied.

That took me by surprise. 'Eh?' I said, eloquently.

'New evidence has come to light that casts doubt over your guilt.' Claiborne managed to make every word sound like a tooth being pulled.

'Casts doubt?' Andrea said. 'You have video footage of the killer shooting Mr Reardon in the face. I would suggest that proves my client innocent beyond any doubt.'

Video footage?

'The video has yet to be examined by our experts, Ms Jarvie. Until such time as we have authenticated the footage your client remains a suspect.'

'If you thought there was any doubt over this footage you wouldn't be dropping the charges and letting him go,' Andrea said.

'As I said, Ms Jarvie, this new evidence casts doubt over Mr Harper's guilt. With that in mind it would be negligent to pursue a case against him while ignoring other avenues. At this point in the investigation we will be considering all possibilities. And yes, that includes the possibility that Mr Harper is in fact guilty.'

Claiborne got to her feet but Andrea wasn't finished. She stood and fixed the taller woman with a hard look. 'My client gave you a description of Sean Reardon's murderer. You have three witness statements describing the same man and saying he entered the building with a gun. You have video footage showing that man shooting Mr Reardon in the face. There is no doubt over my client's innocence and continuing to harass him over this matter would be ill-advised, Detective Claiborne.'

'I'll decide who I investigate, *Ms* Jarvie,' Claiborne hissed back. She stalked to the door and turned with her fingers on the handle. 'You still shot someone, Mr Harper. By your own admission.'

'Self-defence,' I said. 'Tell you what, let me know when you find him and I'll ask him if he wants to press charges.'

Claiborne stopped in the doorway. 'I would strongly advise you to contact us should you learn anything about this man's whereabouts.' She stepped out of sight, leaving us with only the angry clip of her heels along the corridor.

The gorilla lumbered back in and looked at us with a face like fizz, his shoulders hunched up towards his ears like he wanted to bench press us till we squealed a confession. Andrea took no notice of him and eased out of the plastic chair with a grace more suited to a ballroom than our current location. I shuffled after her as she glided through the doorway.

Andrea had already taken care of the formalities and all that was left for me to do was sign for the return of my possessions. I threaded the laces back into my trainers and my belt through my jeans, put my potentially-deadly watch back on my wrist, and returned my wallet and phone to my pockets. With my possessions returned we left the building and emerged into daylight. I turned my face to the warmth of the sun and let it burn away the cobwebs and ghosts of the night before. I realised Andrea was speaking and I tuned in.

'...and bring me the original blackmail letter. With a bit of luck Reardon left his fingerprints all over it.'

I pulled her into a relieved hug, squeezing the air from her. She fought me off with a grin. 'Get off, you big soppy beast.'

When I finally put her down she carried on. 'And don't pay any attention to Claiborne. She's just gutted that her case has fallen apart in record time. There's no way they can pin this on you. Not now.'

'I don't know how you pulled that off,' I said, 'but thanks. I owe you yet another one.'

Andrea waved it away. 'Nothing to do with me. I just told Claiborne what we had.' She pointed behind me. 'You called it right, Harper.'

I turned and screwed up my eyes against the sun. On the other side of the street a woman leant against the door of an eight-year-old Hyundai Accent. She wore a navy top with thin straps and her legs were disappointingly hidden beneath baggy khaki combat trousers. The sun's rays lit her long dark hair, giving it the appearance of polished mahogany. Her arms were folded and a tired smile toyed with the corners of her mouth. I turned back to Andrea and found she was walking away. She called back over her shoulder, 'And stay out of trouble!'

I crossed the street and stood in front of Jessica Brodie. She had always been stunning and even the dark shadows beneath her eyes couldn't detract from her beauty. She'd lost weight, I noticed, which she might be happy about, but saddened me to see, for I knew the reasons behind it. But even with a few pounds off she still had the kind of curves that turned men's heads sideways and women's eyes green.

She blinked and I was sure I felt the draft from her long eyelashes as their movement drew me into her eyes. I looked into two deep, warm, brown pools, and wondered how deep the Jessica I used to know had sunk.

'Hell of a job, Jessica,' I said.

'I'm used to pulling your arse out of the fire.'

'What can I say, you're a wonderful human being.'

She opened the car door. 'Hungry?'

I realised I was ravenous. 'Like I said, wonderful.'

*

We stopped off at a bakery and bought sandwiches then drove to my flat in Paisley and sat at the kitchen table where I demolished my sandwich in a disgustingly short period of time. Jessica picked at hers and I wondered if she'd already eaten or if she had yet to regain her appetite. She pushed it away and began to fill me in.

'Andrea came to my door last night and told me you'd been lifted. Said you'd been on a case and someone had been shot, that you were the prime suspect and the cops weren't buying the story you gave them. She reckoned it wouldn't stick, not once the forensics were in, but she wanted you out of there as soon as possible.' Jessica picked an apple from the bowl in the centre of the table and began rolling it in both hands. 'She said you told her to ask me for help.'

'I did.'

'Why?'

'I didn't trust anyone else.'

'Mack?'

'Has everyone forgotten that asking Mack to look into this would be like slicing a loaf with a grenade?'

Jessica put the apple down, picked it back up again. She wouldn't look at me. 'Andrea didn't want me involved, did she?'

'No. She didn't.'

'I don't blame her, I wouldn't have either.'

I didn't say anything. There was nothing to be said. I had trusted her when even she wouldn't have trusted herself. And I'd been vindicated.

'Anyway,' Jessica said, placing the apple back in the bowl and looking at me now. 'I went out there and had a nosey. Told the cop outside that my elderly uncle lived in the building and I needed to make sure he was okay after all the drama.'

'And he fell for that?'

'He only seemed to care that I wasn't a reporter. Once he'd established that he just waved me in.'

'Sharp as a tack, I see.'

She shook her head in wonder. 'To be fair though, the dead guy's flat was still crawling with SOCOs, so it's not like I could've got in there anyway. But the rest of the stairwell was clear, so I just went up and down chapping doors and asking the neighbours if they'd seen or heard anything. Most of them hadn't, but there's a family with three wee boys on the floor above the dead guy. The cops had already been to their door, but the wee buggers just blanked them.'

'I think I met them.'

'Anyway, the little darlings were playing outside when they saw a guy go into the close with a gun in his hand. The description they all gave matched your description of the killer.'

'How did you get them to talk to you if they blanked the cops?'

'Told them they might get on the telly.'

'Lying to children? Jessica Brodie, I am appalled.'

'TV's the only authority these wee sods recognise. Might as well use it to our advantage.'

'Speaking of which, how the hell did you get hold of a video?'

'You mean they never taught you that at P.I. school?' Jessica said with feigned surprise. 'Guess they must have kept that for the ones with real talent.'

I rolled my eyes. 'Yeah, yeah, you're number one.'

'Glad you realise it.' Jessica smiled, but it wasn't a real one, not yet. There was too much pain there still. She leaned forward, focusing on her story. 'The guy across the close from Reardon is in his seventies. Gets harassed by those three brats almost every day. As usual there's nothing the police can do so he decides to get some evidence. He bought himself a tiny wee camera and stuck it above his door. Just a budget thing, not very high-spec, and no sound, but it does the job. It's connected to his telly so he can record whatever they're up to. He's had it a week and he's caught them on it five times already.'

'Five? The little shits.'

'Don't be ungrateful. Those little shits got you out of jail.'

'Wonderful children. I won't hear a word said against them.'

'Seems the wee horrors always come back several times, so the old boy presses record after the first thump at his door, and he catches them on camera the next few times, until they get fed up for the day. Not long before Reardon got shot they rattled the door and he started recording.'

'Yeah, I passed them on the stairs.'

'I know, I saw you arrive.'

'How good a recording is it?'

Jessica took a small, rectangular piece of plastic from her pocket and flipped it to me. 'You tell me.'

I caught the memory stick in mid air. 'You took a copy?'

'Would you have trusted the cops with the only copy? Imagine Darroch got his hands on it. He'd have Photoshopped your head onto the killer's and had you making Nazi salutes and clubbing baby seals on your way out the door.

'Anyway, you're not the only one with techy friends,' Jessica continued. 'I took it to a guy I know and he made me that copy before I gave the original to Andrea.'

'It's probably on the internet by now, then.'

'No, he knows better. Plus, he owes me a few favours.'

Owed favours or not, I couldn't see many men saying no to Jessica. I went into the spare room that doubled as a gym and an office and turned on the computer, trying to ignore the faint, ridiculous, feeling of jealousy.

I sat in the chair in front of the computer and Jessica brought a chair from the kitchen. She placed it beside me and we sat in silence as we waited for the computer to start up. I realised I was about to watch a man's life being ended, and yet I was excited about seeing it because it cleared me of the same crime. A feeling of shame flushed through me as I realised I hadn't given any thought to the fact that a man was dead.

I tried to put that thought from my mind and turned to Jessica. 'How've you been sleeping?'

'Fine.' It was too quick, too defensive.

'Really?'

Jessica shrugged but didn't look at me.

'Still having the nightmares?'

'Wouldn't you?' More defensive.

'Maybe you should see someone,' I suggested.

Now she looked at me, though her expression dripped derision. 'I'm not sure I'd be able to trust a therapist. But thanks for the suggestion.'

I held my hands up in surrender. 'Fine, okay, that was a crap idea. But you can't go on like this, Jess. You're sleeping at weird hours, if at all. You're having nightmares, you're depressed...'

'I'm not fucking depressed!' Jessica pushed her chair back violently and stood up. She began to pace the room.

And your temper's out of control, I didn't say.

Jessica stopped pacing and looked at me. 'The nightmares are a natural response to a fucked up situation, they'll go away in time. And my sleep pattern's a mess because I'm not working just now. Once I find a job and get back into a routine I'll be fine.'

'I offered you a job.'

'I want a job on merit, Harper. Not because you feel sorry for me.'

'For Christ's sake...'

The computer beeped to signal it was ready.

I held the memory stick up. 'You got me off a murder charge, Jessica. In one night. Believe me, it's on merit.' I connected the memory stick to the computer and opened the folder that showed its contents. There was only one file: a video clip, as promised. I hesitated, waiting for Jessica to sit back down. She finally did, though her folded arms told me she still wasn't happy. I wasn't either, and I wondered how we'd ended up like this.

I opened the file.

A new window opened on the screen, a high-angle shot of the landing between Reardon's flat and his neighbour's. The neighbour's door was beneath the camera and wasn't visible, though you would be able to see anyone outside it. Reardon's door was clear however, as were the first few steps leading downstairs. The video had only been playing a few seconds when I appeared at the top of the stairs and had my brief conversation with the old man. His head disappeared from the bottom of the screen as he returned to his flat and I turned to knock silently on Reardon's door.

The video was grainy, as I expected with something this low-budget, but Reardon was clearly recognisable when he opened his door. So was the fact that I shoved him inside his flat. While we waited for the gunman to appear a sudden thought occurred to me. 'Why didn't the neighbour give this to the police? They must have interviewed him.'

'Said he forgot about it at the time, what with all the excitement. More likely he was pissed off that the cops haven't helped him out with his bratty neighbours, so he didn't help them out.'

'Very public-spirited.'

The gunman appeared on screen at that moment and I paused the video as he turned to the camera. I had seen him twice before, but the first time, on the subway, I was too intent on following Reardon to pay any attention, and the second time had passed in a blurred fight for survival.

He was about my height, but heavier in the shoulders, arms and chest, and wore a tight black t-shirt to emphasise the muscles beneath. His right hand hung at his side, a gun clearly visible. I stared at his face, committing it to memory, trying to imagine what he might look like without the goatee, or with a hat or wig. When I was certain I would recognise him I restarted the video and watched as he checked the stairway leading upstairs was clear and turned back to Reardon's door. He knocked and stepped back, right arm extended at shoulder height, the gun an inch from the door.

The door opened and Reardon's face was visible for a split second. There was a flash and his face dropped out of sight. The gunman kicked the door wide open and charged into the flat. There were two more flashes and I shivered as I remembered how close those bullets had come to finding their mark.

The screen remained still for a time until the killer came running from the flat holding his left shoulder and disappeared down the stairs. Seconds later I followed, the gun now in my hand. Not long after that Reardon's flat became a police convention.

I turned to Jessica in amazement as the video continued to play. Despite our argument she couldn't completely contain the look of pride at what she'd accomplished, especially in such a short space of time. And at that time of night, when she must have had to drag people out of their beds, I couldn't imagine what she might have had to beg, promise or threaten to get people to cooperate with her. How could she think I'd offered her a job out of pity?

I had no idea how to thank her for what she had done and I felt like a first-class arsehole for ruining what should have been a moment of triumph for her. As I turned to face her, to try to put my gratitude into words, Jessica saved me once again.

'You're right,' she said. 'I am pretty amazing.'

Chapter Nine

Tiredness crept up on me then, sandbagging me after my disturbed night. Jessica tried to usher me off to bed, but I fought her off long enough to run a cold shower, standing under the freezing spray until the stale sweat and haunted dreams were sluiced down the drain. I dried off and lay on my bed, thinking off Jessica watching television in the living room. Her presence was a comfort and I wondered if the events of the last twenty-four hours might bring us closer again. Or if my attempts at forcing her to confront her problems would push us further apart. But she was here, still, and as I drifted off to sleep I held onto that like a lifebelt in the deepest ocean.

And suddenly I was catapulted back to consciousness. The sun still shone through the window, but lower. Much lower. I grabbed my watch from the bedside table and saw I had slept for hours. I swung my legs over the side of the bed and heard the noise again: a thumping at my front door.

I yanked on a pair of jeans from the floor as a warning bell rang in my mind. I threw a t-shirt on over the jeans and hurried into the hallway where Jessica was opening the door. I wanted to tell her not to. I wanted to warn her that no-one in my building bothered to close the external door properly, that it could be anyone on the other side of that door, that there was a killer out there who knew what I looked like and knew I was a witness to murder.

But I was too late. The door opened.

It wasn't a killer. But when I saw the blonde at the door and the look on Jessica's face I almost wished it had been.

Nicole Dunbar eyed Jessica slowly from head to toe, then

flicked her expensively-styled hair in dismissal and stalked past her. 'You found the blackmailer, then?' she said to me.

'Yeah.'

'And now my father's a murder suspect.' Nicole smiled coldly. 'Nice job, Harper.'

Behind her my front door slammed. Nicole and I both turned towards the sound. 'That's your client?' Jessica's voice sounded like she'd bitten into a sandwich and found a slug. A slug that was in the middle of taking a dump.

'Oh, didn't he tell you?' Nicole's feigned astonishment fooled no-one.

'No, he did not.'

I sighed and pinched the bridge of my nose as a headache arrived at speed. 'And neither did Andrea, apparently.'

'You thought I knew?' Jessica asked me. 'And what, I didn't mention it because I was fine with it?'

I opened my mouth, closed it again. Tried again, realised I resembled a goldfish and gave up. I walked into my living room and flopped heavily onto the sofa. Yesterday I had seen a man shot in the face, fought for my life and been charged with murder. Today wasn't shaping up to be much of an improvement.

Nicole strolled in after me and stood at the window, the low sun igniting her hair like a stolen halo. She was slim and petite, dressed in a crisp white shirt, skinny dark jeans and summer sandals. Her large blue eyes brought back memories and her soft, full lips made my heart tell my head to shut up and come back later. Whatever I thought of her – and there were times that opinion had been lower than a snake's belly – she was gorgeous. Problem was, she knew it.

Jessica followed her into the room and leant against the door frame. She looked calm, but her clenched fists betrayed her. She had never liked Nicole: had always – for reasons I couldn't fathom – felt inadequate around her, and, after the last few months she'd endured, seeing Nicole here, now, in my home, was a surprise she didn't need.

'What's going on, Harper?' Jessica asked.

I looked from one to the other, caught between two women I

had known strong feelings for, and who hated each other with a passion. There was no way to keep them both happy. I had known that from the moment Nicole had entered my office the previous morning. And still I had chosen to help her.

So what did that say about where my feelings lay?

'Nicole's dad is missing, Jess. He was being blackmailed, and Nicole hired me to find him and make sure he's safe.'

'She's paying you?' Jessica asked, looking from me to Nicole. I nodded as Nicole gave her a look that suggested no money had changed hands. Jessica blanked her and asked, 'What was the blackmail about?'

Nicole jumped in before I could answer. 'A mistake, that's all. My father's done nothing wrong.'

'The note suggests that your father paid the blackmailer at least once. Innocent people don't tend to cough up.'

I had tried to be gentle but Nicole's eyes narrowed in anger. 'He's done nothing wrong.'

Jessica peeled herself from the doorframe and walked into the middle of the room where she looked down at me. 'You sure this is a good idea, Harper?'

I wasn't sure. Not even remotely. Not about letting Nicole back into my life, and certainly not about hurting Jessica. But again, Nicole answered before I could gather my thoughts. 'And why wouldn't it be?' she asked, stepping away from the window.

Jessica waved an airy hand. 'Oh, I don't know. Past performance maybe?'

'*Our* past has nothing to do with you, does it? You're just the friend.'

'Which puts me a step above the paycheque.'

I rolled my eyes and began to wonder if dodging those bullets yesterday had been the better choice. I looked back at the catfight as Nicole tilted her head to one side and studied Jessica thoughtfully. Against her better judgement Jessica finally snapped. 'What?'

'Oh, nothing,' Nicole replied sweetly. 'I thought for a second you'd lost weight. My mistake.'

There was silence in the room as I waited for the explosion. It never came. Instead Jessica swept up her purse and keys from the table and left the room. A second later the door slammed like she was trying to demolish the building.

I looked at Nicole with distaste and waited for some sign of shame or regret. Then I caught myself. This was Nicole. Did I expect her to change the habits of a lifetime?

'You know,' I said, 'you can be a real bitch sometimes.'

'Perhaps. But I've yet to make anyone in your family a murder suspect, so I'd say I've got the moral high ground here.'

'Sit down.' I waved at the sofa opposite.

Nicole gave me a stubborn look. 'Did you throw my father to the police to get back at me? Is that it?'

'For once, Nicole – just once – try to imagine the whole world doesn't revolve around you, okay? Now sit down.'

She surprised me by doing as I asked. She might have surprised herself too, since it was something of a first.

'Listen, Nicole. You hired me to find your dad because you wanted someone you could trust. Now you have to trust me. I found the man who was blackmailing him. Minutes later someone shot and killed that man and tried to kill me. What did you expect me to say to the police? How exactly was I supposed to explain my presence at a murder scene?'

Nicole looked off to the side and I recognised the gesture. She knew she was wrong but couldn't, or wouldn't, bring herself to acknowledge it. A moment later she looked back at me and her face was clear and open, as though she had apologised for her outburst and the air had been cleared between us. It had always been that way with Nicole.

'Okay,' she said, her tone suggesting that I had apologised and she had magnanimously accepted. 'They told me the blackmailer's name was Sean Reardon. What do you know about him?'

'He's a lowlife.'

'Is that it?'

'You only hired me yesterday, Nicole. Do you think I just fire names into Google?' I paused and swallowed my annoyance. 'Did you recognise the name?'

'Of course not.' Nicole tutted like she was offended. 'And what about the man who shot him? Do you know anything about him?'

'Nope.'

'Nope?' She looked at me from beneath her brows. 'So you know nothing about the blackmailer or the man who killed him?'

'I've been locked up since I was shot at, Nicole. Little things like that tend to hamper an investigation.'

'I've spent a rather uncomfortable few hours with a Detective Inspector Claiborne myself. She thinks my father hired this man to kill the blackmailer. Did you give her that idea?'

'She's not stupid. As soon as the blackmail was mentioned that's an obvious conclusion. But she also maintains that I'm not entirely in the clear.'

'Why did they let you go then?'

'Jessica found evidence that they'd missed.'

Nicole dismissed that with a roll of her eyes. Whether it was aimed at Jessica or the police I wasn't sure. Probably both.

'You're going to find this killer,' she said. It didn't sound like a question.

'The police are looking for him.'

'No, they're looking for my father. And if they find him they'll try and pin this on him.'

I nodded. I knew from experience how it could go. 'To find the killer I'll have to investigate your father.'

'Fine.'

'I'll need to speak to people close to your dad. Friends, colleagues... One of them might know what this is about.'

'No.'

'What do you mean, *no*?'

'I mean, no, you don't need to speak to his friends and colleagues.'

I leant towards her as though that might help me understand. 'You want me to find your dad, but you want me to do it without talking to anyone he knows?'

Nicole ran a finger along the neckline of her shirt as she changed tactics. Subtlety was never her strong suit. 'Listen,

The Forgotten Dead

Harper,' she purred. 'This whole blackmail thing's bullshit. We both know it. But mud sticks, you know? I want my father back, but I'm not going to help some snivelling little shit destroy his good name from beyond the grave. And if you speak to people he knows that's exactly what will happen. If my father comes back to find his career and reputation are ruined through malicious rumours, it won't be because of me, okay? Or you.'

'What about the blackmail?' I asked. 'Don't you want to know what it was about?'

Nicole sighed and ran a hand through her hair. 'In an ideal world you'd have found him, broken his bloody legs and made him tell you. But he's dead, and my father is being blamed for it, so let's just concentrate on finding the killer.'

I looked at Nicole for a long time, trying to work out what she really wanted. I knew how willing she was to harbour a grudge. Would she really be satisfied with me identifying the killer and clearing her dad? Or had she mentioned leg-breaking to open me up to the idea of violent retribution?

'Why did you come to me, Nicole?' I asked.

'Because my father's gone missing?' She tried to look confused but was fooling no-one.

'There's plenty of investigators in the phone book. Why me?'

She didn't hesitate. 'Because you're a good man.'

'Not good enough,' I replied, thinking of the way she'd walked out on me.

Nicole picked up on something in my tone and sighed again. 'Whatever happened between us is in the past. You're not a petty man, and I know you'll help someone in trouble, even if it's not what you want to do.'

I almost believed her, but I knew there was more to it. 'You think I'll keep the blackmail under wraps, don't you? Whatever it was about, you think I'll cover it up.'

A look of frustration came over her face, but was quickly smothered. 'Like I said, you're a good man. If you find something, I know you'll do what's right.'

Which didn't really answer my question. Or maybe it did.

Nicole continued. 'And I can trust you not to try and

blackmail my father if you do find something. Could I be that sure about anyone else?'

I had to concede that point. 'So you need me.'

'Definitely,' she whispered, as her fingers returned to the neck of her shirt.

'But I can't speak to any of your dad's friends or colleagues?'

'Nope.' And suddenly her tone was playful. 'And I'm in charge. Now, will you help me or not?'

It was my turn to stand and walk to the window. I squinted against the slowly dying sun as the river trudged past beneath it like golden syrup, its waters lower than I had ever seen. A couple strolled by on the far bank, hand in hand, fingers entwined like miniature lovers, oblivious to everything and everyone around them. I had been like that once, and some days I felt I could be once again.

My focus shifted to Nicole's reflection in the glass. I studied her and thought about our past. It wasn't every day a beautiful woman asked for your help. You'd think a guy would be only too happy to help. But then, it wasn't every day that the beautiful woman in question was the same one who had ripped your heart from your chest and crushed it beneath her cloven hoof.

Certainly makes you think twice.

And Nicole Dunbar was beautiful, no arguments. I hadn't forgotten that over the last twelve months, but when she had walked into my office yesterday – and watching her golden reflection in the glass now – I could almost smell the scent of her skin and feel it pressed against mine. And she knew it.

I could see it in the way she lounged on the sofa, her slim legs crossed to show them off, an extra button unfastened on her white shirt, giving just a hint of lace. Like I said, subtlety and Nicole were barely on nodding terms. Manipulation on the other hand... well, they were old friends.

She was playing me, and I knew it. The real problem was that part of me was enjoying it.

I pushed the mental images away, knowing if I dropped my guard I could end up in trouble. The kind of trouble that feels pretty good until you're in so deep you can't find your way out.

I looked at the way the sun caught her hair, the white shirt against her tanned skin, the shine of her lips as they parted in a knowing smile. I'd love to say I stayed on the case to help a man in trouble, to protect someone in need, but I'd only be lying to myself. I spread my hands in surrender and stepped into trouble.

'Fine,' I said. 'I'm all yours.'

Chapter Ten

I pressed the buzzer for the third time, leaving my thumb against it for a good ten seconds. A few seconds after I let go there was a click and a voice snapped, 'What?'

'It's Harper. Let me in.'

There was silence for a few moments and I wondered if Jessica was still there. I'd waited till ten o'clock to come here, though I could have come at any time and been unsure of finding her either awake or at home. The last few months had seen her sleep pattern fall into disarray, leaving her asleep at midday and wide awake in the early hours. I was taking a chance coming here anyway after Nicole's arrival at my door last night.

Eventually the buzzer sounded and the lock released with a click. I climbed the stairs to the top floor where Jessica's door was slightly ajar, hesitantly pushed it open and called her name.

'Kitchen,' she replied

I entered the kitchen and found Jessica leaning against the oven with a cup of coffee held tightly in both hands. She wore a thin vest and shorts topped off with a thick scowl.

I tested the water. 'Hey.'

'What time did you kick the bitch out this morning, then?'

It seemed there were sharks in the water.

'She left not long after you.'

'Shame. Hope I didn't spoil the mood. Good luck to you both. I hope you're very happy together.'

'Jessica, pack it in.' My voice was hard and she didn't like it. She slammed the coffee cup down on the counter behind her, her temper frayed already.

'I'm not fucking stupid, Harper!'

'Then stop acting it!'

We stood facing each other and I wondered how we had slipped so far from the comfort we used to know. Jessica's teeth were gritted, her jaw set, her eyes afire.

'Look, Jessica, I need you. And I need you to be you. You're letting Nicole under your skin. If she could see you now, she'd be laughing at you. You're better than that. You're better than her.'

Her eyes still burned me, but her jaw softened. She picked up her coffee mug and a cloth and mopped up the spilt liquid. She threw the cloth in the sink and eventually asked, 'Why did you agree to help her?'

'Because she needs help. Her dad's in trouble, and I don't think she realises juts how much. I don't like her dad, never did, but he still deserves help.'

'What about the bitch? How do you feel about her?'

I paused – perhaps a fraction too long – then tried to be truthful. 'I don't know. I want to help the Nicole I used to know, the Nicole I loved once.'

Was that true? Who knew? It's hard to be truthful when you don't know what the truth is.

Jessica nodded, like I'd confirmed something. I had no idea if that something was in my favour or not. 'She's long gone, Harper. I don't think she ever actually existed.'

'Maybe not. But I think doing this will tell me, one way or the other.'

*

'How long's he been missing?'

'Nicole spoke to him last Thursday night, so a week at the most,' I replied. 'She got worried when he didn't return her calls so she went round on Monday, found the blackmail letter, and came to see me first thing Tuesday morning.'

We were sitting in Jessica's living room now, me in an armchair with my back to the window, her on the sofa opposite finishing a bowl of cereal. She had showered and dressed in jeans and a plain white t-shirt, tied her hair back in a ponytail, and applied make-up to cover the puffiness beneath her eyes. It was simple, but the effect was breathtaking. When she'd come back into the room and asked me to fill her in on the case it was all I could do to remember what case she was talking about, far less talk her through everything I knew.

'And of course,' she said, pointing an accusatory spoon at me, 'we don't know if he's spoken to anyone else since then, because the bitch won't let us speak to anyone he knows.'

'I'm not happy about it either,' I said. 'But she's writing the cheques, so she calls the shots.'

'Up to a point.'

'To a point,' I agreed.

Jessica glanced down at a photocopy of the blackmail letter lying on the sofa beside her – I'd delivered the original to Andrea first thing this morning – and said, 'You realise she's asked you to look into this because she thinks you'll cover up the blackmail, right?'

'Yes. I'm not as daft as I look.'

'You couldn't possibly be.'

'Anyway, Nicole told me there are messages on her dad's answering machine from the three people he knows best. None of them seemed concerned, so it doesn't look like he spoke to anyone in his usual circles.'

'What does your gut tell you? Ran off or was taken?'

'Ran off.' I didn't hesitate. I'd thought about it enough. 'Reardon expected him to be at the meeting, so he had nothing to do with it. I think Gordon was scared. He knew there was someone dangerous involved and he legged it before they got close to him.'

Jessica nodded her agreement as she swallowed another mouthful of cereal. 'Tell me about Gordon Dunbar.'

I gathered my thoughts then told Jessica the little I knew. 'Gordon is a doctor, a GP, has been for about twenty years, worked in A&E before that. Now he works in a wee surgery in Giffnock, lives there too. Was married, but separated from his wife when Nicole was thirteen, so that would be nineteen years ago. She died a few years ago.'

'Suspicious?'

'Don't think so. It was cancer.'

'You never know, especially with him being a doctor.'

'True. But when she died, they had barely spoken for years. I don't think he'd have had enough access to kill her without raising suspicion.'

'Fair enough,' Jessica conceded, placing her empty bowl on the coffee table between us. 'Might be worth bearing in mind though. He was being blackmailed over something after all. And despite what Nicole says, he's guilty. It's obvious from the letter that he paid up at least once.'

I nodded thoughtfully. 'That's the key, isn't it? Find out what the blackmail was about and we'll find the killer. We need to investigate both Gordon Dunbar and Sean Reardon, find out more about the blackmail through one of them.'

'Any chance that Reardon's death and the blackmail of Gordon Dunbar are unrelated?'

'The killer followed me and Reardon from George Square, when Reardon was there to be paid by Gordon. Too much of a coincidence.'

'That's what I thought,' Jessica agreed. 'You take Gordon and I'll take Reardon. I don't imagine Nicole would be too happy with me sniffing around her dad.'

'Probably not. That's why I emailed you the info Brownstone sent me on Reardon.'

'Already? You're sure of yourself.'

'I was sure about you.'

Jessica flushed and looked away, embarrassed. Then she seemed to be considering something, finding the right words. Finally she asked, 'You sure this is a good idea, Harper?'

'Why does everyone keep asking me that?'

'She messed you up the last time.'

'We were together then. This is business.'

'Can you keep it that way?' Jessica's eyes were hard again and I felt my conviction waver in the face of her stare. 'Because if you can't, I'm out.'

'You know the real reason I agreed to stay on this case?'

Jessica raised her eyebrows in a *do tell* gesture.

'Someone tried to kill me, Jess. And I want to know why. I want to find him and I want to break his fucking neck. That's my priority. He tried to shoot me and that really pisses me off.'

Jessica looked at me for a few seconds then said, with a straight face, 'You'd think you'd be used to it by now.'

She laughed then. It wasn't truly heartfelt, and wouldn't be for a while, but it held a kernel of the deep, throaty laugh that had always turned my legs a little weak. She leant forward and held out her clenched fist. 'You want to find him?'

I bumped my knuckles against hers. 'Oh, yeah.'

'Then let's go get him, tiger.'

Chapter Eleven

We split up and I headed to Giffnock while Jessica returned to Ibrox to speak to Reardon's neighbours. She'd already spoken to most of them, but that was about the shooting. This time, armed with the information provided by Brownstone, she would be asking about Reardon himself.

I found the right street and spotted Nicole's three-year-old yellow Beetle parked half on the kerb outside a three-bedroom detached house in blonde sandstone. I pulled my black Honda Civic in behind the Beetle and noticed the time on the dashboard clock. I was more than half an hour late and a small, petty part of me was quite happy about that.

I climbed out of the car and walked up the driveway, noting the parched grass and bushes wilting in the sweltering midday heat. The house itself was in good condition and, given the area, likely to be expensive, as was the BMW 5 Series sitting at the head of the driveway. Of course, neither meant that Gordon Dunbar had ready access to disposable cash. Or that he would be willing to part with it to a blackmailer.

Nicole stood on the top step, one hand holding the door open, the other shading her eyes against the sun. 'You're late.'

I nodded to the red BMW. 'Is that his only car?'

She nodded. 'Why wouldn't he take it?'

Because he doesn't want to be found.

'I don't know yet,' I lied.

I followed Nicole into the house and stood in the kitchen door as she filled the kettle. Her jeans were spattered with paint and I wondered if she'd been in her studio this morning or if she'd simply thrown on something comforting and familiar before she left home.

'Coffee?' Nicole asked.

'No, thanks. Still don't drink it.'

'But it's nice to be asked, right?' she said with a smile.

I smiled too, despite myself. Here she was, pulling my strings again, and I was already rolling over to have my belly scratched. So much for willpower.

I told her I was going to take a look around and wandered off. But not before I'd spotted the two empty bottles of Glayva on the counter by the kitchen door and the almost empty bottle of store-brand whisky by the window. Nicole had never mentioned her dad being a big drinker, but all of the bottles were clear of dust. Had Gordon had a party recently? If so, he'd managed to find a lot of people that drank Glayva and not much else. Or, perhaps more likely, something had driven Gordon to drink heavily, starting on the liqueur he normally favoured, and ending up on the supermarket whisky when he admitted to himself he only wanted it for the effect.

I scrutinised the rest of the ground floor for anything else that seemed out of place. Nothing did. Not even by millimetres. The room was sparsely furnished, every edge perpendicular or parallel to the next, and everything told me something about the homeowner, as I'm sure Gordon had intended. From the thick encyclopedia of wines on the coffee table, to the bonsai tree on the mantelpiece and the alcove full of classic books with their uncracked spines; everything was carefully chosen to convey an image of sophistication. It was a show home, not a real home, and yet all it showed me was that I'd been right about Gordon Dunbar all along.

I had met Nicole's father several times during our relationship, and even the first was once too often. I was never sure if the feeling was mutual; the man seemed too enveloped in his own smugness to care about me one way or another. Perhaps being entirely wrapped up in yourself was a family trait.

In truth, although I had instinctively disliked Gordon, my opinion had been coloured from the start. I had learned enough from Nicole about both her parents to read between the lines and I had lived through enough of the aftershocks to know it was their use of her as a pawn in their perpetual game of psychological one-upmanship that had screwed Nicole up and created her skewed vision of her own importance. To use an old cliché, I blamed the parents. Problem was, so did Nicole. I had long given up hoping that she might move on from that.

Given all that, it was no surprise that this was the first time I had been in Gordon's home, and now, walking around, examining his possessions and looking for a clue to where he might have gone, or even to something of his personality, I found only what Gordon wanted his visitors to see. Which, in reality, told me only that he was as superficial as I'd suspected. I gave up on the ground floor and opened the door to the basement, where I found only cobwebbed junk that hadn't been disturbed in a long time. I closed the basement door and climbed the stairs to the upper floor.

I gave the bathroom a quick look over to rule it out. With a family like mine I was never surprised with the places things could be found, but Gordon had apparently been more traditional with his storage solutions and I found nothing.

It was a similar story in Gordon's bedroom. The bed was neatly made and, as Nicole had told me, appeared to have been undisturbed for several days. The chest of drawers by the bed contained nothing but neatly folded clothes and the wardrobe held more clothes with two rows of shoes on the floor. I was starting to feel like I was searching a movie set.

The first of the spare rooms contained nothing but a neatly made bed and a bookcase stuffed full of everything Stephen King and John Grisham had ever written. Obviously the literary snob in Gordon didn't want these on display downstairs with the Dickens' and Keats'.

It was the third bedroom where I finally found something interesting. The single bed and small bedside cabinet held nothing of interest, but the desk by the window had two large drawers, both full of hanging files, all conveniently labelled with everything from *Bank Statements* to *Credit Card* to *Phone Bills* to *Council Tax* to *Insurance*. Every little piece of the minutiae of modern life had a file bearing its name, and each was impeccably organised, in chronological order, starting with the most recent and dating back two years.

Did I mention how much I liked Gordon Dunbar?

I pressed the power button on the computer and leafed through the files while I waited. Most of them were of little interest to me. I kept out the files containing the phone bills, credit card bills and bank statements and returned everything else to the drawers.

Gordon's most recent bank statement was dated two weeks ago and showed less than two thousand pounds in the account. Nowhere near enough to pay off the blackmailer. I scanned the statement and saw a healthy salary being paid in, so where was all the money?

The answer lay in the dozens of withdrawals Gordon had made. A hundred pounds here, two hundred pounds there: too many and too frequent for them to be payoffs for any kind of extortion. Plus, I'd found one large payment that was almost certainly the blackmail payoff. Almost four weeks ago Gordon had withdrawn five thousand pounds. No other, similarly large amounts were listed, suggesting Reardon had been paid only once.

So what were the smaller withdrawals?

Whatever they were, they explained the lack of funds in the account. The balance showed a steady depletion over the last two years, the monthly salary acting only as a sticking plaster on a severe wound.

The withdrawals were all from various cash machines but there were three that appeared frequently. One, according to the statements, was located on Sauchiehall Street, and another on Renfrew Street – both in the city centre – but the third bore a label that meant nothing to me. I kept the most recent statement, folded it up and stuffed it in the back pocket of my jeans.

The credit card statements told me that Gordon regularly withdrew cash from those too, and that he frequented those same three cash machines most often. They also told me that he had almost twenty grand of debt spread across four cards. I returned them to their file and gave the phone bills a cursory glance, pushing them aside for the moment.

The computer was up and running now and looking for a password. I went to the door and called to Nicole, asking her to come upstairs. She trotted up a minute later, taking just long enough to let me know she was still the boss.

'Do you know your dad's password?' I asked.

Nicole came to the desk, bent at the waist and leant across me to type it in. Her neck was within inches of my lips, her still-familiar perfume floating in the suddenly heavy air between us. I closed my eyes to the smoothness of the skin that was only a kiss away, and waited for her to straighten up. It took a remarkably long time to type in an eight-character password.

'You okay?'

I opened my eyes and saw Nicole's amused face closer than expected. I flinched and she repeated her question.

'Yeah, fine. Just a bit warm in here.' I straightened up in the chair and focused on the screen.

'Anything else?' There was a flirtatious tone to Nicole's voice and I gave myself a mental kicking for letting my guard down.

'Actually, yes.' I grabbed the phone bills like a man in quicksand reaching for a hanging vine. 'Can you go through these and label any you know?'

Nicole took the bills for the last three months and left the room. I heard her footsteps going downstairs and blew out a long breath.

I began trawling through Gordon's computer and found I was wading through a lot of junk. From what I remembered of Gordon he hadn't been the most technically astute, and the evidence before me suggested he had used his computer mainly for completing paperwork relating to his job. His browser history showed a small number of websites visited semi-regularly, though nothing that seemed promising, and certainly nothing that he could be blackmailed over. It looked as though

Gordon was firmly of the generation that didn't trust his computer. I knew how he felt – I was from the, *If it doesn't work give it a dunt,* school of thought.

I hunted around some more and found nothing of further interest. That left me with the curious cash machine withdrawals, unless something promising turned up in the phone bills. I shut down the computer and returned the room to the way I'd found it. I went back downstairs and found Nicole sitting on the kitchen worktop, head down, hair hanging over her face like a sad five-year-old. I wondered if this vulnerability was for show or if she was genuinely upset. I wanted to go to her and take her in my arms, to comfort her and tell her it would be alright. But the warning bell was ringing. I stopped in the doorway and kept a safe distance.

'How did you get on?'

Nicole looked up, apparently surprised to see me in the doorway. She slid down from the counter and walked past me into the dining room, took a seat at the table where a small book lay open showing two pages of names and phone numbers. I sat opposite and she passed me the annotated bills and talked me through the numbers she'd found in her dad's phone book. There hadn't been many calls at all, and most of the ones that had been made were to a few friends and colleagues – the very people I couldn't speak to. I told Nicole that I would have to take the statements with me and check out the remaining numbers. She wasn't happy about it, and reminded me to be careful who I spoke to. I asked her to reconsider the restriction she was imposing on me and received only a withering glare in return. I then asked for a recent photograph of Gordon. She went to a drawer in the sideboard and flipped through a packet of photographs, took one out and passed it to me.

'That one's about a year old, but he still looks exactly the same.'

Gordon hadn't changed a bit since I'd last met him. He had dark brown hair, greying at the temples and balding prominently on the top, and a face dominated by a thick brown moustache. I knew that he was mid-fifties and, judging by the photo, he looked every day of it. What the photo didn't show was that he was shorter than average and slightly built but for a burgeoning belly. I took a second to fix a clear picture of Gordon in my mind, trying to see him without the moustache as that was the easiest change to make.

Nicole interrupted my thoughts by asking what I was going to do now. I told her I had a few leads to follow, but didn't elaborate. I wasn't going to tell Nicole anything I might find until I knew what I was dealing with.

Before I left, I said, 'What's he done, Nicole? Why doesn't he want to be found?'

She stared back at me defiantly. 'Nothing. I don't know why he's scared, but he's done nothing wrong.'

'He's done something or he knows something, Nicole. Something serious. A guy blackmailed him over it and that guy ended up dead. Your dad could be in real danger.'

'Then find him!'

'I'll find him quicker if you tell me the truth.'

'I am telling you the truth.' Moisture filled her eyes and she was almost pleading now. 'I'm worried about him, Harper. Please find him. He's done nothing wrong.'

'How can you be sure?'

'Because he's my father! Isn't that good enough?'

'No.' I sighed and rubbed my palms over my face, wiping away the thin sheen of sweat that had begun to build in the heat. 'I'll tell you now, Nicole. Whatever this is, I can't guarantee I can keep it quiet.'

'Fine,' she said. 'I know you'll do the right thing.'

She turned away, but not before I saw the look that said, *And that'll be whatever I tell you to do.*

Before this was over, one of us was in for a surprise.

Chapter Twelve

I got back into my car and quickly wound down the windows before I passed out from the heat. I took Gordon's bank statement from my pocket. It didn't matter what Nicole said, I knew Gordon had been involved in something, and as far as I was concerned, the proof was in his bank records.

I checked again the three cash machines that Gordon seemed to frequent most often and memorised the notations listed beside them on the statement.

CPTLNK 27 RENFREW ST

CPTRBOS BOTHWELL STR

CPTLNK GLASGOW – DCE

The first was certainly straight-forward: the LNK told me that the cash machine was part of the Link network, and the rest was the ATMs street address – 27 Renfrew Street. The second was a Royal Bank of Scotland ATM located somewhere on Bothwell Street, while all I could tell about the third was that it was a Link machine in Glasgow. If I needed to I could ask Brownstone to find out more.

It looked almost certain though that none of the ATMs were anywhere near Gordon's home or workplace, and yet he visited them regularly. It was a fair bet that whatever Gordon was spending the money on was located near to those machines. And an even better bet that it was something he could be blackmailed over. My first thoughts were prostitutes

The Forgotten Dead

and drugs, and neither could be ruled in or out without more investigation.

I put the car in gear and headed for the city centre.

The traffic was sluggish in the lunchtime heat, as though everyone had decided it was just too damn hot to hurry anywhere. It took far longer than normal to reach Glasgow and when I finally got there I was only too glad to park the car at the bottom of Renfrew Street and get some air, hot and dry as it was.

I walked up the street, checked the building numbers to make sure I was on the right side, and kept my eyes open for a cash machine. I'd only walked a few hundred yards when the red and blue Link logo caught my eye. The doorway beside the ATM had a brass 25 fixed to the frame confirming I had the right machine. I turned to look around for any clues to what Gordon might have spent his money on, and when I turned one-hundred-and-eighty degrees I almost laughed out loud at how obvious it was.

On the other side of the street was Glasgow's newest casino: Dice. Four floors of gaming tables, slot machines, bars and a restaurant. Somehow I didn't think Gordon had been coming here for the steak.

I returned to my car and moved it from the side of the road to Dice's expansive car park. The building was impressive, all sleek metal and glass, an ultra-modern newcomer to Glasgow's theatre district. I doubted the nearby Theatre Royal and Royal Concert Hall saw it as competition for their business, but the grand opening had been delayed twice over vocal objections to another casino in the city. If I had a pound for every time I'd heard the term *tax on the poor* I could have bankrolled the place. Funny how the same objectors had no problems playing their own half-dozen lottery tickets every week though. Guess that's different somehow.

I stepped through the automatic sliding doors and into an air-conditioned reception that could only be described as heavenly. If the hordes on the street found out how cool it was in here the place would be overrun with people happy to stick a few pounds in a fruit machine just to stop sweating for ten minutes.

The reception desk was a long silver block with a smiling man in a suit behind it. Call me a cynic, but I was fairly sure I heard him make a *ka-ching* noise at another mug entering the premises. I strolled over, enjoying the cool air, and said hello. I didn't ask him about Gordon Dunbar in case he tried to stop me talking to other members of staff. I'd ask him on the way out if need be.

The receptionist gave me a quick rundown on where everything was located. Electronic gaming on the ground floor, main gaming floor on the first, restaurant and smaller gaming area on the second, private members' area on the third, bars on each level, did I mention the main gaming floor was on the first, just at the top of that escalator?

I prised myself away before he started a find-the-queen scam right there on the reception desk. I pushed through the doors into the casino and stopped to look around. The ground floor was smaller than I had expected it to be, though the central two-storey sculpture of two gold-coloured dice and the pair of escalators that sandwiched it occupied a large portion of the available space. Despite this the management had still managed to cram in an impressive number of electronic poker, roulette and fruit machines. Even at one o'clock on a Thursday afternoon, in the middle of a heatwave, there were people hunched over machines, methodically ploughing coins and pushing buttons with all the excitement of using a kettle.

I remembered my first trip to a casino – and the disappointment when I realised it was nothing like a James Bond movie. This was more of the same; ordinary people chasing money they'd never win, or a short-term buzz they'd only end up chasing again five minutes after it wore off.

This wasn't the floor I wanted though – there were virtually no staff here, and none that had any interaction with the punters. I rode the escalator to the first floor, ascending alongside the massive dice. As I reached the first floor I looked around and saw the going was slower up here, with only five customers spread around the whole gaming floor. Several tables were occupied only by the croupier. That would at least make it easier to ask the staff a few questions.

I headed for the bar and ordered a can of Irn-Bru. While the barman poured the drink into a glass with all the urgency of a sloth on industrial action I looked around and noticed a stand-alone cash machine at the far side of the room, placed very conspicuously near the toilets where everyone would pass it at some point. That explained the third ATM Gordon was fond of: LNK GLASGOW – DCE. Presumably he used the one across the road more often as this one would almost certainly incur a withdrawal charge. Until he was chasing his bets of course and this one became too convenient to ignore.

Of course, that was assuming Gordon did indeed come here to gamble. For all I knew at this point he was meeting high-class hookers for a cocaine-fuelled orgy.

I paid for my drink and walked to the nearest unoccupied gaming table where a middle-aged man stood idly spinning a roulette wheel as though that would tempt us to part with our cash. I pulled up a seat and dropped a twenty on the table. The croupier slid it through a slot in the table and placed a small stack of chips in front of me. I put half on black and watched the wheel spin. It came up black. I took that as a good sign and began to make small talk.

Or at least, I tried. The dealer wasn't the chatty type, giving me a definite *shut up, I just want my shift to be over* vibe. I ditched the small talk and took the photo of Gordon from my pocket. I placed it on the centre of the roulette grid and slid it towards him.

'Recognise him?'

The dealer looked at the photo and rolled his eyes. 'Oh aye, I recognise him alright. Most folk in here would.'

'He's a regular then?'

'Why the interest?'

'He's missing. I'm a private investigator and I'm trying to find him.'

'Is he in trouble?'

'I don't know. That's why I need to find him.'

The croupier turned and spun the wheel and I watched the ball bounce after he tossed it in. He didn't look at me during the spin and I could almost hear the gears turning in his head. Finally he turned back and fixed me with a calculating look. 'He's a regular.'

'How regular?'

'Few times a month. Sometimes more, sometimes less. Depends how well he's doing, like most of them.' His voice oozed disdain. 'Likes his roulette, so he does. Maybe a bit too much, if you catch my drift.'

I did. It wasn't all that subtle.

'What's he like when he's playing? Quiet? Chatty?'

'Starts off quiet. By the time he's had a few drinks he loosens up.'

'How many drinks are we talking about?'

'A lot.' He dipped his head and his voice grew quiet, almost conspiratorial. 'Between you and me, I think he might have a problem.'

'Is that so? Was it the heavy drinking and the chronic gambling that tipped you off?'

The croupier held his hands up defensively. 'Hey, it's not my call. As long as they're not abusive they can play. It's up to the bar staff when they stop serving drinks. And the Gamble Aware signs are all over the place. People need to take some responsibility for themselves, you know?'

I held my own hands up, a gesture of apology. 'You're right, you're right. So, when does he come in? Any particular night, any particular time?'

'Could be any night. He's a late one. Eleven at the earliest, sometimes doesn't show up till the wee small hours. Like he's been lying in bed and all of a sudden the bug's bitten him.'

'He's got the bug then?'

'Oh aye, something terrible. Doesn't know when to walk away, chases his bets, gets worse when he's drunk… His bank balance must be taking a hiding.'

'When did you last see him?'

The dealer screwed up his face in thought. 'Couple of weeks, I think. Must be due back in soon.'

'What makes you say that?'

'Oh he needs his fix, don't you worry about that. He'll be in soon.'

I thought about that and knew he could be right, assuming Gordon was simply in hiding. People are creatures of habit, and, most of the time, when they go into hiding it's their habits that help track them down. Gordon, if he was as hooked on casino gambling as the croupier would have me believe, could very well be back here at some point.

'How about you give me a call when he shows up?' I said.

The dealer sucked air through his teeth like a mechanic giving an estimate. 'Don't know… that could get me in bother…'

'Let's cut the crap,' I said. 'How much do you want?'

To his credit he didn't even bother trying to look offended. 'Five hundred.'

I laughed. 'Get real. He's not that important. And you've already told me everyone else in here knows who he is too. Maybe I should ask some of them.'

'Believe me, none of those arseholes would help you. And I'm here every night. If he comes in, I'll spot him. For four hundred.'

'One.'

'I can't take any less than three hundred. Honestly, my boss would skin me alive if he knew I was doing this.'

'One,' I replied. 'Or I'll find some homeless guy and sit him outside with a half-bottle and twenty-pee for the phone box.'

The croupier blew out a long breath. 'I need half up front.'

'No. You might want it, but you don't need it. This is money for nothing.' I stood up and slid one of my cards onto the table, scooped my chips into my hand. 'You call me as soon as you see him. He's still around when I get here then you get your hundred.'

'What if he's gone by the time you get here?'

'Then you don't get paid.'

I left the table and took my chips to the cash desk, walked away eighteen pounds up and with a spy on my side. I didn't bother with the rest of the staff. No sense in attracting the attention of management or security when I'd already found a source. Despite the croupier's whining I knew he'd call as soon as Gordon stepped onto the gaming floor. A greedy spy was always better than one who simply wanted to help. The greedy ones made sure they delivered.

I stepped outside and the blistering heat hit me like the blast from a furnace. The air conditioning had made me forget just how warm it was on the street. I crossed the car park, eyes squinting against the sun and its reflected glare slanting off car roofs and windows. The glare was so bright I almost stepped in front of a white Renault Laguna as it raced towards the exit. I stopped abruptly and chided myself for being so careless. Back in the car I put it out of my mind and decided to uncover the extent of Gordon's gambling.

*

There were six other casinos in Glasgow, and I visited each of them in turn. From the edge of the River Clyde to the Merchant City and back into the shopping district. The first I visited was the latest chain casino on Bothwell Street, which I found located near the end of the street, not far from the M8 off-ramp, and directly across the street from a Royal Bank of Scotland cash machine. It seemed I'd found Gordon's other favourite casino.

As I'd hoped, two employees – a barman and a croupier – identified Gordon as a regular, giving me virtually the same information as the dealer in Dice had, including the drinking. They were both part time so I doubled up on spies and made the same arrangement with both of them: one hundred if they called when Gordon showed up.

I visited the other five casinos with less success. Three produced no-one who recognised Gordon, while a couple of staff in the others thought he looked familiar. Going by the ATM withdrawals though, it appeared Dice and the casino on Bothwell Street were his preferred venues. As much as I couldn't guarantee he'd return to either I was satisfied I had done what I could to cover that possibility.

Now I just had to figure out what the connection was between his gambling and drinking and the blackmail. There had to be one. Was he blackmailed because of the drinking and gambling? Had he done something while drunk and Reardon had found out about it.

I left the last casino and began to walk back to my car. It was late afternoon and the sun, though it had lost some of its sting, was still hot on my skin. Its rays still bounced off the parked cars around me and this time I was careful when stepping onto the road.

It was only as my mind flashed back involuntarily to my near-accident outside Dice that I noticed the vehicle sitting near the exit of the car park. A white Renault Laguna.

The light was in my eyes, obscuring both the number plate and whoever was inside the car. Was I being paranoid? Lagunas were relatively common cars, but even so, what were the chances of two old-style Lagunas of the same colour being so close to me in two casino car parks within a few hours?

I started towards the car quickly, hoping to get a look at the driver. When I was forty yards away it suddenly reversed round a row of parked cars. I broke into a run as the driver put it into first and accelerated away from me.

The car was out of the car park and had turned a corner in the direction of the Clyde before I could reach the exit. I slowed to a stop, frustrated at having seen nothing more than the make and model of the car.

One thing I could be certain of though; I wasn't the only one searching for Gordon Dunbar.

Chapter Thirteen

There's a funny thing about paranoia; it's far better to think you're paranoid than to realise you're not.

The Laguna had unsettled me. No matter how I tried to rationalise it, the reaction when I walked towards it confirmed this was no coincidence. I considered briefly that it could be the cops, keeping an eye on me, not as convinced of my innocence as I would have liked. It was a possibility, certainly, but so was that of it being Sean Reardon's killer, or accomplices of his. And that possibility troubled me far more. I had seen Reardon killed without a word of warning or a moment's hesitation, and I wasn't naïve enough to think the same couldn't happen to me.

I had been in spots like this before. As Jessica had joked, there had been more than one person in the past who'd wanted to kill me. Some of them had been hard men and women, some not so tough, some had been almost boringly normal, and others had been fully fledged, howling-at-the-moon sociopaths. I had no idea which category my current fan or fans would fall into. All I knew was I wanted someone on my side who was capable of out-crazying most of them.

I went to see Mack.

*

The gym was quiet when I arrived at the small grey building a little before six. Only one vehicle – Mack's huge Navara – sat in the car park, though the roads outside the industrial estate were busy with workers heading home from the other companies based there. Mack's gym – still without a name after all these years –

had been a long-disused trade warehouse before he bought it and began to teach martial arts there. It was quiet now, presumably between classes, but usually the place echoed to the thud of fists and shins, knees and elbows as they hammered bags and pads. It wasn't fancy. It was tough and hard and so were those who trained there in Mack's own brutal brand of Muay Thai boxing. The lack of name wasn't a problem; the gym maintained business through word of mouth among those who took their fitness seriously and wanted to improve their skills, and it kept the posers away – those who think they're working hard because they've bought themselves a gym membership and go once in a blue moon wearing a carefully coordinated outfit. Mack took great delight in making that type throw up during their first class. None of them tried a second.

I passed through the small reception and made my way to the main hall. Mack was in the ring on the left hand side of the hall, feet on the top rope, running rapidly through a series of steep press-ups. He rattled off another fifty or so then lifted his feet from the rope, rolled forward and stood up in one fluid motion. He was smaller than me, by a couple of inches and maybe a stone in weight, but, where I was in good shape, Mack looked as though he could jog to Belgium or kick down a tree without breaking more than a light sweat. I tried not to suck my gut in.

He pushed his sandy blonde hair out of his eyes and said, 'They let you out then?'

'Justice occasionally prevails.'

Mack made a face but declined to comment. 'What did Jessica find?' he asked instead.

'Video footage of the murder.'

It took a lot for Mack to look impressed but that managed it. 'She back on form, then?'

'It's early days.'

Mack nodded. He knew how difficult some things could be to get over. We were seventeen when his girlfriend, Katie Jarvie, was murdered in woodland in our village of Lochbridge. And still seventeen when Darroch, then a Detective Sergeant, had somehow convinced the Procurator Fiscal that he had a case against Mack. Only Andrea's testimony that I had been with her at the time of the killing saved me from being on trial with him. After the Not Proven verdict freed him to face the condemnation of the community he joined the army and left his childhood home. He'd never been back. But neither has Katie left him. Or Andrea, or me, for that matter. Each of us was changed by Katie's death and the events that followed. But none of us more than Mack. Part of him didn't so much die that day as combust in a pure flame that had yet to burn out. In truth, he scared me at times, both for the torture he inflicted on himself and for the things he was capable of.

Stewart was right. One day it would burn him up.

For now though, his thoughts were on Jessica. 'If I'd killed that bastard she wouldn't have had to save me and she wouldn't be going through this shit.'

His voice and his eyes were so neutral most people wouldn't have realised the extent of his pain. But I saw it. My mind flashed back unbidden to that night, to the shine of metal and the flow of blood. I tried to shake it off, but it lurked in the edges of my vision like the beginning of some malignant migraine.

'And if we hadn't gone after her she'd have been dead,' I told him. 'You saved her too.'

Mack didn't respond. What I said was true but it wouldn't convince him. He expected himself to be invincible and anything less was unacceptable in his eyes. I tried to take his mind off it by telling him about the case, about Jessica and the people she would speak to today, and about the white Laguna that had been following me.

'It's not the cops,' he said when I'd finished. 'They wouldn't have driven away. They'd want you to know they were following you.'

'I know. It has to be the killer.'

'Or someone else you don't know about yet.'

'It's complicated enough already, thanks very much.'

Mack sat on the edge of the ring. 'You didn't come out here just to fill me in. What's the plan?'

'I'm going to see McKenzie. Thought you might be interested.'

The flatness in Mack's eyes lifted. 'You thought right.'

*

I called a number I'd been given some months ago when Innes McKenzie had *asked* me to do him a favour. I met him three times, and never in the same place. As the most powerful criminal in Glasgow for the last few decades he'd acquired more than his fair share of enemies, most of whom would happily kill him at the first opportunity. So he moved around. I doubted anyone, other than Mason, his right hand, knew where he was all the time.

It took a while but eventually McKenzie must have given the nod and I was given a location where I could meet him. I drove, with Mack sitting bolt upright in the passenger seat, trying not to get his hopes up in case a violent confrontation didn't materialise.

We found the address, just off Anniesland Cross, and I felt my pulse quicken as we turned through the gates of a funeral home. I suspected that McKenzie had his fingers in almost every type of business there was, but something about him having ready access to coffins and incinerators made me nervous.

We followed a long curving path through parched looking trees and came to a stop outside a low red-brick building that looked more like an office block than a place of rest. It was now after seven o'clock, and, while glad there wouldn't be any grieving relatives on the premises, I would have been grateful for a few more witnesses to our presence.

We got out of the car and walked up to the door, which opened before we reached it. A tall, thin man stood with his hand on the door while a shorter man eyed us suspiciously as we stepped inside.

'Harper,' I said to them. 'McKenzie's expecting me.'

'You carrying?' the short one asked.

'Carrying?' Mack snorted.

'Something funny, arsehole?' The short guy reached one hand behind his back, a challenge on his face.

'Not yet. But when I take whatever it is you've got behind your back and stick it up your arse I might just piss myself laughing.'

Good old Mack. Always willing to help a possibly volatile situation live up to its potential.

The short guy narrowed his eyes while the taller one closed the door behind us and reached behind his own back. Before anything could kick off another door opened at the end of a short hallway and a very average man walked through it. He was somewhere in his forties, with a slight paunch, his hair short, dark and beginning to grey. He was dressed very plainly in dark trousers, polished black shoes and a light blue shirt and navy tie.

Mason had been McKenzie's enforcer and hitman for nearly twenty years and yet he didn't have a single conviction to his name. Part of that might have been his non-descript appearance which enabled him to drift past unnoticed, but mostly, I was certain, it was his ability to help witnesses forget they'd ever seen him.

He walked towards us and the two other men froze. I understood the reaction; the first time I met Mason he put a gun to my back and our relationship had only deteriorated from that point. I was wary still, but he no longer induced the same cold dread in me that he once had – a result of becoming personally acquainted with my own mortality – and he didn't like that. He also didn't like that McKenzie had turned to me for help and that I had delivered.

'Find something to do,' Mason said to the two men.

'That one's carrying,' the short one said, pointing at Mack.

Mason swivelled his eyes to the short guy and spoke in his eerily soft voice. 'And you think I need your help?'

The short man looked as though his bowels had just loosened, while his taller companion looked away to distance himself from the confrontation.

'Leave,' Mason said.

The two men left quickly through the front door.

'Quite the management style you've got,' I said.
'What do you want?' Mason asked.
'McKenzie's expecting us,' I replied.
'I'm well aware of that. Why do you want to see him?'
'Let's cut the crap,' Mack said. 'You want to act the tough guy so you're going to try and intimidate us like you do with those two clowns. But we're not that easily impressed. You want to find out why we're here, you take us to McKenzie and he can tell you later over cocktails.'

Mason's jaw tightened almost imperceptibly. He looked between Mack and I for several seconds before he spoke. 'One of these days McKenzie is going to forget about you two. But I won't.'

'You going to send us Christmas cards?' Mack asked.

Mason looked at him like a mechanic sizing up a second-hand car. 'How's your back these days? Fully recovered?'

'Better than ever.'

'Really? Maybe we'll find out.' Mason's lips curled slightly as he turned back to the interior door. We followed him through the door and into a wood panelled corridor with a plush red carpet. Several doors led off the corridor before Mason led us through one at the far end.

A solidly built man in his late-sixties sat behind a large oak desk, his hair short and white, his moustache nestled comfortably under a flattened nose and cold grey eyes. A rotating electric fan sat on one corner of the desk, ruffling his plain white shirt each time it pointed in his direction. Mason closed the door behind us and McKenzie gestured for us to sit at the desk opposite him.

Mack sat down first and I followed, trying not to look at the hand that had waved us to our seats. The two smallest fingers on McKenzie's left hand were fused together; the result of a firebomb that had killed his wife and son and left him with scarring that ran the length of his arm up to his neck. It was irrational, I knew, but somehow it made him more sinister, as though it was an outward sign of the corruption and malice that resided within him.

McKenzie tapped the damaged fingers on the desk and dispensed with any pleasantries. 'What do you want, Harper?'

I cleared my throat and tried to remind myself that this man owed me a favour. It was easier said than done when I thought of the deaths he was reputed to be responsible for over the years.

'I need your help finding someone,' I finally said.

McKenzie's eyes narrowed with suspicion, while Mason spoke quietly from behind us. 'Thought you were the private dick?'

I didn't speak, and Mack, thankfully, remained silent. After a moment McKenzie finally spoke. 'Who are you looking for?'

'A man who tried to kill me.'

'Could be just about anyone, surely?' McKenzie smiled, but there was nothing recognisable as humour in his expression.

I wasn't going to tell McKenzie the full story so I told him what I thought I could get away with: I was working on a case and one of my witnesses had been murdered. I certainly wasn't going to mention blackmail and risk McKenzie trying to grab a slice of that action.

'Why do you think I'll be able to find this man?' McKenzie asked.

'I shot him as he ran away. He can't go to the hospital, so he needs someone who'll patch him up without asking too many questions. I want you to ask around and find out who's been treated for a bullet wound in the shoulder.'

'That's it?'

'Just a name and address. That's it.'

'What's in it for me?'

This was the moment I'd been dreading. I'd expected it, even though we both knew he owed me.

'You owe me, McKenzie. I found your daughter's killer.'

'And I offered you a substantial sum of money. Which you turned down, if you recall.'

'Sometimes my morals get the better of me.'

McKenzie sat back in his chair, a look of mock surprise on his face. 'Morals? After what you did?'

'I did say sometimes.'

McKenzie sat forward again, folded his hands on top of the desk and leaned towards me. 'And this will make us even?'

I took that as a yes. I stood up and walked to the door, turned the handle and opened it, my eyes never leaving McKenzie's. Mack followed, his eyes on Mason.

'No,' I said. 'But it's a start.'

Chapter Fourteen

I dropped Mack off at the gym after we'd left McKenzie's funeral home and called Jessica for an update. 'Any luck?' I asked.

'None. Reardon's neighbours all knew him by sight, but that was about it. He'd only been there a month or two, since he got out of prison, so they didn't know anything about him. Seems the kind of close where no-one saw nothing anyway, thanks very much officer.'

'Back to square one then.'

'Maybe not. I checked Brownstone's file on him and called the cop that arrested him last. Figured they might know anyone he was involved with. She agreed to meet. I'm waiting on her now.'

'She agreed?'

'It's Sam Taylor. Think I might have got the sympathy vote.'

Sam Taylor was a Detective Sergeant who normally worked with DI Stewart. She'd been involved in the investigation at the start of the year and knew how big a role we'd played in bringing it to an end. More to the point, she knew exactly what we – and Jessica in particular – had been through.

'Where you meeting her?' I asked.

'The Maltings, round the corner from Pitt Street. She'll be here in half an hour.'

'So will I.'

*

I found Jessica sitting alone in a booth in the back corner of The Maltings. The small bar was quiet, with only a few hardened drinkers willing to forgo the still warm daylight of a beer garden for the dinginess of the Maltings interior. There were three men sitting alone, one at a table checking the betting form in a newspaper, the other two spaced well apart at the bar, and another two men occupied a table on the other side of the circular bar, their heads bowed in conspiracy.

I checked them all out as I slowly made my way to Jessica's table. While there was no way they could have followed me and somehow made it into the pub before me, could I be certain Jessica hadn't been followed? My paranoia had been kicked into overdrive by the Laguna following me earlier and I was in no mood to take chances.

I took my seat beside Jessica so we both faced into the bar with a wall at our backs.

'Apparently,' Jessica said, sliding a beer towards me, 'it's not paranoia if they really are out to get you.'

I looked at her blankly.

'You scoped out every guy in here on your way in. Unless you've switched teams, I'd say you're feeling edgy.'

I lifted the beer to my lips and took a long swallow. Then I told her about the Laguna and the certainty that I had been followed. She thought it over and said, 'I'm pretty certain that everyone in here is a cop.'

I knew a lot of police officers drank here. Perhaps that was why I didn't. Strathclyde Police might have merged into Police Scotland, and its former headquarters on Pitt Street might have closed but old habits die hard, especially among cops. Even so, I was surprised Jessica was so sure. 'You been checking them out?' I asked.

She rolled her eyes. 'Not in that way. I just like to know who's nearby.'

'And you call me paranoid?'

'I'm not paranoid. I just don't trust anyone.'

And no-one can blame you.

Fortunately Jessica changed the subject before either of us had to give too much thought to why she didn't. 'What did Nicole tell you?' she asked.

'As little as possible.'

'Is she being difficult just because she's a nightmare, or is she hiding something?'

'She probably is hiding something. Something small that she thinks doesn't matter, or that we don't need to know. But I'm sure she doesn't know what her dad's been up to, and I think she's genuinely trying to limit the damage for him. And showing me who's boss, I suppose.'

'And you're going to let her?'

I took Gordon's folded up phone bills from my pocket and handed them to Jessica. 'I need you to check out each of these numbers, find out who they belong to, see if there's anything worth looking into.'

'What about the ones with names beside them?'

'Especially those ones. Let's see if Nicole is telling the truth.'

'And if she's not?'

I didn't say anything for a few moments, and when I did I looked Jessica in the eye. 'Then we decide what to do next. Together.'

Jessica held my gaze for a few seconds before looking away and clearing her throat. Something in my words had unsettled her, and I wondered if I had reached out too far too soon.

When Jessica spoke she was focused on the case again. 'You really think he'll go back to one of those casinos?' she asked.

'At some point. Addicts need their fix, whatever their drug is. Gordon's seems to be gambling.'

'He might get his fix elsewhere.'

'He might. But his computer showed no traces of any gambling websites, so it looks like he prefers to waste his money in person. Of course, he might go to a bookies, but there must be thousands of them in the city, so I'll have to make do with the casinos. They seem to be his comfort zone.'

'Fair enough,' Jessica nodded. 'Now, more importantly, how do you think this person in the Laguna got on to you in the first place?'

This was something I'd given some thought to. 'They might have been at George Square, either to meet Gordon Dunbar for the payoff, or to catch up with Reardon, and they saw me follow him. Or they were waiting at Reardon's home and saw me there. But I don't know how they could be on me now, without waiting outside Helen Street for the cops to let me go and then following me home.'

'Or they followed Nicole to you, saw you were a PI and thought it might be worth their while following you. If Gordon Dunbar is hiding it's from these guys. And if they're looking for him they could have staked out his home waiting for him, then decided to follow Nicole when she showed up there.'

'It's possible.'

'It's more likely. That's how they're following you now. They saw your office, they got your name, and they presumably know where you live.'

I was saved from contemplating that comforting thought by the arrival of a short, stocky woman in a once-white shirt and black trousers. Taylor stomped towards us, her thick eyebrows knotted, her square jaw jutting out in anger.

'You never said he'd be here too,' she threw at Jessica before dumping herself on the seat opposite us. There were deep shadows under her eyes and when she lifted her arm to signal the barman I saw a large damp ring of sweat.

'I missed you too, Sam. How's tricks?'

'I've been working since three a.m., it's been about a thousand fucking degrees for most of that time, I haven't eaten since ten a.m., some bastard lawyer got his obviously guilty shitbag client off a rape charge today, and now I've got to listen to your pish and I can't even have a fag while I'm doing it. How's that sound?'

'I'm getting mixed signals…'

'Piss off and get on with it.'

'Thanks for meeting us,' Jessica said. 'We appreciate it.'

Taylor's scowl softened slightly as the barman appeared beside us and dumped a double vodka unceremoniously in front of her. She turned and looked up at him and his outstretched hand. 'What? Oh, bugger off. Stick it on my tab.'

'So you do know you've got a tab?' the barman retaliated. 'Any chance of paying it?'

'Any chance of giving me peace?'

The barman muttered something under his breath and turned back to the bar where he stared daggers into Taylor's back. She remained unfazed, even when she took a big hit of the straight vodka. She closed her eyes as though in prayerful thanks.

Jessica cleared her throat and Taylor's eyes opened. 'Oh, aye, what was it you wanted?'

'Sean Reardon,' Jessica said.

'He's dead,' Taylor replied.

'We know,' I said.

Taylor put her glass down on the scarred table and looked at me. 'Heard you were in the frame for it too.'

'*Frame* would be the appropriate term,' I told her.

She gave a snort of amusement. Whether it was with me or at me I was unsure. 'Surprised Claiborne let you go. She usually likes to get what she can from a man before she cuts him loose.' She finished that off with a lascivious wink.

Jessica leaned forward in collusion. 'Are you suggesting Inspector Claiborne is a maneater?'

'Oh, she's been cocked more times than John Wayne's gun,' Taylor replied.

'And yet she let you go, Harper,' Jessica said. 'That's got to be a blow to your ego.'

'He's a man, his ego's bloody bulletproof,' Taylor said. Her hands were already twitching, giving away how desperate she was for a cigarette, despite smelling like she'd smoked half a pack on her way here. 'Probably did more damage to Claiborne's ego when her case fell apart. I hear she was raging.'

'Serves her right for locking up an innocent man,' I said. Even to my ears I sounded like a huffy child.

'Oh, dry your eyes,' Taylor said. 'You were found at a murder scene. What do you expect, a pat on the head and a box of Quality Street?'

Taylor rolled her hand toward her in a *give-it-to-me* gesture. Jessica had given her a brief rundown on the phone, but I went through it again in more detail. Even so, I didn't tell her any more than necessary, and I certainly didn't tell her about my visit to Innes McKenzie. When I finished she looked at me as though I was an idiot.

'You sure you've got the right guy?'

'Reardon?' I said. 'Definitely.'

Taylor shook her head in wonder. 'Then he must've picked up a copy of *Blackmail for Dummies* while he was inside. I nicked him a while back for stealing a charity box – a charity box for fuck's sake! Definitely a special needs case. Now, what, eight months later, he's graduated to extortion?' She shook her head again. 'I'm amazed he managed to scrawl the note legibly enough to blackmail anyone. What colour crayon did he use?'

'He didn't strike me as the sharpest tool in the box,' I admitted.

'You noticed then?' Taylor's voice dripped sarcasm. 'So, what was the genius blackmailing your client about?'

'We don't know yet,' Jessica said.

Taylor gave us a derisive snort. 'Some detectives.'

'Does he run with anyone a bit smarter then?' Jessica asked. 'Someone who could pull this together?'

'Doubt it. He's the kind of guy no-one really wants to associate with. Why cut your take by involving someone you don't need? And why risk the whole thing by bringing in some useless twat who's had more convictions than he's had baths?'

'Then why is he dead?' I asked.

Taylor threw her head back and barked out a humourless laugh. 'Christ knows. It could be anything with some of these lowlifes. Half of them would kill each other over a two-draw fag end.'

The mention of cigarettes seemed to remind Taylor how long she had gone without one. She downed the remainder of the vodka and stood up. 'More than likely you've ballsed up and got the wrong guy.'

'Maybe Reardon was the one with the goods on our client?' Jessica suggested. 'Maybe he brought someone else on board. Someone who decided he didn't need Reardon anymore, figured he was a liability and put him away.'

'That would imply Reardon was capable of intelligent thought in the first place though. And I don't believe in fairy tales.' She jammed a cigarette between her lips and spoke round it. 'But hey, what do I know? I'm only a copper.'

'Well, that's true,' I said

'Fuck you, Harper,' Taylor grinned. She turned and headed to the door, lighter clenched desperately in her hand, its flame already tickling the cigarette end. Suddenly she stopped in mid-stride and came back to our table, looked at Jessica. 'You said on the phone he was blackmailing a guy called Dunbar?'

'Gordon Dunbar,' Jessica said.

'It sounded familiar, so I looked him up...'

'Hey!' came a shout from the bar. 'You can't smoke in here.'

'Piss off, I'll just be a minute,' Taylor threw back. 'Anyway, this Gordon Dunbar bloke, we had him in a while back.'

'For what?' I asked.

'Hit and run. Just up the road actually. Ran over some woman on Woodlands Road. Well, it was his car, but he got off with it. Claimed the car had been stolen.'

'Had it been?' Jessica asked.

'No idea. Don't care, wasn't my case. It'll be rotting in a pile of paperwork somewhere. Added to the ever-growing pile of unsolveds.'

Taylor decided she'd delayed her nicotine fix long enough. She turned away from us and headed for the door, a deep draw already filling her lungs and soothing her temper.

'Sam,' I called after her. 'When was this?'

'About six weeks ago.' DS Taylor grinned round her cigarette and absently flipped her middle finger in the direction of the glaring barman as she backed through the door to the street. 'Why? Think it's related?'

Chapter Fifteen

'Well that's clearly just a coincidence.'

'Obviously,' I agreed. 'Guy gets questioned by the police, two weeks later he gets blackmailed over an entirely unrelated matter, a month after that he gets blackmailed again, and the blackmailer gets shot in the face. That could happen to anyone.'

'Happened to me last week.'

There was a pause as we pondered just how ridiculous that was. Then Jessica voiced what had begun to scratch at the edges of my mind.

'Nicole must have known about this,' she said quietly.

'Yeah, she knew alright.'

'You going to ask her about it?'

'Not yet.' I ran a hand through my hair and thought about the lies I had been told. 'I want to know more about it first.'

Jessica nodded her agreement. 'Not much we can do about it tonight though.' She caught the barman's eye and made a circular motion over our beers. A minute later two beers appeared in front of us and Jessica paid the barman. 'So, what's been happening?' she said, attempting a smile. 'Apart from extortion and murder, of course?'

I felt the tightness in my jaw loosen as Jessica reached out. I sat back and let go of my anger at Nicole. She wasn't here and Jessica was. There would be plenty of time to be angry with Nicole tomorrow.

For tonight, I put her out of my mind and took the hand that Jessica had reached out. This woman had proven her worth to me time and again, and despite being on the floor, she had picked herself up off it when I needed her most. Her troubles hadn't vanished, and she might still be more fragile than either of us cared to admit, but she'd taken her first steps on the path back from a very dark place.

But none of that mattered at that moment. Not the terrible things that had happened in the preceding months. Not Nicole, not her father, and not Reardon or his killer. All that mattered was that we sat side by side in a dimly lit bar and reignited the fading embers of our friendship.

*

I awoke early the following morning. Earlier than I wanted to after staying in The Maltings later than was sensible. My head was foggy and my tongue was thick with far too much alcohol, but I climbed out of bed quickly, as though I could will myself to feel bright and peppy. I forced myself into the spare room and tortured myself through half an hour of intense exercises, finishing with a solid five minutes on the punch bag that hung in the corner. By the time I had finished I was dripping with sweat but the mist in my brain had cleared and the two litres of water I'd downed had shaved some of the fur from my throat. By the time I'd endured a cold shower, dragged a razor across my face and brushed the night from my teeth, I'd begun to feel like today might not actually be a journey through all nine circles of hell. Maybe just the first five or six.

I booted up my computer and searched the internet for information on a hit and run on Woodlands Road. Results popped up immediately and presented me with reports from most papers that covered the area. The Evening Times was first, but only had the bare facts – that a fifty-three-year-old woman had been struck by a car on the night of May 29th – and an appeal for witnesses. The Herald did better, identifying the vehicle as a red BMW – the same make and colour as the car in Gordon Dunbar's driveway – and asking witnesses to call the number provided if they had any information. The article also named DI Denise Claiborne as the investigating officer. The bloody woman was haunting me.

Fortunately, the Glasgow News – a paper whose normal worth was found when wrapping it round a fish supper – came up trumps, giving the name of the victim as Mrs Daphne Hillcoat, and quoting a witness, Mrs Susan Miller.

God bless the Glasgow News and its total disregard for privacy.

I made a note of the names and began the usual searches, starting with electoral roll and council tax records. It didn't take long to locate an address for Daphne Hillcoat, but I could only narrow my list to six Susan Millers, any of whom could be the correct one.

I called Jessica. It rang for some time before she finally answered with something that sounded like, 'Ummph?'

Her next word, after I said my name, was far clearer. So were her feelings at being woken before lunchtime.

'What do you want at this godforsaken time?' she demanded.

'It's half-nine, Jessica.'

'Shit. Really?'

'You okay? You weren't that bad when we left the pub.'

'I had a couple when I got home. Shouldn't have mixed my drinks.'

My first reaction was to warn her about going down that road again. But who was I to talk? I was the one who had happily sat drinking with her in the pub till midnight. I bit my tongue and said nothing for fear of undoing all the repair work we had undertaken on our friendship the previous night. Instead I told her what I had found out about the hit and run and that I needed her help.

Jessica gave me a long sigh. The kind of sigh that says you just want to curl up on the sofa and if you die from your hangover that might not be such a bad thing.

I began to count to ten in my head, figuring if I got there I was on my own. On the count of eight Jessica said, 'What do you need?'

I smiled in relief. 'Can you check out the Susan Millers, see if you can find the witness? I'm going to speak to the victim first then I'll see how far you've got and help with the rest.'

'I take it you expect me to get out of bed for this?'

'That would be helpful, yes.'

The last thing I heard before she hung up was, 'You're a bastard, Keir Harper. An irredeemable bastard.'

*

It took twenty minutes for me to reach the small village of Bridge of Weir and ring the doorbell of Daphne Hillcoat's semi-detached house. The door was answered after a few moments by a small, nervous looking man in his fifties who raised his eyebrows in lieu of speaking.

I introduced myself and handed him a card. 'I'm looking for Daphne Hillcoat. I wanted to ask her a few questions about the accident.'

'Oh... well...' he stammered. 'I'm sorry, that's out of the question.'

'Who is it?' a voice bellowed from within the house.

'No-one, dear,' the man replied.

'Hardly, Trevor. The bell didn't ring itself, now, did it?'

I waited. The voice within the house clearly held more sway over him than anything I could say.

'Someone asking about the accident,' he finally said.

'Accident? What bloody accident? That was no accident! Get them in here.'

Trevor closed his eyes and his shoulders slumped: a posture I'd bet he assumed regularly. He ushered me inside the house and into a small, overly-furnished living room.

One wall of the room was occupied by a sofa currently functioning as a bed, on which sat a solidly built woman with a round face and red cheeks. Her hair was short and curly, yet flattened on one side where she had been lying on it. She was sitting upright, a blanket across her lap despite the heat outside, and her right leg, encased in plaster, resting on a footstool. Her right arm was similarly plastered and a foam collar encircled her neck. Despite these injuries she looked in good spirits.

'Ah, you're the chap asking about the *accident*?'

'Yes, ma'am,' I said. She looked the type who'd appreciate a bit of ma'am-ing. 'My name's Keir Harper, I'm a private investigator.'

'A detective, eh? Have those plods finally admitted defeat and called in some help?'

'No. They don't know I'm here.'

'Really?' She gave me the beady eye for a moment then snapped, 'Tea, Trevor. We have company.'

Trevor left the room like a kicked dog.

I hated tea, and wasn't wild about the way Daphne Hillcoat spoke to her husband, but I'll put up with a lot if it brings a few answers with it.

She made a show of shuffling an inch further upright, huffing and puffing like she was scaling Ben Nevis. I spoke with forced concern. 'How are you feeling, Mrs Hillcoat?'

'Oh, I'm well enough,' she said, her voice the softest I had yet heard it. 'No point in complaining, is there? Who'd listen? Just got to get on with it, haven't you?'

I nodded sympathetically. 'Will it be long before you can return to work?'

'Work?' She looked aghast. 'Oh, absolutely. If I'm ever able to return, that is. I shall soldier on, of course, but while the spirit may be willing, if the flesh is weak...' She tailed off, then treated me to an in-depth account of the injuries she sustained in the hit and run – broken arm, broken leg, whiplash, various scrapes, cuts and bruises – and the treatment that followed, including more personal details about her hospital stay than I cared to know.

'And I do so hate putting other people out,' she finished. 'Trevor! Where's that tea?'

Somehow I managed to maintain an expression of mild interest and understanding at her predicament. I was amazed at the fact she had told me so much without actually establishing why I was here. It seemed to occur to her at the same time.

'Perhaps you could tell me your interest in the incident, Mr Harper?'

'I'm trying to trace a missing person and it was his car that hit you. Do you recognise the name Gordon Dunbar?'

Daphne Hillcoat nodded vigorously, despite the foam collar. 'Of course. The police asked me that. Not that it meant anything to me, you understand. It does beg the question: why haven't they arrested him? That maniac could have killed me.'

'I don't know that yet, Mrs Hillcoat. But it's possible someone else was driving the car at the time. Can you tell me everything you remember about the incident? Something might help me find him and might help me determine exactly who was driving the car.'

Trevor appeared in the living room at that point, a tray bearing two cups of tea and a plate of biscuits held in his hands. He put the tray down on a side table and passed one cup to his wife and the other to me before placing the biscuits on the arm of the sofa beside Mrs Hillcoat. He picked up the tray and left the room quickly. If he'd walked out backwards with his head bowed I wouldn't have been surprised.

Mrs Hillcoat reached for a chocolate biscuit and dunked it in her tea. She sucked the tea off it noisily and took such a large bite of her biscuit she almost lost a fingertip. 'I seem to remember the police saying he was a doctor,' she mused through a mouthful of crumbs. I could almost see the pound signs floating in her eyes. Too many mornings watching TV adverts for no-win no-fee claims.

I took a sip of the tea for show, managed to suppress my gag reflex, then took out my notepad and tried to prod her back on track. 'It was the 29th May, is that correct?'

'I'll never forget that date,' she said dramatically. She took a deep breath and began what I suspected was a well-rehearsed story. 'I had been visiting a friend of mine – Irene McCafferty, lovely woman, bit slow – and was returning to my car, around nine-thirty. I remember the time because I'd deliberately left Irene's while it was still light, rather than walk to my car in the dark.'

'Very sensible.'

'Quite. I crossed Woodlands Road about half way down, near that ridiculous statue, and stood on the traffic island in the middle waiting for the cars to pass. Then I heard a car engine roaring.

When I turned a red car was speeding towards me. Before I could react it swerved up onto the island and hit me on the side of the leg. My leg broke instantly, of course, and my arm broke either when I hit the bonnet of the car or when I landed on the road. Goodness knows how I survived. The ambulance must have got there very quickly. Of course, I've always been made of stern stuff.'

I doubted Trevor would dispute that.

Daphne Hillcoat reached for another biscuit to help her get over the trauma of reliving her brush with death. I noticed she hadn't offered the plate in my direction yet. Maybe they were for medicinal purposes only.

'Were you able to tell the police the make of the car that hit you? Or its number plate?' I was hoping for something more specific than the vague *red BMW* the papers had mentioned.

'Hardly! Not with my life flashing before my eyes. Only that it was red. I believe one of the witnesses confirmed the exact model.'

'Did you get a look at the driver? Or anyone else in the car?'

'Oh, it was just the driver, there were no passengers. And I got a good look at him alright. That's how I know it was no accident, you see. I saw the look on his face as he aimed for me. That's right – *aimed.*'

'Can you think of anyone who would want to hurt you, Mrs Hillcoat?'

'Me? Why would anyone want to harm me? I think the devil just wanted to hurt someone and I happened to be his first opportunity.'

'Could you describe him for me?'

'Absolutely. I'll never forget that wicked face. It was a thin face, and he had a long, thin nose and pointy chin. There was a scar too, on his left cheek, just underneath his eye, sort of cross-shaped – strange the things you notice as you're about to die. Oh, and he had the blondest hair you'll ever see. It was practically white.'

'You're quite sure about those details?'

'Of course I am.' Her voice was indignant, offended at me questioning what was no doubt a very practised description.

'Well, Mrs Hillcoat, if that's the case,' I said as I stood, 'it definitely wasn't Gordon Dunbar who ran you down.'

'What? It must have been. It was his car, for goodness' sake. Who else could it have been? Why would they have his car?'

I placed my still-full tea-cup on a table and made for the door. 'I don't know, but I'm going to find out.'

I passed Trevor in the hall and gave him a sympathetic roll of the eyes while his wife loudly demanded answers from her makeshift bed. The door closed behind me but did nothing to block Daphne Hillcoat's foghorn voice. I wondered briefly if Trevor had the number for the Samaritans.

Back in the car I called Jessica. She answered quickly and told me she had just finished speaking to Susan Miller.

'Already? Did you get her first time?'

'Yup. Started with the one who lived closest to the hit and run, figured she might have been on her way home.'

'Why didn't I think of that?'

'Because you can only aspire to be as good as me.'

'Yeah, yeah. What did she tell you?'

'That the hit and run was deliberate. She's adamant the car swerved towards the victim, who was standing on a traffic island. Said there were no other cars on that side of the road, no pedestrians, dogs, nothing that might have caused him to swerve accidentally.'

'Did she get a number plate?'

'No, just that it was a red BMW. One of the cops told her they'd backtracked through CCTV footage around the area, got the number plate, and traced it back to its owner. That's as much as she knew about that though.'

'What about the driver? Did she see him?'

'Clear as day. Some skinny guy with a white-blonde Teddy boy quiff and big sideburns. Definitely not Gordon Dunbar. And she confirmed there was only one person in the car.'

'That's what the victim said too.'

'Any reason why someone would want to hurt her?'

'Just her husband. But he's probably too scared of her. One of these days, maybe.'

'So it's all about Gordon then.' There was silence for a few seconds before Jessica spoke again. 'If Gordon wasn't driving, or even in the car, we still don't know what the blackmail's about. But the hit and run and the blackmail must be connected. No-one has that much bad luck.'

'Yeah, they must be. And I know someone who's not telling me everything'

'Going to see Nicole?'

'Yeah. And this time she's going to tell me the truth.'

Chapter Sixteen

I banged on the door with my fist, the glass panels shaking under the pressure. Music was playing within the small house but even without the competition I would have been pounding on this door. A curtain twitched in a window next door. Others would soon join in if that door wasn't opened. In this small residential estate in Crookston, on the very edge of Glasgow's suburbs, this might have been a flurry of excitement for bored, stay-at-home parents and the retired.

Suddenly there was a shimmer of movement behind the glass and the door swung open. Nicole's angry face looked out. An angrier face looked right back at her.

'We need to talk,' I said.

'Before or after you break my door down?'

'Either. But whichever it is you're going to tell me the truth, Nicole.'

She turned from me without a word and stalked through her house to the conservatory overlooking the postage-stamp back garden. A small sofa was pushed back against one wall, an armchair against the other, the centre of the room occupied by an easel with a canvas propped on it, facing the light. Nicole stood before the easel, wiping a brush with a stained cloth. She was buying time, collecting her thoughts and wondering how best to manipulate me.

This time it wouldn't work. I watched her as she moved slowly around the canvas, her paint-spattered jeans and vest, her hair tied loosely back, and I felt none of the stirrings I had before. Anger was my ally now. It would keep me focused and protect me from Nicole's machinations.

The Forgotten Dead

Finally she turned, and, inclining her head toward the canvas, asked, 'What do you think?'

I considered the canvas, the wash of reds and blacks, the thin streak of yellow sprayed across one corner like sunlight's last breath, and again I felt nothing. There had been a time when Nicole's paintings had excited me, when I had looked at them and been able to see the things she described, the things that she and I both wanted me to see. Now, despite her continued success, I saw only another addition to the wardrobe of a deluded emperor.

'I don't get it,' I said.

Her lips tightened. 'Fortunately you're not an art critic.'

'True,' I conceded. 'Guess I should stick to what I know.'

'And what would that be?'

'When people are lying to me.' I sat down on a cushioned wicker chair in the corner.

'For Christ's sake, Harper, we've been through this.' She threw the brush on the floor to show just how angry she was.

'Enough of the tantrums, Nicole. I'm the one who's pissed off, so stop trying to make yourself the victim.'

'You're pissed off? How do you think I feel? My father's missing, very likely in danger, and you're pissing about insulting me! Why's this taking so long? Are you dragging it out just so you can stay close to me?'

'Shut up and get your head out of your arse!' I jumped to my feet and grabbed her by the arms. 'Why didn't you tell me about the hit and run?'

Her mouth fell in surprise. It took her several seconds to find a denial. 'What are you talking…'

'Don't bother, Nicole. You know exactly what I'm talking about. Six weeks ago your dad's car was involved in a hit and run. Two weeks later he paid off a blackmailer, and four weeks after that he's missing and his blackmailer is dead. These aren't coincidences.' I let go of her and stepped back. 'So why didn't you tell me?'

'Because I wanted him found, not dragged through the mud!'

'And you didn't trust me?'

'I did – I do – but I don't trust anyone else. What if someone heard you were asking about it? It's past now, there's nothing to be gained from dredging it up again.'

'But he didn't do it. Witness statements proved it wasn't him.'

'Mud sticks, Harper. You know that.'

'Oh, come on. No-one would've believed he was involved. So what was he really worried about? People finding out what he was doing while his car was nicked?'

'What are you talking about?' Nicole looked away, but not before I saw embarrassment in her eyes.

'Was he drunk? Did he get wasted and pass out while someone took his car and ran over an innocent woman with it? That wouldn't fit with his image, would it?'

'He's not a drinker.' Her voice was so quiet I doubted she even convinced herself.

'He is. Maybe only recently, but he is. And he was gambling too.'

Her reaction was telling. The drinking was old news, but the gambling shocked her. 'What do you mean?'

'He's a regular at casinos in town. A few hundred pounds at a time. More than one person told me he's a big drinker.' I watched her carefully for signs of deceit. 'What happened? What got him drinking?'

She shook her head, still stunned. 'It must be the blackmail. He got stressed out and started drinking. Maybe gambling too.'

'He was drunk the night his car was stolen. Two weeks before he paid the blackmailer.'

'He might have got the demand for money before that,' Nicole argued. This time she didn't deny that Gordon had been wasted when his car was stolen.

'True. But his bank statements show that he's been gambling for over a year.'

'Okay, so he was gambling...' I could almost hear the gears turning as Nicole sought the correct spin to apply. 'And this Sean Reardon found out about it and blackmailed him and he started drinking because he was so worried.'

'Why would he care if people knew he was gambling? It's not illegal.'

'He's a well-respected doctor. It could damage his image.'

I wasn't buying that. The man was image-conscious, but he was a doctor, not a public figure. And there was a bigger problem with that theory. 'If that's the case, who killed Reardon? And why? The only reason to kill him would be to protect your dad.'

'He must have been blackmailing other people at the same time. My father wasn't rich, he couldn't get much from him.'

Nicole could well be right about more blackmail victims, but Reardon's killer was at George Square before he was at Reardon's flat, which connected him to Gordon Dunbar's blackmail.

Our time together might have given Nicole the ability to pull my strings, but it also helped me read her. And now the scales had fallen from my eyes I could see there was something else she was keeping from me. I had no idea what, but it was time to push harder.

'He could be a rich man if he wasn't pissing it all away on boozing and betting,' I said, my tone deliberately harsh.

'Fuck you, Harper. You don't know anything about him.'

'I know trying to drink your problems away is pathetic. And gambling all your money away for the sake of a quick buzz is nothing short of stupid.'

'You bastard.' Nicole's voice fizzed with anger. 'You don't know what he's been through.'

'Oh, don't I?' I laughed in amazement. 'Because the cops talked to him about a hit and run? I know exactly what it's like to be accused of something you didn't do. You know what I call that? A weekday. And it's usually a lot more serious than a stupid wee accident. Did I start drinking and throwing my hard-earned money about like a fanny? No.'

'Maybe if you'd been mugged as well you would have!'

I had to count to ten to stop myself screaming at her stupidity. Then I carried on to thirty. 'When was your dad mugged?' I finally asked.

'A couple of months ago.' She was subdued now, realising she'd been goaded into opening up.

'And you *honestly* thought that was unrelated to him being blackmailed?'

'Yes!' Nicole came to me and put her hands on my chest. 'He hasn't done anything wrong, so the blackmail must have been a mistake. Once you accept that the rest of it's just bad luck.'

'Are you serious?' When she nodded I could only shake my head in wonder. 'Do you want him found, Nicole? Because you're doing everything you can to hinder me.'

'Of course I want him found.'

'Then open your eyes.' My voice was firm and I gripped her arms again. 'Someone is trying to take your dad's life apart.'

'Why?'

'I don't know, because you've done nothing but lie to me. Whoever it is, you're helping them.'

'I... I'm...'

Ah, Nicole. Still wouldn't know an apology if it bit you on the arse.

'Just... don't bother,' I said. 'Tell me about the mugging.'

'I don't know much about it, he only told me a couple of days later when I saw he was injured and asked what had happened. It was in the city centre. He took a shortcut through one of the lanes off Buchanan Street and some coward sneaked up and attacked him, took his wallet and phone. There wasn't much in his wallet though, and he cancelled all his cards before they could be used, so whoever did it didn't get much for their trouble. The phone was a new one though, and pretty expensive, so it's long gone.'

'How badly hurt was he?'

'A black eye, some cuts and bruises, a lump on his head. Nothing serious. It hurt his pride more than anything.'

'I need the date.'

'Let me check.' Nicole went into the kitchen and came back with a small purple diary. 'Let's see... he was supposed to be coming to the opening of my show on the Saturday night, so I went to see him that morning. Ah, here we are, my show was the 19th May, and it happened the night before. So, Friday the 18th.'

Eleven days before the hit and run. 'What time?'

'About ten o'clock, I think.'

'Did he report it?'

'He said there was no point, the police would never find the mugger. I made him call them anyway. I hated the idea of someone getting away with something so cowardly.'

'Did they find the guy?'

'Not that we heard. I doubt they will.'

I doubted it too. And I doubted much effort had been given to such a minor crime. If I was right about that, I might have an avenue to explore that the police hadn't bothered with. I asked Nicole for the number of the phone that was stolen. She got her mobile from a side table and read her dad's number from it.

'How will that help?' she asked.

'I don't know if it will yet. If it was a good one he might have hung onto it, you never know.' I put the pad away and fixed her with a hard look. 'So what else haven't you told me?'

'That's everything.'

'That you want to tell me? Or everything there is?'

'I know you don't believe me, Harper. But that's it, there's nothing else.'

'You told me that before, Nicole. And you lied then.'

She stalked toward me and stopped with her chest almost touching mine, her breasts rising with each heavy breath. 'I was protecting my father.'

'No, you were putting him in danger.'

'He's a good person, Harper. He hasn't done anything he could be blackmailed over. Accept that and you'll see the rest of it is coincidence. He's had a bad time of it recently. I need you to help him out of it.'

'Then you need to be honest with me. And you need to accept that, good person or not, he's done something he doesn't want people to know about.'

Nicole shook her head, refusing to believe the truth in my words. I gave up and walked to the door. I opened it and, against my better judgement, looked back at the woman I had once loved. There were tears glistening in her eyes and this time I believed they were real.

'Just find him, Harper. Find my father. Please.'

'It was your father who went missing, Nicole. But it might be a different man who comes back.'

Chapter Seventeen

I left Nicole's home with the burn of regret in my throat and the feeling of something having slipped from my fingers; that phantom feeling of having lost something and yet being unsure what it could be.

I called Brownstone from the car as I trudged along the M8 back towards the city centre and my office. She answered quickly as always. 'Brownstone.'

'I need another favour,' I said. 'Is there any way you can trace a phone just from the number and tell me where it is?'

'To give you a physical location?'

'Yeah.'

'No problem. I assume you don't want the technical details?'

'You'd only make my head explode.' I read out the number Nicole had given me. 'How long does it take?'

'Depends on the service provider. Shouldn't be too long, I'll get back to you.'

I hung up and hoped, against the odds, that the mugger hadn't ditched the phone, or, if he'd sold it, that it hadn't changed hands too many times. While I was waiting I placed another call. This time the phone rang several times before being answered by a very tired voice. 'Stewart.'

'It's Harper,' I said.

'Well, well. How's life on the outside?'

'No-one's tried to kill me in a couple of days, so that's a bonus.'

'Must be a personal best. Anyway, I don't imagine this is a social call, so what do you want?'

'You're so cynical,' I replied. Then after several seconds of silence, I added, 'I need some information on a mugging.'

'What do you think I am, directory enquiries?'

'Come on, I just need to know if anyone got lifted for it. I don't want access to the file.'

'Good, because you wouldn't be getting it.' He paused and I heard him exhale a long breath. He didn't want to give information to a civilian, but he knew I'd got results before. 'Is this connected to that murder?'

'It might be. Or it could just be a coincidence.'

'I need more than that.'

'The guy who was being blackmailed was mugged a couple of months ago. I want to know if it's related.'

'Is that all? That's a bit thin.'

Unless you know about the hit and run.

'Got to cover all the bases,' I said. I told him when and where Gordon was mugged and he grudgingly agreed to look into it. I hung up the phone just as I finally reached the city centre.

I parked outside my building and left behind the confines of my car-cum-oven for the relative coolness of my office. I threw the windows open wide to let what little air there was outside limp half-heartedly into the room. I lay on the sofa against the wall and tried to ignore the faint smell of damp that still persisted after I had flooded the place a few months back. I turned the case over in my mind, looking at it from every angle, but found only more questions.

Stewart was the first to phone back, after only fifteen minutes.

'Okay, I've checked it out and no-one was arrested for that mugging. Or questioned for that matter.'

'Any witnesses?'

'None. Even the victim didn't get a look at him. And the CCTV didn't pick it up either. It's been a dead case from the start. From what I gather the victim realised that too and didn't press it. He wasn't badly hurt and only lost a tenner. He probably chalked it up to experience and decided to stay out of dark alleys.'

'Thanks, Stewart. You're a shining example to the rest of the force.'

'Just make sure you get in touch if this turns out to be more than just a coincidence. I don't want you running around playing vigilante again.'

'Perish the thought,' I said as I hung up.

I was grateful to Stewart for getting back to me so quickly, but I was no further forward. I was now relying on Brownstone to work her magic and find Gordon's phone, or for McKenzie to hear about someone seeking under the counter treatment for a gunshot wound. Brownstone only took another ten minutes.

'Found it,' she began. 'On the corner of Duke Street and Armour Street and hasn't moved since I picked it up.'

'You're a genius.' I was already up and heading for the door. 'Let me know if it starts to move.'

I climbed into the car and shot off, tearing down the hill onto Sauchiehall Street and dialling Jessica as I accelerated through an amber light.

'I've got a lead,' I said when she answered. I explained briefly about the mugging and Gordon's phone being stolen and gave her the location Brownstone had given me.

'I'll be there as soon as I can,' Jessica said. 'And remember, whoever has the phone probably isn't the mugger so take it easy.'

'I know, I know. Call me when you're in the area.'

I disconnected the call and concentrated on negotiating city centre traffic without killing myself or anyone else. It was a short drive but there were no guarantees the person with the phone wouldn't have left by the time I got there.

*

I parked on Duke Street, a hundred yards back from the junction with Armour Street and walked the rest of the way. Perpendicular to Armour Street, Duke Street continued in an unbroken wall of tenements. The opening of Armour Street, however, consisted of a boarded up electrical store and a pub, The Wellington.

I checked my phone and saw Brownstone hadn't called again: my target hadn't moved yet. I turned the phone to silent and made sure the vibration was switched on, put it back in my pocket and entered the pub past the territorial gaze of two old smokers bookending the doorway.

The Wellington was a drinker's den. Nothing fancy, nothing new, just a few dedicated drinkers concentrating on good, solid boozing, and one bored barman reading a paper on the bar. The only sounds came from the occasional short tune from the fruit machine trying to tempt some lucky punter into losing a few quid and the murmur and hiss of the TV hanging in the corner alternating between Sky Sports News and a screen full of static.

I glanced around casually as I made my way to the bar and ordered a pint. I suspected ordering anything softer in here would have immediately drawn attention to me. I paid the barman and chose a single table in the far corner that let me view the entire bar. I sipped from my pint and let my eyes drift round the pub.

Other than the barman there were five people in the long thin room. At the end of the bar nearest me an elderly man sat hunched over a large whisky, his swollen red nose mere inches from the rim of the glass. At the far end was a much younger man drinking a pint of lager. In his late-twenties, scrawny, with a greasy complexion and lank, dirty blonde hair, his clothes hung loose in a manner that screamed smackhead. His gaze jumped from television to fruit machine to his fellow drinkers with a drug-induced edginess.

Another man sat at a table by the fruit machine, a pint glass clutched in his hand as he emptied it down his throat. He was forties, big and balding, with a belly that strained at his t-shirt and had long ago defeated his waistband. Nearer me sat two women, each with a bottle of beer before them, their faces hard and frustrated at lives that had not lived up to expectation. They might have been late-thirties or they might have had rough paper rounds. They sat in silence save for the occasional gulp of beer and rustle of pages turning in their magazines.

No-one in the bar came close to matching the description of the hit and run driver.

If it was Gordon's mugger who still had the phone I had to rule out the two women and the pensioner, leaving only the junkie, the fat man and the barman himself; a middle-aged man who gave off such a lethargic aura it was difficult to imagine him mugging anything livelier than a corpse.

There was an easy way to find out who had Gordon's phone, but I decided to wait till Jessica got here. I took out my phone, switched it to Silent mode, and typed a short text message telling her where I was and asking her to wait outside.

Five minutes later my phone buzzed with a text message from Jessica confirming she was in place. I typed Gordon's number into my phone and dialled, then put the phone back in my pocket and my hands on the table in clear view.

I watched the room from the corners of my eyes and waited for a reaction. A loud musical tone started up at the far end of the bar. The nervous junkie nearly slid off his seat as the phone in his tracksuit trousers began to ring. He fished it out and looked at the screen. It wouldn't tell him anything, my phone number was blocked for outgoing calls. He looked at the screen suspiciously, the unanswered call still playing a dance version of some eighties monstrosity – doubly horrific – until the barman looked up like a peeved sloth and asked if he was going to answer it. Finally he answered the call. I heard him *Hello* several times, as we all did, then with a *Fucksake* he hung up and stuffed the phone back into his trackies. As he did so something else almost fell out. He caught it in time and shoved it back in, but not before I recognised it as a flick knife.

He took a few more sips of his pint as his thought process moved slowly to a conclusion. I could almost see the moment it hit him. He jerked upright, his eyes widening. Slowly he turned his scrawny neck and looked around the bar, scrutinising every one of us. I pretended I hadn't noticed, but the two women were less keen on being started at.

'Fuck ye lookin' at, Jason?' one of them demanded.

'Fuckin' perv,' her pal chimed in.

'Want a fuckin' photie?'

And so it went on. I tried not to smile. This was working out better than I could have hoped for. Poor Jason could have sat here all day nursing a pint, but not with these two harpies on his back.

Sure enough, after a few moments of arguing back and forth, the junkie downed what was left of his pint and stormed out with his middle fingers raised at his antagonists. As soon as he cleared the door I had my phone out dialling Jessica.

'He's just left,' I whispered. 'Grey vest, black and white trackies.'

'Got him,' she answered. 'Heading west on Duke Street, coming toward me. Skanky looking bastard, isn't he?'

'Just keep an eye on him till I catch up with you. He's got a knife and he's a junkie. He'll be unpredictable.'

'I can cope with a smackhead, Harper.'

'Jessica, the guy's got a knife. Just wait for me.'

'Gotta go, he's almost here.'

She hung up.

I raced for the door, no longer caring what anyone thought, and barged through it into bright sunlight, startling the two smokers. Their muttered expletives rolled right past me as my eyes strained against the harsh light, until finally I saw Jason the junkie, a hundred yards along the street, his back to me.

And standing in front of him, smiling widely, was Jessica.

Her lips moved but I heard no words. I hurried towards them, willing his edginess to remain under control.

Jessica reached out and her hand rested flirtatiously on the junkie's left arm. He looked down at it, his shoulders tensed in surprise. I wondered if she'd gone too far and quickened my pace, all but breaking into a run.

Then his head lifted and he looked into Jessica's face. The fingers of his right hand twitched as they crept slowly towards his pocket, fumbling at the edges of the material.

I broke into a run and shouted Jessica's name as his skinny fingers slid inside the pocket and gripped the knife.

Chapter Eighteen

My trainers pounded the pavement as I desperately tried to reach Jessica in time. The smackhead turned at my shout, his eyes wide as he saw me charging towards him. His hand came out of his pocket, empty as he held it up to ward me off.

He turned back to Jessica, realisation dawning in his eyes at the same time as disappointment; as though he'd really thought he'd scored with her. His eyes flicked wildly between us and he tried to run. Jessica grabbed his shoulder and spun him towards the mouth of an alley lined on three sides by crumbling brickwork and devoid of anything but discarded rubbish, broken glass, and the stench of urine. She followed him in with a two-handed push in the chest, sending him stumbling into the alley where he was hidden from the street by high walls and their deep shadows.

Jessica turned and looked at me like I was an over-protective parent. 'What the fuck's wrong with you?'

'He was going for his knife,' I told her.

She looked at the scrawny specimen standing slack-jawed and frozen in the alley and gave a derisive snort. 'The dirty wee bastard was getting a hold of something alright, but it wasn't a knife.'

'Oh.'

'I can cope, alright?'

I held my hands up in apology as the junkie found his voice. 'What dae yous want?' he said, his voice pure nasal ned.

I looked at Jessica and she held out a hand, deferring to me as this was my case. 'You mugged a friend of mine,' I said. Until proven otherwise I'd work on the assumption that this was the mugger.

'Naw, man, I don't dae shit like that.'

'Yes you did. And you're going to tell me about it.'

'Fuck you, ya prick. Ah'm tellin' ye nothin'. Get oot ma fuckin' way.'

He tried to push past and I shoved him backwards.

'Ah'll no' tell ye again. Get oot ma fuckin' way.' His hand slid back into his pocket and this time it came out with the knife. He pressed the button on the handle and a short blade shot out. 'Or ah'll fuckin' cut ye.'

'Is that all you've got?' Jessica said. 'A three-incher?'

'You an' all, ya cow,' the junkie said.

I saw a darkness cloud Jessica's face and felt a crackle in the air. Her voice was so soft I could barely hear it. 'You want to guess what happened to the last guy who pulled a knife on me?'

Before the junkie could answer Jessica's left foot shot out, kicking him in the stomach and folding him forward. She bounced her foot off the tarmac and kicked him in the side of the head with her shin, sending him thudding against the wall. She grabbed his knife hand and twisted it up his back.

'Drop the knife or I'll stick it in your kidney,' she hissed in his ear.

He dropped the knife and I stepped in to kick it away.

Jessica grabbed the back of his greasy hair and rammed his head off the wall, then kicked his legs out from under him, dragging his face down the rough brickwork as he slid to the ground and tried to decide which part of his battered body to cradle. Jessica crouched beside him and whispered. 'You want to know what happened to him? I killed the fucker. Caved his head in with a rock.' The junkies eyes looked up at her in terror as she picked a half brick from the ground beside her. 'So, are you going to help us?'

His mouth was working but no sounds were coming out. I took the expression on his face as a yes. Jessica did too. 'Good man,' she said. Then she pushed him onto his side and took the phone from his pocket and a wallet from his back pocket. She stood up and threw the phone to me, opened the wallet and took out a driver's licence.

'Jason Teague,' she said. 'Is this your current address? Doesn't matter, we'll find you if we need to. So don't even think about lying to us.'

Teague lay on the ground, his mouth hanging open, his eyes wide, nodding his cooperation. 'Ah... Ah won't, ah won't.'

I looked on in slightly-shocked wonder. Jessica had, in the space of ten seconds, disarmed a belligerent, aggressive junkie and terrified him into a state of stammering cooperation. In truth she had scared me too.

Jessica looked at me and inclined her head towards Teague. I stepped forward and stood over him, holding the phone out for him to see. 'Where did you get this?'

'Took it aff some bloke,' Teague sniffed.

'Who?'

'Dunno. Just some bloke.'

'You took his credit cards too. They had his name on them.'

'Cannae remember. Never used them.'

I took the copy of Gordon's photo from my pocket and held it up. 'Is this him?'

Teague looked at the ground, eyes jumping from side to side as he thought of a lie. Jessica thumped the half brick loudly against the wall. Teague jumped and looked at me rather than Jessica. 'Eh, aye... aye, that was him.'

I couldn't believe our luck. Or the stupidity of this guy to keep the phone after he'd stolen it from Gordon. He must have been away having a piss when they handed out brains.

'Why didn't you use the cards?' I asked. 'Seems like a lot of trouble for the tenner in his wallet.'

Teague looked away again, his eyes darting to the mouth of the alley as though help might suddenly appear. When none came he answered, 'Was telt no' tae.'

'By who? The guy you mugged?'

'Aye right.' Teague scoffed at my stupidity, then quickly swallowed it when he looked at Jessica. 'The guy that paid me to mug him.'

Jackpot.

'Who paid you?' Jessica asked.

'Dunno. Just some bloke.'

'That's the second time you've said that.' Jessica got in Teague's face and cracked the side of his head with an open hand. 'Get more helpful. Quickly. Or I'll come round to your shitty little bedsit and pump you full of the mankiest fucking heroin I can find. You want to be an organ donor? Fine, keep your mouth shut. Otherwise, start talking.'

Teague swallowed hard. 'Ah dunno! Honest. Never seen him before and he never telt me his name. Just came up to me in The Welly, bought us a drink, got talking and he asked if ah wanted to make a few hundred quid. Just hud tae hit some bloke a couple of times then piss off with his wallet and stuff.'

'And it had to be this guy?' I said, waving Gordon's photo.

Teague nodded vigorously. 'Telt me whit he looked like, where and when ah'd find him on his own. Gie'd me a hundred up front and another when ah handed over the bloke's wallet.'

'He didn't want the phone?' Jessica asked.

'Nah. Telt me to bin it. Said if he found out ah'd selt it on he'd gie me a kicking.'

'So why didn't you bin it?'

'Fucking earned it, didn't ah? Ah'm no' chucking that away. Thought, gie it a few weeks till he forgets aboot it, then flog it for a few notes.' Teague smirked at his entrepreneurial skills, still ignorant as to how we had found him and why his mysterious employer had wanted the phone binned. Relying on Teague rather than destroying it himself might have been his first mistake.

'How did you get in touch with the guy who paid you?' I asked.

'Didnae. Telt me when to do it, said he'd be in The Welly the day after. He wis, he coughed up, and ah huvnae seen him since.'

'What did he look like?'

Teague's eyes screwed up in concentration as he tried to dredge up through a chemical haze an image of a man he'd met twice two months ago. The effort was so obvious that I would have believed him anyway, even if I hadn't already heard the same description very recently.

'Dead tall bloke, right skinny. Weird hairdo, like Elvis, big sideys and everything, but pure white.'

Jessica and I looked at each other. This was the man we were looking for. But if Teague hadn't seen him in two months he wasn't coming back here.

'Did he tell you how he knew where the victim would be?'

'Naw, just gie'd me the street and the time. He wisnae dead sure of the time right enough, hud to hang aboot for ages. Just as well it's dead down there at that time of night.'

'Wait a minute,' Jessica said. 'Where did he tell you to go?'

I'd picked up on it too. Gordon had supposedly been mugged in a lane off Buchanan Street at ten o'clock. No-one could call that street deserted at ten p.m. on a Friday night.

'Whiteinch,' Teague said. 'He telt me the bloke drove a red BMW, and parked it near the bottom of South Street. Gie'd me the reggie plate an' all.'

'What time was he supposed to be there?' I asked.

'Sometime between twelve and one. Bastard didnae show up till nearly two. Just aboot froze ma nuts aff waiting on him. Gie'd him a few extra dunts for that. Fucker.'

We'd got as much as we were going to get from Jason Teague: the man who hired him had left him with almost nothing to tell. Before we left I gave him a description of Sean Reardon and asked if he recognised him. The blank stare was all the answer I needed. We turned away from Teague and were leaving the alley when we heard him call out.

'Haw, that's ma stuff.'

I held up the phone. 'This?'

'Aye.'

'No. It's not,' I told him.

Jessica turned and walked back to him. 'You want your wallet?'

Teague nodded and Jessica opened the wallet, took the notes out and folded the wallet closed. She threw the wallet in his face and counted through the money.

'Eighty quid,' she said. 'Where'd a smackhead like you get eighty quid?'

Teague's eyes roamed the ground rather than look at Jessica.

'You mug someone else?' she asked, kicking his leg. She held the notes up and tore them in half. Teague watched in horror as she tore them in half again and again, until she was left with a handful of once-valuable confetti. She threw the shreds in his face. 'Get a fucking job, Jason. And remember – I can find you any time I like.'

Jessica turned and stalked past me, out of the alley and into the sunlight. I looked at Teague, in a heap on the floor, covered in shredded money, with a look on his face like he'd just been hit by a whirlwind.

'Hell of a woman, isn't she?' I said with a slightly scared smile.

*

I caught up with Jessica where she'd parked her green Hyundai behind my car. She climbed in and wound down the window. 'Whiteinch?' she asked.

'See you there.'

Jessica accelerated away from the kerb. I got into my Civic and headed after her. We turned left onto the High Street and drove south, then west before crossing the river and followed the north bank of the Clyde past the huge glass roof of the St Enoch shopping centre, along the Brooomielaw and past the financial district. We followed the Clydeside Expressway past the Big Red Shed and the Armadillo that made up the SECC before turning off into Whiteinch.

Up ahead Jessica turned onto South Street and pulled in to the kerb. I pulled up behind and killed the engine, got out and met her at the door of her car. We both stood and looked around. The street stretched far ahead of us yet all we could see were a carwash, a discount furniture showroom, a timber company, and plenty of empty warehouses.

'What would he be doing down here at two in the morning?' I asked.

'There's bugger all down here at any time of day,' Jessica replied.

'Let's take a walk. Maybe there's something further up.'

'I wouldn't bet on it.'

We started walking along South Street and found nothing that looked anymore likely than what we had already seen. We headed back and wandered round all the side streets and again found no more clues as to why Gordon Dunbar would be down here in the early hours of the morning.

'Whatever it was, it wasn't legal,' I said. 'That's why the mugging had to be here. So he couldn't go to the cops. Whoever's behind this wants him to feel helpless, wants him to know they can get to him and there's nothing he can do about it.'

'But he did go to the police.'

'He fed them a pile of crap though. And even then he only called them when Nicole forced him to.'

'If you believe anything she says, of course.'

'I did. This time.'

Jessica raised a sceptical eyebrow. I didn't try to convince her, it would only sound weak. But then she added, 'Actually, I checked out Gordon's phone bills. There's nothing there. And the names she gave all matched.'

'Well, well. She can tell the truth,' I said.

'I'm as surprised as you are.'

We stood for a few more moments, looking around in silence. I wanted to talk to Jessica about the beating she had given Teague, but I couldn't find the words to do so without sounding like a hypocrite. I had done the same, and worse, and would do so again no doubt. But that's why I was concerned: I didn't want Jessica to succumb to the same violence that I had seen control my actions in the past.

But when I looked at her, gazing calmly down the street, I saw a friendship that had almost drifted away from me once, and the coward in me wasn't willing to risk that.

In the end, what I said was, 'You know, if you killed him with an OD, they wouldn't transplant his organs.'

Jessica looked at me for a time, before finally shaking her head. 'Did he, or did he not shit his breeks?'

'I believe he may have soiled himself, yes.'

'Then it did the job. So screw you, Captain Pedantic.'

'Just thought you might appreciate some feedback.'

Jessica smiled at that, and for a moment I managed to forget she had scared me too.

'What now?' she asked.

'I'm coming back tonight. I want to see what's here at two a.m. on a Friday night.'

'Whatever it is, someone's willing to kill over it.'

'Oh good. I'd hate to get out of bed for nothing.'

Chapter Nineteen

We arranged to meet again later and went our separate ways. Having no idea what might be waiting for us in Whiteinch once darkness fell, and having been shot at once already this week, I called Mack on my way home and asked him to join us. He agreed as soon as I mentioned the possibility of violence. He probably started counting the hours as soon as I hung up.

I was counting the hours too, trying to judge how much sleep I could squeeze in. I wanted to be in position in Whiteinch by ten o'clock when the sun would be setting, and it was already past five o'clock when I parked outside my flat. I climbed out and was walking towards the building when I got the feeling I was being watched. I spun round quickly.

DI Claiborne stood with her arms crossed and an eyebrow raised in amusement. 'Highly strung, aren't we?'

Like I said, haunting me.

'Someone did try to shoot me the other day,' I replied. 'You maybe heard about it.'

'Rings a vague bell.' She looked up and down the short cobbled street that ran along the front of my building, as though worried someone would see her consorting with the enemy. 'We need to talk. Can I come in?'

'Officially or unofficially?'

She held up her arms in mock surrender. 'I come in peace.'

Against my better judgement I agreed and opened the door to let her in. We climbed the stairs to the first floor and I showed her into my living room while I quietly said farewell to any hopes I had of a few hours kip. Claiborne politely stood in the centre of the room while I quickly opened windows in the living room and kitchen in the vain hope of creating some sort of movement in the turgid air. I realised she was still standing and asked her to take a seat, watching with interest as she folded her tall frame into the corner of the sofa.

'Are you off-duty or on?'

'Off, technically.'

'Beer? It is Friday night.'

'I suppose it is. Why not, then?'

I took two beers from the fridge and popped them open, passed one to Claiborne and sat in the armchair opposite with the other one.

'I hope you won't tell anyone I was drinking beer in the presence of a murder suspect?' she said. She removed her glasses and there was a flirtatious sparkle in her eye as she spoke. A sparkle that brought to mind Taylor's verdict on her fellow officer.

'As long as you don't tell anyone I was drinking beer with a cop.' I found to my surprise that my response was said with a smile rather than the scathing sarcasm I'd expected.

Claiborne smiled and tilted her head back, her long neck stretched upwards as she took a swig from the bottle. In that moment of relaxation I saw how attractive she was.

I had to focus. 'So, did you come round to tell me I'm no longer a suspect?'

'Not exactly. I'm not clearing you of any involvement just yet. You might not have shot Reardon, but you were there, and that makes you a person of interest.'

'Person of interest?'

'It's a technical term.'

'For what? A suspect?'

Claiborne tutted with good humour and decided not to respond to that. 'Actually, I came to see you because I got a call from your friend, DI Stewart.'

'Did you now?'

'Apparently you're still investigating Sean Reardon's murder. I'm fairly certain I told you to contact us if you found anything.'

'But I haven't found anything yet.' I took a drink and savoured the cold beer. 'As soon as I do, you'll be the first to know.'

'That's very public-spirited of you.'

'I'm a concerned citizen.'

'I could pull you in, you know.' Claiborne ran a finger round the rim of her bottle, and I wondered if she was trying to make me misinterpret her words. 'Obstruction of justice,' she clarified.

Somewhere a warning bell rang, reminding me that this was a police officer, and as such, virtually my natural enemy. I sat back and gave her an open look. 'Gordon Dunbar was mugged two months ago. I thought it seemed a little coincidental, figured it might be related to the blackmail somehow. So I called Stewart.'

'That's a bit of a stretch, is it not?'

'That's what Stewart said too. I thought it was worth looking into anyway.'

'And?'

Like I was going to tell her. 'It's not just a cold case, it's frozen solid and stuck at the back of the freezer behind the ice-cube trays and three inches of frost. Wee run of the mill mugging in the city centre, not much taken, victim not badly hurt...' I shrugged. 'Nothing was done at the time and it's too late now.'

Claiborne studied me, searching for the lie in my words. She'd do well to find it; my poker face was strapped on tight.

'Your turn,' I said.

She slipped her glasses back on then stood and walked to the window where she looked out over the anaemic trickle that was masquerading as a river. 'You know I can't discuss the case with you.'

'And yet you're here. And you don't have your big hairy pal with you.'

Claiborne laughed, a high, fragile note. 'Sergeant Rowe would definitely not approve of me being here.'

'Think you're getting too close to the enemy, does he?'

'He usually does.' She smiled. 'If you listened to him you'd think I wasn't always chasing the bad boys to put them away. He says I change men more often than he changes his underwear.'

'That I can believe,' I replied, then realised how it sounded and added, 'About his standard of personal hygiene that is, not your... relationships.'

Claiborne looked at me over the top of her glasses, her eyes sparkling with amusement. 'Why, I do believe you're blushing, Mr Harper.'

I finished the beer and put the empty bottle on the table while I tried in vain to regain my composure. I cleared my throat. 'So, you were about to fill me in on your end of the case.'

'Was I really?' Claiborne drained the bottle and got to her feet, handed it to me and patted my cheek with her hand. 'Cheers.'

'Any time.'

Claiborne smiled, her eyes shining. 'I look forward to hearing from you.' She left the room and walked to the front door. 'When you hear something, that is. You being a concerned citizen and all.'

'Of course. I've got Crimestoppers on speed dial.'

Claiborne stopped in the open doorway, took a card from her pocket and held it out between two long fingers. 'Now you've got me too.' She stepped into the close and disappeared down the stairs.

I walked into the living room and stood at the open window, listening to the clip of Claiborne's heels as she strode towards a blue Volkswagen Passat and watching the sunlight set fire to her dark red hair. I was unsettled by her visit, but not in the way I usually was after contact with a member of the force.

The Passat pulled out into the road and disappeared from sight. I released a slow breath and went to the bathroom to run a cold shower.

*

'Are you daft?'

'It wouldn't be the first time it's been suggested. Why?' I asked.

The three of us sat in my car, submerged in a pool of darkness between streetlights on South Street in Whiteinch. It was eleven o'clock and the sun had long since burned its way below the horizon. Our view took in most of the length of the street, albeit large parts of it were shrouded in darkness. There was even less to see than there had been that afternoon.

Mack was in the backseat, leaning forward between Jessica and I, while Jessica sat with her back to the passenger door and stared at me like she was wondering when I'd had the lobotomy.

'You think a cop came to your home, off-duty, just to ask a couple of pointless questions and do some flirting?' she asked

'No. I think she was trying to trip me up, and she's probably used to using her looks to do it.'

'But you didn't fall for it because you've such high morals.'

I gave that one about as much attention as it deserved.

Mack had been quiet for a while, but he chimed in now. 'Maybe she just wanted laid. Taylor did say she was a maneater.'

'For God's sake don't feed his ego,' Jessica said.

'Apparently I'm still a *person of interest*, so that might be a wee bit unprofessional on her part.'

Mack sat back in his seat. 'She did imply that she likes the bad boys.'

'Hey,' I protested. 'I'm one of the good guys.'

'Who shoots people and turns up around dead bodies.' Mack's face was expressionless as he wound me up. 'Could be a potent combination for a frustrated female cop.'

'She didn't strike me as frustrated. I'd imagine if she wants it she gets it.'

'Enough!' Jessica called. 'Jesus, it's like sitting with a couple of teenage boys.'

'You wish,' Mack said quietly.

Not quietly enough, as he realised when Jessica reached over the top of her seat and clipped him on the head.

We were silent for a time after that. Jessica yawned loudly and I fought the urge to follow suit. We were both tired. I had been kept awake by Claiborne's visit and the uneasiness it had instilled in me, and Jessica had forgone sleep in favour of collating a file on Teague which she had emailed to me. As tiredness began to paw at me I wished I had it now, if only to give me something to focus on. Not that I would have been able to read it in the darkness within the car, but straining to read each page might have kept me awake.

Mack didn't seem tired, as usual – presumably sleep was for the weak – and he seemed determined to keep the conversation going. 'So who do we think this guy with the white hair is?'

'Someone who hates Gordon,' I said. 'That's all we know so far. Hates him enough to use his car to run somebody over, pay somebody else to mug him, and Christ knows what else.'

'We have to assume he's behind the blackmail too,' Jessica said. 'It's obviously connected, and Taylor was adamant Reardon didn't have the brains to pull it together.'

'So Reardon was just the fall guy,' Mack said.

'It's looking like it,' Jessica agreed. 'Teague obviously is, so why not Reardon?'

I stared out of the window at the deserted stretch of South Street while I thought about that. 'If this new guy's the one behind it all though, and he's paying lowlifes to do his dirty work, why would he do the hit and run himself?'

'Maybe someone else hired him and he sub-contracted some of the work,' Jessica suggested.

Mack shook his head in the darkness of the back seat. 'Too complicated. Using scum like Reardon and Teague as a buffer is fine, but you wouldn't pay someone to pay someone else. And if you're not the guy at the top of the food chain you're not getting enough money out of this to waste any of it on unnecessary help.'

'It also explains why Gordon hasn't come home yet,' I said. 'Someone is trying to destroy his life, and he knows they're still out there.'

All we had to do now was find him.

*

We settled into a long period of quiet. The only sounds were those of the sparse traffic that sped past from the Clydeside

Expressway before disappearing along Dumbarton Road. None of it turned in our direction and South Street remained deserted.

According to Teague it was almost two a.m. before Gordon had shown some common decency and turned up to be mugged. Even if nothing happened it would be several hours before we would be able to concede we had wasted our time.

It had seemed like a lucky break, finding out that Gordon had been mugged on a Friday night, on the very same day of the week. That surely gave us a better chance of discovering what Gordon had been down here for. But what if whatever it was only happened once a month? Or he'd only come here for a one-off rendezvous?

I was weighing up the possibilities when a pair of headlights turned onto the far end of South Street. The silence in the car thickened as we watched the twin beams of light head in our direction.

I glanced at my watch: ten past one. Five hundred yards away the headlights turned and the vehicle, a big four-wheel drive, stopped perpendicular to us. A figure climbed out of the passenger side and removed a padlock and chain from a chain link fence. He pushed the gate open and the car rolled through the gap. I expected the gate to be closed but it was left open as the car disappeared round the far side of a large concrete block of a building. The street lights nearby were out, presumably broken deliberately, and we could determine little else about the building.

'Go in or wait and follow them when they come out?' Jessica asked.

'Go in,' Mack said immediately, to no-one's surprise.

'Let's give it a few minutes,' I said.

Despite Mack's derisive snort I was glad we did. Five minutes later another car turned onto South Street, at our end this time, and drove to the same building, cruising straight through the gap and round the corner of the building.

'Could be some kind of deal,' I suggested

That didn't look likely when ten minutes later another two cars showed up in convoy and a fifth appeared shortly after.

'What the hell is going on here?' Jessica muttered.

Suddenly a square of light blazed from the corner of the building as a door was opened. It was extinguished quickly but not before we saw two men standing in front of the building. 'Security,' Mack said.

We watched in amazement as another dozen cars arrived within the next fifteen minutes. Suddenly South Street was a buzzing metropolis. 'So much for nothing to do down here,' Jessica said. 'The place is heaving.'

'We're obviously mixing in the wrong social circles,' I said.

The newest arrivals parked their cars at the front of the building and beams of torchlight flashed across figures as they exited their vehicles and made for the concrete block. The glimpses we caught were long enough only to confirm that each figure was male and that several were carrying kitbags.

'Well, it's not a brothel,' I said. 'I haven't seen a single female yet.'

'They could have been in the first couple of cars,' Jessica pointed out.

'Not enough for this many guys. You'd be doing some serious porridge stirring in there.'

'Nice image. Thanks for that,' Jessica grimaced. 'Any chance of getting your mind out of the gutter long enough to figure out what's going on here?'

'It's an underground fight club,' Mack said.

'What?'

'A fight club. You know, bunch of people get together to watch a few guys beat the shit out of each other.'

'How do you know that?' I asked.

'How do you think?'

'You never mentioned it.'

'Ah, well, you know the first rule of fight club.'

'Very funny.'

'Are you sure?' Jessica asked.

'Yup. Haven't been here but I've seen it loads of times in places like this.'

'I can't see Gordon Dunbar stepping into the ring,' I said.

'Hardly,' Mack said. 'There's some real hard bastards at these things. But there's also a hell of a lot of gambling.'

I'd been sure Gordon's gambling was confined to the casinos but it looked as though I was wrong. Why else would he be here? And yet I couldn't picture him here, couldn't imagine how he had become involved in something like this. I said as much to Mack.

'Who knows?' he said. 'But there's nothing else down here, is there? That's why they chose here. Nice and quiet, no-one to call the cops. Mind you, there'll be some fat lazy cop taking a nice wee backhander to turn a blind eye.'

'So what do we do?' Jessica asked. 'Do we go in?'

'Me and Harper do.'

'Oh really?' Jessica gave Mack the stink eye.

'Don't go in a huff. This is almost exclusively men only. You'll get the odd wannabe-WAG, but they've been brought by some paper gangster who thinks that's the way to act the big man. You'd only draw attention to us. And with the money involved here, the guys in charge aren't the welcoming kind.'

Jessica folded her arms in annoyance but her silence was an admission that Mack was right. In a way I was relieved. It was difficult enough to keep Mack under control most of the time, and now that Jessica seemed to have developed a hair-trigger temper I didn't fancy trying to keep a leash on both of them.

Mack and I gripped the door handles and checked to make sure there was no-one around before slowly opening the doors. There were two soft clicks as the locks released, then we stepped out of the car in darkness – I had long ago taken the bulbs out of the courtesy lights that would blink on when the doors opened – and hurried to the side of the nearest building where we began to walk along the street in the shadows cast by the high wall.

Our aim was to go in through the front door, so we didn't try too hard to disappear into the darkness. But still, I didn't want anyone to see where we had come from. I wasn't entirely comfortable leaving Jessica behind, but, if I'd learned one thing today it was that Jessica was more than capable of looking after herself. I should probably be more worried about the prospect of my car suffering collateral damage if someone pissed her off while we were away.

We walked at a relaxed pace, as though we were on our way to a party we'd been invited to. Despite our casual stride our eyes were constantly scanning the shadows around us, our ears alert for the slightest noise.

'How dangerous are these people?' I whispered to Mack.

'Most of them, not at all. They're here to see some fights and throw a few quid around. But the ones in charge, they don't fuck around. If they think you're a threat they will hurt you.'

'Are they killers?'

'Probably.'

We reached the concrete block that had been the centre of all the activity and we turned in through the open gate and passed the parked cars. Two shadowy figures stood in front of the building, no doubt watching our approach intently. When we were twenty yards from the building a beam of light blazed through the darkness, simultaneously illuminating and blinding us both.

We didn't break stride, but my muscles tensed as we walked into the light.

And whatever lay behind it.

Chapter Twenty

'This is private property,' said a deep voice from behind the light. 'I suggest you turn around.'

We didn't turn around.

'How's it going, lads?' Mack asked, his voice relaxed. 'First fight hasn't started yet, has it?'

'It will in a minute,' said a second voice; a high, ratty thing. 'Soon as I teach you to do as you're told.'

'That's a shame,' Mack replied. 'I hoped the first fight would last longer than three seconds. You might want to phone your ambulance now.'

Mack was a huge loss to the diplomatic corps.

'There's no need for that,' the other, more reasonable, voice said. 'But we will call the police if you don't leave.'

Mack barked a short laugh. 'No you won't.'

The torch lowered to point at the ground, painting a small yellow circle between the two men. I blinked my eyes rapidly and looked away, into the darkness, letting my eyes adjust to the dim light. 'Won't we?' the deep voice said. 'And why's that?'

'Because Ricky would put you in the hospital,' Mack said. 'If you're lucky.'

Ricky? Who's Ricky?

There was silence for a few seconds, then the owner of the deep voice pushed open a door behind him. A shaft of light spilled out into the parking area. Now that I could see the man I almost mistook him for a bear dressed in workout gear.

He was well over six feet, with a wide chest and long, muscular arms, dressed in black tracksuit trousers and a short-sleeved grey sweatshirt. His skin was dark, his features Asian, and his hair long, thick and black.

The bear held the door open and told us to go in. But before we could the other bouncer stalked over to the door and stood in our way. 'What the fuck are you doing?'

He had spoken to his colleague, but his angry eyes glared at us from beneath a dark beanie hat jammed over long brown hair. He was early twenties, and small, but he looked fast and wiry, like a good flyweight. Heavy stubble covered his jaw beneath a crooked nose that suggested he might not be that good a flyweight after all.

'What's the problem?' the bear asked.

'I don't recognise them.'

'You don't recognise most folk that come here.'

'They look like trouble.' He ran his eyes up and down both of us, head to toe. 'Probably cops.'

The big guy looked at him with disgust. 'And if they were, you just gave them more of a reason to want to take a look around, you fucking idiot.'

'Look, lads,' Mack said. 'We just want to see a few fights, okay? If you two want to leather each other, fine, but can we at least stick some money on it?'

They both looked at Mack. The bigger one, who was obviously in charge, out here at least, then gave the flyweight a hard look until he raised his hands in surrender and stepped aside. But he wasn't happy about it. He glared at us as we walked past, doing his best to intimidate us. It didn't work.

I waited for him to do something else. I knew the type; already boiling with anger and the desire to prove something, he wouldn't take this well.

'Door at the end, and down the stairs,' the big guy said as we walked past.

Mack and I walked along a corridor and opened a door leading to a flight of stairs. We took the stairs down to the basement level and walked along another corridor, through a double door and into bedlam.

The huge area we entered covered the entire floor space of the building and was dominated by four rows of six concrete pillars that supported the upper level of the building. The floor was scarred, chipped and cracked concrete, the walls the same. The lighting was provided by battery powered lights screwed into the sides of the pillars, seemingly at random intervals. The effect was to leave some areas in darkness while others were brightly lit and long shadows linked the two.

A large crowd was gathered in the middle of the room, where a makeshift cage, approximately the size of a boxing ring, had been erected between the four central pillars. The cage was eight feet high, open at the top, and badly made from what looked like old bits of chain-link fence that had been stolen and fastened together. The shoddy nature of the cage only made it more dangerous; there were plenty of sharp edges, and more than one area that was dark with something other than rust. Within the cage were two men, barefoot and wearing only shorts. One of them had the other bent over in a headlock and was pounding his fist into his opponent's head. A third man I assumed was a referee stood in the corner watching with disinterest.

A tall black guy with a shaved head and tight t-shirt stood beside the door we had just come through. He watched us silently as we looked around, until Mack looked at him and asked, 'How much?'

'Twenty each,' the man replied.

I dug my wallet out and handed forty pounds to him. He took the notes and stuffed them into a small bag that hung round his waist as Mack and I moved away towards the crowd.

Around the cage stood several dozen men and, as Mack had suggested, I counted only three women among them, each harder faced and shorter-skirted than the last. There were far more people here than we had seen arrive and I guessed there was another access road we didn't know about.

The crowd around the cage were a mixed bunch, some dressed smartly in suits, others in jeans and t-shirts, but each of them was bathed in a thin layer of sweat in the suffocating heat of the basement. The walls ran with condensation, making them look as though they were sweating, giving the impression that the whole building was alive.

No-one seemed to care about the heat though, or even to be aware of it. Everyone was focused on the fight and hurling enthusiastic expletives. In one corner stood a table with a small, bookish man seated at it, a metal tin and several sheets of paper before him. On either side of him stood two large men, their arms folded, their eyes glaring at anyone who came near them. I assumed from their watchful gaze that this was the bookmaker and the tin before him contained a considerable sum of money.

Beside the table was an easel with a blackboard propped on it, like a restaurant's specials board. A list of names was scrawled in chalk, indicating eight fights. And behind all of that, on the wall, hung a long, hand-painted banner proclaiming this to be *The Blood Shed.*

'Nice name,' I said.

'Catchy,' Mack agreed.

There was a sudden collective roar as one of the fighters hit the concrete floor on his back and the other landed on top of him, driving a flurry of punches into his face. The man on his back lay still, his head snapping from side to side with the blows. After a horribly long time the referee stepped over and pulled his assailant off, hoisting the winner's arm aloft to signal his victory.

Several people in the crowd punched the air while several others threw pieces of paper on the floor in disgust. No-one seemed concerned that the man on the ground was still motionless.

I looked at Mack. 'You used to do this?'

'Yeah.'

'When?'

'A while back.'

'Why?'

'To vent.'

'Why did you stop?'

'I vented enough.'

'You sure?'

Mack decided to circle the cage rather than respond. I went

The Forgotten Dead

with him, checking out the crowd as he educated me on the underground fight scene.

'Scotland's got a tradition of good boxers,' he began. 'Benny Lynch, Ken Buchanan, Jim Watt. But what about the guys who can't make it? The guys who only know fighting? They can take a minimum wage job or they can sign on the dole. Or they can come somewhere like this and make better money.'

'That's who fights here then?'

'Them and the ones who can't fight legitimately, for whatever reason. And the ones who just need to fight. Like me, back then.'

'Who's Ricky?'

'Ricky Bruce. Or Ricky Bruises, as he's known. He ran the place when I was fighting. He had the monopoly on fight clubs then. I took a punt that he still did.'

'I'm assuming he didn't get his name because he bruises like a peach.'

'Not exactly. Thing is, anyone can set up a club like this. Provided you've got the balls to do it, the money to pay off the cops, and the muscle to fight off anyone who tries to take it from you. If Ricky's still in charge he's been running this for nearly ten years. Since the guy that used to run it fell off a roof. That tells you all you need to know about him.'

'Fell?'

'No-one was ever willing to say any different.'

I looked around, at the crowd waiting for the next fight, at the queue forming at the bookie's table, at the water running down the walls, the patches of dried blood on the floor of the ring, interspersed with dots of fresh blood from the last bout. 'How much money are we talking about here?' I asked Mack. 'It doesn't look like a goldmine.'

'Well there's the entrance fee. Fifty people and you've pulled in a grand already. Obviously it doesn't cost much to set the place up. Rig up some lights, a few ropes – or a cage – a couple of cheap-shit tables, and your only costs really are the fighters, the bouncers, and paying off any cops that come sniffing around. The cops are probably the biggest cost. They're always happy to stick a few quid in their pocket, but they're greedy bastards.'

'Police Scotland's finest?' I said. 'Never.'

'Most of the money, as usual, comes from the betting. Ricky's basically the bookie, and bookies never lose. There'll be people here chucking hundreds around. Do this a couple of nights a week, maybe in a couple of venues, he'll be raking it in.'

Mack stopped as a man walked through the crowd and a couple of others separated two sides of the cage to let him enter. He was flabby and his eyes were glazed. Mack must have sensed my surprise and continued my education. 'You get two guys who might be completely different heights and weights, have had a hundred fights or no fights. You get boxers, martial artists, street brawlers, guys who just think they're hard... as long as you can throw a punch and take one back they'll let you fight. And people will watch. Boxing is boring these days – when was the last time you saw a good fight?' He gestured towards the cage. 'And this nonsense is to cash in on the popularity of the UFC, but that's crap as well. Most of the time they're rolling around on the floor cuddling.'

'People want to see blood.'

'Exactly. Every person in here wants to see someone get messed up, and the chances of it happening are very good.'

'How many people did you mess up?' I asked.

My voice must have indicated my distaste and Mack's voice was hard when he replied. 'No more than I have done when I've been helping you out.'

He was right. I held up a hand in apology as a second man entered the ring and the sides of the cage were closed and fastened behind him. This one was thin and his eyes darted around like he was high.

'How the hell did Gordon get involved in this?' I said, almost to myself.

'He's a gambler,' Mack said simply.

'I'm going to ask around, see if anyone recognises him.'

'Try and keep a low profile then. And if you can't manage that, and someone does try to kill you, don't dare finish it before I get there.'

The Forgotten Dead

'I'll dodge bullets till you show up. I'd hate to ruin your night.'

I moved away from Mack as the ref started the fight and the scrawny guy lunged at his opponent who swatted him away with a wild backhand. Technical it certainly wasn't. But by the way the crowd was baying I doubted any of them cared.

As long as there was blood.

Chapter Twenty-One

I kept an eye on the staff as I moved through the crowd, but they too seemed more interested in the fight. It often happened: the longer a place remained secure the lazier the security got. I'd already tried to speak to half a dozen people and not one of the bouncers had noticed. I kept moving, attempting to speak to several more people, but everyone was too intent on the fight to give me more than a grunted response. After a while without progress I found myself getting distracted too, stopping to watch as the skinny guy, his face smeared with his own blood, kicked his opponent in the groin and stamped on him while he was on the floor. The end of the round saved the prone man from a worse beating.

I was surprised to see the fight broken into rounds, but when I saw a rush towards the bookies table I realised why breaks were allowed. I moved on, hoping I might get some answers during the brief lull in violence. By the time the fighters were ready to leave their corners I was still no further forward and sorely pushing my luck.

'Anything?' Mack asked as he appeared beside me.

'Not yet.'

'Come on, I want you to meet Benny Buchan.'

I followed Mack through the crowd to a quieter space thirty feet back from the cage. On the way he told me that Benny Buchan had been a fighter all his life. He'd fought hard and with class and had won the admiration of his fellow boxers. The problem with Benny, according to Mack, was that he'd used the same defensive tactic as Rocky Balboa: he blocked punches with his face. Even in the fights he won Benny took a lot of punishment, and over the years, through numerous concussions, the effects became obvious.

It reached the point where, for his own good, no-one would let Benny fight.

No-one with any scruples that is.

Somehow, Benny discovered the existence of the illegal fight clubs. Maybe he'd always known they existed. To a man with no other skills and no alternative means of income, these clubs must have looked like a lifeline. In reality, fighting in these unregulated clubs, where the medical attention was non-existent, sent Benny's mental health into a downward spiral. He became a joke figure where once he had been a respected athlete, carrying out menial odd-jobs, taking a pittance in wages as he clung to the fringes of the only community he'd ever known.

Ahead of us an old man stood leaning against a pillar, his eyes on the cage. It was obvious Benny had been a fighter, even if Mack hadn't told me, and just as obvious that he hadn't been the best. He was old now, and that explained the once-solid form having turned to fat, but his nose had been broken so many times it was a shapeless mass, his eyes were unfocused, and his ears were puffed and permanently swollen, the left one sticking out as though indicating an intended turn. At first glance he could have been the poster boy for the ban boxing types.

But what other life would they have given a man like that? Would they have denied him the chance to compete in a sport he loved? Would they have deprived him of his only chance at earning a living? Would they have put food on his plate when he was unable to do so himself?

We reached the old man and Mack introduced me. 'Benny, this is Harper, a good friend of mine.'

Benny looked up, his blue-grey eyes clouded with doubt and confusion. He stared for a second, trying to focus his eyes and his mind, then suddenly the mist cleared. 'Mack! How are you, son? Haven't seen you in ages.' He grabbed Mack's hand and shook it vigorously.

'Harper, this is Benny Buchan. Legend round these parts.'

'Benny Bucket,' Benny corrected.

'That's not your name,' Mack said, a hint of anger in his voice.

Benny glanced down at the bucket of water that stood at his feet. 'That's what they call me, that's who I am.'

'Anyone who calls you that is a disrespectful wee prick who'll never be half the man you are.'

Benny glanced at the bucket again, staring into the murky water as though it were keeping a secret from him. 'What kind of man does this job?' he asked mournfully.

I saw a pained expression cross Mack's face before he put a gentle arm across Benny's once-powerful shoulders and guided his eyes away from the bucket onto me. Mack said to me, 'Benny looked after me when I first started in this kind of place.'

'Oh, I don't know about that, son. I think you'd have done just fine on your own.' Benny looked embarrassed but the small smile that crept onto his face showed how much the comment meant to him.

Mack told Benny that I was trying to find someone, and I took the photo of Gordon from my pocket and held it out to him. He took it from me with an unsteady hand and held it close to his face. He gazed intently at it for a good while before slowly shaking his head.

'What's his name?' he asked.

'Gordon Dunbar.'

Benny looked at the photo some more, holding it mere inches from his face now. After a time he shook his head again. 'Looks familiar, but there's a lot of faces come here.'

'No problem,' I said, taking the photo back. 'Thanks for taking a look.'

'Sorry, son,' he said to Mack.

'Don't worry about it, Benny' Mack told him. 'There's another guy we're looking for too. We don't have a picture though.'

I gave Benny the description of the man who'd hired Teague and who'd run over Daphne Hillcoat in Gordon's car, but he shook his head and looked crestfallen again.

Mack was thanking Benny for trying when we realised a

group of six men were walking towards us from the crowd. Benny's eyes darted to the ground as though they couldn't see him if he didn't make eye contact. Mack and I turned to face them, bracing ourselves for a confrontation.

The men stopped in front of us and spread out into a loose semi-circle. The tall black guy from the door stood on the left with the two bouncers from outside beside him. On the right were a fat guy with his arms folded over his beer belly, and a hulking brute with a wild mane of hair that merged seamlessly into his straggly beard.

The sixth man was dressed differently from the rest. He wore expensive looking charcoal trousers with an electric blue shirt, its sleeves rolled up once, its collar open wide to show off a thick gold chain. He stepped forward from the centre of the group and smiled, his face sharp and threatening as an axe blade, and ran his fingers back through his shoulder length brown hair, taking the opportunity to flex and impress us some more.

He was big alright, probably only an inch or so taller than I was, but several stones heavier. He had the broad shoulders, wide chest and thick arms of a gym freak, though I suspected he was one who had spent as much of his thirty-odd years in front of the mirror as he had on the weights.

'How are you, James,' he said to Mack, still smiling that fake smile. 'It's been a while.'

'Not long enough, Ricky' Mack replied.

Ricky cocked his head, as though unused to anyone talking back to him. Though if he'd known Mack it couldn't be an entirely new experience.

'I hear you've been asking a lot of questions,' he said.

'Just one,' I said.

Ricky pursed his lips in annoyance that neither of us were intimidated by him. 'Who are you looking for?' he finally said.

I took the photo from my pocket and held it up for Ricky to see. 'Gordon Dunbar.'

Recognition flashed across his face.

'Benny,' Ricky said. 'How about you get to fuck and do your job?'

'Right, sorry, Mr Bruce,' Benny said. 'Right you are, I'll just...'

'Move, you old retard!'

We all watched Benny scuttle off with his bucket slopping dirty water at his heels. The fat bouncer smirked like the school bully and I decided if this kicked off I'd ram that smile down his throat.

Ricky looked back at Mack. 'Stop looking for him.'

'No,' Mack said.

A ripple of surprise and excitement flowed through the other five men. Ricky spread his hands though, showing how relaxed he was about the whole situation. 'I don't have a problem with Gordon. He's got nothing to fear from me. But you keep looking for him you're going to get hurt.' Ricky hiked his shoulders and lifted his hands. 'Where's the sense in that?'

'Hurt, as in shot in the face?' I said. 'Like Sean Reardon?'

'Whatever you think you know, you don't know shit,' Ricky growled.

'I know Gordon Dunbar is scared to come home, even though the guy blackmailing him is dead. And I'm going to find out why.'

'You think so?' Ricky smiled his shark smile again. 'I'll give you this chance, and this chance only, to walk away from here and forget everything you *think* you know.'

'No,' Mack said again.

The flyweight we'd met outside lost his patience and charged forward. He threw a spinning kick, his heel missing Mack's face by an inch. A smile crossed his face, convinced he had Mack with his speed, that it was sheer luck he hadn't connected. He stepped in again and snapped a side kick at Mack's face.

Mack's hand shot up from his side and caught the foot, stopping it dead. He pivoted and stood on the flyweight's standing foot, then wrenched his kicking foot towards the roof. There was a howl of pain as his groin tore and his standing leg buckled. Mack let go of the foot and stepped backwards as the guy collapsed to the floor in agony. Mack ignored him and looked impassively at Ricky.

The Forgotten Dead

'I could do this all day, Ricky,' he said.

The fat bouncer was nearest me and he unfolded his arms and rumbled towards me. I stamped on the inside of his knee, toppling him forwards till I met his face with an elbow. He rolled sideways and I punched him hard in the face, dropping him onto his back where he lay cradling his broken nose as blood leaked through his fingers. He wasn't smirking anymore.

The shaved head took a step forward and Mack kicked him once on the outside of the knee, then, as he stumbled, kicked him again in the ribs, and drove an elbow into his face. He went down like someone had cut his strings.

Three down.

The people at the back of the crowd had started to turn towards us. Ricky realised it too and decided enough was enough. His hand went behind his back and produced a gun. He held it loosely by his side, but the look on his face suggested he would dearly love to empty it into us.

'Like I said,' Ricky hissed, 'one chance only.'

'You think we're going to drop this, Ricky?' Mack asked.

'I think you better. Or the first time I see you without two hundred witnesses I will fucking shoot you.'

Even we knew when discretion was the better part of valour and we began making our way to the door. I led the way while Mack kept his eyes on Ricky and his remaining two bouncers as they followed us. By now the eyes of everyone in the room were on us, and no doubt hoping for more carnage. As we neared the door I saw Benny through a gap in the crowd. It was between fights and he stood in the cage, mopping up the blood from the previous bout. He looked up and made eye contact with me, though he gave no sign of recognition.

We passed through the double doors and climbed the stairs. Ricky and his goons followed until we were outside. As we moved away from the building, Ricky called out to us one last time. 'You're playing with the big boys now, James. Next time you come looking for a fight, you best bring more than your fists.'

I pulled Mack's arm, dragging him into the night before he

felt compelled to prove a point. We walked away, and, in the darkness, with our backs turned, I tensed for the impact of a bullet between my shoulder blades. But none came.

We reached the car, where Jessica was in the driver seat ready for a quick getaway if one had been necessary. I climbed into the passenger seat and Mack slid into the back. Jessica started the engine and pulled away from the kerb, turned the car off South Street and towards the Clyde Tunnel, all the time checking no-one was following.

'Well,' Jessica said, when she was certain we were clear. 'Anything happening?'

'Nah, it was pretty quiet,' Mack said.

Chapter Twenty-Two

I slept late the next day and didn't make it to my office till after ten. I spent half an hour checking out Jessica's file on Jason Teague, and treating myself to several jaw-cracking yawns. Shortly after I'd finished wading through his criminal record, the intercom buzzed. I wasn't expecting anyone, and I was all too aware that at least one person still had a reason to want me dead. I went to the door of the flat and warily pressed the button on the intercom. 'Yes?'

'Open up.'

The voice was slightly distorted, but still recognisable. And it still sent a small shudder through me. I reluctantly pressed the button to release the outside door lock, opened the flat door and watched as Mason entered the building. He stood at my door, close enough that I could feel his breath. I told myself I had no reason to fear him, but somehow, standing alone in this quiet hallway, with no witnesses, it seemed like hollow bravado. Nevertheless, I looked him dead in the eye and said, 'You got a name for me?'

'We're not doing this out here.'

I stood my ground in the doorway. 'What, you want a cup of coffee? Maybe a Caramel Wafer?'

Mason leaned in closer still. 'Watch your tongue. Sooner or later it's going to talk you into something it can't talk its way out of.'

'Probably,' I conceded with a nod. There was a part of me that knew a showdown with Mason was, at some point, inevitable. Admitting that seemed to pacify him a little. I asked for the name again.

'Laskey,' he said. 'Craig Laskey. One of the less morally-afflicted doctors in the city pulled a bullet from his shoulder on Tuesday night.'

The timing was perfect. It had to be the gunman.

'Where can I find him?' I asked.

'Why don't I just do your job for you?'

'You obviously know where he is, so it would be easier if you just told me, wouldn't it?'

He stared a little longer, as though giving me the address was admitting defeat. McKenzie had sent him here to give me information though, and that was what he would have to do, however much it pained him. I waited him out.

'23 Langton Avenue, Pollok.'

'Anything else I should know?'

'Like what? Whether he's single?' Mason's lip curled at one corner. 'You've got a name and address and that's all you're getting. Think yourself lucky I didn't bring over the bullet they took from Laskey's shoulder and put it through your head.'

We stood and looked at each other for a few seconds, my heart hammering as blood surged round my body. Finally I said, 'Always a pleasure, Mason, never a chore.'

'Remember, Harper, one day you'll fall out of favour with Mr McKenzie. And that's the day you'll vanish.'

Mason turned abruptly and stalked from the building, the door closing almost silently behind him. I shivered in spite of the heat and immediately closed and locked the door to the flat. I went to my desk and made a note of the gunman's address on my pad then picked up the phone and dialled Jessica.

'Meet me at the gym,' I said when she answered. 'I've got a name and address for Reardon's killer.'

'You'll be calling your new lady friend on the force then,' Jessica said.

'Maybe after I have a friendly chat with him.'

'Friendly?'

'We've got a lot to talk about. Like the time he tried to shoot me. I really want to talk about that.'

*

'Tell me again why we don't just kick the door in and grab him by the throat?'

We'd spent seven hours watching the address Mason had given me and Mack had lost his patience some time ago. This was the second time in the last hour he'd called my phone to make a plea for more immediate action.

'Witnesses?' I suggested.

'Witnesses shmitnesses,' Mack muttered and hung up.

Langton Avenue was a long, sloping street of terraced houses between a block of flats at the top of the hill and a small grassy area beside a corner shop, bookies, and rundown pub at the bottom end. Number 23 was a third of the way along the street, just at the bottom of the slope where it levelled out. I was parked outside the flats among another half dozen cars where I had an unobstructed view down the hill to the front of the target building and the battered old Ford Fiesta that sat outside. We'd agreed earlier that, since I was the only one Laskey could recognise, I should be the furthest away. Jessica was parked on a parallel street watching the back of the house and Mack had spent several hours in the bookies before migrating to his current position lurking in the pub next door. He couldn't see the target, but if Laskey left on foot either Jessica or I would alert Mack who would then follow him.

It had been a long day, made longer still by the heat. The back of my t-shirt was damp and stuck to my skin like it had been pasted on. Jessica had reported similar discomfort, while Mack took great delight in confirming the temperatures in both the bookies and the pub were quite pleasant.

I'd met Jessica and Mack at the gym that morning and given them what little information I had. Before leaving the office I'd done a little digging into Craig Laskey and found he had convictions for, among other things, armed robbery and GBH. His record was clear of murder charges, but I doubted Reardon's was the first life he had taken.

I then checked the address Mason had given me and found it was owned by a man named Anthony Pellini, who'd lived there for three years. Another quick search revealed Mr Pellini had previous convictions for housebreaking, theft, robbery, and reset of stolen goods. Just the kind of scumbag Laskey might be hiding out with.

At the gym I'd given Jessica and Mack descriptions of both Laskey and Pellini. Jessica had of course seen Laskey on the video she'd found, but the quality hadn't been great. The only description of Pellini that I'd been able to dig up was vague – mid twenties, five-five, slightly built, short ginger hair – but it was all we had. The three of us memorised the descriptions then looked at a map of the area and estimated the best places to set up our surveillance. Mack then presented us with keys to two of the cars he kept in his car park for various extracurricular activities. I had once asked Mack why he kept untraceable cars parked outside his gym and, though the answer had been deliberately short on details, it had been enough to prevent me ever asking again.

Sometimes ignorance really was bliss.

We'd arrived shortly after one o'clock and taken up our current positions; Jessica in an old Rover on the parallel street, while I sat at he top of the hill in a clapped-out Nissan. We weren't concerned about Laskey recognising our vehicles, but there remained the possibility that at some point today we might have to take action that the police would frown on. If that happened Mack would have the cars scrapped before anyone could connect them to us.

The flats beside me had been largely deserted – presumably everyone was already out taking advantage of another scorching day – and, with the exception of one hardy soul pushing a lawnmower across his grass and trimming his hedges, Jessica's street was similarly quiet. The bookies, by contrast, had been fairly busy. It looked like the kind of place where punters went in at lunchtime and stayed for hours, and Mack had done exactly that before moving to the pub shortly before the bookies closed for the day.

Before entering the bookies Mack had walked past number 23 hoping for a glimpse of Laskey but had seen nothing more than the glow of a television in the front room. After the first couple of hours passed without incident we all became very aware that Laskey, if he'd ever been here, could be long gone.

I picked up the files I'd brought with me, hoping to distract myself from such negative thoughts. I was comfortable that I had become sufficiently attuned to my environment that anyone approaching or leaving number 23 would register with me, even if I wasn't concentrating fully on the house.

I'd already trawled through the information Brownstone had sent on Reardon, and had read Jessica's file on Teague several times this morning, but it occurred to me that I had been looking for clues to who had hired them to hurt Gordon, for connections to this mystery man, and not for connections between Reardon and Teague themselves.

They were lowlife scum, seemingly willing to do anything for a payday, however meagre. They were from different ends of the city – Reardon living in Ibrox, Teague in Dennistoun – had attended different schools, and had, for what few days honest work they had done between them, been employed in different jobs. But there must be some connection between them, something that had caused them both to be chosen by the white-haired man. Teague certainly didn't know him – Jessica's terrifying display would have loosened his lips on that account – and it seemed unlikely that Reardon would have either. The white-haired man was too careful for that.

The answer had come as I waited for a glimpse of Laskey and mulled over what I knew about him. Including his previous convictions.

Prison.

Reardon and Teague had both served time for various offences over the years, and I wondered if this was where they had come to the white-haired man's attention. And sure enough, on flipping through the files, I found they'd both served time in Greenock prison earlier this year, overlapping in February and March. I checked the rest of their records to be certain, but that two month window was the only time Reardon and Teague had been in the same prison at the same time.

I called Brownstone and asked if she could give me a list of everyone who'd served time in Greenock prison in February and March this year and had since been released. She told me it wouldn't be a problem and I asked her to email the list to me along with photos if possible. When I used the phrase *if possible* she just gave a little tut, as though I'd insulted her, which I probably had.

She hung up and I put the files back on the passenger seat. I returned my full attention to the house at the bottom of the hill, and waited for the man who'd tried to kill me once and would do so again if I gave him half a chance.

Chapter Twenty-Three

In the end, the wait had been shorter than I'd feared. At quarter to three the front door had opened and I had my first sighting of Craig Laskey since I'd looked at him down the barrel of a gun as he made his getaway. I pulled my binoculars off the seat beside me and watched Laskey close the door behind himself and limp down the path. He wore knee-length white shorts and a tight black t-shirt, his eyes hidden behind a new pair of wraparound sunglasses. A white bandage ran from the middle of his left forearm up beneath the sleeve, while the back of his right hand was covered by a large plaster and his face bore numerous cuts and bruises.

I put the binoculars down and called Mack's mobile on my phone while I picked the walkie-talkie from the door pocket beside me with my other hand. Since Mack could hardly sit in the bookies or the pub with a walkie-talkie in front of him this was the easiest way to keep us all informed of developments at the same time, though I would have to relay Mack's words to Jessica if they were important.

Mack answered the call and I pressed the transmit button on the walkie talkie and said, 'Target on the move, heading west.' I released the transmit button. Unlikely as it was that either Laskey or Pellini was listening in on our transmissions, we were careful to give nothing away that could compromise us.

'All quiet this side,' Jessica said. I was holding the walkie-talkie and the phone close enough that Mack could hear her.

'Is he on his guard?' Mack asked.

'Doesn't look he's expecting anyone,' I said as I watched Laskey hobble along the street in Mack's direction. For all the awkwardness in his walk, he certainly didn't carry the tension or wariness of a man in hiding. Had he been any more ambivalent to his surroundings we could have set up the stakeout on deck chairs in the front garden.

Laskey reached the grassy area at the end of the row of houses and cut across it, past the bookies and the pub and headed for the corner shop. He pushed open the door and stepped inside out of sight. I pressed the transmit button and said, 'He's in the shop.'

Jessica and Mack both acknowledged and then were silent again. All we could do now was wait till our target reappeared. A couple of minutes later the door opened and Laskey appeared, a six-pack of beer in a cardboard carrier under his right arm and a carrier bag in his right hand, full of, judging by the shape, more beers. The way he was carrying them looked awkward enough to suggest that his left arm was out of action. Interesting.

'Target in sight. Heading east.'

Moments later Laskey turned through the gate of number 23 and let himself in the front door with a key.

'Target back home.'

'Then let's go,' Mack said.

I thought about it – God knows I wanted answers as soon as possible – but it would be rash. There were too many reasons why we should wait. And we now had another one. If Laskey planned on drinking those beers tonight that could make things easier. Providing we got to him before he was too far gone to answer our questions. Of course, for all we knew he had five or six mates in the house who would be sharing his beer. And since we knew Laskey could get hold of a gun and was willing to use it we needed more information before we went in.

'It's too light' I said. 'Too big a risk of someone seeing and identifying us. Plus, we still don't know how many people are in there.'

'And?'

'This guy is probably armed, and he's already shown he's willing to kill. That's enough to deal with. I don't fancy going in there and finding there's fifteen of them sharing a house that could double as an armoury.'

'I remember when you used to be fun,' Mack said and hung up.

'You didn't see Reardon's head spread across his hall floor,' I said aloud, though no-one could hear.

I tried to put that image out of my mind but it refused to budge. It was half an hour before I managed to move it from the forefront of my mind and that was only when Jessica radioed to confirm Laskey wasn't alone. She was watching Pellini, standing on the back step smoking a cigarette and enjoying the late afternoon sun. I called Mack and relayed what Jessica had said, then asked him if he was attracting any unwanted attention.

'Nah,' he replied. 'I'm a chameleon.'

We chatted a little longer, until Jessica confirmed Pellini had returned to the house. From then on it was quiet at the target house, and silent between the three of us. The area around me got busier after five o'clock as people began to return to their homes for dinner. No-one paid me the slightest bit of attention.

At five to six Mack left the bookies just before it closed and wandered next door to the pub. I envied him the opportunity to have a nice cool drink and use the bathroom. Jessica and I might well be suffering from dehydration by the end of the day since we were trying to limit our water intake and subsequent need to use a toilet.

My phone rang and when I answered I heard Mack's voice at a slight distance say, 'Ahhh, that's a nice cold beer.' Then the call disconnected.

Bastard.

My stomach was beginning to rumble now. We'd grabbed some petrol station sandwiches and a few bars of chocolate on the way here this afternoon but, as with water intake, it was advisable to only eat when absolutely necessary on surveillance. Breakfast felt like a long time ago.

At ten past seven a white Peugeot 106 turned into Langton Avenue and crawled along hesitantly before stopping outside number 23. I lifted the binoculars again and watched a young guy in t-shirt, jeans and a baseball hat climb out, open the back door and lift out a white plastic bag with red Chinese lettering on the side. He looked at the front of the building again, presumably checking the number, then walked up the drive with the bag in his hand. I focused on the bag, looking for the name of the restaurant but there didn't appear to be one.

The door was opened by a short, skinny, ginger guy who paid the delivery driver, took the bag and disappeared inside. The driver climbed back into the 106 and drove off.

I dialled Mack and lifted the walkie-talkie at the same time. 'Target's have just had dinner delivered.'

'Are you taking the piss?' Jessica said.

'Me too,' was Mack's reply. 'Steak pie. And it's some size, I don't know if I'll be able to finish it.'

Not wanting to suffer alone, I relayed this to Jessica.

'You're both evil bastards,' Jessica complained. 'My stomach's started digesting itself.'

'Anyway,' I cut in, 'the delivery bag looked too small to have more than two meals in it. So unless there's a houseful of anorexics down there it's just the two of them.'

There was silence for a few seconds, then Mack said, 'Better hurry up and finish my dinner then.'

I didn't bother relaying that to Jessica. Instead I said to Mack, 'I need you to get hold of a phone book. The pub has a flat above it so chances are there's a phone book kicking around somewhere.'

'Are we going to beat him to death with a phone book?'

Mack sounded so keen on the idea I hated to let him down. 'I want you to text me the numbers for the nearest Chinese takeaways.'

'Are you that hungry?'

'I'm going to make sure there's only two of them in there. And maybe get them to open the door.'

'Don't suppose I get to finish my pie first?'

'You suppose correctly.'

I hung up, then radioed Jessica and filled her in and sat back to wait for Mack's text. My stomach was grumbling less loudly now, due partially to excitement and partially to the petty satisfaction that Mack wouldn't be able to enjoy his food yet.

Eight minutes passed before my phone vibrated with the arrival of a text message. I picked it up and looked at the list of seven names and phone numbers. Mack would have listed them in order of proximity to our target, with the last few on the list probably too far away to be likely. With any luck I wouldn't get that far.

Luck seemed to have my back. After I struck out with the Jade Garden and the Lucky Dragon, my third call, to the Golden Star, hit the bullseye.

'Golden Star,' said a bored voice.

'The name's Pellini. I just got a delivery, but I don't think it's right.' If this was Pellini's house I couldn't see any reason why he wouldn't use his own name.

'What's the address?'

'23 Langton Avenue. It just came about ten, fifteen minutes ago. Young guy in the white Peugeot dropped it off.'

I heard the sound of the phone being placed on a hard surface then there was nothing for several seconds before the monotone returned. 'Pellini, Langton Avenue. One chicken fried rice, one chips and curry sauce.'

I put surprise in my voice. 'Is that what he ordered? Ah, sorry mate, my pal phoned it in, I'd asked him to get me something else.'

'That's what was ordered.'

'No worries, mate, I'll see him about it.'

I hung up smiling. Two meals suggested there were only two people in the house. And I had an idea how to get them to open the door. I radioed Jessica and told her what I had in mind then called Mack and did the same.

All we had to do now was wait for darkness.

Chapter Twenty-Four

By half past ten it was fully dark and the three of us were beyond impatient. We had no idea what we'd be stepping into when we entered that house, only that it wouldn't be a polite sit-down chat and that's why I'd insisted we wait for darkness to cover our movements. If nothing else, the target house and those around it all had their curtains and blinds drawn by now, providing us with an easier approach.

I called Mack and gave him the signal. Twenty seconds later I watched as he left the pub and walked round the corner away from me. I got out of the car and began to walk down the hill. As I neared the bottom of the slope Jessica's car turned into the far end of the street and drove towards me. Mack would now be lurking at the back of the house with Jessica's radio in his hand.

I opened the gate to number 27 and cut across their grass till I was close to the building then climbed the small fence into number 25's garden. I crouched and scuttled under the window before climbing another small fence into the property of our target. I took a thin pair of leather gloves from my pocket and put them on just as Jessica pulled up outside.

Jessica made a show of checking something in her hand and looking at the front of the house, then, apparently satisfied that she had the right place, she cut the engine and got out. She opened the gate and walked up the path with a ten pound note clutched in her hand. I stood to the side of the door with my back pressed against the wall where no-one within could see me. Jessica stopped at the door and rapped her knuckles against it.

I held down the transmit button on the radio for two seconds as previously arranged. Mack would now move towards the back door.

Ten seconds passed with no response from inside. Jessica knocked again.

This time we heard movement and a voice from behind the door. 'Who is it?'

'Golden Star, Mr Pellini,' Jessica said. 'The driver made a mistake with your change earlier. I've brought the rest of it.'

There was a pause, then we heard the door being unlocked and the security chain rattle as it was taken off. Pellini's greed had got the better of his caution.

The door opened and I heard a voice say, 'Mistake?'

'The driver should have given you another tenner. Sorry about that.' Jessica held out her left hand, the ten pound note waving in the light breeze. Her face was neutral, her eyes focused solely on Pellini, despite the fact I was standing only eighteen inches from him.

I held my breath and felt the brickwork rough against the back of my head as I pressed myself flatter against it, willing him to reach for the money, waiting for fingers to appear past the edge of the wall and snatch at the bait held in Jessica's hand.

A moment later Pellini's hand shot out, grasping for the money. Jessica was quicker though and her left hand grabbed his wrist and yanked it towards her, pulling him off balance and driving her knee into his stomach. The wind left him with a rush of air and Jessica spun him round and wrapped her arm tightly round his throat. She whispered in his ear and after a shocked pause Pellini held up one finger to indicate there was only one other person in the house. Jessica whispered again and he pointed towards the living room at the front of the house.

I pressed the transmit button twice quickly and moved in through the open front door. Jessica dragged Pellini in behind me and shut the door quietly with her foot. I barged through the door to the living room at the same moment the sound of breaking glass came from the back of the house.

Laskey was watching the television beneath the window. His head snapped round as the door crashed against the inner wall, his fingers instinctively reaching for a gun on a side table. I ran at him, head down, my only goal to stop him picking up that gun.

He was halfway to his feet when I hit him at full speed. My shoulder ploughed into his chest, pushing him backwards over his armchair and into a dining table that screeched across the floor as the two of us fell in a heap. Behind me the gun clattered to the floor.

I tried to get to my feet but Laskey had wrapped his right fist in my t-shirt and was holding me down. His left arm lay uselessly at his side but he aimed a headbutt at my nose, connecting instead with my shoulder as I threw my head to the side. He pulled back for another but I punched him hard in his injured shoulder and he howled in pain. I was about to throw another punch when something appeared in front of me and connected with Laskey's face. His grip loosened but didn't fall away until Mack stamped on his face again.

I got to my feet as Laskey tried to open his eyes and see through the blood that covered his face. He hauled himself up into a sitting position against the leg of the table and looked from Mack to me. Then he looked past us and saw Pellini on his knees with Jessica's arm round his neck in a stranglehold, his eyes bulging.

'Watch him,' I said to Mack. 'He caught me with that dead duck routine the last time.'

'Better make sure he isn't faking it then,' Mack said. He took a step forward and stamped on Laskey's face once more, driving him to the floor. He rolled onto his side and spat blood on the floor.

'You don't know who you're fucking with,' Laskey managed, his voice a gurgle through the blood in his mouth and nose.

'Yes we do,' I replied. 'You're the man who tried to kill me.' I leant down and picked up the gun, walked over to Pellini and pointed it at him. Jessica let go of him and pulled on a pair of gloves, making sure he saw her do so. Pellini's face whitened as he realised the significance.

I gestured to Mack and he left the room to check there really was no-one else in the house.

Laskey had pushed himself upright again and he looked at me through dazed eyes. This time I didn't think he was putting on an act. 'What?' he said. 'I'm supposed to be scared? Fuck you, arsehole. Soon as you leave here I'll find you and I'll finish what I started.'

'No you won't. By the time we leave here you'll be lucky if you can walk.'

'Big talk,' Laskey said. 'Can you back it up?'

I knew I could. I had in the past. What I wasn't sure about was whether or not I was willing to walk that road again. I hoped it wouldn't come to that.

I turned to Pellini and said, 'How'd you enjoy the X-Trail? Nice drive?'

His eyes alone confirmed that he had indeed been Laskey's getaway driver. And that made him as complicit in Reardon's murder as the man who pulled the trigger. And by extension, as complicit in the attempt to kill me.

'Why did you shoot Sean Reardon?' I asked Laskey.

'Don't know what you're talking about,' he answered as he struggled to his feet.

'The guy you shot in Ibrox on Tuesday. Just before you tried to shoot me. Why?'

Laskey was standing upright now, buoyed by my failure to shoot him. 'Fuck you.'

'Look what I found!'

I turned and saw Mack enter the room with a thick phone book held aloft. He strode towards Laskey and swung the book two-handed into his face. It connected with a thud and Laskey staggered back against the table. Mack swung it again and Laskey fell to the ground.

Mack threw the phone book on the table and grabbed hold of Laskey's injured arm and began pulling him towards the kitchen. 'Bring that other twat as well,' he called over Laskey's pained howls.

'I'm not arguing with him when he's like this,' Jessica said. She hoisted Pellini to his feet and dragged him to the kitchen. After a few seconds I reluctantly followed.

Laskey was slumped against the front of the cooker and Pellini was sprawled against the back door, beneath the jagged hole where Mack had broken the glass and reached through to turn the key.

Mack was at the sink, filling a kettle from the tap. He turned and placed it back on its stand and switched it on. 'You might as well start asking,' he said. 'It'll take a couple of minutes to boil.'

I raised an eyebrow in question.

'You've got questions, they've got answers. And in two minutes I'll have a litre and a half of boiling water.'

Pellini's eyes darted around the room as he desperately looked for a way out. Mack noticed and said to him, 'One of you will answer our questions. Whether or not you do it before you're permanently disfigured is up to you.'

I handed the gun to Jessica and walked out of the kitchen. Mack followed and looked at me blankly.

'What are you doing?' I asked quietly.

'Finding out why these pricks tried to kill you.' Suddenly he looked angry. 'Why, what did you bring us here for?'

'Not to torture anyone.'

'They'll talk.'

'And if they don't you'll just pour it away?'

Mack's steady stare told me what I already knew.

'So you thought we'd roll up, ask a couple of questions, they'd cough their guts up and we'd move on?' He shook his head in amazement. 'You know better than that, Harper. We've been here before.'

'I know that. But how many times can we do this?'

'As many as it takes.'

'We can't.' I rubbed my gloved hands over my face and blew out a long breath. 'Don't you feel it? Every time we do something like this we become more like them. Every time we find ourselves on their level we get further away from the people we once were.'

Mack's voice was level but his eyes burned with the fire that had been consuming him for years. 'I don't know about you,

Harper, but there isn't much difference between the man I was, the man I am, and the man I want to be.'

'There needs to be.'

Mack stuck his head quickly into the kitchen to check Jessica was still in control, then stepped forward and stood right in front of me, his eyes boring into mine. 'The last time we were in this situation you were the one doing the damage. You didn't stop till you got answers. What's different now?'

'People I loved were in danger then. They aren't now.'

'What about Gordon Dunbar?'

'I don't want anything to happen to him, but... when it was you and Jessica... I couldn't think straight. I felt like someone was going to have to die, and I'd do whatever it took to make sure it wasn't either of you.'

Mack's finger thrust toward the kitchen like a sword. 'That guy in there is a killer. He killed Reardon and he tried to kill you. And if you think that was his first time round the dancefloor you're kidding yourself. Take a look upstairs. This place has more guns than an eighties action movie.'

'What?'

'There's a pile of them in a cupboard in the back bedroom. Maybe they're selling them, maybe they're planning a job, who knows. Point is, these are some bad, bad people we're dealing with. And if we don't put them down hard they *will* come after us.'

'You think torturing them will stop that?'

'Scaring the holy fucking shit out of them will stop that. These are bad people, Harper, but they're as scared of a crazy motherfucker as the next man.'

'Well aren't I just lucky to have the craziest motherfucker on my side?'

'It's black and white, Harper. These people tried to kill you, and that puts them firmly on the black squares.'

I was about to respond when we heard a shout from the kitchen, followed by a cry of pain. We rushed in and found Jessica standing over Laskey, his t-shirt bunched in her hand, smashing the butt of the gun repeatedly into his face.

I stepped forward and pulled Jessica back, took the gun from her hand and turned it on Pellini to make sure he wasn't trying to escape. He wasn't. He was cowering in the corner, eyes screwed shut in terror, pressing his head into the wall as though he could make himself invisible if only he pressed himself hard enough against it.

Jessica shoved past me and kicked Laskey's injured shoulder. 'Who wanted Reardon dead?'

Laskey groaned and slid sideways into unconsciousness. Jessica's eyes searched the room like a tidal wave looking for a ship to break over. She found it in Pellini.

'Who wanted him dead?' she shouted.

'I don't know,' Pellini whispered.

'Yes, you fucking do,' Jessica said. She grabbed the kettle of boiling water and crossed the room to him. She held up the kettle and poured a little on the leg of his jeans. Pellini howled and pulled his legs up against his chest.

Mack and I stood motionless as we watched Jessica tilt the kettle again. I lowered the gun. She had him so scared he wasn't going anywhere.

'The next lot will need a skin graft. Who called the hit?'

My mouth was dry as I watched and I had the taste of something foul in my throat. But I said nothing. Jessica was getting answers and that's why we were here. I just hoped Pellini talked before she crossed a line she couldn't come back from.

'It... it... Ricky Bruises. It was Ricky Bruises. He told us to kill Reardon.'

'Why?'

'I... I don't know. We don't get told that. Just that we were to take him out.'

'Tell me everything you know,' Jessica said.

'But he'll... Ricky'll kill me.'

'Would that be before or after you get your skin grafts?'

Pellini whimpered and pushed himself further back against the wall, tears leaking from his eyes. I reminded myself that only a few days ago this man had been involved in a murder. And almost involved in mine.

Jessica held the kettle above his head. 'Last chance.'

Chapter Twenty-Five

Pellini talked, of course. With the fear Jessica had instilled in him it wasn't in doubt. The only problem was trying to interpret his words through the tears and snotters.

He told us how Ricky Bruises had ordered him and Laskey to watch an address in Giffnock, that he wanted to find the homeowner – a man named Gordon Dunbar – as well as the person who was blackmailing him. Pellini claimed – and Jessica had him too terrified to lie – that Ricky hadn't told them what the blackmail was about.

When a young woman – Nicole – arrived and let herself into the house on Monday, Laskey called Ricky who identified her as Dunbar's daughter and instructed them to follow her, presumably in the hope that she would lead them to Gordon. Instead she led them to me. After another phone call Ricky told them to follow me instead of Nicole, since she had presumably hired me to find either her father or the person who was blackmailing him.

Pellini told us how they followed me to George Square and watched me follow Reardon to the subway. While Laskey got on the subway with us Pellini called Ricky and told him what had happened. Ricky ordered them to follow us both until they found where Reardon lived and to then kill both of us and recover from Reardon's home and our bodies anything that looked like it might relate to blackmail. Laskey, as I thought, had waited until his getaway driver had caught up before entering the building and opening fire.

After their escape Pellini had switched cars and torched the X-Trail before driving Laskey straight to the kind of doctor you could rely on to keep his mouth shut. Unless Innes McKenzie was asking him questions. But then, everyone answers McKenzie's questions. Sooner or later.

By the time he was finished we were no further forward on the reason for the blackmail or why the blackmailer was killed. All we had established was that Ricky Bruises, for some reason, seemed to want to protect Gordon Dunbar. The question was why?

When Pellini finished spilling his guts I acted quickly to make sure neither Mack nor Jessica – I was no longer sure who scared me the most – took matters any further. I took them aside and explained the plan that had come to me almost as soon as Mack mentioned the cache of guns upstairs.

Unfortunately for Pellini the plan required him to be unconscious. Fortunately for Mack he was elected to do the honours. Seconds later both our targets were out cold. I retrieved the guns from upstairs and we made sure Pellini and Laskey's fingerprints were on each and every one of them before I took them back upstairs and left them on the bed in plain sight. When I got back downstairs Mack was handing Jessica a mobile, one I knew would be untraceable and its pieces scattered in bins across the city within the hour.

Jessica pressed three numbers and held the phone to her ear. When the call was answered she immediately made a bid for an Oscar.

'Help! Oh, please God, help. I think they're killing her!' Pause. 'She's screaming, and I saw a man at the back bedroom window with a gun. Please, hurry!' Pause. '23 Langton Avenue, Pollok. Please! Before it's too late!'

Jessica hung up the phone and we gave her a mock round of applause.

'Too much?' she asked.

'Not at all,' I replied. 'You've got to sell it or the audience can't buy it.'

We checked each other for blood and made sure we were clean, then Jessica walked out the front door, leaving it clearly open, while Mack and I left through the kitchen. We began walking along the pavement until Jessica pulled up beside us in the Rover and we climbed in.

A minute later Jessica parked at the top of the hill beside the Nissan I'd spent the best part of the day in. We waited in silence, watching the shaft of light that was the open front door of the house at the bottom of the hill.

The police arrived quickly. The armed response unit pulled up short of the building and officers in bulletproof vests armed with machine guns approached the house issuing warnings while others presumably approached from the rear. There was no response and the officers went in.

It was some time before we saw what we were waiting for, but the sight of Laskey and Pellini being led from the house in cuffs made the three of us smile. Mack's fist appeared between the seats and Jessica and I bumped our knuckles against it then against each others.

Whatever misgivings I'd had while in that house, the fact remained that two dangerous men were now in police custody, and, with the amount of guns in that house, all bearing their fingerprints, the chances of them avoiding jail time for firearms offences were small. I didn't know what the police would make of the scene, and didn't care too much. Knowing how they liked their easy answers I suspected the whole thing would be chalked up to an arms deal gone wrong.

I'd give them a couple of days to link Laskey to Reardon's murder and if they didn't then another anonymous tip-off would be on the cards. All they had to do was match the blood he'd shed in Pollok to that he'd lost in Ibrox and, along with the video Jessica had found, he was going away for a long time.

I felt a deep weariness descend on me then. It had been a long day and at the end of it I was unsure we were any further forward. I needed to rest before I thought more about Gordon Dunbar and Ricky Bruises and the ties that connected them to a dead man.

I got out of the car and climbed into the Nissan while Mack got into the front of the Rover and Jessica reversed back and turned onto the road, taking the two of them away into the night.

I put the car in gear and headed home, all the time wondering if what we had accomplished here today had been worth the cost. Two dangerous men might be on their way to prison, and put there by their own deeds, but was the violence we had inflicted on them and the answers we received worth the discolouration of my soul?

I wished for some seconds that I could see the world as Mack did, in pure monochrome of blinding whites and deafening blacks, but I knew I would never be able to. My world was built on shades of grey, where one blended into another and left me unsure of my footing or even which end of the spectrum I belonged to.

A red light loomed ahead and I slowed the car to a stop. I glanced to the side, my gaze resting on the empty eyes of my reflection. I looked deep into them and asked myself once more if I thought the cost would prove to be worth it.

I found no answer and a chill crept across my skin as I realised my damnation or salvation would already be complete before I did.

*

I picked Jessica up on the way to my office the following day. I could have gone through Brownstone's emailed list in the comfort of my own home, but I preferred to keep my home and my work separate as much as possible. Jessica had called to say she'd help me go through it and I was glad to accept the offer. I don't think either of us expected it to be a long list, but she was reaching out and I was willing to meet her halfway.

Since she'd got in the car a little after midday, however, Jessica had been quiet and withdrawn. At first I put it down to tiredness after our long day yesterday, but soon realised there was more to it. I asked if she was okay and got a mumbled *yes* in response. I decided not to push it and drove on in silence, hoping she'd fill the void in conversation.

It didn't take long. Whatever was bothering her was too troubling to simply set aside.

'How did you sleep last night?' Jessica asked.

I took my eyes off the road for a second to glance at her. It hadn't sounded like a throwaway question. 'Fine,' I replied. 'Just crashed out really. It was a long day.'

Jessica was quiet again. After a minute I asked how she had slept.

'Not well.'

'Something on your mind?' I asked.

'Just the small matter of torturing a man with boiling water.'

'They're killers, Jess. Laskey tried to kill me, and both of them knew that's what they were going there for. They've done it before, and they'd do it again. They brought it on themselves.'

'You sound like Mack.'

I laughed inwardly at the irony. Just the previous night I had been on the other side of this conversation, and now I was arguing against my own misgivings. I knew why: I wanted to soothe Jessica's pain.

And yet, I realised I was pleased at her discomfort. Not that she was suffering, but that she hadn't become completely blasé about the violent urges she was feeling. She had scared me when she interrogated Teague, and even more so with Laskey and Pellini. I had looked at her then and wondered how far she would slide and if she could find her way back.

Now, looking at her, tired and puffy-eyed after a sleepless night spent worrying about the violence she had inflicted on another human being, I felt hope.

'Doesn't it bother you?' Jessica asked.

'Of course it does. I hate the things we have to do sometimes. And I worry what it does to us.'

'I've changed, Harper.' Jessica looked out of the side window, unable to look at me. 'Ever since... you know... I still feel that rock in my hand sometimes. I still feel his skull give way...'

'It's trauma, Jess. It's natural to feel that.'

'But sometimes it feels good.' Then she turned to look at me, and when I took my eyes from the road I saw the fear in her eyes. 'Is that natural?'

For a time I didn't know what to say. We drove on in silence, along Great Western Road, down onto Woodlands Road, and past the scene of Daphne Hillcoat's brush with death before I could speak.

'Jessica, listen to me. You took a life, but you saved at least two. And the life you took was that of an evil man. How many more lives would he have taken if you hadn't stopped him?'

'I know that,' Jessica said quietly. 'Intellectually, I know that. But...' she hesitated, searching for the right words, 'you ever just feel like you've given up a bit of who you were?'

I nodded. 'All the time.'

'And what about last night? If Pellini hadn't talked I know I would have poured that boiling water on him. And Teague, when we spoke to him – if he hadn't talked I don't know that he'd ever have walked out of that alley. What does that say about me? What does that say I've become?'

'We spend most of our time in the grey areas, Jessica. Nothing's straightforward for people like us. But we still have to do it. Someone told me once that bad shit was still going to happen, and asked what I was going to do, let it?' I thought often of the woman who'd said those words to me and what had become of her. 'And she was right. It's a heavy price we pay, but I can't walk away from it. And I don't think you can either.'

Jessica smiled a sad smile. 'So your advice is to suck it up and get on with it?'

'No.' I shook my head as I manoeuvred the car through Charing Cross and onto Sauchiehall Street. 'I can't give you advice. It's all I can do to keep my own head straight. But the one thing you have to cling to is the fact that it bothers you. It's when you don't think it's a problem that you should worry.'

'I know that too, but it didn't help me sleep last night.'

I pulled the car into the kerb outside my office and cut the engine. I took the key from the ignition and turned to face Jessica. 'What's stopping you sleeping? The things you've done or the things you think you might do?'

'The things I might be capable of. I can justify the things I've done without much difficulty, but I'm scared of what I might end up doing one day. I took a life that had to be taken. But maybe next time I'll be wrong. What if doing it once makes it come easier and quicker the next time? What if I can't control myself?'

Jessica reached for the handle to open her door but I grabbed her hand and squeezed it till she looked at me. 'You won't cross the line,' I said. 'You're too good for that.'

Jessica tried to smile but it was forced and didn't stick. She turned away but I didn't let go of her hand until she turned back to face me. 'Trust yourself, Jessica. Trust yourself the way I trust you.'

There was a moistness in her eyes and her lips had curled inwards to quell the first hints of a tremor. 'I can't trust someone I don't like.'

Jessica opened the door and got out quickly, already distancing herself from the things she'd revealed. I sat in pained silence for several moments before I looked out of the window and saw Jessica standing at the door to the building with her back to me and her shoulders slumped.

I took a deep breath and tried to gather the pieces of my heart together again.

Chapter Twenty-Six

We entered my office and Jessica lay down on the sofa. This was no indication of her state of mind; this was her usual pose when visiting my office, regardless of the reason. I stood in the centre of the room and just looked at her for a moment, hoping for some inspiration.

In the end, all I could think to say was, 'We need to talk about this, Jess.'

'You're right,' she replied, without looking at me. 'We're no further forward, are we? To finding Gordon, or why he was blackmailed, I mean. Despite everything we did yesterday.'

Her voice was deliberately casual, as though the conversation outside had never taken place.

'About you,' I said.

She rolled her head to the side to look at me. There was nothing in her eyes now, no sign of the sadness she had revealed outside. 'Is that going to help find Gordon?'

'It might help find you.'

'I'm right here, Harper. Right in front of you where I've always been.' She looked back to the ceiling then, as though she'd revealed something else she hadn't planned to. 'Can we concentrate on the case?'

I watched Jessica withdraw again and knew she'd revealed as much as she would today. She needed a friend alright, but at this moment, she needed one who knew when to remain silent.

I sat down and switched on the computer. If Jessica wanted to focus on the case then that's what we would do. For now.

'We know Gordon is connected to Ricky Bruises in some

way,' I began. 'Ricky confirmed that himself. And we know Ricky ordered the hit on Reardon.'

Jessica continued to stare at the ceiling, her fingers now drumming on her thigh. 'Then it must be something to do with the fight club. Maybe Reardon was blackmailing Gordon over his gambling?'

'He could've been. Maybe he saw him there, figured he was supposedly respectable and thought he could take him for a few quid.'

'Why would he pay?'

'To protect his reputation?'

We were both unconvinced by that.

'There must have been better targets there than a GP,' Jessica argued. 'Someone he could have got more money from.'

'Maybe Gordon looked like an easy target. One who couldn't put up a fight.'

'Possibly. But why is Ricky looking out for Gordon? He's making shit-loads of money down there, why would he care about a small-time gambler?'

I put my feet up on the desk while I waited for the computer to start up. I thought about Jessica's question and found only one answer. 'To protect himself and his business. If Reardon tried to expose Gordon, he'd have to expose the club too. It doesn't sound like Ricky Bruises is the kind of guy to take that risk.'

'Then why not just warn him off? Maybe break a leg or something. Killing him seems extreme.'

'A warning? To stop anyone else trying the same sort of thing.'

'You don't sound convinced,' Jessica said.

'I'm not,' I admitted. 'To believe that you'd need to forget about Reardon being hired to blackmail Gordon, about Teague being hired to mug him, and about his car being stolen and used to run down an innocent woman.'

'Well, when you put it like that...' Jessica was quiet for a few moments, her fingers continuing their backbeat to her thoughts. Then she turned to face me and asked, 'Why hasn't Gordon come home yet?'

'No idea, remember?'

'I mean, if this was just a simple case of blackmail, and Gordon was hiding from him, he should have come home by now. Reardon was killed almost a week ago. It's over.'

'He might not know he's dead. It's been in the papers, but Gordon might not have known his name.'

'True. Or maybe he knows someone else is involved. Maybe he knows it's not a simple case of blackmail.' Jessica swung her legs to the floor, sat up and leant forward. 'What was he hoping for when he ran off? Did he think the blackmailer would get fed up and go away? He couldn't stay away forever.'

'People don't always think rationally in stressful situations.'

'Also true. But what if he knew he only had to stay away for a while? What if he knew the blackmailer wasn't going to be around to blackmail him for much longer?'

'He knew Ricky was going to kill him?'

'It's a possibility.'

'If that was the case he didn't need to go into hiding. He could have arranged to meet Reardon, identified him for Ricky and his mob then walked away and waited for it to show up on the news.'

'Not if he wanted to tell himself he didn't know it was going to happen.'

Now that was plausible. In fact, convincing yourself of something despite overwhelming evidence to the contrary was something of a Dunbar speciality.

'But,' Jessica continued, '*if* that was the case, he would definitely know Reardon was dead and he'd be home by now. Unless he knows someone else is involved.'

'Which brings us back to the guy with the white hair.'

The computer had loaded up now and I logged into my email account. Among the usual spam offers of Viagra and warnings that various bank accounts I didn't have needed my urgent attention, was a single email from Brownstone, sent the previous afternoon. There were nine files attached, each labelled with a series of digits I assumed were the individual's prison number. I opened the first one.

It was a large file and took a few minutes to open on my less than state of the art computer. While we waited I became aware that it was another stiflingly hot day. The same thought must have struck Jessica for she went to the small kitchen and came back with two cans of Irn-Bru from the fridge. She handed one to me, opened hers and perched on the edge of the desk. I pressed the can to my forehead, savouring the coolness of the metal and trying to ignore the fact that Jessica's thigh was six inches from my right hand. I willed the file to open before I ran out of places to avert my eyes to or the willpower to do so.

When the file finally opened I sat forward abruptly, grateful for the distraction. There were several pages in the file, but the first thing I saw was a photo of a very fat, bald man.

'That's not our boy,' Jessica said.

I closed it and opened the second file. This one opened far more quickly now that the computer had warmed up, and we were presented with a picture of a middle-aged Asian man with a thick beard. Another miss.

I opened each file in turn and quickly ruled them out. Bodybuilder, black man, elderly man, thin guy with white hair...

And there he was, just as Daphne Hillcoat and Susan Miller and Jason Teague had described him: a thin, sharp face with a long nose, a small cross-shaped scar beneath his left eye, and a quiff and sideburns so blonde they appeared almost white.

I scrolled down the page until the man's name became visible.

'Frankie Dent,' I said. 'Well, well, Frankie. Haven't you been a bad lad?'

'What was he in for?'

I scrolled down further, then laughed, short and humourless. 'Get this – his last conviction was for running someone down and killing them.'

Jessica's eyebrows lifted. 'Mrs Hillcoat might be luckier than she realises.'

I read further through the file. 'Christ, he only did seven months for it.'

'For killing someone?'

'I don't know why we're surprised. He'd have got more for ripping off some rich bloke.'

'Right, put your soap box away.'

I shrugged an apology and continued to scan Frankie Dent's file. 'Looks like he's got a temper. Assault, aggravated assault... pretty much every kind of assault you can think of.'

'That's what I love most about this job. You meet such lovely people,' Jessica said wryly. 'Does it give an address?'

'Yeah, there's one in Barmulloch. What are the chances of him being there?'

'Slim. There a phone number?'

I read the number out and Jessica dialled. When the call was answered Jessica put on a sing-song call centre voice. 'Good afternoon, may I speak with Mr Dent please?'

After a pause she continued. 'Oh, I'm terribly sorry. Perhaps the name's been taken down wrongly. The first name definitely looks like Frank though, is there a Frank there?' Jessica leant across me so she could see the computer screen. 'No? Hmm, perhaps they've given me the wrong phone number. Is this 35 Zena Street?'

Another pause, longer this time, then Jessica said. 'Thanks you for your help, very sorry to bother you.' She hung up and turned to me. 'The house is owned by an elderly lady named Moira McArthur and has been for years. I spoke to her carer, a woman named Karen, who told me that as far as she's aware there has never been anyone named either Frank or Dent at that address.'

'Don't they check these things?'

'Apparently not.'

'Any chance it's an elaborate cover?'

'I doubt it. I could hear the old lady in the background, even before I used the name Dent. We'll need to find another address for him.'

An hour later we'd found nothing and exhausted every one of our usual computer-based methods for tracing someone. There were no details of known associates in Brownstone's file and, although we found plenty of information on him prior to his most recent incarceration, he had apparently vanished since then.

I leaned back in my chair and ran my palms over my face in frustration. Jessica was standing at the window now, her eyes closed against the brightness of the sun, her fingers pulling at her lower lip. Eventually, without turning or opening her eyes, she spoke. 'He likes running people over, doesn't he?'

'Sorry?'

Jessica turned and opened her eyes. 'When did he kill that person?'

I looked through the file and found it. 'May last year. Got sent down in September, released at the end of April this year.'

'And a month later he does it again, only this time the victim survives.'

'What's your point, caller?'

'Has he done it before that?'

I scanned Dent's file again. 'Not that he did time for. But he could have done it and got away with it, just like he did with Daphne Hillcoat.'

'Maybe.'

'You don't believe that. What are you thinking?'

'We agreed that Daphne Hillcoat was chosen at random, right? Just the wrong place at the wrong time. Dent wanted to bring the police to Gordon's door and that's how he did it. But why a hit and run?'

'He'd seen it before,' I said. 'He ended up in prison after running someone over, so he tried to do the same to Gordon.'

'He's relying on someone getting the number plate, no-one getting a description of himself driving the car, and Gordon having no alibi. That's a lot to hope for. There's easier ways to frame someone. Stash some drugs in his car or something.' Jessica smiled wickedly. 'Maybe a pile of guns.'

'He knew Gordon didn't have an alibi though. Gordon was wasted that night, and I've got to think Dent knew that before he took the car. He was probably watching him and waiting for his chance.'

Jessica sat on the edge of my desk again. 'What about the rest of it?'

I sighed, realising what Jessica was getting at. 'I think you're right. I don't think Dent wanted Gordon to go to jail. I think he's got an agenda and he's messing with him until he can fulfil that agenda.'

'Exactly. He's planned this from the start. Probably spent every day in prison working on it. He saw Reardon and Teague and pegged them as the kind of lowlife scum he could rely on to do a small job without trying to cut themselves a bigger slice of whatever he had planned.'

'The mugging was well planned,' I agreed. 'He chose Whiteinch so Gordon couldn't involve the cops without linking himself to an underground fight club and he told Teague exactly when Gordon would be there.'

'Nothing's random with this guy. That's why I think the hit and run must be significant. And if it's not the victim, and it's not the location, it must be the very fact it was a hit and run.'

I turned back to the computer and checked the information on the killing Frankie Dent had been imprisoned for. 'Victim was a guy named Steve Kelsey. Frankie hit him on May twelfth last year in Scotstoun. Arresting officer was a DS Malcolm Rowe.' I involuntarily pictured Claiborne's sergeant, complete with stained shirt and pieces of food in his beard. 'This sounds like the kind of case even he could cope with.'

There was no further information in Brownstone's file and I began searching the internet for details of the incident. The first newspaper article I found fleshed it out a little. Kelsey had been crossing the road in the middle of the afternoon, just a few streets away from his house in Scotstoun, when a car driven by Frankie Dent collided with him, knocked him underneath the car and dragged him several yards along the street. Kelsey had died of his injuries on the way to hospital. And that was as much as the papers seemed to feel Steve Kelsey's life was worth.

I continued searching, looking for a smaller, local paper that might have delved deeper into the victim's background. I was glad I did, for there, halfway through an article in a local paper that covered Scotstoun, Whiteinch and Yoker, was the phrase, *former amateur boxing champion Steve Kelsey*. I read those words aloud.

'There's another one of those coincidences we don't like,' Jessica said.

A former boxer, who lived and died in Scotstoun, practically in the shadow of an illegal fight club.

'Yeah, that's one hell of a coincidence.'

Chapter Twenty-Seven

Over the next few hours we pieced together Steve Kelsey's life and found nothing to suggest we were on the wrong path.

Kelsey had joined the army straight from school and spent his entire length of service involved with the army boxing team. He'd done well and, after leaving the army, had taken up amateur boxing and earned a reputation as a tough, if not technically proficient fighter. He turned professional only to find his career come to an abrupt end before his first fight. A late-night brawl at a taxi rank left another man with brain injuries and Kelsey serving two years in prison. He'd lost his boxing licence and been unable to regain it. The years since then had seen Kelsey bounce from one job to another, from one charge to another, and from one prison sentence to the next, until, at the age of thirty-eight, he'd been dragged under the wheels of Frankie Dent's car.

In short, Steve Kelsey was exactly the kind of man who'd jump at the chance to fight in the Blood Shed.

That's why I called Mack. It took several minutes for him to come to the phone. I assumed he was teaching a class the technically correct way to remove a man's spine with one hand. When he picked up I told him what we'd found.

'Steve Kelsey,' he said thoughtfully. 'Don't know the name, but I've been out of that loop for a long time.'

'Who's in the loop that would be willing to talk to us?'

'Benny will talk. What he can remember is a different matter though. I'll track him down when I've finished this class. I'll get back to you.'

I hung up and told Jessica what Mack had said.

'Not a lot we can do till he gets back to us then,' she said. She glanced at the clock and saw it was after half past five. 'Takeaway?'

I nodded agreement.

'Then you can help me prepare for my interview.'

That stopped me thinking about my stomach. 'What interview?'

'Didn't I tell you? I've got a job interview tomorrow.'

'Where?'

Jessica looked down, embarrassed. 'Scotspy.'

'Really? But...'

'Don't say a word! I know they're a bunch of ambulance chasers, but I've got bills to pay, alright?'

'No, of course... hey... I mean, good luck.'

'Thanks,' Jessica said stiffly. I took the takeaway menu from a drawer and scrutinised it intently. 'And maybe divorce cases and compensation claims won't be as... confrontational, as some of the cases we work together.'

I couldn't look up from the menu. I knew I should tell her to screw that job, to work with me instead, to work where I knew she belonged. But she'd turned me down once, and she wasn't any less likely to think it was charity on my part now than she had done then.

I felt the dull weight of regret and helplessness settle in my stomach. When I most wanted to reach out to Jessica and talk her out of her depression I had said nothing and sought refuge in a case. And when I most wanted to reach out and tell her how important it was to me that we worked together, I again said nothing.

How did we end up here?

*

Mack called back within an hour, by which time I was comfortably stuffed and the smell of Chinese food hung as thick in the office as my continuing sense of failure. Jessica was lying on the couch with her eyes shut, her chest rising and falling with the rhythm of her breathing. Rather than preparing for her interview she had opted to catch up on some of the sleep she missed last night. I could find no such peace, resigned instead to watching her and desperately hoping for some insight that would help me bridge the gulf between us.

She jerked awake as the phone rang and looked blearily over at me as I picked it up.

'I've found Benny,' Mack said.

'Will he talk to me?'

'If I'm with you. But he won't talk in front of Jessica. Benny's old school, he won't talk fighting if there's a lady present.'

'That's alright, Jessica's not a lady.' I ducked as a plastic fork flew over my head. I told Mack I'd pick him up and ended the call. Then I told Jessica what Mack had said.

'Sexist arseholes,' she muttered. She got up from the sofa and stretched her back. 'Fine. Drop me at home. I'll prepare for my interview alone.'

Say something. Anything.

But once again I said nothing.

*

Thirty minutes later I'd dropped Jessica off at her flat and swung by the gym to collect Mack. He gave me directions then sat back and we drove in near silence. The only thoughts running through my mind concerned Jessica, and for all Mack was a true friend, I couldn't discuss this with him, since Jessica's worry was essentially that she was becoming Mack.

I saw the sign for the pub up ahead and pulled into the kerb. 'Is Benny safe talking to us?' I asked.

'Yeah. I doubt Ricky gives him a second thought.'

'And if you're wrong? If Ricky punishes him for talking to us?'

'Then I'll kill him.'

We got out of the car and headed for the pub, which looked to have come from the same mould as the Maltings, where Jessica and I had met Taylor. It was an old-fashioned drinker's den where the few customers who were currently huddled over their glasses were more concerned with drowning their sorrows, or any other emotion they might be in danger of feeling, than they were with décor or ambience.

Benny was seated on a stool at the end of the long bar. We walked towards him and Mack forced a smile onto his face. 'Benny! Good to see you again.'

The old man looked up, his blue-grey eyes clouded with doubt and confusion. He stared for a second, trying to focus his eyes and his mind, then the mist cleared. 'Mack! How are you, son? Here, pull up a seat, let's have a wee dram to celebrate.'

Benny looked as though he'd done a fair bit of celebrating already.

'How about we grab a booth, Benny?' Mack said. 'Have a proper chat, eh?'

'Aye, good idea, son.'

Benny half slid, half stumbled from his bar stool. Mack caught his elbow gently and held him upright before leading him to a booth in the back where the pub was quiet. I bought a round of drinks, beers for Mack and I, whisky for Benny. I paid the barman and carried the drinks to the table where Mack was trying to engage Benny in conversation.

'Cheers, son,' Benny said to me as I placed the whisky in front of him. Then he looked to Mack. 'You not going to introduce your pal?'

Something sad flitted across Mack's eyes. When he spoke it was with a softer, gentler voice than I could recall him ever using. 'Benny, this is Harper, he's a friend of mine. Harper, this is Benny Buchan.'

'Benny Bucket,' Benny corrected.

'That's not your name.'

Benny didn't argue this time. He finished the whisky he had been drinking when we came in and reached for the fresh one.

'I heard you were a great fighter, Benny,' I said.

Benny put the whisky down and smiled. 'Aye, well, I wasn't bad, son. Wasn't the best, but I threw a few good punches, I can always say that.'

Mack cleared his throat to get Benny's attention. 'Benny, have you ever heard of a guy named Steve Kelsey? I think he used to fight a couple of years ago. After my time, but I thought you might remember him.'

'Kelsey...' Benny looked thoughtful, his eyes drifting down towards his glass. 'Kelsey....' He brightened and looked up. 'There was a Kevin... now, what was his second name?'

'No, not Kevin,' Mack said. 'Kelsey. Steve Kelsey.'

'Kelsey? Why didn't you say so?' Benny took a drink. 'Was he a fighter?'

I felt my hopes get up and leave, slamming the door behind them. I could see why Ricky Bruises might never consider Benny a threat. Anything he knew was likely lost forever in the maze his mind had become.

Mack wouldn't give up though. I suspected he saw in Benny what, but for the grace of God or simple good fortune – whatever you chose to call it – could become of anyone who'd spent their life fighting. Perhaps he looked at Benny and saw the dread spectre of a future self. Mack would never be in this position, he was too good to suffer the punishment Benny had over the years, but treating Benny with kindness appeared to be a talisman for him, guarding against the possibility of a similar fate.

'Steve Kelsey. Fought in the last couple of years?' Mack's words were infused with an increasing desperation that spoke of his need to believe Benny's mind could still function. 'He was killed a year ago. Someone ran him down.'

And there it was, like a light being flicked on.

'Oh, Killer Kelsey! I remember him.'

'What do you remember about him?'

'Oh, he's dead now. Got hit by a car.'

I willed myself to remain patient.

'Is that right?' Mack said. 'Can you remember what happened?'

Benny shrugged his big shoulders. 'Just one of those things, you know? An accident. Happens all the time.'

'Was there ever any suggestion it wasn't an accident?'

'Don't think so.' Benny took another drink, burped quietly to himself. 'I'm sure the guy that hit him went to jail, but I didn't hear anyone say it was deliberate.'

'Would anyone have a reason to hurt Kelsey?' I asked.

'No. Not outside the ring, anyway.'

'You sure, Benny?' Mack asked.

'Of course I am.' Benny straightened his back indignantly. 'I might be old but I've still got my faculties, son.'

'Of course, of course,' Mack said soothingly. 'We just thought there might be more to it than an accident.'

'Well there might be, I suppose. If you go in for all that kismet nonsense.'

'Kismet?'

'Aye, fate, destiny. What do they call it now?'

'Karma?' Mack suggested.

'Aye, that's it. Karma.'

'Because of that guy he hurt in the taxi rank years back?' I asked.

'What?' Benny looked at me as though I was high. 'No. Because of the lad he killed last year.'

Chapter Twenty-Eight

It took a while to get Benny back on track after that bombshell. It took me several seconds to gather my thoughts as well. Fortunately Mack was quicker to recover.

'Who did he kill, Benny?' he asked.

'Another drink, lads?' Benny asked, his words aimless, directed at anyone who cared to listen.

'Who was the man he killed?'

Benny lifted his empty glass and rotated it, searching for some hidden pocket of alcohol that was defying the laws of physics.

'Benny,' I said urgently, 'listen to me. We need to know who Kelsey killed.'

Mack put his hand on my arm and nodded towards the bar. I took the hint and got up, taking a deep breath and composing myself, then getting another round of drinks. When I sat back down and slid a beer and a whisky to the other side of the table Mack pulled both of them nearer himself. Not so that he was obviously withholding the whisky from Benny, but far enough that the other man followed it with his eyes.

'Remember Killer Kelsey, Benny?' Mack asked.

Benny looked up in surprise, like he hadn't realised there was a person at the end of the hand holding his drink.

'Killer Kelsey,' Mack continued. 'Good fighter. Couldn't believe it when I heard he'd been run over and killed.'

'Aye, that was a shock,' Benny said. 'Mind you, after what happened I doubt there were many who shed a tear.'

'Really? What happened?'

'Oh, it wasn't really his fault, you know? Could have

happened to any of us. I think it was the way it was dealt with that got to folk though.'

'What was that?'

'A sad day.' Benny shook his head. 'A sad day all round.'

'I heard he killed someone,' Mack said.

'Who told you that?'

Mack remained uncharacteristically patient. 'A few people.'

'Are they talking about it now then? Everyone was well warned at the time – talk about this and you're the next one off the roof.'

Mack decided this was the time to loosen the floodgates. He slid the glass of whisky to Benny. 'So what is it we're not talking about?'

Benny smiled and took the glass. He took a dainty little sip then placed the glass on the table with the air of a man who's just tasted the finest drop of his life. Then he spoke.

'The night Daniel Dent died,' he said.

I could have kissed the old soak.

'When?' Mack asked.

Benny's eyes narrowed in concentration as he tried to dredge a memory from the swamp of his brain. 'Last year. About the end of April, if I remember right.'

I figured the odds on that would be pretty long but said nothing. Benny carried on, oblivious to my silent scepticism. 'It was just a normal night, you know. These things always are, there's never any warning, anything off-balance. They just happen.'

'That they do,' Mack said encouragingly.

Benny nodded sagely. 'Now, you've got to understand here, I picked Daniel for the fight, and I know what I'm talking about. But he was off the pace and Kelsey took him apart, right from the first bell. Destroyed him. Daniel was like a punchbag on legs.'

'Had he been doped?' Mack asked.

Benny shrugged again. It seemed to be a standard response to any question. He took advantage of the interruption to take another drink. 'Maybe,' he said, after a quick swallow. 'It happens.'

My phone vibrated twice in my pocket, signalling the arrival of a text message. It could wait. 'What about the ref? Why didn't he stop the fight?'

'Because he'd have got his legs broken.' The look Benny gave Mack said *where d'you find this clown?*

Mack explained it to me. 'The longer the fights last the more the fighters get hurt. The more blood is spilt, the better the show. The better the show, the more money comes in. Ricky isn't going to let anyone stop a fight. As long as both men can stand the fight continues.'

'And Mr Bruce was there that night, so it would never have been stopped,' Benny added. He lifted his glass, took a small sniff and looked at the liquid within as though seeing something he'd failed to recognise before. 'Dent's problem was his heart. If he'd stayed down they'd have given the fight to Kelsey, but he kept getting back up. Didn't know when to quit.'

'So Kelsey just battered him to death?' I said.

Benny raised one finger and pointed it at me, leaning forward to make his point. 'Daniel was still breathing when he left the ring. Kelsey didn't know he'd killed him till later on. If they'd phoned an ambulance right away…' Benny shrugged yet again.

'But they didn't because they didn't want to put the club at risk,' I said.

'He knew the risks…'

I cut him off. 'Tell me about Daniel Dent.' Benny seemed to be in an extended state of coherence, but who knew how long it would last.

'Good fighter. Had a shot at going pro, but you know the old story: couldn't keep his thieving mitts to himself. Got a criminal record and couldn't stop adding to it.'

'How old was he?' I asked.

Benny made a face and waved a hand as though plucking a figure from the air. 'Thirty-two? Thirty-three? Somewhere around there. Still a young guy. And a good looking big bugger as well. He wasn't shy about telling everyone how much the ladies liked the bad lad in him. Especially the ones you would expect to know better.'

'Do you know the name Frankie Dent?' I asked.

Benny looked blankly at me, shook his head and finished his whisky. 'Doesn't ring a bell.'

'Did Daniel have a brother?'

'No idea.'

I asked a few more questions but lucidity was deserting Benny Buchan, turning his memories to fine sand held in an open hand. Before he drifted away from us completely I asked what happened to Daniel's body.

'I don't know. They must have just dumped it.'

'Did anyone report his death?'

'No. They took him through the back, so most people didn't know he was dead till later, if at all. And everyone knew it had to be kept quiet or Daniel Dent wouldn't be the only one getting buried.'

'So the police were never involved?'

Benny laughed, a short bark that sounded more like an insult than a sound of amusement. 'The police knew alright. Police was there most nights. Maybe not that night, but most nights, and they knew Daniel Dent very well. Very well indeed. Oh, the police knew alright. They just couldn't do anything, not without letting on they were there. Not without biting the hand that feeds them.' Benny choked out a bitter laugh and slammed his hand down on the table. 'Police just turn their backs and whistle while men die at their feet.'

*

'How old is Frankie Dent?' Mack asked when we were back in the car.

'Forty-one.'

'Then they're brothers.'

'Or cousins.'

Mack shook his head. 'Feels like a brother thing. Kelsey killed Daniel, Frankie killed Kelsey.'

I checked my phone and saw the text message I'd received was from Jessica.

Checked out Barmulloch – dead end. Going to sleep. Call you tomorrow.

I considered texting a good luck message back then decided against it. She might be asleep by now. I figured I'd do it in the morning. Or that's how I justified it to myself at least.

I returned the phone to my pocket, started the car and pulled away from the kerb. 'So where does Gordon fit in?' I said to Mack.

'Maybe he witnessed it.'

'Then it would be Ricky Bruises wanting to kill him, not Frankie.'

'Unless Frankie thinks Gordon could testify that he had a motive to kill Kelsey.'

'If that was the case the time to kill him was before he went to trial for Kelsey's death. Gordon obviously didn't testify or Frankie would still be inside.'

Mack was silent for a few minutes then said, 'Ah, fuck it. This is giving me a headache. Drop me back at the gym, let me work it off.'

We drove in silence the rest of the way, lost in our separate thoughts. I dropped him at the door of the gym and headed for home. It was past nine o'clock when I locked the door to my flat behind me and slumped onto the sofa. No sooner had my backside hit the cushion than the phone rang, its unexpectedness startling me.

I grabbed the phone from the cradle. 'Hello?'

'I hear Mr Laskey's looking at some serious jail time. His pal too. Something to do with a load of guns.'

It was McKenzie.

'Is that so?' I said. 'Pity, I hadn't got around to seeing him yet.'

I got to my feet and crossed to the window. Someone had been watching, waiting for me to arrive.

'Someone did,' McKenzie said. 'And they fucked him over like it was their sole mission in life.'

'I doubt I'll shed any tears.' I scanned the street. There was no one there. Not that I could see, at any rate.

'Who else knows I gave you Laskey's name?'

'Just two friends of mine. They're solid, you don't need to worry about them.'

'You guaranteeing them?' he asked.

'Yes.'

'Then it's your funeral if anyone hears I was involved in this. No-one is going to think I've played a part in someone getting lifted.'

'You know I can be trusted.'

There was quiet on the line for a few moments. McKenzie did indeed know I could be trusted. I had found his daughter's killer and I had helped him exact his revenge, and, in doing so, bound us by a secret that would destroy both of us should it be revealed.

Eventually McKenzie spoke again, and his voice cut through me when he did. 'You seem to think the more you know about me the safer you are. I'd advise caution on that score.'

'Mr McKenzie, the less I know about you the happier I am. No offence.'

'None taken. Just make sure I don't ever have a reason to take offence. We're even, and that's the end of it.'

'Actually...' I began.

'What?' McKenzie growled.

I felt the tension as a palpable thing through the phone line. And yet, I couldn't let the chance pass by. The whole journey home the idea had been gnawing at my brain and I had tried to disregard it. And I wasn't sure why. When it comes to finding someone I'll use whatever means I can, and whatever source I deem necessary. It's never mattered to me whether that source is a computer record or a heroin junkie. And yet, despite being unable to find Frankie Dent through other means, I continued to overlook a possible resource.

Was my reluctance to use Innes McKenzie indicative of the fear he instilled? Did I think he would react more badly now that he presumably thought he'd repaid the favour he owed? Or was my fear not of McKenzie himself, but of what he represented, and what associating with him said about me?

There was no guarantee that McKenzie would be able to locate him of course, but Frankie Dent was a career criminal, living below the radar since his release from prison, and McKenzie had connections in even the darkest corners of the underworld.

I decided he was unlikely to kill me for asking a favour. I hoped.

'I want you to ask around, see if you can get a location for someone.'

'What the fuck do you think this is?' McKenzie shouted. 'You think I'm running a fucking charity here? Some sort of Lost & Found for pricks?'

'A quick favour, that's all.'

'I've done that for you already, remember? That's us even.'

'Is it?' I said. 'I would have found Laskey myself, given time. You just made it quicker. Do you think saving me a day or two is on the same level as me finding your daughter's killer?'

Neither of us said anything for several seconds, during which all I could hear was McKenzie's laboured breathing. When he finally spoke I could tell he was still angry, but at least he was listening. 'Don't fucking push it.'

It was a warning, but with McKenzie warnings came with the territory, and at least were a step below a threat. I wondered if what I'd said had got through to him. I remained silent, hoping he would make the next move.

'Why can't you find him?' he asked eventually.

'He's been keeping a low profile since he got out of prison, making it tough to trace him. I figured you might know someone who knows someone who knows this guy, Dent.'

'Dent?'

'Yeah. Frankie Dent.'

A pause. Then, 'Tell me about him.'

I felt a little of the tension leave me as I told him everything I could about Frankie Dent without revealing anything about the case. I might be willing to use the devil where necessary, but that didn't mean I trusted him.

When I finished McKenzie was quiet for a while. A hand was placed over the receiver and I heard the faint sound of muffled speech in the background. That could mean only that he was consulting Mason, who was unlikely to agree to anything I'd asked. I prepared myself for a refusal.

But McKenzie came back on the line and, to my surprise, agreed to put the word out and let me know if anything turned up. 'Not that I'll be going out of my way, understood?'

'Understood.'

'You're a pain in the fucking arse, Harper. I wish to fuck you'd taken the money.'

When he hung up I sat down and looked at the phone and, despite my misgivings, felt a sense of optimism. When Mason had arrived at my home several months ago with a holdall containing a substantial sum of money I had been tempted. Sorely tempted. But in the end my soul could not let me accept that money. He had appeared a fortnight after I found the person who killed McKenzie's daughter, and the thought of what had almost certainly happened within those two weeks was more than I wanted to be reminded of. The money was tainted, and not just with McKenzie's deeds, but with my own.

In the months since that day, in my weaker moments, when the bills mounted up, I had occasionally regretted my decision. It hadn't been a lottery win – he wasn't that grateful, or generous – but still I fantasised about life being just a little bit easier. Then I closed my eyes and saw the reasons I had turned it down.

Now, finally, I was seeing the unexpected benefits of my decision. Though I was certain I would eventually regret the favours I had asked of McKenzie.

I sat back on the sofa and flicked on the television. Nothing grabbed my attention within the first few channels and I'd started to drift when the intercom sounded. I sat upright, suddenly alert. I wasn't expecting anyone; Jessica was at home in bed, getting plenty of rest for her interview with those Scotspy divorce-chasers, and Mack was at his gym killing a punch bag. I looked at my watch and realised half an hour had sneaked past while I briefly shut my eyes. I got up and went to the window again. Darkness was closing in but it was still light outside. I was looking for a clue to who was at my door and I found it in the blue Passat parked beside my car. I went to the intercom just as it buzzed for a second time, lifted the handset and said, 'Yes?'

'Open up. This is the police.'

Chapter Twenty-Nine

The voice was stern and commanding, leaving me silent for several seconds as all sorts of paranoid thoughts rushed through my mind. When I said nothing the voice came again. 'Open the door. This is the police.'

'What, all of them?' I asked.

There was a pause before Claiborne replied using her normal voice. 'Yes. I hope you've got plenty of biscuits.'

I pressed the button to unlock the door. Despite knowing that her arrival here was unrelated to my conversation with McKenzie, I couldn't shake the uneasy feeling that brought a sheen of sweat to my forehead. I wiped my face with a towel on the way to my door, opening it just in time to see Claiborne appear at the top of the stairs, immaculate in figure-hugging jeans and an olive green shirt.

'Working undercover?' I asked.

'Not yet,' Claiborne replied as she walked into my living room and took the same seat as before.

'Can I get you a drink?'

'Another one of those beers would go down pretty well'

I got two beers, passed one to Claiborne and sat down warily opposite. 'So, Detective, what can I do for you?'

'Oh, please, we're well past that, aren't we? It's Denise.'

I didn't so much hear a warning bell at that point as an air-raid siren.

'Any luck finding the elusive Gordon Dunbar?' she asked.

'You'd be the first to know, Denise.'

Claiborne smiled, took a slow sip of beer. 'You know,

I've met Mr Dunbar's daughter a few times now, in the course of our investigation. Pretty little thing, isn't she?'

I kept my voice neutral. 'Nicole's an attractive woman.'

'That's an understatement. If I was a bloke I'd be all over her. Yet you've moved on. Why is that?'

'What exactly are you getting at, Detective Inspector?'

Claiborne laughed. 'Oh, it's back to full titles already, is it? You're very defensive, Private Investigator.'

'Cops do that to me.'

'Even delicate lady cops?'

'I don't imagine you got this far by being delicate,' I said. 'I gather you've pissed off Innes McKenzie quite a bit too. I don't imagine you managed that by being delicate.'

Claiborne's smile dropped for a second. 'McKenzie is scum, Harper. Don't forget that. And don't believe all the stories you hear.' The smile blinked back into place. 'One or two of them aren't true.'

I allowed that a small laugh then we sat quietly for a minute. It was a surprisingly comfortable silence. Her response to McKenzie's name had been convincing and she hadn't tried to keep the subject on him, convincing me that her presence here so soon after my phone call was pure chance.

Eventually Claiborne spoke. 'Look, Harper. In all honesty we're getting nowhere with this case. We can't find the gunman – we found the getaway car, burnt out and useless from an evidentiary point of view – and we can't find a motive for anyone to want Reardon dead. Apart from the blackmail you told us about. That means finding Gordon Dunbar is extremely important to us. If any of the stories you heard about me are true, it's the one that says I'll do what it takes to get results.' She looked me steadily in the eye. 'I need your help to bring Gordon Dunbar in.'

I was silent for a few moments, returning her gaze, searching for the lie, the catch. The trap.

'What makes you think I can help?'

'Nicole Dunbar,' Claiborne said. 'She knows more than she's telling. I'm not saying she's involved in anything, but she knows something that might help us. She won't talk to me, to any of us, but she'll talk to you.'

'I don't know that she would.'

'Oh, come on. She obviously still has feelings for you. And I think you feel something for her.'

I wasn't going to admit to Claiborne that she was right, and neither was I going to confess that I had no idea what that something might be. Instead I asked if Gordon was a suspect.

'Yes.'

I shook my head. 'He didn't do it.'

'I know that. I saw the video your friend found. I saw the man who pulled the trigger.' She paused and got to her feet, took a walk to the window and looked out on the fiery tones of the setting sun. 'Did you know Gordon Dunbar withdrew five thousand pounds from his bank account on the eighteenth of June?'

'That was the blackmailer's first demand.'

Claiborne turned to face me. 'Or payment to a hitman.'

'You've got to be joking.'

'It's a possibility, Harper. You can't deny that. And I don't have the luxury of ignoring possibilities. I have to consider them. If you don't like it help me prove it's wrong.' She paused to finish her beer. 'How can you be so sure Gordon Dunbar didn't order that hit?'

Because I know who did.

I looked at Claiborne standing before me and fought the urge to tell her about Frankie Dent. To tell her about Daniel Dent and Steve Kelsey and let her and her colleagues figure out what Frankie was up to. Name them all and let the cops sort it out.

Except Claiborne was right. I *did* have some kind of feelings for Nicole, and until I knew exactly what her dad's involvement was in all of this, I couldn't step away from it. For whatever reason, I felt I owed her that much.

I also knew that they had Reardon's killer in custody on another charge, and hoped they would realise it soon. If they didn't I'd make an anonymous call and help them piece it together. Surely then Gordon would be off the hook.

Claiborne's expression changed as I thought it over. Her eyes narrowed, her jaw hardened. 'You know something, don't you?'

'I don't know anything.'

'Bullshit. What is it?'

I got up and took my empty bottle to the kitchen, dropped it in the bin. Claiborne followed me into the kitchen. 'Don't you dare lie to me, Harper. You know something and you'll tell me if I have to drag you into an interview room and sweat it out of you.'

'If you thought you could you'd have done that already.' I took the bottle from her hand. 'I think it's time you left, Detective Inspector.'

*

Claiborne left, and in rather a worse mood than the last time we'd parted company. I watched from the window as she stomped across the street to her car, got in, slammed the door, and roared angrily away. I turned from the window and fell back into the sofa, lifting my feet up onto the coffee table and stretching out. I lifted the remote control for the stereo and pressed play, shutting my eyes as the music began. Within seconds I could feel my eyes begin to close. I didn't fight it.

Some time later my eyes snapped open, my brain on high alert. Something had woken me, but I couldn't place it. Was it the sound of something breaking?

Inside or outside?

I rolled off the sofa and walked softly to the window, pressed myself against the wall and peeked out.

I saw immediately what the noise had been. The rear left window of my car was broken and beside the car lay a football. Twenty yards away, beneath a streetlight, two boys, maybe twelve or thirteen, looked around guiltily to see if anyone had seen them.

I almost laughed as the tension drained from my body. A broken window was a hassle I could do without, but preferable to the first thoughts that had gone through my head when the sound of breaking glass had woken me.

Still, I didn't want to fork out for a new window just because two kids couldn't find their shooting boots. I went to the door and unlocked it, stepped into the close and felt something cold and hard against my neck.

'How about we just go right back inside, Mr Harper?'

Chapter Thirty

I stepped backwards into the flat and Frankie Dent walked in after me, his gun never leaving my neck. He closed the door behind him with his foot and walked me backwards into the living room.

'Sit on the sofa and put your feet on the table,' he said.

I hesitated, until a fast punch to the gut doubled me over. When the gun cracked against the top of my head I lurched sideways and the room tilted. Frankie gave me a push, sending me stumbling back against the wall. When I lifted my head again the gun was pointing at my face.

As I stood there waiting for Frankie to pull the trigger he spoke again, his voice still perfectly reasonable. 'I said sit down.'

I did as I was told, staggering toward the sofa and collapsing into it, grateful for its support.

Now that I was in a position where I couldn't possibly make a quick move – if I'd even been able to form the thought – Frankie relaxed a little. He sat in the armchair opposite, the gun resting on his knee, but still pointing at me. When my head stopped spinning I was surprised to see he hadn't changed his appearance at all. There was little he could do about the cross-shaped scar beneath his eye, but he still had the almost-white blonde hair in the old-fashioned Teddy boy quiff and the long sideburns, just as he did in the photo from his prison records. I wondered what that said about him; did he think he wouldn't be identified or caught, or did he simply not care if he was?

The arms protruding from the short sleeves of his loud checked shirt were long and thin, as was the neck sticking out of the collar, but there was something about Frankie Dent that told me he'd be stronger than he looked. He was calm at the moment, but I'd already had a glimpse of the rage at his core.

'You know who I am, right?' he said.

'Frankie Dent.'

'And you're Keir Harper, so now we're all best pals, aren't we?'

'Most of my friends don't smack me around or point guns at me.'

'I bet you a whole bunch of other people do though, don't they? I can tell, 'cause it ain't bothered you at all.'

I lifted a hand and gingerly touched the top of my head where the gun had connected. Electricity shot through my scalp and brought my stomach up to meet my throat. When the feeling dissipated I looked at Frankie. 'I wouldn't say not at all.'

'You know what?' Frankie smiled, and it seemed genuine. 'I bet even some of your pals have pointed guns at you.'

'First time anyone's used kids to help them get to me though. There are laws against child labour you know.'

'There's laws against lots of things I've done, Mr Harper.'

'Well, you've notched up a few just since I opened my door, so that sounds about right.'

'And I'm prepared to add to my tally, don't doubt it. So I'll keep this short and sweet: I want you to back off. I want you to stop looking for me, and I want you to stop looking for Gordon Dunbar.'

'And if I don't?'

'Listen to me, Mr Harper. I don't mean you no harm, and that's a guarantee you can take to the bank. I've got a plan and I intend to carry it out. As long as you don't interfere with me doing that we'll go our separate ways and that'll be that. You can take that as a guarantee as well.'

'And if I interfere with your plan?'

'I'll kill you.'

'Is that guaranteed?'

Frankie's face was impassive. 'I'm in your home, Mr Harper. You've got a sore skull and a gun pointing at you and I ain't even broken sweat.'

A sliver of something cold ran up my neck, bringing the hairs to attention. I had rarely seen anyone as convinced of anything as Frankie was that he would kill me should the need arise. I dug deep and found some lingering bravado, hoped it would give Frankie pause for thought. 'Next time I'll be expecting you.'

'Everybody shuts their eyes sometime, Mr Harper. Everybody. I suspect you'd like to be one of the ones that opens them again. Best way to do that is to forget all about me, and all about Gordon Dunbar.'

'I can't forget, Frankie. I know what happened to Danny...'

'DANIEL!' Frankie roared. He jumped to his feet and punched me hard across the jaw with his free hand. The position I was seated in left me unable to do anything but take the shot. It was a solid dig, and the backhander he followed it with was no pale imitation. The throbbing in my head was back with a vengeance, and my ears rang like someone had replaced my brain with a bell and set it swinging. I looked up and blinked rapidly to bring my vision back into focus. Frankie was standing over me, the gun pointed at my face; his own face twisted in fury like someone had flipped a switch in his mind. 'My brother's name was DANIEL!'

I looked up at him as steadily as the hammering of my heart allowed. His breathing was laboured, his chest heaving, his jaw jutting out like the prow of a ship. I swallowed hard and watched his eyes. It was a long thirty seconds before Frankie's breathing returned to normal and he stepped back. He lifted his left hand to his jaw and clicked it to the side, rolled it a couple of times and looked away dismissively. 'You don't know nothing.'

I took a risk. 'I know Steve Kelsey killed Daniel. And I know you killed Kelsey.'

Frankie sneered. 'Well, ain't you a smart cookie? Tell me something, Mr Harper, do you know why I'm looking for Gordon Dunbar? Do you know what he did?'

'Not yet.'

'Not yet,' he chuckled, calm and reasonable once more. 'Well, I must say, I do admire confidence.' Frankie settled back in the armchair, the gun once more on his knee, but bouncing slightly now: small, rapid movements that told me how much tension remained in the hand holding the weapon. 'Do we have an ETA for this knowledge?'

'Any day now.'

Frankie stuck out his bottom lip and nodded several times, like he'd considered my words and realised I was probably right. 'I'd imagine you'll get there. But see, here's the thing,' he scratched his head absently, a man engaged in casual conversation. 'I don't think you'll figure it out quick enough.'

'No?'

Frankie gave a wide, slow shake of his head. 'Hell, it's better if you don't. I don't want to kill you. You strike me as the kind of guy I could have a beer with.'

I wondered if I'd misheard: a possibility, since my ears were still buzzing from the blows he'd landed. Or maybe Frankie was more than a little unbalanced.

'Maybe if you left the gun at home,' I said.

Frankie laughed and slapped his knee like he was in a pantomime. 'You see?' He shook his head a few times as though what I'd said was just too funny. He chuckled a little more to himself, then looked up quickly. 'I got to tell you, man, from your side of the fence, Gordon just ain't worth going in the ground.'

'You sure he's worth it from your side?' I asked

'A man who won't die for something ain't fit to live. Martin Luther King said that and he was a smarter man than I'll ever be.' Frankie was sitting forward again, his eyes focused, all trace of humour gone. 'In a cell, in a box, it don't matter any more what happens to me. Rest easy though, if you leave me in peace I'll return the favour. If not, well, you might just be dying for a man who ain't even worth a wet fart.'

I met Frankie's eyes, trying once more to tell him I wasn't scared. And yet I was. When I looked into those eyes I saw no fear, no trepidation, no sense that he had anything to lose. Nothing but a quiet and steady conviction that when the time came he would either kill or be killed. I'd been there before. It wasn't a place I was in a hurry to revisit.

'What happened to Daniel was rough, Frankie,' I tried. 'But this isn't the way to fix it.'

Frankie sat back in the armchair and laughed again, though it was forced this time. 'That's a good one, Mr Harper. That really is. Maybe some other fool would believe it, but me? Well, I look at you and I see you and me ain't so different. I look at you and I see vengeance written through you like a stick of rock. Tell me, Mr Harper, you got a brother?'

I thought of Mack, of the things he'd done for me, the times he'd risked his life. And I thought too of the times I had done the same for him, the times I had bent my own morals and ignored my conscience to stand by him.

'Yeah,' Frankie said. 'You do. Not blood maybe, but there's a bond. A strong one. One you wouldn't forget if some pack of bastards had laid him down to die.'

I didn't deny it.

Frankie got up and stepped over to the door. 'That's what I thought. Maybe now you'll leave me to do what I got to do.'

'You don't have to, Frankie.'

Frankie stopped with his hand on the door frame and looked back at me. 'Like Daniel used to say, we don't get to pick the things we got to do.'

And then he was gone. I heard the front door open and close but I didn't pursue him. For all the violence and threats Frankie had issued, he hadn't meant to inflict any serious harm on me tonight – if he had I might well be dead by now. Instead, it felt almost as though our conversation had taken place under a white flag – a brief respite from the thunder of battle – and I was in no hurry to return to the carnage.

I crossed to the window and watched as Frankie exited the building, turned and flicked a casual wave at me before walking off. I watched him go, his white-blonde hair tined amber by the streetlights, till he turned a corner and disappeared from view.

Somewhere in the dark a white flag was being lowered.

*

I slept only fitfully, my mind in turmoil, my body soaked in sweat as I thrashed against the covers and the heat of the muggy night. I was troubled by the fact I'd been held up at gunpoint in my own home, but not by fear that Frankie would return, not tonight at any rate. He had offered me a way out and I believed he meant it. I was certain that if I did actually drop the case I would never see him again. He was clearly unbalanced – violently so – but for some reason I believed him when he made his promises. That however, was bad news for Gordon Dunbar.

And that was the other side of the coin that rattled inside my skull all night: the knowledge that Frankie could well be right. I had felt the rage that Frankie now felt: that flammable, all-consuming urge to destroy, to annihilate that which had stolen from me. I had felt its caress on my neck and heard its poisonous whispers in my ear. I had turned away from it, but the darkness remained, waiting, biding its time till it would whisper to me again.

And *vengeance* was the word on its lips.

*

Nicole answered the door quickly, yanking it open as though she expected to see Gordon on the doorstep. A quick shake of the head told her I had no good news yet and she turned and walked through to the conservatory, her small shoulders dipped.

She stopped in front of the easel, her back to me, contemplating the canvas she was working on. After a few moments she reached out robotically and tipped the easel over, sending it and the canvas crashing to the floor. She turned and looked at me with tired eyes. 'It's fucked, isn't it?'

'I'm no art critic.'

'I wasn't talking about the painting.'

'I know.'

I reached out and took her in my arms. She buried her head in my chest and held on tight. We stood like that for several minutes and in all that time I hardly took a breath. Eventually I felt a spot of dampness seep through my t-shirt.

Suddenly she pushed me away and pressed the heels of her hands into her eyes, pushing the tears away. She took a breath and pulled her shoulders back, bracing herself. 'Right, come on, out with it.'

So I told Nicole about the man who wanted to kill her father and his visit to me the previous night, about the illegal fight clubs, about Ricky Bruises and Steve Kelsey and Daniel Dent. I watched for a sign that any of the names were familiar to her, but there was nothing.

When I finished it was some time before she could find her voice, and even then it was muted with shock. 'This can't be real.'

'I'm sorry, Nicole. It is.'

'First you tell me my father is a drinker, then he's a gambler. Now he's involved in some sort of illegal boxing? This is crazy!'

I waited her out. There was no point in trying to convince her of the truth in my words. She would either believe me or she wouldn't.

I stood and watched as Nicole wandered aimlessly from one side of the room to the other, muttering to herself about how crazy this whole thing was. She crouched down to pick up the easel and set it upright, bent again to pick up the canvas and placed it carefully on the frame. She stood and looked into its black and red depths as though the truth lay in there. After a time she saw something, in the painting or in herself, and her shoulders squared as though she had accepted it and now it was time to deal with it.

Nicole turned and spoke briskly. 'Do you know why this man wants to harm my father?'

'Not yet. But I'll find out.'

Nicole barked a harsh laugh. 'Oh good! Tell me, will it be before or after he shoots my father?'

'Nicole, listen to me,' I said. 'You need to think about calling the police.'

'Are you serious? Do you want to screw up his life?'

'I'm trying to prolong it. I was under the impression that would be a positive thing. Call me traditional.'

'And you think calling the police would protect him?' Nicole gave me a dubious look. 'This man doesn't sound like he's particularly worried about being caught. And even if they do catch him it doesn't sound like there's enough evidence to charge him with anything, far less convict him.'

This was the answer I had expected. It was the same one I would have given, but I had no right to make the decision for Nicole.

Nicole stepped closer to me, put a hand on my chest. 'I don't want the police, Harper. I want you. I want you to protect me. Like you used to do.'

I swallowed hard, suddenly very aware of the heat from Nicole's hand. 'I can't...'

'Remember that time on the train, the drunk guy that tried to grab me?'

I remembered alright. I had been pretty drunk myself and I'd given him more of a beating than he either needed or deserved, and I'd always been ashamed of that.

'I need someone to be there for me like that. Like you were. Like you could be again. I didn't realise...'

I grabbed her arms, creating a space between us. 'Nicole, listen to me. I can't guarantee your dad's safety. If this man finds him before I do he'll kill him. It's way past the time to be worrying about his reputation and high time we focused on saving his life.'

'Then save it!'

I turned away in exasperation. She was playing me again. 'I know what you want me to do, Nicole. What you hope I'll do. But I can't. I won't hurt someone unless I've no other option.'

Nicole grabbed my arm and spun me towards her, fixed me with her scared eyes. 'Harper, if you don't find my father soon, we'll be out of options. I don't want to live with knowing he died because we failed to take action. Do you?'

*

I left Nicole's house and drove to my office, trying to cast off the shroud of manipulation that hung across my shoulders. I thought about Jessica and wondered what time her interview was at, before realising I was as uncomfortable thinking about that as I was thinking about Nicole.

I opened all the windows in the office to let in what little breeze there was. The sun still shone and the air was thick and humid, but at least the drive here had been bearable, since my car was now missing a window. I lay down on the sofa and stared at the ceiling, wondering what subconscious part of my brain had made me emulate Jessica's usual pose. Was I telling myself that I wanted her here to help me figure this out?

I pushed that thought from my head and tried to focus on the case. I went through the facts I knew for certain, hoping something would shake lose. All I came up with – again – was that Gordon had been involved in the fight club, run by Ricky Bruises, and that Daniel Dent had been killed there by Steve Kelsey, who had in turn been killed by Daniel's brother, Frankie. And for some reason Frankie wanted to kill Gordon, meaning he blamed him, at least partially, for Daniel's death.

There were only three people who definitely knew what had happened and why Frankie wanted to kill Gordon. One of them was missing, and the other two had already refused to tell me, so where did that leave me?

I was pondering this, and the more pressing question of where to get lunch when my phone rang. I answered and Mack's voice came over the line, thrumming with something dangerous.

'He went after Benny.'

Chapter Thirty-One

Someone must have tipped Ricky off, as Benny was admitted to hospital only a few hours after we'd spoken to him the previous night. Mack heard about it through an acquaintance who'd helped him locate Benny in the first place. I suspected that acquaintance had called Mack to make sure he wasn't in the frame for tipping Ricky off. No-one wanted to face Mack when he was angry.

I picked Mack up and drove to the Southern General. I made him wait at a distance until I had sweet-talked the nurses into letting us in to see Benny, but even still I could see them casting suspicious glances in his direction as he barrelled along the corridor to Benny's room like a heat-seeking tornado.

Benny was asleep when we entered, giving us a chance to take in the bandages swathed round his skull, the cuts across his face and neck, the badly broken nose and the black eyes. And that's just the injuries we could see at first glance. His arms were hidden beneath the bedclothes, and the frame that held the blankets up off his legs told us there had been serious injuries inflicted on the lower half of his body.

Benny stirred and began to come round, still groggy from the medication. He shuffled in the bed, bringing an expression of pained anguish to his face as he lifted his left arm, encased in plaster, from beneath the covers. When he looked up at us he saw the look of fury on Mack's face. His own face showed a clarity I hadn't seen before and I wondered if the night in hospital had dried him out, or if it was simply that fear and pain had focused his thoughts.

'Don't,' Benny croaked.

Mack stood with fists clenched, a face of granite, like some horror movie gargoyle waiting to come to life and tear someone's head off.

I pulled up a plastic chair and sat in Benny's line of sight. 'How bad is it?' I asked.

'Bad enough.'

'Permanent?' Mack asked.

There was a long pause, heavy with consequence. Benny finally broke it. 'Maybe. They don't know yet.'

Mack's fist clenched again, the knuckles bone white.

'What happened?' I asked.

'Doesn't matter, does it, son? It's happened now. No turning it back.'

'I'm not letting this go, 'Mack growled.

Benny turned and looked at him with a deep weariness. 'Is that going to help me walk?'

'It'll make sure some other fuckers don't.'

'When did they get you?' I asked.

'Maybe half an hour after I got home.' Benny blinked a few times and tried to pull himself upright. He gave up before he got far and lay back breathing heavily. 'Got a chap at the door. Soon as I opened it five of them piled in.'

'Five?' Mack was incensed by their cowardice.

'Was Ricky Bruises there?' I asked.

Benny laughed bitterly. 'He wouldn't have missed that, son. No way. He was the one who did my knees.'

'I want their names,' Mack said. 'All of them.'

'No.' Benny shook his head weakly.

'He did this to you because you spoke to us.'

'Don't blame yourself.'

'I don't,' Mack said. 'I blame that bastard Ricky. And I'm going to tell him that as I pull his fucking kneecaps off.'

'And what will you do when they come back for me? Once was enough. I'm not taking this again.'

'He won't come for you again.'

'Why not? You going to kill him? 'Cause if you don't...'

I cut in before Mack could answer. 'Have you spoken to the police, Benny?'

'Nothing they can do. I've no idea who done this, didn't get a look at them, don't know nothing.'

'They buy that?'

'They don't give a toss. And it wouldn't surprise me if they already know what happened.'

'What do you mean?'

'You think a place like the Blood Shed operates without drawing any attention? Ricky's been buying off cops for years. Some of them show up for the fights, some for the gambling, some just to collect a wad of Ricky's cash.'

'What cops?' Mack asked.

Benny gave him a steady glare. 'No chance. You think they'll go any easier on me?'

'Then I'll get their names from Ricky,' Mack said.

'He's too well-protected,' Benny said. 'You won't get near him.'

'Just tell me where to find him.'

'You won't...'

'TELL ME!' Mack roared, banging his fist down on the windowsill.

For the first time Benny looked scared of Mack, as though he'd only just realised what he was capable of. He looked to me for support, for sanity.

I stood and took hold of Mack's elbow, whispered in his ear. He looked at me through eyes clouded with rage. I nodded and he reluctantly headed for the door. When it closed behind him I looked at Benny.

'Ricky pulled the pin, Benny. You can't stop Mack exploding now.' Benny looked at the closed door as though he expected it to be thrown open again at any moment. 'I can find Ricky, but it'll take time and Mack won't wait. You either tell me where to find Ricky or he'll go to the Blood Shed and tear it apart.'

'There's too many of them there.'

'You think that'll stop him? Tell me. Give him a fighting chance.'

Benny closed his eyes, took a heaving breath. When he opened his eyes again they were wet. 'First thing I thought when they fucked me up was that Mack would go after them. And I was glad. I wanted him to kill them. But not anymore. That lad's got enough pain in him already. I don't want him to kill anyone... Can you stop him?'

I thought about my answer, about whether to lie or tell Benny the honest truth. Eventually I said, 'I can try.'

Benny didn't answer for some time. He seemed to be wrestling with his conscience, torn between his desire for revenge and the guilt he knew he would feel if Mack were to kill Ricky Bruises. Finally he reached a decision, his eyes closing in resignation.

'He's got a place up the back of Milngavie. Flash place, overlooks the golf course. Place that mugs like me have paid for.'

'You got the address?'

Benny described how to find Ricky's home, seemingly surprising even himself by being able to do so. Perhaps his memory had been jump-started by an unconscious desire for revenge.

I headed for the door, but stopped as he called to me. 'He won't be alone. He never is. Like I said, he's smart.'

'They're never as smart as they think they are.'

I stepped into the corridor and closed the door behind me. Mack was pacing a ragged circle under the wary eye of two nurses. He stopped when he heard the door click shut. 'Did he tell you?' he asked.

'Yeah.'

'Just tell me where. You don't need to get involved.'

I found myself echoing the words of Frankie Dent. 'We don't get to pick the things we got to do, Mack'

*

It didn't take long to reach Milngavie – one of Glasgow's more affluent suburbs – and find the split level detached villa that Ricky had bought with the blood of his fighters. The house sat alone at the top of a slope, like a castle occupying the highest land, its white walls and Tudor windows bouncing the sunlight back at us. Mack and I sat in my car at the bottom of the slope, looking up at the L-shaped house for signs of life. Other than the gleaming black Porsche Cayenne parked outside the twin integral garage there was no suggestion anyone was at home.

'What do you want to do?' I asked. I could only hope I'd get a chance to ask Ricky a few questions before Mack tore his throat out.

'Go in there and beat the shit out of him.'

I nodded. 'Yeah, I'd guessed that much. Do you want to wait and see if he's home? Wait till he's alone? Or you want to just march up there and chap on the front door?'

'You can sit here and wait if you want. But I'm going up there to pull Ricky's lungs out through his fucking ears.'

Mack got out of the car and began slipping on a pair of gloves as he walked quickly up the hill. I got out and followed, fumbling with my own gloves as I caught up with him. 'Benny said he was never alone, Mack.'

'Then there's no point waiting for him to be on his own, is there?'

It's hard to argue with logic like that.

We stepped off the road onto the long monoblock driveway that led to the house, ending at the two garages that faced us from the base of the L. To the left of the garage a dozen steps led up to a front door and the long side of the L. My eyes flitted from one window to the next but each was rendered opaque by the sunlight glinting off the glass.

Mack passed close by the Cayenne and carried on round the right-hand side of the building. I waited with my back to the wall between the garage doors while Mack checked around the building. He returned after a minute. 'There's a side door to the garages. It's unlocked.'

I followed him round the corner to the unlocked door. He paused, gloved hand on the handle. 'Sure?'

Sure about doing this? Or sure I can keep you under control?

'Sure,' I replied.

Mack pushed down the handle and swept inside, moving left. I followed him in, moving right, making separate targets for anyone lying in wait. The room was dim, the only light coming from a small window on the opposite wall and fighting its way through a thick film of dust. I stopped and waited for my eyes to adjust to the gloom, listening for the sounds of movement or breathing. By the time I was able to see basic shapes around me I had decided we were alone.

Until I took a step forward and kicked someone.

Chapter Thirty-Two

Mack appeared at my side as I studied the dead man I had almost fallen over. He lay on his back, head near the exterior door, legs splayed in the direction of a small staircase leading up to an internal door. His left arm was trapped beneath his body, the right thrown to the side. His head was caved in at the temple, the indentation of a blunt object clearly visible beneath the blood. It didn't take the cast of CSI to identify the blood-stained hammer lying beside him as the murder weapon, or the open tool box against the wall as its source.

'He's not been dead long,' Mack said. 'Whoever killed him could still be here.'

I looked quickly around the twin garage though there were precious few places to hide. The racks of shelves along the rear wall, and the collection of gardening equipment beside the door we had entered through left the silver BMW parked in the middle of the room as the only possibility. Mack dropped into a press-up and looked underneath the car, then got up and looked in the windows and shook his head.

'So, did Ricky do this?' he said, dusting his palms. 'Or did someone else come looking for him too?'

'I don't see Ricky leaving dead bodies lying around his house. Someone else was here.'

'Or still is,' Mack said. A calmness had come over him, holding his fury in check until he'd established what new, unexpected danger we now faced. He climbed the short flight of stairs and took hold of the door handle. He eased it open and we stepped quietly inside. We stood at one end of a hallway that led past the glass front door of the house to a staircase to the upper level. Along the hallway were four internal doors, two on each side. All of which were closed.

Mack pointed to the nearest door, on the right hand side of the corridor beside a small table bearing a lamp. He stepped forward and quietly opened the door wide before flowing through the opening and quickly scanning the room while I watched our backs. It was a small bedroom, apparently unused for some time, with nowhere to hide but beneath the bed or in the wardrobe. Mack checked both places quickly and came back to the door.

One down.

At the next door I took the lead and eased the door open as quietly as I could before darting inside, my eyes scanning Ricky's kitchen and coming to rest on another body lying in front of the fridge. He lay face down, with several bloody holes in the back of his tracksuit top. Two knives were still embedded in his flesh, one between his shoulder blades, the other in the vicinity of his right kidney.

Mack nodded in the direction of a magnetic knife rack above the cooker, the two empty spaces as obvious as the fact the knives were a perfect match for the ones in the dead man's back. 'He likes to improvise, doesn't he?'

We moved on with greater urgency, clearing the remaining two rooms on the ground floor, a spacious lounge and a small bathroom, and by the time we stood at the bottom of the staircase, my t-shirt was pasted to me with a sweat that had nothing to do with the summer heat.

Mack put his back to the wall and started up the stairs, keeping his feet to the edges of the stairs where they were less likely to creak. He moved slowly, his eyes constantly scanning the upper level for signs of movement. It was a full minute before he reached the top and beckoned me to follow.

I climbed the stairs quickly and stopped beside him in another hallway. In keeping with the ground floor of the house there were again four doors, two on each side, and two dead bodies. The first lay six feet from us, and I recognised him as the big Asian bouncer from the Blood Shed. He lay in a pool of blood, his

The Forgotten Dead

hands still clutched against his slashed throat where they'd tried in vain to hold his life together. At the far end of the hallway, slumped beside the open fourth door was the second body. The thick stubble and the beanie hat jammed over his greasy hair told me it was the other bouncer from the door of the fight club. The screwdriver embedded up to its handle in his right ear told me he was dead.

From within that last room a voice suddenly called, 'Come on in!'

We reacted instinctively, pressing ourselves back against the wall on either side of the staircase.

'The door's open!' shouted the voice.

I looked at Mack and he shook his head, pointing in turn at the other three doors. He was right: only a fool would turn his back on rooms he had yet to clear. We checked the other rooms as quickly as we could, one of us going in while the other covered our backs. By the time we had cleared the third room, all of which turned out to be bedrooms, the voice had become impatient.

'Any time you're ready!'

By now we were pressed against the wall beside the door. I risked a glance into the room, pulling my head back quickly.

'It's Frankie Dent,' I whispered to Mack. 'And he's got a gun on Ricky.'

'Guess that makes me and him friends then.'

'For God's sake, come in,' Frankie called. 'Mr Bruce doesn't have all day.'

I prised myself off the wall and stepped through the door into Ricky's study. Mack followed me in and stood off to the left while I went right. The room was smallish, its walls bare except for a calendar and a clock. The only furniture in the room was a large wooden desk in the centre, its back to a window overlooking woodland in the distance, and a comfortable looking leather chair behind it.

I wasn't sure how comfortable Ricky was in the chair at this moment since his arms had been taped to the armrests with the same thick white gaffer tape that bound his broad chest to the back of the chair. I couldn't see his legs but assumed they were similarly restrained.

Behind Ricky stood Frankie Dent, one hand on Ricky's shoulder, the other holding a gun to the back of his neck. Ricky's eyes were wide with fear, sweat running freely from his temples and mingling with the blood that smeared his face. His split lips quivered beneath his broken nose.

'*Now* you know what it's like playing with the big boys, Ricky,' Mack said.

'F... fu...' Ricky tried, before Frankie cracked the butt of his gun down on Ricky's head. Ricky's eyes slid sideways with the blow and I felt a quick pang of sympathy: my own head still throbbed from a similar dunt.

'How about you just hold it right there, lads?' Frankie said. 'Just take it real easy or I'll shoot Mr Bruce.'

'No skin off my nose,' Mack said. 'Long as someone kills him.'

Frankie's eyebrows crept upwards. 'Is that right? Well you won't mind letting me get on with my business then, will you?'

'What business is that, Frankie?' I asked.

'Revenge, Mr Harper. None of this best-served-cold nonsense for me, no sir. Get it while it's hot, that's what I say.'

'Daniel died over a year ago,' I pointed out.

Frankie had crouched down and was looking for something on the floor, the gun still pressed against Ricky's head. He stopped and looked up at me. 'Being in prison can seriously interfere with a man's plans, Mr Harper. Unfortunately this reptile got an extra year he wasn't entitled to. Still, we're here now, so that'll soon be rectified.'

Frankie stood up again, a polythene bag in his hand.

'What are you doing, Frankie?' I asked.

'What he did to Daniel.'

And with that he jammed the bag down over Ricky's head and twisted a roll of gaffer tape round his neck, sealing the bag tight and holding it in place.

Ricky bucked and strained against his bonds but they held firm. His eyes widened still further, his mouth gaped, sucking wildly. Instinct made me start forward, but Frankie was quick. He already had the gun aimed, though not at me. Instead he held it at arm's length, pointing straight at Mack's face.

'You're either a brave man or you're a fool, Mr Harper. Sometimes there ain't much difference, I suppose. But you come one step nearer and I *will* shoot your friend in the face.' Frankie turned to Mack then. 'Nothing personal.'

'It wasn't when you were pointing the gun at that prick,' Mack said. 'Now you've made it personal.'

'I didn't invite you to this party. In fact, I seem to remember telling Mr Harper to butt out or I'd have to kill him. I thought he'd heed the warning, but...'

And that's when Frankie pulled the trigger.

The bang was deafening in the small room, drowning out the sound of the bullet thumping into the wall behind Mack. For a second I couldn't breathe, far less move, until Mack turned to look at the bullet hole and I realised Frankie had fired just wide of his head. Frankie still held the gun on Mack, almost daring him to make a move.

'You can't talk me out of this,' Frankie said, checking his watch. 'I will have my revenge and I don't care if I'm neck deep in bodies by the time I do. The only question is whether or not you two think this parasite is worth joining the pile for.'

We all looked at Ricky, still gulping for air, oblivious to anything but his own dwindling oxygen supply. We all knew he wasn't worth dying for – and might well have deserved to die – but Frankie's retribution was too cold-blooded for me to accept.

'For Christ's sake, Frankie,' I said. 'If you want to kill him, just shoot him. Why torture him first?'

Frankie didn't answer. He leaned forward and made eye contact with Ricky through the condensation on the inside of the plastic bag. He didn't say anything, just stared at Ricky, communicating some unspoken message to his victim whose breathing accelerated in response. Within moments Ricky's head began to wobble and finally fell forward as he passed out.

Frankie lifted his free hand and looked at his watch again. I wondered if he, like Laskey, had an accomplice picking him up. I decided I would ponder that later, when no-one in my immediate vicinity was suffocating to death. I turned my attention back to Ricky Bruises and Frankie saw the look that crossed my face.

'Don't be a hypocrite, Mr Harper,' he scolded. 'You came here to put Mr Bruce in the hospital, maybe even the mortuary, for all I know. So what's the problem? Your friend seems happy enough.'

I looked at Mack who was staring intently at Ricky's now-inert form and the plastic bag that was no longer inflating and deflating. The red mist that had descended when he'd seen Benny's crippling injuries had dispersed when Frankie took his revenge for him. 'Happy might be overstating it,' Mack said.

'Maybe,' Frankie said. 'But you've accepted there's nothing you can do about the situation. You're a pragmatist, my friend, and I respect that.'

Frankie took another look at his watch. 'Okay boys, time I was getting a move on. Mr Harper, please join your friend.' He waved the gun from me to Mack. 'Quickly now. Sooner you do that, sooner you can make some misguided attempt at saving Mr Bruce.'

He was right. There was nothing I could do while he had the gun, and the longer I delayed his departure the bigger the risk there was to Ricky Bruises' life. I moved towards Mack as Frankie stepped around the desk and towards the door, keeping a wary eye on both of us.

'I don't kill anyone I don't need to, but if I do need to, I don't hesitate and I don't lose any sleep. But you step aside and let me walk out of here and that's that.'

'Till you find Gordon Dunbar,' I said.

'I swore Gordon Dunbar would die, Mr Harper, and I'm a man of my word. He's already dead, he just hasn't realised it yet.'

With a final satisfied glance at Ricky Frankie stepped into the hall and pulled the door closed behind him. I lunged at Ricky, pulling at the plastic bag, tearing it open with my fingers. I fumbled with the drawers of the desk, searching desperately for something to cut the tape with. My hands closed on the handles of a pair of scissors and I fished them out, cutting wildly at the tape until I was able to pull Ricky free of the chair and lie him flat on the floor.

As I began mouth to mouth I realised Mack had yet to move. I looked up at him. 'Christ almighty, Mack. Call an ambulance!'

'Why?' he asked. 'I was going to kill him anyway.'

'Are you serious? You're actually okay with this?'

'I was fine with coming up here and beating him to death, so yeah. What's the difference? Dead is dead.'

Mack sat on the corner of Ricky's desk, calmness personified.

I stared at him for several seconds; seconds that Ricky could ill afford to lose. When I spoke it was without accusation or recrimination, just a simple fact. 'The difference is we need to feel something. Because if we don't all we've got to fill us up is anger and revenge and those will eat their way through us like a plague. And then what will we be?'

Mack was motionless for a moment, then he reached into his pocket. He took out his phone, looked at it for a moment, and dropped it on Ricky's chest.

'You can borrow my phone,' he said as he walked out of the room.

Chapter Thirty-Three

"And you just stood there and watched?"

'We're allergic to bullets,' I replied.

Claiborne stalked away from me, put her hands on her hips and stared past the police officer at the end of the driveway. I figured she was counting to ten. A little later I upped that estimate to thirty. When she finally turned round and walked back to us her face showed no emotion.

'Tell me again why you were here.'

'I thought Ricky Bruises might know something about Gordon Dunbar.'

'And you just happened to turn up at the same time as this other guy, this Frankie Dent?'

'Pretty much.'

DS Rowe hoisted up his belt, only for it to be forced back down by his gut. 'Sure you did. Total coincidence.'

'What do you think happened, genius?' Mack said. 'We called you to turn ourselves in then changed our minds when you got here?'

Rowe turned his beady eyes on Mack. 'You got something to say, pal?'

Mack cupped his hands round his mouth and shouted in Rowe's face. 'You're a fat, incompetent slob.' Then he dropped his hands and spoke normally. 'Clear enough?'

Rowe's face coloured behind his beard and he took a step towards Mack. If he was trying to intimidate him with his bulk he was wasting his time. 'Maybe a night in the cells will sort you out,' he said.

Mack laughed. 'I doubt it.'

'Shut up, the pair of you,' Claiborne spat.

Rowe looked embarrassed, where Mack just looked amused. Claiborne glared at me like she was torn between slapping on the cuffs or just slapping me.

I spread my hands in a gesture of openness I hoped would disguise my lies. 'I found out about this guy Ricky, that he might know something about Gordon. So we came out here to ask him. When we got here the door was open, so we went in, found a couple of dead bodies, then found Frankie Dent holding a gun to Ricky Bruises head.'

'And you let him put a bag over his head and try to suffocate him.'

I gritted my teeth. 'Like I said, getting shot in the face didn't seem like a very appealing alternative.'

'How did you find out about Ricky Bruises?'

'Gordon was a gambler. And not a very good one. I spoke to a guy who said Ricky Bruises was the man to see for a loan.'

'Does this guy have a name?'

'John. He didn't give me his surname. Didn't want Ricky on his back.'

Rowe snorted in disbelief. Claiborne paid no attention to him and asked, 'Where did you speak to this *John*?'

'The casino on Sauchiehall Street.'

'What did he look like?'

I made up a description and Rowe grudgingly jotted it down while Claiborne stared at me like a human lie detector. Two hours had passed since the ambulance had arrived and tried to save Ricky's life. When I had called for an ambulance I had asked for the police too, for even I accepted that there was no way to keep them out of this. A police car had arrived minutes after the ambulance, with a couple of uniforms who quickly realised they were out of their depth and called for backup. Claiborne and Rowe appeared on the scene shortly after and were followed by the duty doctor, the pathologist and someone from the Procurator Fiscal's office.

We'd taken a seat in Ricky's lounge under the apprehensive eye of a uniformed constable while the paramedics worked on

Ricky before whisking him off to hospital. The other bodies had been pronounced dead and, after an initial examination, taken to the mortuary.

As for Ricky, we were still unsure if he would live or die. If he regained consciousness he could corroborate our story. If he didn't we were relying on the white-clad Scene of Crime Officers drifting around the house to find the evidence that would back us up.

'Sergeant,' Claiborne said to Rowe, 'find out if this Frankie Dent exists.'

Rowe lumbered off, his tail between his legs. Once he was out of earshot Claiborne leaned in close. 'You know I could take you in, don't you?'

'You did that before and you had to let me go,' I said. 'And you know this wasn't us. Rowe's going to come back over here and tell you all about Frankie Dent, and you're going to have to find him before he kills anyone else.'

'Why didn't he kill you two?'

'We're not on his list,' Mack said.

'What list is that?'

'Don't know, but Ricky was on it and look what happened to him.'

'What's the connection between Ricky Bruises, Frankie Dent, Gordon Dunbar and Sean Reardon?'

I hiked my shoulders. 'If I had to take a stab in the dark I'd say Gordon was gambling, and losing, so he borrowed from Ricky to pay his debts. Reardon found out about the gambling and tried to blackmail him, but Ricky felt the money Reardon was squeezing Gordon for was his and put a hit on Reardon.'

Claiborne looked at me while she thought that over. It was plausible, at least, and probably not that far from the truth. 'What about Frankie Dent?' she asked.

'No idea.'

Claiborne pinched the bridge of her nose. 'Why don't I believe…'

'Inspector,' Rowe called. Claiborne turned and saw him gesturing to her.

'Don't you two go anywhere,' she said, before striding towards Rowe. He spoke softly to her and after a few moments they both walked back to us, the inspector's mouth a tight, thin line. 'Okay, so Frankie Dent is at least a real person.'

'Brilliant, you can get on with looking for him then,' I said.

'It's a long way from him existing to him being responsible for this carnage.'

I gestured toward the nearest SOCO. 'I'm sure your wee elves will turn something up that puts him here. But since you don't have any reason to keep us here, we'll just head off.'

Rowe looked like he wanted to argue, but wasn't willing to risk Claiborne's wrath again today. Claiborne didn't look any happier about it. 'You know more than you're telling me, Harper,' she said. 'And that pisses me off. You don't want to piss me off.'

'Seems like I just can't help pissing people off, Inspector.'

Claiborne pursed her lips, like she was trying desperately to hold back something one of us would regret. I glanced over her shoulder as a uniform approached. She followed my eyes and turned to him. The uniform took that as an invitation to speak.

'Just heard from the Southern General, Ma'am. Mr Bruce is alive, but they think they're looking at severe brain damage. A complete vegetable, most likely.'

'Jesus,' Rowe said softly. 'Fucking brain damage? Just like that guy they dug up. Fuck me.'

Claiborne whirled round on the spot and gave Rowe a look that would have burned a hole in Superman's chest. Her voice cut through him like a band saw. 'When you've quite finished discussing operational matters, Sergeant, perhaps you could get these two out of my crime scene.'

With that Claiborne took the uniform by the elbow and led him off for a tongue-lashing. Rowe watched her go, his face colouring again. When he looked at us our faces were split with the broadest of grins.

'Someone's going to get their bum skelped,' I said.

'Shut the fuck up,' Rowe growled. He shepherded us off Ricky's property and pointed down the hill. 'Go on, piss off before I think of something to arrest you for.'

Mack turned to me and spoke in a stage whisper. 'I think we're safe for a couple of days then.'

I called after the already retreating DS Rowe. 'Who did they dig up?'

He ignored me and kept walking. I tried again but there was still no answer. The uniform standing guard on the perimeter of the crime scene looked at me blankly. I didn't bother asking him and followed Mack down the hill instead.

*

After we left Mack and I didn't speak of our disagreement at Ricky's house. I had no idea what to say and I suspected he had nothing to say on the matter. I dropped him back at his gym then took my car to a garage owned by a guy who owed me a few favours. He repaid one of them by replacing my broken window. When that was done I headed home and made a sandwich for dinner. It wasn't much but my appetite was shot anyway. As it was, I couldn't get the image of Ricky out of my head long enough to eat more than a few mouthfuls.

I binned the remains of the sandwich and took a beer from the fridge. I popped it open and took a gulp that tasted of something rotten. I had watched a man being tortured and had done nothing to stop it. I knew on an intellectual level that there was nothing I could have done. Had I tried, Frankie would have shot Mack. And had Mack tried Frankie would have shot me. But knowing there was nothing to be done, and living with it are entirely different matters.

I tried to rest for a few hours, but sleep would not come, nor would relaxation. Frankie Dent rampaged through my thoughts like a malevolent storm. I realised he scared me, for I could not determine his plan. I knew only that he held terrible fates in store for those who had done him wrong, and that thus far I had been unable to do anything to knock him off course.

When I closed my eyes I saw the polythene bag, clouded with condensation, Ricky's breaths drawing the bag inwards as he sucked desperately at what little air there was. I saw his arms and chest strain against the tape as he knew his life was about to end.

If you want to kill him, just shoot him.

And then it came to me, and I wondered how I had taken so long to understand: Frankie didn't shoot Ricky because he didn't want him to die.

What they did to Daniel...

There were quicker and easier ways to kill someone than strapping them to a chair and jamming a bag over their head. And Frankie had left enough bodies in that house to prove he was proficient in several of them. I knew then why he had checked his watch, and it was nothing to do with being picked up by a getaway driver. Instead Frankie was being very particular about how long Ricky was deprived of oxygen for. With the result that Ricky had suffered severe brain damage.

Just like the guy they dug up.

The guy DI Stewart had told me about. The one they found in the Campsies. The one who'd been buried alive about a year ago.

Daniel Dent.

Chapter Thirty-Four

I turned it over in my head a few times and knew it was right. Daniel Dent had been seriously injured in the fight at the Blood Shed before being taken out to the Campsies and buried. I wondered if Ricky and his goons knew that Daniel wasn't dead or whether it was sheer ignorance that led to him being buried alive. Perhaps they simply didn't care.

Whatever the circumstances, I was certain it was Daniel Dent's body that had been found over a week ago. And that Frankie Dent blamed Steve Kelsey and Ricky Bruises, and, seemingly, Gordon Dunbar, for his death.

It was obvious to me now what Frankie's aim had been when he butchered his way through Ricky's home. Although everyone else in the house had been killed with brutal efficiency, Frankie had deprived Ricky of oxygen for a very specific time, and then left, allowing him to be resuscitated. Had Mack and I not arrived Frankie would in all likelihood, have removed the bag and called the ambulance himself.

Inflicting brain damage on Ricky was clearly his intention, but how could Frankie be certain that his method would have the desired effect? The human brain is a complex machine and I doubted there could be such a thing as a defined period of oxygen deprivation that would guarantee irreparable brain damage yet stop short of death.

Did he need certainty? Was it enough that retribution was conducted in the appropriate way? If Ricky had died, would Frankie have been satisfied that the man responsible for his brother's death had spent his final few minutes in terror and fighting for every last molecule of air? If, by some miracle,

Ricky had survived without any adverse effects Frankie would, I was sure, have cranked up the vengeance mobile once more and happily gone back for seconds.

But why the difference in the levels of punishment? Why had Kelsey been run over and killed instantly, where Ricky had been tortured and sentenced to an existence worse than death?

I thought about the timing of the incidents. Daniel had died, according to Benny Buchan, around the end of April last year. Frankie Dent had run over and killed Steve Kelsey on the twelfth of May. Was it simply a case of Frankie killing Kelsey in a rage? Had he seen Kelsey unexpectedly and taken the opportunity when it presented itself, whereas, with Ricky and Gordon, he'd had seven months in prison to plan his vengeance?

But even if that were true, the prolonged, intricate plan he'd seemingly laid out for Gordon – from the hired mugger and blackmailer, to stealing his car for the hit and run – didn't mesh with breaking into Ricky's home, killing four men and suffocating him to the point of irreversible brain damage.

I stood up and walked to the window, looking out over the darkened river on the far side of the parked cars, the amber streetlights giving it a sickly look as it meandered past. That river had been affected greatly by the heat of the last few weeks, and I believed something similar had happened to change Frankie's plan. Only in Frankie's case, the surge of the river had increased exponentially.

But what had changed? That Frankie had revealed himself to me, even come to my home, suggested things weren't going exactly to plan, but I was under no illusions that he had ditched the plan because it had been ineffective. On the contrary, Frankie seemed to be the only person things were going even remotely well for.

It seemed the only occurrence that had been outwith his control was Gordon going into hiding. But he must have considered that a possibility of his actions, so surely he had a contingency. Frankie had seemed patient until recently – prepared to recruit others to do his dirty work while he remained largely in the shadows. And yet he had begun to unravel over the last few days.

And then I realised. The discovery of Daniel Dent's body. That was an unexpected event he had no control over. Something about that discovery had steered him onto a new path. But what?

I picked up the phone and dialled DI Stewart, oblivious to the lateness of the hour. The call went straight to his answering machine and I left a message telling him I had a name for his corpse.

I sat back on the sofa and put my feet up on the coffee table, thinking about my theory while I waited for Stewart to call back. Somewhere at the back of my mind I knew I should call Jessica and ask how her interview went. I told myself it was late now, that she might be asleep, and I shouldn't wake her, but it was a poor excuse. I was merely putting off the inevitable moment when she pulled further away from me.

*

Some time later I jerked awake with the ringing of my phone. I lifted my feet down from the table, stiff joints groaning in protest as I fumbled for the phone. I found it between the sofa cushions and jammed it to my ear.

'Harper,' I mumbled.

Even in my freshly-awoken state I was surprised it wasn't DI Stewart.

'Mr Harper? This is Doug.'

Doug? Who the hell's Doug?

'The croupier? From Dice?'

'Oh. Hi, Doug.'

'That guy you were looking for, you still interested? 'Cause he's here. Right now. At the roulette table.'

I was on my feet, car keys in hand, stiff legs forgotten. 'I'm on my way.'

'Don't forget my hundred quid,' Doug called urgently.

'You want it, make sure he doesn't leave before I get there.'

*

The clock in the car read 00:43 as I gunned the engine and roared out onto the road, the adrenaline kicking in as I closed on my quarry. Going to the casino was a stupid move on Gordon's part. He'd managed to lose himself and now he was sticking his head above the parapet for the sake of a game of roulette. But that's why I'd made the rounds of the casinos, and that's why I'd offered money to the croupiers: people get themselves caught by their own stupid habits.

I had the windows down, enjoying the coolness of the night air after the stifling heat that had been the norm recently. The roads were quiet and I was able to ease through red lights when I could see it was safe to do so. The car behind me doing the same was a big tip-off that I was being followed.

Its headlights were bright, preventing me from seeing the occupant or even the make of car. All I could determine was that it was a light-coloured saloon, probably white. And that it was following me. Now that Ricky Bruises was out of the equation I had to assume it was Frankie Dent.

As I left Paisley I went right round the roundabout at the top of Renfrew Road and took the first exit at the second opportunity. The other car didn't follow and turned off toward Glasgow instead.

I stopped in the middle of the B&Q car park and waited for it to come back round. It didn't. I couldn't wait any longer or Gordon might leave the casino. I headed back to the roundabout and took the exit for the M8 leading to Glasgow.

No sooner had I hit the motorway than a white saloon appeared in my rear-view mirror. I wasn't sure where it had waited – probably in the petrol station forecourt near the top of the slip road, hidden behind another vehicle while it waited for me to pass – but it was behind me now and any lingering doubts had been extinguished.

Losing a tail on the motorway is difficult, unless the sheer volume of traffic separates you from your follower. At quarter to one on a Monday night there was no chance. I could have come off the motorway and tried to lose the tail but time was crucial in getting to Gordon. I had no option but to let the car follow me until we reached the city centre.

Ten minutes later I crossed the Kingston Bridge and turned off for Charing Cross. I swept through the junction, hoping there wouldn't be any police around. My luck held as I turned onto Sauchiehall Street. Had this been a Friday or Saturday night the street would have been heaving with revellers and cops and I wouldn't have got far at this speed.

Glasgow city centre follows a grid pattern, with most of the streets running one-way only, as though the city was determined to confuse unfamiliar drivers. This end of Sauchiehall Street was formed by two lanes of eastbound traffic with cars parked on either side, until it hit the pedestrianised section at the junction with Blythswood Street and forked north and south. I had driven these streets so often I knew their layout as well as I knew the inside of my own home. If I could get a head start on the car behind me I could lose it in a matter of minutes. All I needed was something to give me a little distance.

Up ahead I saw a Hackney cab indicating that it was about to pull out from the left hand kerb. I stamped on the accelerator and flew round it as it pulled into the left lane. Another taxi sat idling in the right lane, hazard lights flashing as it waited for a pickup from one of the many bars on this stretch of road. I swerved around that one too as the car behind accelerated and tried to get through the gap between the two taxis. He didn't make it and had to slam on the brakes. A quick glance in my rear-view told me the Hackney had stopped, presumably to allow the driver an opportunity to tell my pursuer what he thought of him. I didn't wait around to find out. I kept my foot down and hurtled round the corner onto Blythswood Street.

By the time I'd turned another two corners I was certain I'd lost the tail, but still I took a convoluted route through the city to Dice, checking my mirrors all the time for the light saloon. When I pulled up in the car park of the casino I switched off the engine and waited for more than a minute. Once I was certain there was no longer anyone following me I got out of the car and entered the building.

I headed straight for the escalator and rode it to the first floor, all the while scanning the faces around me for any sign of Gordon. There had been few enough people on the ground floor but the first was almost deserted. I counted no more than six customers spread around the gaming floor and none of them were Gordon Dunbar.

Standing at an empty blackjack table and looking agitated was the croupier I'd made the deal with. He saw me and a look of annoyance crossed his face. When I reached him he hissed, 'He's just left! For Christ's sake, what kept you? I want my money, it's not my fault...'

'When did he leave?' I interrupted.

'A couple of minutes ago.'

Why didn't I see him outside?

'I want...'

'Shut up. Did you actually see him leave the building?'

'No, I can't from up here. But he finished his drink and went downstairs. Where's my...'

'Are there toilets downstairs?'

'Yes. On the left of the front doors.'

I turned and hurried for the escalator, ignoring the cries behind me. His greed was low on my list of priorities.

I clattered down the escalator and made for the toilets, bursting through the door, no longer concerned with calling attention to myself. There was one startled man standing at a urinal and no one else in sight. I moved along the row of cubicles, pushing each of them open in turn and found no-one else.

'Was there anyone else in here?' I asked the guy at the urinal.

'Eh, aye, a bloke was coming out as I was coming in.'

'Short guy? Fifties? Going bald?'

The man looked at me nervously, turning slightly away to shield himself. 'Aye, that sounds right.'

I spun round and barged back out of the toilets, making for

the exit. A man in a suit came towards me, shoulders back ready for trouble. He put his hand out to stop me.

'Excuse me, sir…'

I batted his hand down and shoved him aside and barrelled through the front doors. He wouldn't follow: he'd be happy enough that I'd left the premises. I glanced around the car park and saw a man forty yards away, heading for the street, his head dipped, shoulders hunched. There was no one else in sight. As he passed under a streetlight I called his name.

'Gordon!'

To his credit he didn't turn, but even at this distance I saw him stiffen, saw a slight misstep in his walk. He started walking again, faster this time. I was about to break into a run when I heard the roar of an engine being gunned and the squeal of tires.

A white car shot out of a parking space and along the front of the building at speed. I could see now it was a Renault Laguna; the same car that had been following me the first time I visited the casinos to look for Gordon. It turned towards the street and came up on Gordon from behind as he started to run. He was too slow. The car reached him and was passing on his left when the driver's door was thrown open, catching him in the back and knocking him to the ground in a heap.

The Laguna sat down on its nose as the brakes were slammed on. I was halfway there when Frankie Dent climbed out of the car and grabbed Gordon by the collar, swung him roughly against the side of the car and took a gun from his pocket.

Frankie pressed the gun into Gordon's neck and smiled at me.

'We've got to stop meeting like this, Mr Harper. People will start to talk.'

Chapter Thirty-Five

I stopped fifteen feet away and looked at Gordon's terrified face. He'd shaved off his moustache but he was still easily recognisable. Which made his decision to come here even more stupid.

'You're a fucking idiot, Gordon,' I told him.

He looked at me in confusion, obviously expecting me to be on his side. I might not have wanted him to die, but right then I felt like slapping some sense into him.

'The man's right,' Frankie agreed. 'You lost yourself. Then you got itchy, needed a wee shot of the wheel. Just as well, I was getting fed up waiting for Mr Harper to find you.' He paused a second, then punched Gordon viciously, as though it had slipped his mind to do so before now.

I took a step forward, reflexively, and Frankie screwed the barrel of the gun harder into Gordon's neck.

'Easy,' Frankie said. 'I've told you, I don't want to shoot you. I respect you, man. Way you lost me back there, that was smooth.'

'Not smooth enough.'

Keep him talking, keep him here...

'I played the odds,' Frankie smiled. 'Pardon the pun. Figured you might be heading for a casino again. Couldn't be the one on Sauchiehall Street, you wouldn't have come off the motorway so close. Didn't think it was much further away either, just in case the good doctor pissed his money away too soon.' He shrugged, almost embarrassed. 'You make your own luck, I guess.'

Gordon seemed to have recovered a little from the shock. He had begun to whimper and plead with Frankie. 'Please... please... I didn't...'

'Shut your fucking mouth!' Frankie shouted. He pulled the gun from Gordon's neck and cracked him across the side of the face with it. Before I could move the muzzle was nestled in the skin beneath Gordon's chin once more.

'I'm taking him, Mr Harper. Don't try and stop me.'

'I can't let you do that, Frankie.'

He looked at me with raised eyebrows that said, *Okay then, stop me.* When I did nothing he hauled Gordon to his feet and pushed him roughly towards the back of the car. He popped the boot and began pushing Gordon inside with one hand while the other kept the gun trained on me.

'You made a smart decision back at Ricky's place. Don't ruin it now.'

My mind flashed back to that decision, and the thoughts that had plagued me since. Again, it seemed I had no choice. But again, a man's life lay in my hands. Could I stand by and watch Frankie Dent destroy another human being?

Frankie seemed to read my thoughts. In fact, it seemed he'd predicted them, because then he played his ace.

'You let Gordon Dunbar go, you get Nicole Dunbar back.'

Even in that split second of shock I saw Gordon tense, saw his jaw gape as the words hit home. Then he reached into the boot and grabbed something long and thin and began to lift it.

But Frankie Dent was too quick. He smashed the grip of the gun into Gordon's face as he turned, then again, sending him toppling into the boot, dropping what I then saw was a shovel. I was still reeling from the mention of Nicole's name and couldn't react quickly enough. By the time my heart had begun to beat again, Frankie had the gun pointed at me again and was scooping Gordon's legs into the boot with his free hand.

'You won't touch her,' I said. 'She didn't do anything.'

'Ah well, guilt by association, you see.'

'What kind of bullshit is that?'

Frankie slammed the boot lid and walked backwards to the open driver's door. 'Okay, fine. It's your fault. You happy? I only took her so you'd back off. So you want her back, you let me do this. Or her blood's on your hands.'

I walked alongside the car as Frankie climbed in and closed the door. The window was already down and he rested the gun on the sill, aimed at my stomach.

'You need to accept, right now, that you can't save two Dunbars. You get one, or you get none. So take your pick.'

'Where is she?'

'Here's the deal. Nicole dies at six a.m. if I don't get back to her first. Okay? So all you got to do is just back off. I'll do what I got to do with Gordon and be back with her long before she's in any danger. That's a guarantee.'

'Frankie, there's cameras all over this place. They'll identify you and they'll find you.'

'And?' Frankie looked genuinely puzzled. 'What else am I going to do? Settle down and start a family? Watch some soaps, some of that reality pish, maybe take the dog for a walk? You may have noticed I'm not that kind of guy.'

'You could be,' I said. I thought back to the words Stewart had spoken to me the night this had all begun. *Sooner or later, it'll burn you up.* 'Don't let your past rule you, Frankie. Just let it go.'

Something haunted passed through Frankie's eyes then. He put the car in gear and released the handbrake, eased up on the clutch and set the car rolling. As the car pulled away Frankie looked me hard in the eyes. 'You can bury the past, Mr Harper. But some fucker always digs it up. We can but hope that some things stay buried a good while longer.'

His eyes stayed on me even as he put his foot down, only looking away as the Laguna shot out into the road. I ran for my car to give chase. Frankie Dent might have claimed to be a man of his word but I wasn't giving him that trust when two lives were at stake.

I reached my car sat and swore a blue streak when I saw the two slashed tyres. I pulled out my mobile and called Mack.

'Yeah?' he answered, as alert as if it was mid-afternoon.

'I need you to pick me up. I found Gordon but Frankie Dent got there first. He slashed my tyres and took Gordon.'

'What is it with folk slashing your tyres?'

'Christ knows, but it's pissing me off.'

I told Mack where I was and he said he'd be there in ten minutes. Then I called Jessica.

Jessica took longer to answer, and sounded significantly less alert than Mack had.

'I need you,' I said. Then I told her everything. 'I need you to find Nicole. Mack and I are going after Frankie.'

'Do you know where he's taking Gordon?'

'I've got a rough idea.'

*

Mack's huge black pickup swung into the casino car park ten minutes after he'd hung up. He slammed on the brakes and I jumped into the cab, yanking on the seatbelt as he spun the car around.

'Where to?' Mack asked.

'Great Western Road,' I said as the car bounced out into the street. I thought of the shovel in the car boot, of Frankie's desire to inflict the same fate on Daniel's killers as he suffered, and of his hope that *some things stay buried a good while longer*. 'We're going to the Campsies.'

Mack accelerated towards Charing Cross and through the junction without stopping for traffic lights. Traffic was sparse at this time of night but even still we almost sideswiped a Corsa on the way through. Mack turned the car onto Woodlands Road and up Park Road before blasting out onto Great Western Road. From here it was a straight shot to Anniesland Cross where we would either turn towards Bearsden and Milngavie, or carry straight on to Dumbarton.

We needed more information. My phone was still in my hand but I hadn't made the call yet. I had to make sure we got there first. Now it was safe to dial DI Stewart's number.

When he answered it was with the tiredness of a man several hours past the end of his shift with no end in sight.

'It's Harper,' I said, ignoring the sigh from the other end of the line. 'I need to know where that body was found in the Campsies. The one that was buried alive.'

'Is that what your message was about? You know who it was?'

'Yes. But I need to know exactly where he was buried or you're going to be digging up another body. And this one's going to be breathing soil too.'

The tiredness was gone in an instant. 'Explain.'

'Gordon Dunbar has been abducted by a man named Frankie Dent. Dent blames Gordon for the death of his brother, Daniel. Daniel Dent is your corpse, and Frankie's going to get his revenge by burying Gordon in that same hole.'

'Are you sure about this'

'Positive.'

'Then I'll get people out there.'

'There's no time. I need to know where it is.'

'I'm not having a civilian involved in this. Just sit tight and I'll deal with it.'

'There isn't fucking time! Frankie's got a fifteen minute head start on us and he knows where he's going. By the time you lot get there Gordon Dunbar will be dead. Now tell me where you found the body!'

Stewart was quiet for a moment. I wanted to yell some more, to talk him into it. But for once I was smart and kept my mouth shut.

Finally Stewart said, 'Don't get involved unless you have to. If Dunbar's life isn't in imminent danger you keep your distance, okay?'

'Fine.'

Stewart let out a sigh, like a man forced into a decision he really didn't like. 'You know Strathblane?'

'Well enough.' I covered the receiver with my hand and told Mack to take a right at Anniesland Cross.

'Come into Strathblane from the south, and take the A891 east. About a mile along that road there's a left turn. Follow that road about six hundred yards until you see a gate on the right. On the other side of that there's a dirt track that ends after a few hundred yards. There's a clearing through the trees straight ahead. That's where we found the body.'

I thanked Stewart and hung up, cutting off yet more warnings about getting too involved. As we hit Anniesland Cross and Mack spun the wheel I considered everything that had happened so far and wondered how I could get any more involved.

Then I thought about the last time Mack and I had headed into the countryside to save a life. As deeply involved as we'd been on our way there, by the time we walked away we'd been changed forever.

As the pickup barrelled along the road to a place that might change us even further I watched the darkened roads disappear under the tyres and knew there was no going back to the person I had once been.

This wasn't the time to worry about that. All I could worry about now was Frankie Dent's assertion that he didn't care what happened to him as long as he had his revenge. He wouldn't walk away, and this time neither could I.

A grave had been dug.

But who would remain standing after the grave was filled?

Chapter Thirty-Six

'Just killing them would have been a lot easier, don't you think?'

'Yeah,' I agreed, 'but that's not the revenge Frankie needs.'

I'd explained the whole thing to Mack, or my understanding of it at least, as we tore through the night. We passed Bearsden and Milngavie in a blur, hoping not to attract the attention of any police cars. Not that we would be stopping, but we didn't want them arriving in the Campsies with us.

'He's making it hard for himself with all these games he's playing. Why not just wait at Gordon's house for him one night, grab him as he's getting out of his car, and bring him up here? All that crap with the blackmail and paying that other clown to mug him, doesn't seem like his style.'

'I think something's changed,' I said.

'What?'

'I don't know, but something's changed his plan. Something to do with Daniel's body being found.'

'He already knew he was dead though. That's what started this whole thing.'

I didn't reply. Mack was right, but still I was sure that something to do with the discovery of Daniel Dent's body had changed things. The original plan seemed to have made provision for Frankie getting away clean, but now he didn't seem to care what happened to him. What had changed that?

I didn't have much time to think about it though. We'd reached Strathblane and Mack had turned the car onto the A891. We were close now, and I willed Gordon to hold on. And prayed I hadn't got the whole thing completely wrong.

As though he'd read my thoughts, Mack asked, 'How sure are you he's brought him here?'

'Less than I was ten minutes ago.'

'What about Gordon's involvement in Danny Dent's death? Figured that out yet?'

'Nope. But I'm hoping we'll find out in a few minutes.'

At that moment we spotted the turning and Mack swung the car into it. The road rose steeply from that point as we wound our way up into the hills. We rolled down our windows and were quiet from there on, listening for any sounds that might help us find our quarry. Even in the still of the hot summer night we could hear nothing over the sound of our engine. I hoped it wouldn't tip Frankie off to our approach. But if he wanted to run, he wouldn't be able to drive past us, he'd need to drag Gordon across country, and that would be slow and noisy.

As the road stretched ahead and curved around a steep, forested embankment, the gate appeared on the right, propped open as though inviting us through. The pickup bumped and jostled its way through the gate and onto the dirt track. The moon was bright tonight and Mack killed the lights, using the ambient light to see the path. It ran uphill for a hundred yards then cut sharply to the right. A few hundred yards later it cut back to the left and as our eyes adjusted to the gloom we saw the shape of a car at the far end.

Mack stopped the car in the middle of the path, blocking that escape route, and we got out, covering the rest of the distance on foot. We stopped beside Frankie's white Laguna and found it was empty. Mack took a knife from his pocket and stabbed it into all four tyres in turn. The air left them quickly as the blade was withdrawn and within seconds the car was sitting on four completely flat tyres.

'Kwik Fit must love us,' I said.

'We're keeping the economy going,' Mack said as he put the knife away.

We turned to the woods ahead of us as a scream cut through the stillness. We looked at each other and Mack pointed at himself and made a curving motion with his right arm. I nodded and ran directly for the woods as he took off to the right at a diagonal.

I hit the tree line and came to a halt against a thick tree. I waited a second and stole a glance around its trunk. There was no-one to be seen. I began to move again, picking my way through the trees, stopping now and then to check my surroundings. As the trees began to thin sounds came to me; sounds that chilled me. The sounds of metal scraping against earth.

I reached the edge of the trees and looked across a vaguely circular clearing, maybe twenty feet across at its widest point. The moon shone down brightly in the open space, showing me a hole in the ground with a pile of earth beside it and Frankie Dent bent over the hole. Frankie straightened up and the light of the moon glinted off the point of the shovel for a second before he returned to his task. He threw in two more shovelfuls and stopped, stabbing the spade into the pile of earth before stamping his foot into the hole. The night air was still and the sound of Gordon's groan carried to where I stood.

I watched Frankie pick up the shovel again and thought about the things he'd done to reach this point, and I thought of the gun he'd pointed at me several times already. I thought too, of what Gordon had supposedly been involved in, and, for the briefest of seconds, I considered turning away. Mack would be watching from somewhere deep in the woods and I knew he would follow my lead. If I decided Gordon Dunbar wasn't worth the risk we would both leave him to his fate.

I shook it off. Whatever Gordon had done he didn't deserve this. And I would never sleep again if I left him here to die.

I stepped into the clearing.

'You're just digging a hole for yourself here, Frankie,' I said.

Frankie dropped the shovel and straightened up, pulling his gun from his back pocket and levelling it in my direction. For the first time a look of surprise crossed his face.

'Man, you just do not quit, do you?'

'How you doing, Gordon?' I called.

There was a moment of quiet, then Gordon's voice called

back from the hole, quivering with fear. 'Get me out of here! Please! I can't get up, he's cut my legs... Jesus, it... oh God, it hurts!'

'Shut the fuck up,' Frankie said, stamping down into the hole. There was a cry of pain and Gordon fell silent, maybe realising that Frankie could still kill him any time he liked.

'You need to let him go, Frankie,' I said. 'And Nicole. Tell me where she is.'

'No can do. But you walk away now, you'll get her back. I'm a man of my word, remember?'

'I'll walk away if you let Gordon go with me.'

'Not a chance,' Frankie replied. 'This fucking reptile has to die.'

'Then why don't you just kill him? Why all of this?'

'Because he has to die right!'

'Why, Frankie? What did Gordon do?'

'You still don't know?' Frankie laughed and kicked at the pile of earth, sending some cascading down on top of Gordon. 'You're trying to save him and you don't even know what he's done?'

I walked a little closer, stopping when the gun came up again. 'I know Steve Kelsey killed Daniel in a fight at the Blood Shed,' I said. 'So you ran him over and killed him. And Ricky Bruises ran the place. He made money off Daniel's death, so he had to suffer too. But what did Gordon do? He was just a punter. Just some nobody pissing his money away betting on a fight.'

Frankie stared back at me, then shook his head. 'Oh, he's a somebody all right.' He kicked at the soil again, knocking more down on top of Gordon. I wondered how much of him was covered, how much more it would take to bury him completely. And I wondered where exactly Mack was. He would be close, and somewhere out of Frankie's line of sight, but even at the edge of the tree line he was ten feet from Frankie, and I was still seven feet away. And Frankie had a gun.

But he was also standing on some of the soil that had been dug out of the hole. His footing would be unsteady. If I could keep him talking long enough, distract him enough, maybe he'd slip or stumble, and one of us could reach him in time.

'Gordon is innocent, Frankie,' I said. 'He's never hurt anyone in his life.'

The gun thrust towards me and even in the dim light I saw the spark of anger in Frankie's eyes. I just hoped I hadn't pushed too far.

'Is that right?' Frankie demanded. 'Is that fucking right?'

I spread my hands out to the side, telling him that's how I saw it. Frankie took a long, deep breath, filling his chest with air as he debated whether to tell me or just shoot me. When he exhaled the breath the gun lowered and I thanked whoever had been watching over me.

'Well, you got the first bit right. Kelsey killed Daniel in a fight. I found out a few days later and, well, I lost it. Swore all kinds of vengeance. And lo and behold, couple days after that I'm out for a spin and who do I see on the pavement but Kelsey himself. Dead man walking, indeed.'

'So you didn't plan it? You just saw him and ran him over?'

'Didn't plan that one at all. Just took the opportunity when I saw it. Well worth the time it cost me.'

'Time you put to good use planning everything else. The hit and run, the blackmail, the mugging. This.'

Frankie paused to kick some more earth into the grave at his feet. 'What you have to understand, is Daniel was good. Real good. Kelsey was a journeyman at best. And I couldn't figure how some punk like Kelsey could beat Daniel so bad. Then I got the real story.'

I felt a shudder of panic run down me as I watched him kick more soil down on top of Gordon. His time was running out.

'You know what I found, Mr Harper?' Frankie asked. 'I found out Ricky Bruises liked making money so much he rigged some of the fights. Especially the ones that looked a bit one-sided. Ricky liked to tilt things the other way. See, Daniel was so good no-one but a fool would have bet on Kelsey. Except those who knew Daniel had been drugged.'

'Why did Daniel fight if he'd been drugged?'

'He didn't know till he was in the ring. Ricky told him it was a pain suppressant. Something to keep him going a bit longer.'

I edged a little closer. 'I'm surprised he trusted Ricky.'

'He didn't,' Frankie replied. 'But he trusted a doctor.'

Chapter Thirty-Seven

Frankie's revelation rocked me. I'd been convinced that Gordon had somehow been caught up in something by accident or misunderstanding. But the misunderstanding had been mine. I had assumed Gordon was innocent, and now it appeared I was wrong.

'Why would Gordon do that?' I asked feebly.

Frankie looked down at the man in the hole at his feet. A sudden burst of anger coloured his face and he jumped into the hole and stamped and kicked at Gordon several times. I'd taken two steps forward when he raised the gun once more. As he climbed slowly back out of the grave I calculated it was about four feet deep.

I expected more cries for help and screams of pain, but Frankie had either knocked Gordon out or terrified him into silence. For a few moments the night was still and soundless and I was aware only of Frankie's eyes burning me, as though I too was complicit in his brother's death. I couldn't shake the feeling of dread that had crawled into my stomach.

'Let me guess,' I said. 'He ran up gambling debts, went to Ricky for a loan, got in over his head and Ricky said he'd let him off with the debt if he worked for him, helped him rig fights.'

Frankie shook his head. 'He never cancelled the debt. Just went easy on the interest and didn't break his legs. But apart from that, yeah, that's what those fuckers did. Sent men into a ring without a prayer.'

'But why make things so complicated?' I asked. 'Why didn't you just grab Gordon from his front door some night?'

'It was foolproof,' Frankie said bitterly. 'The hit and run, the mugging, they would put Gordon right on edge, really make him nervous. Then the blackmail letter comes, tells him we know he drugged Daniel and helped dispose of the body. By that time he should be too dangerous to let live.'

'You never wanted the money, did you? You just wanted to push him over the edge. You wanted to make him a liability, so Ricky would have to kill him. And when he did that you'd tip off the cops and get Ricky done with murder. And then two of Daniel's killers are dead and one's banged up for life.'

'Not quite. Ricky would've been shivved within a couple of months. I know plenty of guys who'd have done that for a few notes.'

'You didn't expect Reardon to get killed though.'

'Didn't matter. That was just another murder to pin on Ricky when the time came, and one less person that could tie me to anything. Saved me doing it. What I didn't expect was Ricky to let Gordon out of his sight once he knew he was a liability. Fucking idiot. If he'd kept him on a tight leash this would've all been over a long time back and you wouldn't be looking down the barrel of a gun.'

Frankie was right. It was a good plan. Not foolproof, as he seemed to realise, for it had gone wrong, but it would have let him walk away. But something else had changed his attitude, and it wasn't Reardon's murder, which he had taken entirely in his stride, even planned for. It was something entirely unexpected. Something he hadn't allowed for and couldn't let go.

'What changed things?' I asked.

'Well, you cottoned on to me, which wasn't ideal.'

'It wasn't that,' I said. 'It was when you found out he'd been buried alive, wasn't it?'

Frankie took another slow, deep breath as though calming himself. When he eventually spoke it was with the measured tones of a man dangerously close to losing control.

'Thing like that changes your outlook, you know? Thing like that changes everything. Changes what you want to achieve, changes how you feel about walking away. Like suddenly getting away with it ain't the be all and end all anymore. Like making those fuckers suffer's what really counts.'

'And Ricky rigged the fight, which led to Daniel's brain damage, so you made sure he suffered the same. But why are you burying Gordon?' I asked.

'After the fight they took Daniel back to the changing room. They got their pet doctor to take a look at him, and good old Dr Dumbshit pronounced my brother – my only fucking brother – dead.'

'He was!' called a terrified voice. 'He really was...'

'Shut your fucking mouth!' yelled Frankie. 'You think the autopsy was wrong? You worthless fucking...'

'Gordon!' I shouted. 'He was alive when he was buried. How could you get that wrong?'

In the darkness behind Frankie I noticed a shadow move, using the sound of my shouting to cover its movement. I stared at Frankie, willing him to keep eye contact with me.

From the makeshift grave I heard sobbing. 'I... I don't... I'm not...'

'You were drunk, weren't you, Gordon?' I shouted. 'Drunk, and fucked up, and a man who could've lived if you'd sent him to a hospital got buried in a fucking hole in the middle of nowhere.'

'I didn't bury him!' Gordon pleaded.

'You told them he was dead!' I shouted back. 'You might as well have.'

Somewhere in the distance the sound of a siren came to me on the wind. If I could just keep Frankie talking a little longer... But Frankie had heard it too. He knew time was running out on his revenge. He nodded softly to himself, the gun at his side. 'Now you see?' he said. 'You see why this has to happen?'

'Frankie,' I said, 'I know why you think it has to happen, but I can't watch you bury a man alive. No matter what he's done.'

'Then I'm real sorry,' he said in a flat voice, 'but you'll have to join him.'

Frankie raised the gun and pointed it at me. His finger was squeezing the trigger as the shadow hit him from behind and forced the gun up in the air. I threw myself to the ground as the gun fired, the bullet soaring harmlessly into the night sky.

I raised my head and looked to where Mack and Frankie were grappling with each other, fighting for control of the gun. They stood on the loose soil beside the grave, their feet scattering earth into the hole as they struggled. Mack threw a punch into Frankie's gut, doubling him over, then hit him with an uppercut, knocking Frankie onto his back. Somehow he held onto the gun and Mack fell on top of him rather than let go. They landed in a heap on the pile of earth, sending an avalanche of soil down on top of Gordon.

I scrambled to my feet and ran forward, reaching the edge of the hole as the cascade came to a stop. The tip of a shoe was visible at one end of the grave, half a hand at the other, but the soil had packed in so tightly the only movement was a panicked flexing of fingers. I glanced across the hole and saw Mack was astride Frankie, punching his face and twisting the gun as Frankie struggled to keep hold of the weapon.

I looked for the shovel, saw it was trapped beneath Frankie's body and dropped to my knees and tore at the loose soil, throwing it to the bottom end of the trench. I only had moments to clear the earth from Gordon's face. Once he could breathe I could worry about digging him out.

The grunts and thuds of Mack and Frankie's battle came to me over the sound of my heart thumping in my chest. I called out to Gordon with words I doubted he could hear. And the sirens came ever closer.

My digging became more frenzied, scattering soil everywhere, anywhere, in a desperate attempt to find Gordon's face. I was close now. And so were the sirens. Suddenly they stopped and I knew the police would be here soon.

But I couldn't wait. My fingers were raw and bleeding, but the pile of earth in the grave sloped sharply from above Gordon's body and legs to above his face, and I knew he would be free in seconds. At the same time I heard a cry of triumph from Mack as he wrenched the gun from Frankie's grip and stood above him. I waited to hear Mack's voice as he told

Frankie not to move, but instead it was a stranger's voice that cut through the darkness.

'Armed police! Drop the gun!'

There was a sudden pause as all three of us realised we weren't alone. I stopped digging for a moment and glanced round to see two armed police officers facing us, guns drawn and pointed at Mack. Beyond them were another four officers, unarmed but alert, and spreading to form a loose circle around us. Bringing up the rear were DI Stewart and DS Taylor

Mack threw the gun away and raised his hands as Frankie began to struggle to his knees. I ignored the order and resumed clawing at the dirt.

'Don't move!' shouted the voice again. 'All of you, stop moving!

I carried on, hoping they'd hesitate to shoot me in the back. My fingers dug through the soil, scooping it to the side as I heard feet approach quickly from behind. They must have been concerned with what I might be digging up and that concern became obvious when they grabbed me roughly by the arms and pulled me away from the trench. I shouted and struggled against them, telling them a man was dying in that hole, but they were unmoved. I pulled harder and managed to break free, dropping to my knees beside the opening and threw soil aside with increased desperation. The two officers were coming back for me when I suddenly felt my fingers scrape skin and Gordon thrust his face through a last layer of soil, gulping hungrily at the air.

'Fuck me!' called one of the cops. 'There's somebody in there already.'

And that's when I understood. They'd been briefed, but in the darkness they didn't know who was who. They'd seen me digging a hole and Mack beating Frankie at gunpoint and assumed Frankie was the victim, and yet to be put in the hole. I looked up and saw one of the cops had gone to him, helping him to his feet. And in that split second, when all other eyes turned instinctively to the makeshift grave, Frankie Dent saw his chance.

He crouched quickly and scooped up the shovel, swung it in a short arc and chopped the edge of the blade into the police officer's face. The man stumbled back, clutching his face as bone broke and blood spouted forth. Frankie dropped the shovel, pushed the policeman between himself and the armed officers and sprinted into the trees.

The cops holding me had loosened their grip and I pulled myself free, getting to my feet like a sprinter out of the blocks. Mack had freed himself too and we plunged into the woods together, followed by the shouts of the cops. They were behind us, but their reactions were slow, and so were their feet. If we didn't catch Frankie no-one would.

The trees were still sparse here and the moonlight bright enough to show us Frankie's silhouette as he charged between them. He had a good start on us, but we were fit, and I doubted he knew the woods any better than we did. I also doubted he'd planned an escape route, since he'd been prepared to die for his revenge.

What he hadn't been prepared for was going to jail with Gordon Dunbar still alive.

Up ahead Frankie suddenly disappeared from sight. A few seconds later we realised why when we reached the top of a steep slope. We half ran, half slid down the hill after him, bouncing off trees and through bushes that tore at our clothes. Halfway down the slope I saw headlights from far on our left and realised the road passed below us. Frankie must have seen them too, and now he had something to aim for. If he could stop that vehicle he could carjack the driver and escape.

We barrelled on down the hill, a new urgency in our steps as we careered towards the road at the bottom and the headlights grew ever nearer.

Frankie reached the bottom of the slope, cut away from us towards the lights and disappeared into the thick stand of trees at the edge of the road. Through the gaps in the trees the headlights grew brighter as the car approached Frankie's position.

Don't stop don't stop don't stop...

The slope levelled out and we sprinted for the tree line and the glow of lights beyond. We broke through the foliage and saw

Frankie twenty yards further down the road, his back to us as he stepped out into the centre of the road, his white hair luminescent in the brightness of the headlights, his hand raised to stop the car.

For a second nothing changed. Then the squeal of brakes cut the air as the driver reacted. The car swerved hard left, its right corner missing Frankie by two feet, but the surface was loose here and I watched in horror as the car skidded, its back end whipping round towards him.

There was a sickening crunch of metal on flesh and bone as the car ploughed into Frankie's legs. His body folded forward and his face smashed down on the boot before his legs were caught beneath the car and he was dragged beneath the wheels, his head cracking against the tarmac as he fell. The back end of the car rose up as both back tyres rode over his body, leaving him sprawled on the ground, his right leg twisted at an unnatural angle, his left arm folded beneath his body.

I ran to him as the car rocked to a halt facing the opposite direction, dropped to my knees and called to him. There was blood running freely from his mouth and nose, and the angle of his body suggested serious damage. He was alive, but barely.

'Frankie!' I shouted. 'Where's Nicole?'

Frankie's eyes flickered open as Mack dialled an ambulance behind me, though we both knew it was futile. Frankie looked at me with surprise, as though he couldn't believe this was the moment of his death.

'Frankie! You need to tell me where she is. You can't let her die, Frankie.'

But Frankie said nothing. His head turned and he looked beyond me to the car that had done so much damage. I heard footsteps and turned to see DI Claiborne walking towards us, her face ashen as she looked at the injured man.

'Is he... is he alright? I didn't see him. He was on the road. I was looking in the trees. I thought... '

I shook my head, ignoring my surprise at seeing her here. I had more important things to think about. Like saving Nicole Dunbar's life. 'Frankie...'

A cough rattled wetly in his throat and his eyes closed in pain.

When they reopened they locked on mine and poured damnation on me. 'You could have let this go. You could have walked away. But now... now her death's on you.'

Frankie's gaze rolled drunkenly away from me and settled on Claiborne who stood bent over, her hands on her knees like she was going to be sick.

'Fucking cops,' Frankie muttered. 'Bet a cop can fix... fix a hit and run ticket for you. Keep you... keep... you out of jail, right, Ma'am?'

I grabbed Frankie's chin and turned his head towards me. I didn't care about spinal damage – he'd be dead in minutes anyway. 'Where the fuck is she?'

'Fuck you,' he spluttered. The words were followed by a slick of blood that oozed thickly down his chin. I pulled my hand away as he smiled at me with blood-smeared teeth. 'That bastard might still be alive... but he'll suffer when she dies. See how... how he likes losing his only family... A house ain't ever going to be a home after that. And *that*, Mr Harper... is a guarantee.'

'Tell me!'

'What you going to... going to do...? Kill me?'

His voice tailed off into a wet laugh and I looked around impotently as I realised there was absolutely nothing I could threaten him with, nothing I could do to force Nicole's location from him.

And when Frankie drew his last rattling, gurgling breath a few seconds later I felt Nicole slip through my fingers as the secret died with him.

Chapter Thirty-Eight

My despair gave way to anger and I rounded on Claiborne. 'What the fuck were you doing? Why didn't you stop?'

Her mouth dropped open in surprise, and for a second her guilt let her accept my accusatory tone. It didn't last. No sooner had her chin dipped than it bounced right back up again and she fixed me with fiery eyes. When she spoke it was in a cold tone that belied the fury I'd ignited.

'I tried to stop. You may have noticed the fucking skidmarks,' she said through gritted teeth. 'I took my eyes off the road for a second to look for him in the trees. I looked back and he was there. He never gave me a chance. Maybe if you'd caught him before he got that far he wouldn't be roadkill.'

'If *I'd* caught him? I didn't realise that was my job. Isn't that what you lot get paid to do?'

'We would if amateurs like you would stay out of the way.'

'You wouldn't even know his name if Harper hadn't found him,' Mack said.

I turned away and tried to clear the clouds of anger from my mind. I needed to think. I needed to find Nicole. My thoughts were interrupted by the arrival of DI Stewart and three uniforms as they burst out of the trees. I presumed Taylor was in charge up at the graveside.

'Aye, you're just in time,' Mack said, as the cops marched purposefully towards us.

One of them made a beeline for Mack but Stewart waved him away. Stewart walked up to Claiborne with a look of surprise on his face. He softened it with a bit of compassion as he looked at the scene and realised what had happened. 'Are you okay, Denise?' he asked.

Claiborne took a long breath, presumably clearing her own angry mind, before she replied. 'Better than the crash test dummy over there.'

Stewart smiled gently and squeezed her shoulder. 'I called you because the Dunbar case was yours, but I didn't think you'd go to such lengths to clear it.'

'Never underestimate a woman's determination, Greig.'

'How did you end up down here?' Stewart asked.

'Heard the call on the radio saying he'd done a runner when I was almost here, figured there was a chance he'd make for the road so I carried on round the hill.' She rubbed a slightly shaky hand through her hair and looked at Frankie's mangled body. 'He must have seen the car coming and thought he could time it right to carjack me.'

'Looks like he needs to work on his timing,' Stewart said.

Claiborne nodded softly and Stewart turned to Mack and I. 'There's an ambulance on its way, but Gordon will live.'

'Great,' I said. 'We'll see you later.'

'Not so fast.' Stewart put his hand out to stop us. 'We need statements from you. I want to know exactly what happened up there.'

'Then you'll have to wait,' I said. And I told them about Nicole Dunbar. By the time I finished Claiborne was shaking her head and Stewart was looking at me with something approaching exasperation.

'Seriously,' Stewart said, 'is nothing ever simple with you?'

'I'm not the one kidnapping people and trying to bury them alive,' I reminded him.

'Look, we'll get your statements and we'll find her. Leave this to us. We've got the manpower and the resources. She stands a better chance with us looking for her.'

'Don't keep making the same mistakes, Harper,' Claiborne said. 'Going it alone nearly got Gordon Dunbar killed. Are you willing to risk his daughter's life?'

'I'm not telling you not to look for her. Knock yourselves out.

All I'm saying is don't expect us to leave it to you. I'm surprised you lot can find your own arses to wipe them.'

Mack was already heading for the tree line. I turned and went after him.

'Harper,' Claiborne called. 'Get back here and give me your statement.'

I looked back over my shoulder, saw Claiborne take a step towards me. 'I'll talk to you when Nicole's safe. You got a problem with that, you're going to have to arrest me.'

For a second I thought she would, then Stewart put a restraining hand on her arm and I moved away into the trees. Mack was already halfway up the slope and I jogged up behind him, checking my watch as I ran. It was ten past three. Frankie had said she would die at six a.m. if he didn't return to her.

Nicole had less than three hours to live.

I pulled out my phone and dialled Jessica. She answered quickly, her voice breathless with worry.

'You okay?' she blurted out.

'Yeah. We're fine. Gordon's a bit beat up, but he'll live.'

'What about Frankie Dent?'

'He's dead,' I said as we crested the hill and saw the Navara.

'Oh, Christ,' Jessica sighed. 'What happened?'

'It was the cops. Claiborne. He tried to carjack her as he made a break for it. She couldn't stop in time. Went right through him.'

'Did he say anything before he died?'

'He lived long enough to tell me to go fuck myself. Seemed happy enough that Gordon might still be alive, but he'd suffer the loss of his daughter.'

We neared the cars and I saw a cop standing guard beside Frankie's Laguna. I expected him to try to stop us as we passed, but he gave a brief nod and let us pass. Stewart had obviously been in touch.

'You had any luck?' I asked Jessica.

'Still no idea where Frankie's been living. I traced the car you told me about, the Renault Laguna. It was stolen three weeks ago, from a supermarket car park.'

I climbed into the Navara as Mack gunned the engine. He

jammed the car into reverse and floored the pedal, throwing the car back down the track.

'I figured Frankie only had a limited time between causing carnage at Ricky's house and then going to your place to follow you,' Jessica said. 'So I went to Nicole's house to see if I could find out roughly when he'd taken her. Figured I could work out a radius he'd need to have stashed her within.'

'And?'

'Well, her neighbours are a bit snippy. They don't seem to like being woken up at two in the morning. But I did find out that she hasn't been there the last few days.'

'But I met her there yesterday. Sunday morning.'

'Yeah, she's been back and forward, apparently. But she's not been sleeping there. Or so the nosey bint across the street tells me.'

'So where's she been?' I asked.

'I'm on my way to Gordon's place. I figure she's been staying there to feel close to him. Maybe hoping he'll turn up. Or maybe she's realised this is getting serious, figures she'll be safe there since Gordon is off the radar and no-one's likely to look for him in his own home.'

And then it clicked. A voice sounded in my ear, wet with blood and rough with the approach of death.

A house ain't ever going to be a home after that.

Nicole wasn't the only one who figured no-one would bother looking at Gordon's home. Not until it was too late.

'That's where she is,' I told Jessica. 'Get there as quick as you can but don't go in.' I turned to Mack and gave him the address in Giffnock.

'I'll go in if I need to, Harper,' Jessica replied.

'It might be a trap. He said she's going to die at six, so he must have rigged something.'

'Then you better get your arses over there and help me figure it out.'

*

We screeched to a halt outside Gordon Dunbar's house in Giffnock a little under half an hour later, almost hitting the back of Nicole's yellow Beetle. We jumped out and looked up at the house and saw no signs of life. But her car was there. Either Nicole was still inside, or she'd left without her car. And if she'd left without her car it was because Frankie was giving her a lift.

I looked up as my name was called. Jessica was walking quickly towards us across the street, her face flush with excitement.

'You're going to be popular tonight,' Mack said. 'You left anyone asleep?'

'One or two,' she replied. 'But one of the ones I woke up remembers seeing a white saloon car parked outside earlier tonight. Could have been a Laguna, but he couldn't swear to it. Didn't see anyone getting in or out of the car, but it was parked on the street. If Frankie took Nicole away in his car you'd think he'd have parked in the driveway.'

Mack nodded his agreement. 'Definitely. Why risk a neighbour seeing something and calling the cops? Even if he walked her out at gunpoint, it's an unnecessary risk.'

'So she's in there,' I said. I looked at my watch. It was quarter to four. We still had over two hours.

'No need to rush in,' Jessica said as she checked her own watch.

'If you trust him,' Mack said.

'Why would he lie?' I asked.

'Why would he tell you the truth?'

'A fair point, and well presented,' Jessica said.

I looked at Mack for another few seconds and knew he was right. 'Ah, fuck it. Guess we're rushing in then.'

We walked quickly up the driveway and I tried the front door. It was locked. Jessica ran round the side of the building to try the back door but it too was locked. By the time she returned Mack was standing close to the front door, bent at the waist and analysing the lock. Then he straightened up and began pressing against the door at various points where it met the frame. He seemed satisfied and took a step back.

'Take it we don't need a key?' I asked him.

'Not if you don't mind a bit of a racket.'

I spread a hand in the direction of the door. 'Knock yourself out.'

Mack rocked back slightly onto his right foot, bounced it off the path and fired a kick into the door just below the handle. The sole of his foot struck the door with such force it tore the lock free from the frame and catapulted the door back against the inner wall.

I was about to step into the house when the smell of gas hit me like an invisible punch. I stepped back involuntarily as Jessica said, 'He's filling the house with gas? The fumes could kill her well before six o'clock.'

Mack took his phone from his pocket and threw it onto Gordon's front lawn. Jessica followed suit while I looked at them both in surprise.

'I thought that whole mobile-phone-igniting-a-petrol-station thing was a myth.'

'This isn't a petrol station,' Mack pointed out. 'This is a big fucking bomb. You want to take the chance?'

I lobbed my phone onto the grass.

We piled into the house and split up. Mack headed upstairs, calling over his shoulder as he went. 'Those fumes will fuck you up if you give them a chance. Wet a towel and tie it round your face. And see if you can find where to turn off the gas.'

Jessica and I headed for the kitchen, almost stopping in our tracks when we saw the cooker pulled away from the wall, the gas pipe disconnected and hanging loose. Jessica started wrenching open drawers, looking for dish towels. I didn't help. I was too busy looking at the wall behind the door.

'For Christ's sake, Harper. Give me a hand or look for the gas valve,' Jessica said.

When I didn't respond she glanced up and saw me staring at a broken plastic box that hung from the wall. It was the control mechanism for the central heating. The mechanism that determined when the pilot light would ignite. A mechanism whose controls had been broken off to prevent the time being reset. All that remained visible was the time the pilot light was set to ignite at.

'What's that?' Jessica asked.

'The detonator.'

'Fuck. The bastard was going to blow her up at six.'

'No,' I replied, my voice almost inaudible. 'He's going to blow her up at four.'

Chapter Thirty-Nine

Mack came pounding down the stairs just as I was about to call on him. He barged into the kitchen and told us, 'Upstairs is clear.' Then he took one look at the control mechanism hanging from the wall and understood the situation. 'When's it set for?'

'Four.' The microwave read 03:48. 'Under twelve minutes. Assuming the microwave was set to exactly the same time.'

We forgot all about finding towels to wet as panic set in. My head was already spinning from the concentrated fumes in the kitchen, but I figured that might be preferable to it being vaporised if the gas ignited.

Jessica moved to the windows, but Mack stopped her. 'Don't bother. We can't vent this place in time, even if we shut off the gas. We need to find her and get the fuck out of here.'

A quick glance in each room told me Nicole wasn't on the ground floor either. That left only the basement. I grabbed the handle and yanked the door open. All I could see before me were the first few steps of a concrete staircase. The rest was hidden in darkness.

'I'll run out to the car and get a torch,' Jessica said from behind me. 'Don't touch the lights.'

'Oh really, you think?'

'Shut up!' Mack hissed.

We shut up. And then I heard it. From somewhere below us were the sounds of muffled shouts and metal clanking against metal.

'Nicole!' I called. The noises increased in frequency and

volume in response to my shout. I blundered on down the stairs now that I knew she was gagged and wouldn't be able to guide me. I was completely blind. I only knew I'd reached the bottom when my foot jarred against concrete more suddenly than I'd anticipated. The air was clearer down here. The closed door had prevented most of the gas entering the basement. Not that it would do the same for the explosive force the gas would become once ignited.

I kept my hand on the wall and stood still for a moment and prayed for some ambient light to show me my surroundings. My prayers were answered when a blinding beam of light shone down the staircase. The beam swung from side to side, illuminating a dusty room the width of the entire house. The light passed over paint cans and taped-up cardboard boxes before coming to rest on Nicole's terrified figure.

She stood against the far wall, a cloth over her face and chains wrapped tightly around her body from her neck to her waist. I rushed to her and said her name, telling her I was there, trying to reassure her. I realised then that the cloth over her head was actually a wet towel. The wet towel and the closed basement door told me Frankie hadn't wanted Nicole to die from the fumes. If he'd failed in his mission to kill Gordon, he would have still had his daughter as a hostage.

The light from the torch bounced up and down as Jessica and Mack came down the stairs, casting ominous shadows up the wall behind Nicole.

'Ten minutes,' Jessica whispered in my ear as they came up beside me.

I swallowed hard and reached out to pull the towel from Nicole's head. I had braced myself for what might lie beneath but other than a strip of duct tape across her mouth and eyes bulging with fear she appeared unharmed. I ripped off the tape, expecting a cry of pain, but Nicole was oblivious to the patch of raw skin left behind.

'Get me out of here!' she screamed as soon as the tape was free. Her voice was hoarse from hours of attempted screaming, but the fear it held was clear for us all to hear.

'We'll get you out in a minute, Nicole,' I said, as reassuringly as I could.

I took the torch from Jessica and shone it behind Nicole's back. Against the wall was a six foot high metal frame that appeared to be left over from a shelving unit no longer in use. The frame looked strong, the vertical supports screwed into the stone wall at twelve inch intervals, leaving only a small gap behind the vertical supports where the fixtures were attached to the wall. The chains wrapped around Nicole fitted neatly between the wall and the frame and were fastened so tightly there was almost no give when I pulled on them. I shone the torch beam over her body and found three padlocks fastening the chains together. I bent to look at the first and cursed when I saw the key had been snapped off in the lock and a layer of superglue had been poured in around it. A quick glance told me the other two had been given the same treatment. I knew then that Frankie had no intention of letting Nicole live.

I gave Jessica the torch and pulled at the metal frame. It didn't budge. The light swung away from me as Jessica swept it round the basement. 'Where did your dad keep his tools?' she asked Nicole.

'What the hell are you talking about? Who gives a shit? This place is full of gas! Get me out of here!'

Jessica's voice when she replied was calmer than I expected. 'Nicole, keep it together. We'll get you out, but we need tools to do it. Where are they?'

Nicole began sobbing uncontrollably and straining against the chains. 'For fuck's sake, just get me out of here before the house explodes!' she screamed.

Jessica took two steps toward Nicole and slapped her hard. If we lived through this I suspected she'd look back on that moment with fondness. She grabbed Nicole's chin and forced her to look into her eyes.

'Listen to me, Nicole. I don't like you. I think you're a manipulative cow. But I'm here, and I'm going to get you out of this. But I'm not going to die because you can't keep it together and help us. So get your act together or I swear to God we'll walk out of here right now.'

There was a pause that seemed to last minutes before Nicole swallowed and sniffed and gave Jessica a cursory nod.

'Where are your dad's tools?' Jessica asked.

Nicole inclined her head towards the corner opposite. 'O... over there.'

Jessica rushed over and found a dusty, but otherwise immaculate toolbox beside a neat pile of cardboard boxes. She brought it to us and dropped it by Nicole's feet, flipped the catches open and rummaged through the contents. 'Slim pickings,' she said. 'Stanley knife, hammer, some picture hooks and a couple of screwdrivers.'

'Screwdrivers then,' I said. 'Flat head.'

'No need for insults,' Jessica said as she held one out to me. I grabbed it from her and went to work. She handed another to Mack. Then she swore. 'There's only two flat heads. How many screws are there?'

'Five on each side,' I said.

'Please hurry,' Nicole whimpered.

I glanced behind me at Jessica, my hands still turning the screwdriver. She looked back without expression. Nicole was scared, but she didn't know about the timer.

'Don't worry,' Jessica said. 'We'll make it.' I wasn't sure if she was talking to me or Nicole.

'Jess,' Mack said, his voice sharp with urgency. 'How about you go get some more people out of their beds? Maybe get them to a safe distance.'

'Shit,' she replied. 'I didn't even think about the neighbours.'

Neither had I, but Jessica had left the torch on the floor and bolted up the stairs before I could voice my surprise. I spoke to Mack instead. 'How's it coming over there?'

'Not good. The screw heads are tearing.'

'Same here. And the screws are fucking massive.'

Mack leaned over and whispered to me to avoid scaring Nicole even more. 'We don't have time to unscrew them completely. Take them out a couple of inches. That might give us enough leverage to pull the frame out of the wall.'

I nodded and carried on. Two screws were now three inches out of the wall, but still the frame felt secure. I was working on a third and too scared of stopping to check my watch. Maybe I was too scared of knowing how close we were to death.

As the clock in my head ticked on the screwdriver slipped out of the screw head for the umpteenth time, though this time it clanged against the metal frame. I held my breath involuntarily, though any spark created would have ignited the gas long before I'd had time to react, even with the relatively low concentration down here.

'Careful,' Mack breathed.

I slid the screwdriver back into place and brought the screw out the same three inches as the others then moved on to the fourth. Eternities passed while sweat beaded along my forehead and gathered in my hairline. It began to run from my temples and I felt my hands grow slippery.

A voice spoke from the top of the stairs. 'Neighbours are almost out,' Jessica announced. 'Got one lot up and told them to spread the word. They're all gathering down the street. They're safe. One of them's calling 999, asking for everyone but the coastguard.'

'Time check,' Mack called.

Jessica disappeared for a few seconds. When she returned she struggled to keep her voice level. '03:57. You're under three minutes.'

'What?' shouted Nicole. 'Three minutes? What are you talking about?'

I ignored her. We didn't have time to deal with hysterics. As the fifth screw on my side came halfway out I spoke to Mack. 'You've got time to get out if you go now.'

Mack stuck the screwdriver in the back pocket of his jeans. 'Shut up and pull.'

I grabbed hold of my side of the frame as Mack gripped the other. Nicole carried on shouting questions at us, her composure gone as terror gripped her once more.

'On two,' Mack said. 'One – two...'

We pulled with everything we had. I pulled so hard I felt pops in my back and my muscles burn. Just as I thought the thing would never budge there was a shift and the frame moved away from the wall with grudging slowness. We let go, wiped the sweat from our palms and took hold again.

'Jessica,' I shouted. 'Get out of here.'

'Piss off,' she replied. 'You want me out, come up and drag me out.'

'One...' Mack counted, 'two...'

We heaved again, pulling the frame towards us with all our strength. This time it started moving immediately, the screws tearing dust and rubble from the wall as they were torn loose. From somewhere I heard Jessica call, '03:59! Move it!'

And then the frame broke free and came toppling towards us. We caught Nicole with an arm each and stopped her hitting the floor. With an unspoken understanding we flipped the frame onto its back and took hold of it like a stretcher, with Nicole lying on her back, still bound by the chains, tears of sheer terror flowing freely down her cheeks and into her hair.

Mack held the now horizontal supports behind his back and charged for the stairs. I brought up the rear, my feet pounding up the concrete steps, until Mack reached the top and we had to manoeuvre the makeshift stretcher through the narrow doorway and into the hallway. Mack pushed the top end up in the air, turning Nicole vertical again until I was clear of the door, then he dropped the frame back to a horizontal position and sprinted for the front door.

Jessica stood beside the door, holding it as wide open as possible as we ran past. She spun into line behind me, leaving the door ajar for fear of the latch and strike plate triggering a premature blast.

We crossed the lawn at full pelt and Mack hurdled the three-foot high front wall. I cleared it a half second later and we dropped Nicole and the shelving frame to the pavement before hitting the ground beside her at the same time Jessica came over the wall and skidded to a halt.

And then the world exploded.

Chapter Forty

The noise was deafening. A great, booming roar that seemed to roll over us before sucking the air from all around. The early morning darkness was suddenly illuminated as the flames erupted through the roof and walls.

Ten seconds later my ears were still ringing from the blast. But I could hear the faint approach of sirens and the screams and sobs of Gordon Dunbar's neighbours as they looked on in horror at the wreckage that lay behind us.

I pulled myself up on one elbow and looked at Mack and Jessica. They appeared unharmed, though Jessica bore a scrape on her right cheek from where she'd hit the pavement a millisecond before the explosion. I glanced at Nicole and saw she was unhurt. Physically at least. The look of shock in her eyes suggested she'd have trouble sleeping for a while.

Mack got to his feet and looked at the carnage Frankie had wrought. He shook his head slowly and looked down at me. 'And you wanted to trust him?'

There wasn't much to say to that.

Gordon Dunbar's house was destroyed, of course. And the buildings on either side now stood with one end open like a loaf of bread with the crust sliced off. They too would have to be levelled and rebuilt before the pyjama-clad families around us would be able to return to their beds. Once the shock began to wear off Gordon's neighbours started giving us some less than charitable looks.

I didn't care. I was sitting on Gordon's front wall staring at my bloodied, dirt-encrusted hands. I'd been sweating so much during the frantic race to free Nicole that the palms were almost clean. If I looked only at the palms I could just about pretend nothing had happened. But when I turned them over and saw the torn flesh around my fingernails and the soil in the creases of my skin, I realised just how much dirt I was carrying with me. I closed my eyes and tried not to picture Gordon Dunbar's fingers protruding from his grave, or the blood pouring from Frankie Dent's mouth as he lay dying.

All around me was motion. A fire engine sat at one side of the road while two ambulances occupied the other with several police cars parked further back. Firefighters stood in Gordon's garden, cautiously examining the wreckage of the house, while two of them used power tools to free Nicole from her chains. Paramedics had tried to attend to the three of us but we'd been less than welcoming. The fresh air had cleared the fumes from our heads and, other than a few grazes, we were largely unscathed.

A cordon had been thrown up to hold the growing crowd back, but other than that the uniforms on the scene didn't appear to be doing much of anything. They were obviously waiting for a senior officer to turn up, and when one did, I was unsurprised to see it was DI Stewart. He trudged towards me with an expression halfway between anger and weariness. He reached us and stood with his hands on his hips, looking down at me like a disappointed parent, his eyes never straying to Mack or Jessica on either side of me.

'Why, when I heard the word *explosion*, did I immediately think of you?' he asked.

'Psychic premonition?' I suggested.

'Maybe. Or maybe I realised we'd had an attempted burial before the corpse was a corpse and the gravedigger killed in a hit and run, and wondered what you might do for an encore?'

'You make it sound like it's all my fault.'

'I couldn't possibly say that.'

'But you'd really like to.'

Stewart smiled a little, gave a slight nod. 'It would make the paperwork a lot quicker. Just a wee note saying, *Keir Harper did it*. Stick that on Darroch's desk and I can take a holiday.'

'You'd probably make Superintendent,' Jessica said.

'Oh, don't worry,' Stewart said to her. 'I'll pin something on him when I'm getting on a bit and looking for a cushy desk job.' He looked at each of us in turn, then at the wrecked house and finally over at Nicole, who had been helped to her feet by a firefighter and ushered off to an ambulance. 'Anyone want to take a stab at explaining this shambles?'

*

Several hours later I was sitting in an interview room in the Giffnock police office. Stewart sat opposite me with DS Taylor by his side as I went through the story for the umpteenth time. Andrea was by my side, of course, even though I – for once – didn't feel in imminent danger of being framed. There was no need: Frankie Dent was quite clearly the nutjob behind everything, and there were more than enough people to testify to that. Not least of which were the cop scheduled for reconstructive surgery to his jaw and his colleagues who watched Frankie try to take his head off with a shovel.

My concern was with getting the story out in a way that kept the rest of us out of trouble. And I had yet to decide what to do about Gordon.

Stewart sat back and stretched, pushing his arms straight up above his head, fingers linked, palms facing the ceiling. His back popped as he stretched and let out a long yawn. I joined in while Taylor smothered one of her own. Andrea, having spent the night in bed like a civilised person, waited for us to regain our composure. She had to wait a while. It was almost midday and we'd all been on the go for far too long.

I envied Mack and Jessica, who'd already been sent home. We'd agreed before the police arrived at the scene that they would play dumb, claiming I'd called them at the last minute for help and they knew almost nothing about what had happened up to that point. I doubt any of the cops bought it, but there was little they could do about it. Besides, they knew they had the bad guy in a drawer at the morgue anyway, so why waste their time?

It wasn't all one-way traffic either. Stewart revealed as much as he was able. He told me about Gordon Dunbar's injuries, the least of which were a broken nose, a fractured cheekbone and eye socket, several missing teeth and a throat full of soil. The worst of it was the damage to his legs. To make sure Gordon couldn't run away, or even climb out of the grave while it was being dug, Frankie severed the Achilles tendon in both his ankles. He was in surgery at the moment, though with the loss of blood and the possibility of infection from the soil it remained unsure at this point if he'd ever walk again.

When I thought of the fate Daniel Dent had suffered I wondered if that was karma.

It was also from Stewart that I heard the details of Nicole's abduction. As we'd guessed, she went to her dad's house partly to feel a little closer to him, partly hoping he might turn up, and partly because of the finger of fear that had begun to tickle the back of her neck. She thought she'd be safer there, where no-one would think to look for her. Frankie must have been watching her own home and he followed her to Giffnock, catching up as she turned the key in the lock and opened the door, pushing in behind her and closing the door on any potential witnesses. He'd punched her once and she'd blacked out. Then she'd woken up in the basement, already chained to the shelving frame and gagged with duct tape. He explained to her that the house was filling with gas, but not to worry as it wouldn't go off till the following morning at six o'clock.

He'd lied to both of us. So much for being a man of his word.

He'd been talkative, though Nicole tried not to listen as most of it amounted to detailed descriptions of the horrible injuries he was going to inflict on her father. Then he left the basement and returned with a wet towel, explaining that it was to prevent her being overcome by fumes while he was gone. He placed the towel over her head and left.

Some time passed before Frankie returned, though I was surprised to hear he'd gone back to the house at all: it seemed an unnecessary risk. But something seemed to have changed. He was angry, Nicole told Stewart. Furious, judging by the way he stomped around the house. And he didn't speak this time. From behind the towel Nicole couldn't make eye contact, but he was so enraged she wasn't sure if she would have been able to look at him anyway. When he entered the house she'd hoped briefly that it was someone come to rescue her. The silence told her it wasn't. At which point she hoped he'd had a change of heart. Even as the door to the basement was thrown open and he stomped down the stairs she allowed herself to hope. When he grabbed the chains and she felt his fingers reach for the padlocks she dared to envisage freedom.

Then he snapped the first key in the lock. The other two quickly followed. And a few moments later her nostrils registered the pungent aroma of superglue. That's when she realised she was going to die. He thumped back up the steps and slammed the door again. She heard more thumping from the kitchen, which we now knew was Frankie breaking the control mechanism for the heating, and then he was gone and she was left in silence.

Until we showed up and carried her from Frankie's deathtrap.

I had spent most of the last few hours thinking this over and wondering what could have happened to change Frankie's mood so dramatically. Perhaps the pressure of his complex revenge scheme was beginning to take its toll. Maybe he'd begun to worry that Gordon would elude him. Or he might have heard that Innes McKenzie was asking about him and that had piled on more pressure. Whatever it was, at some point after leaving Gordon's house he'd decided Nicole had to die. I wasn't sure what it was, and wondered if I'd ever know.

After a record breaking stretch Stewart dropped his arms and reached for his coffee cup. He looked in it as though someone might have managed to refill it without him noticing since the last time he'd checked and found it dry. Taylor's fingers were flipping her pen back and forth, a clear sign that she was in dire need of another cigarette break.

'So,' Stewart said eventually. 'You still don't know why Gordon Dunbar was being blackmailed?'

'Nope.'

Andrea sighed. 'We've been over this already.'

'And you don't know why Frankie Dent wanted to kill him?' Taylor chimed in.

'Something to do with his brother.'

'You mean Daniel Dent?' Stewart said. 'The man whose body – according to you – was found ten days ago?'

'It would be a sizeable coincidence, would it not,' Andrea said, 'if that wasn't Daniel Dent and Frankie Dent chose that spot by sheer chance.'

'What do you think happened?' Stewart asked me.

'I don't know,' I said. 'You'd have to ask Gordon.'

Taylor snorted. 'Some detective.'

Andrea looked ready to reply but I cut across her. 'Listen. Without me you'd have another dead body that wasn't quite so dead when he was buried, and a killer walking around laughing his arse off at you. So, yeah, I am pretty damn good.' I looked from one to the other. 'We done?'

'Unless you want to tell us the truth.'

'I've already told you the truth.'

'All of it?'

'What I know of it. Gordon should be able to tell you the rest.'

'He's still in surgery,' Taylor said.

'And what would you like me to do about that?' Stewart took the hint and stood up to show me out while Taylor muttered something under her breath.

Stewart, Andrea and I walked through the building in silence. We parted beside the front desk, with Andrea leaving first to get to another client before he incriminated himself beyond even her legal prowess. She gave me a final warning to say nothing without her present then was gone.

As soon as she was out of earshot Stewart asked me one last time if I had anything else to tell him. I took the advice of my legal counsel and said nothing, walking away from him as the door clicked shut between us and Stewart went back to work. I couldn't imagine how much paperwork this case had generated, but he was welcome to it. I stepped outside into the midday heat and screwed up my eyes against the sun. I began to walk, then stopped when I saw a woman leaning against the wall, smoking a cigarette like it was the one thing keeping her from stepping into traffic.

DI Claiborne looked up and tried an unconvincing smile.

'I didn't realise you were a smoker,' I said. Then winced.

Claiborne at least had the decency to look embarrassed for me. 'Sorry,' I said quickly. 'It's been a long night. I'm usually much more witty and suave.'

'You're forgetting I've met you before.' She managed a brief smile before returning to her cigarette. She turned her head and exhaled the smoke downwind of me. 'Yeah. It's been a long one alright. Not one for the scrapbook, I wouldn't say.'

'You okay?' I asked.

Claiborne hiked her shoulders and let them fall like they had been piled high with sandbags. 'Better than Frankie Dent.'

'It was an accident.'

'I'm not sure that makes much difference to ol' Frank.'

I was silent for a few moments. Despite my urge to soothe her with platitudes, to tell her to let it go, I knew how tightly we held onto these slivers of guilt, these blade-like feelings that cut us more deeply the tighter we gripped them. And I also knew why we held onto them so fervently; because letting go of them meant we were less than human. Guilt might tear us apart, but it lets us know we still have empathy. What did we become if we stopped feeling torn by the wrongs we had done? I'd met plenty of those who had no such qualms, and I had no desire to be like any of them. And I didn't want Claiborne to either.

So I remained silent. I kept my mouth shut and stood by her side, to be there should she feel the need to talk. And eventually, halfway through her second cigarette, she did.

'Did he tell you why he wanted to kill Gordon Dunbar?' Claiborne asked.

I stood watching traffic pass, and after a pause, I replied, 'No. I think we'll need Gordon to fill that bit in. I don't really care anymore. Nicole and Gordon are safe and Frankie Dent isn't going to be hurting anyone else. Case closed as far as I'm concerned.' I smiled and glanced over at her. 'Always the cop, eh?'

She let out a short, sharp laugh. 'Here's hoping.'

I winced again, this time at my insensitivity.

'There'll be an internal investigation,' Claiborne said. 'They'll look at what happened and decide how much blame to shovel my way. Then they'll decide how severe my punishment is.'

'It was an accident,' I said again.

'A man died, Harper. The police like to hold someone accountable.'

She was preaching to the choir with that one.

Claiborne sighed and threw her cigarette butt on the ground. She crushed it beneath the toe of her boot and looked at me with defeat in her eyes. 'All it takes is one person to have a grudge against me. One person who thinks I'm a pain in their arse and would rather see me off the force, or demoted, or transferred… just one person, and I'm fucked.'

There was nothing I could say. The internal machinations of the police force were a foreign world to me. Any words I uttered would have been ill-informed to the point of worthlessness.

Claiborne sensed my awkwardness and held up a fresh cigarette, dug from her pocket. 'Hence the fags.'

'There's worse things than smoking,' I said, aiming for light-hearted. 'Not many, but one or two.'

Claiborne blew a plume of smoke into the air. 'Problem is, Harper, we don't get to pick the things we got to do.'

I looked at her for longer than I should have. I reflected on her words and wondered how much truth they held, and how many more truths they hinted at. Frankie Dent felt he had no choice in his actions, as, I'm sure, did Gordon Dunbar. But both of them had been directly responsible for the deaths of others. Now I too was faced with an unpalatable choice. Some of the truth I knew, some of it lay buried still. But, like Daniel Dent, it had found its way to the surface and now it couldn't be forgotten.

And more than one life would be torn apart before the last of the truth had been exhumed.

Chapter Forty-One

I left Claiborne and headed for Central Station. I wondered if my car was still in the casino car park or if it had been towed yet. I'd find out when I could summon up the energy to care. Right now all I wanted to do was go home and shut my eyes for a few days. Strange thoughts and half-formed theories swirled about my tired mind, none of them staying still long enough to grasp. I needed rest before I could make a decision. Anyway, Gordon would be unavailable for some time yet, and I needed to speak to him before I decided whether or not to rip a hole in his life.

I caught a train just before the doors closed and managed to stay awake for the ten minute journey back to Gilmour Street. From there it was a short walk to my flat and I was home just after 1 o'clock. Despite the time I wasn't hungry. I shed my clothes and collapsed into bed where sleep took me instantly.

*

I slept for a solid six hours and woke refreshed. I showered, dressed and sat at the kitchen table while I mulled over what I knew and what I thought I knew. While I'd slept the jumble of ideas and possibilities had settled and merged into something tangible. I knew now what I had to do. I lifted my phone from the table and dialled.

When the call was answered a voice said, 'You found him then.'

'Yes.'

'Then you don't need me.'

'I need to know one thing,' I said. 'Why did you agree to help me?'

'You should have asked yourself that at the time.'

'I did. But I didn't figure it out till now.'

'So now you know everything?'

'Not all of it. I want you to fill in the gaps.'

'Tell me what you know.'

So I did.

And I found out the rest.

*

It was after ten-thirty by the time I reached the Royal Infirmary in the east end of Glasgow. Visiting hours were long past and the multi-storey car park was largely empty. I parked and made my way into the hospital building, found which ward Gordon was in and made my way there. I was hoping it was late enough that the police had either finished questioning him or had been told by the doctors to wrap it for the night.

The ward was quiet and the police officer on guard outside Gordon's room heard me as soon as I opened the door to the ward. When I walked past the nurses desk and into his line of vision he'd already put down his newspaper and was standing waiting for me. I told him who I was and that I wanted to see Gordon. He told me that wouldn't be possible and asked me to leave. I told him to call DI Stewart and clear it with him, and a few minutes later the cop was giving me a dirty look as I pushed open the door to Gordon's room. I suspected that, despite hoping I might get the truth from Gordon, DI Stewart's face almost certainly bore the same expression.

Gordon looked hellish. Each leg was in a cast from knee to toes to keep the leg straight and let the ligaments heal. His face was bruised and cut, a bandage taped across his nose and more swathed around his head. His skin was an unhealthy colour and his blackened eyes were haunted by his brush with death. But, given the number of people Frankie Dent had dispatched with ease, he should feel lucky to still be feeling anything at all.

I closed the door and pulled a plastic chair to the far side of the bed and sat down so I could see Gordon and the door. I looked at him for a long time without speaking. He looked back apprehensively, as though he saw the conflict raging through my mind and had decided to remain silent rather than risk tipping the balance against himself.

'How you feeling, Gordon?' I finally asked.

'Awful,' he croaked. When his mouth opened I saw several gaps where teeth had once been.

'Is that physically? Or have you grown a conscience and the guilt's eating you alive?'

Gordon looked at the door, as though hoping his guard would come in and drag me from the room. I said nothing, just stared at him, waiting for him to tell me how he'd managed to become the catalyst in destroying so many lives.

Eventually he spoke, his voice full of resignation. 'You don't understand.'

'You're damn right I don't. How the fuck could you let a man be buried alive?'

'I didn't know! I thought he was dead. I was blind drunk. They shouldn't have put me in that position.'

'You put yourself in that position, Gordon. What is this, a family trait? Take some responsibility for your own actions.'

'Don't you bring Nicole into this,' Gordon warned.

I put my hand on his plastered right leg, applied a little pressure. Gordon's eyes widened in fear. 'Just... leave her out of it. It's nothing to do with her.'

'She asked me to find you, and she asked me to protect you. I've done both, but now I'm asking myself why?'

'It was just a mistake. The whole bloody thing was just one big mistake. I should never have gone near Ricky Bruises.'

'But your addiction got the better of you. You were losing money hand over fist and still couldn't stop. And once Ricky had his hooks in you he used you. Used you to dope fighters. Like you doped Daniel Dent.'

Gordon looked away as a tear ran down his cheek. I knew the Dunbars well enough by now to know that tear wasn't for Daniel Dent.

'What did you tell him you were injecting him with?'

'Ricky told him it would block the pain.'

'And you didn't disagree.'

Gordon shook his head.

'You lied to Daniel Dent before you injected him with a drug that meant he didn't stand a chance in that fight. You caused his brain damage, Gordon. Ricky might have initiated it, but *you* put the needle in him.'

My voice had risen without me realising and Gordon looked warily at the door as though the cop might come in to arrest him.

'I didn't have any choice,' he hissed.

'How many other times did you drug fighters because you didn't have a choice?' The way he dropped his eyes told me it was plenty. 'And how many times did you stick on a bet and cash in on the rigged fights?' His eyes slid lower still.

I stood up and walked to the window, drew back the thin curtain and looked out. I said nothing for a couple of minutes, just let Gordon stew. After a while I asked, 'What have you told the cops?'

'Nothing. I pretended to be out of it on painkillers the whole time they were here.'

'I spoke to them,' I said. 'But I didn't tell them everything. And you know the only reason I didn't?' I turned back to Gordon and looked at the hope in his eyes. 'Nicole. It would crush her, and I can't do that.'

The wave of relief that swept over Gordon was palpable. 'What will you tell them?'

'I already told them I don't know why Frankie wanted to kill you. They didn't believe me, but that's all I'm telling them.' I paused, let him settle and relax, then added, 'Providing you help me.'

That put a crack in his relief.

'With what?'

'If you help me I'll keep my mouth shut about everything

you've done, everything you've been involved in. You can make up your own story about Frankie and I won't contradict it. But if you don't help me, I'll tell them everything. And you'll go to jail for a long time.'

'Help you with what?' There was desperation in his voice now.

I paused again, though only for effect. I'd known before I entered this room how I was going to play this. I held Gordon's gaze and dropped the hammer. 'There were two of them, weren't there?'

The reaction was exactly as I'd expected. Gordon's face fell and his eyes widened.

'I know there were, so don't lie to me. But I don't know who. I need you to help me.'

'I… I can't. I don't…'

'They'll come for you, Gordon. You realise that, don't you? Do you think you'll be so lucky a second time?'

'I…I…'

'To be honest, Gordon, I'm running out of reasons to look out for you. You've done some terrible things. This is your shot at…' I almost said redemption, but stopped short, unable to even say the word, '…making amends.'

'But I don't…'

'Look, Gordon. You're not in a position to refuse me. I want your help to flush Frankie Dent's accomplice into the open, and you're going to give it to me. Unless you fancy explaining to the cops why you buried a man alive.'

'But I wasn't there when they buried him!'

'That's not what I'll say. And you're the only one left to contradict me. Who do you think they'll believe?'

Gordon's mouth dropped open and he looked at me with renewed fear. 'You can't…'

'Don't fucking bet on it, Gordon. You help me, you get on with your life. You refuse, I'll bury you like you buried Daniel Dent.' I stared into his eyes till he knew how deadly serious I was. 'So, you going to help me or not?'

*

It was almost midnight when I pulled up outside the house on Merrylee Road in the south side. It was a spacious looking semi-detached, set back from the road in a well-tended garden, with a tree in the centre of the front lawn and a blue Passat on the gravel driveway. The householder was clearly someone who valued appearances.

I knocked on the door and it opened after a few moments. Claiborne stood there, a look of mild surprise on her face and a glass of wine in her hand. 'Okay, you've convinced me. You're a good detective. You didn't have to stalk me all the way to my front door to prove the point.'

'I need your help.'

My tone must have been urgent enough for Claiborne instantly stepped aside and told me to come in. She directed me to her kitchen where I took a seat at a breakfast bar and she stood with her back to the sink.

'What's wrong?' she asked.

'Everyone thinks it's over. But it's not.'

'Why? You said it yourself, Frankie Dent is dead, Gordon and Nicole Dunbar are both safe – thanks to you – so what's the problem?'

'There were two of them.'

'What? Dent had an accomplice?'

'I went to see Gordon. He told me Frankie had a partner. That the partner would come for Gordon if anything happened to Frankie first.'

'Was he bluffing? Just trying to scare him?'

'I don't think Frankie knew how to bluff. I think he meant everything he said.'

'Did Gordon tell you who it was?'

'No. He doesn't trust anyone.'

'Not even you?'

'He never did like me. All he would tell me is that he knows who it is, but he won't talk to the police until he's protected.'

'He's still a person of interest to us, Harper. We don't know the full story yet, and until we do he'll be under guard.'

'One guard doesn't seem to reassure him. He thinks he's a sitting duck in the hospital and he wants out. He wants to be taken somewhere safe.'

Claiborne took a long sip of wine. 'I don't know that I can help you. I'm suspended until they finish the internal investigation. Why didn't you go to your pal Stewart?'

'Because there's only one reason Gordon is so terrified and won't trust anyone. He's worried about it getting back to Frankie's accomplice. And if he's worried about the cops leaking it, the only person with that kind of reach is Innes McKenzie.'

Claiborne seemed genuinely shocked. 'McKenzie?'

'And from what I hear, no-one knows him better, or wants to nail him harder to the wall, than you do.'

Claiborne strolled to the window and looked out over her darkened back garden. Or maybe she was just looking at her reflection, seeing her image in the newspapers, on TV: the women who brought down Glasgow's godfather.

She turned back to me. 'If he's that scared of McKenzie why would he talk to us when he's in protective custody?'

'He's not going into protective custody. I'm going to bust him out.'

Claiborne looked at me as though I'd lost my mind. 'And you think I'll help you with that?'

'It's your best chance of nailing McKenzie. Maybe your only chance. Bring him down and no-one's going to be kicking you off the force.'

Claiborne ran a hand through her hair as she thought about it. Then she gave a curt nod. 'Fuck it. What's the plan?'

Chapter Forty-Two

I sneaked a look through the glass panel in the door and surveyed the ward. I couldn't see the guard from this angle but knew one would still be in place. Nothing had changed since the previous night when I'd been allowed in to see Gordon.

Two rows of five rooms lay at either side of the ward, with hallways laid out between them in the shape of an H. Storage areas separated the two longer corridors, with the central bar of the H that linked them also home to the nurses' desk. The door, were I now stood, was at the bottom left of the H. Gordon's room was at the top right, out of my sight. I wondered if the police had requested the room furthest from the door to protect Gordon, or if it was intended to make it harder for him to leave unexpectedly. Either way, from where I stood I could not see the door to his room, or his guard. And, more importantly, the guard could not see me.

It was almost ten-thirty and the ward was as quiet as it had been last night at this time. A lone nurse sat at the desk, head bowed as she ploughed her way through a pile of paperwork. Everything looked exactly as I'd hoped; there was no need to change the plan. I gripped the folded wheelchair in both hands and waited.

Right on ten-thirty the phone at the nurses' desk rang. The nurse dropped her pen in a gesture of annoyance and lifted the receiver. She listened for a few seconds, said something back, then placed the receiver on the desk. She pushed back her chair and stood up, stretching her back as she did so. Then she turned and walked towards Gordon's room.

I was through the door and easing it closed almost before

she'd disappeared from sight. I walked quickly to the far end of the corridor where I was hidden from the nurse and the guard. I'd scrutinised the ward thoroughly the previous night after leaving Gordon's side and had discovered the last room in the central section was a storage area with a door at either side, giving access to both sides of the H. And since it was used to store only bedding and other non-medical equipment, the doors weren't locked.

I opened the door and stepped through, closing it silently behind me. I hurried to the other door and stopped with my ear to it, listening intently. By now the nurse should be telling the police officer on duty that there was a call for him from Detective Inspector Claiborne. He might be surprised, he might wonder why she hadn't called him directly, but he wouldn't fail to take the call.

I just had to hope that when the guard went to the phone that the nurse didn't decide to check up on Gordon while he was away. Or come into the storage room for something. I was banking on her pile of paperwork being sufficiently large that it created a gravitational pull and dragged her back to the desk.

A moment later my worries were eased when I heard two sets of footsteps walking away from me, heading back towards the nurses' desk. I counted their steps until I estimated they were almost there, then gently opened the door and risked a glance along the corridor just in time to see the back of a police uniform turn the corner. The nurse was nowhere in sight.

Claiborne wouldn't be able to keep Gordon's guard on the phone for long. I darted across the hallway into his room with the wheelchair still under my arm, closed the door behind me and put the wheelchair down and unfolded it. Gordon was sitting upright in bed, dressing gown wrapped tightly around his body over t-shirt and loose shorts, his plastered legs jutting out in front of him. He looked at me with a question. The look I gave him in return left no room for argument.

I picked Gordon up and lowered him into the chair, then cracked open the door and stole another glance towards the nurses' desk. At the edge of the wall I saw the black short sleeve of a uniform and the hint of an elbow. There was no time to hesitate. I pushed the wheelchair across the corridor and pulled Gordon's door closed behind me with a click that seemed far too loud in this silent hallway.

I leaned over Gordon and pushed open the door to the storage room and wheeled him in, closing it behind us. Gordon looked ready to speak but I silenced him with a glare and listened for footsteps. It was almost another minute before I heard the guard return to his post. I'd no idea what Claiborne had said to him, and didn't really care. Maybe she'd spent the whole time flirting with him. She seemed to be good at that when it served her purpose.

Whatever she'd said, she'd cleared the way for me to get Gordon out of his room. Now I had to get past the nurse again.

On the opposite side of the H from Gordon's room were two rooms that were completely hidden from anyone seated at the nurses' desk. A third was partially obscured but I would only risk that one if absolutely necessary. What I needed was for one of the occupants of those first two rooms to be sound asleep. And for me to be able to determine that from the corridor I was hoping for a heavy snorer. Fortunately, as anyone who has spent a night in a hospital will testify, every ward has several window-rattlers, and the guy in the first room seemed to be impersonating a chainsaw.

I left Gordon in the storage room and crept across the hallway into the snorer's room under cover of his bear-like grunting. I took the half empty water jug from the bedside table and poured it on the floor beside the bed, then laid it on the ground as though he'd knocked it over. Then I pressed the call button and darted back across the hallway into the storage room and closed the door.

The nurse didn't seem in any hurry and at least a minute passed before she shuffled into the snorer's room. I listened for a break in the snoring that would signal her awakening him and when it came I wheeled Gordon into the corridor and walked quickly for the door. The nurse would be concerned over why her patient had knocked his water all over the floor, called for a nurse, and then gone straight back to sleep, or perhaps lost consciousness. By the time she straightened that out we'd be long gone.

I swung the wheelchair round in a circle just before I reached the swing doors at the entrance to the ward and pushed my way through it backwards, pulling Gordon along and keeping a wary eye on the room at the end of the corridor. The doors had closed behind us and I had only just stopped them from swinging when, through the glass panel, I saw the nurse step out of the room and walk back towards the desk, shaking her head and obviously far more concerned about being interrupted than she was about her patient's welfare.

*

We were silent and tense as we made our way through the hospital. I wheeled Gordon as quickly as I could without attracting attention. Fortunately no-one seemed remotely interested in what must have looked like just another patient being taken somewhere by a concerned friend or relative. In a matter of minutes we made it to the car park entrance and were suddenly alone. I found a ticket machine, paid for my parking and pressed the button to call the lift. Just then my phone vibrated once in my pocket. I took it out and read the short text message. Gordon was sitting with his back to me and remained oblivious. Adrenaline began to fire through my body.

Gordon was getting increasingly jumpy the longer we stood there. His head spun from side to side, looking for any sign of someone following us.

'Are you sure this is safe?' he asked.

Now that I had him out of the ward I had no reason to pander to him. So I told the truth. 'No.'

'What?' Gordon's head whipped round and he looked at me over his shoulder.

'In fact, I'm almost certain it's unsafe. You might well get a bullet in the head before the end of the night.' I spread my hands to show just how honest I was being.

Gordon looked at me in horror for several seconds. Then he

closed his mouth and its corners twisted into a forced smile. 'Ha ha, Harper. I suppose you think that's funny, scaring me senseless after everything I've been through. Very good, have your little joke.' He turned back to the lift as it reached our floor and the doors opened with a ping. Shaking his head in disgust he said, 'Let's just get a move on, shall we?'

Don't say I didn't warn you...

I pushed the wheelchair into the lift, spun it round to face the doors and felt a tremble in my fingers as I pushed the button for the top floor.

The lift didn't stop on the way up and in a few seconds the doors opened once more. I pushed Gordon out into a largely deserted car park. There were four cars parked near the far end of this level – including my own – and only one near this end, a silver Skoda Octavia parked twenty yards ahead on our left. The ramp from the level below opened out on our right, and at the far end another ramp led back down. As I walked towards the parked cars I noticed Gordon peering nervously down the ramp, searching the gloom below for signs of movement. There was nothing, and he seemed to relax as we got nearer the cars.

With the Octavia behind us my own Civic was now closest, parked on the left hand side, six bays from the far wall. A shiny Rover 45 sat four spaces further along on the same side, and a dingy looking Vauxhall Astra, was parked on the right hand side, halfway between the Rover and my Honda. The last car was an old Citroen Synergie people carrier parked in the farthest corner where the light was poor. Perhaps it was the dim light combined with the tinted rear windows that had caused the driver such difficulty in parking in a straight line. As it was the rear of the car pointed at a slight angle back down the row towards my car on the other side.

I glanced over each vehicle in turn and found nothing to worry about, which was, in itself, something to worry about.

Gordon, it seemed, was equally concerned. 'Can we hurry up, for God's sake?' he muttered. 'This place is...'

His words ended in a strangled cry as a figure stepped out from the shadows behind the Synergie and walked toward us.

Gordon pushed back in the wheelchair, his fingers gripping the arms in panic as Detective Inspector Claiborne strode toward us.

'Denise?' I said, surprise in my voice. 'What are you doing here? I thought I was to call you when I had him somewhere safe.'

Claiborne didn't look at me. She had eyes only for Gordon as she pulled a gun from behind her back and levelled it at him. 'Safe? Now why would I let you do a silly thing like that?'

Chapter Forty-Three

There was silence in the car park as the gun loomed large before us. Gordon appeared to be too busy trying not to have a heart attack to speak, and I was too busy edging away from him. It was him, after all, that she was here to kill. I was merely collateral damage. If she could only take one of us out I hoped she'd follow her heart.

Claiborne stopped eight feet from us; too far for me to reach, too close for her to miss. Her red hair was tied back and stuffed under a beanie hat, her slim figure hidden beneath a baggy hooded top, and maybe that would be enough to fool the cops when they looked back over the CCTV footage after finding our dead bodies. And beyond that, the malevolence in her eyes when she looked at Gordon rendered her almost unrecognisable from the beautiful woman I thought I'd known.

'Is this your way of telling me you're not interested anymore?' I asked.

'Did you ever really think I was interested?' she replied with a faint smile.

'No. I thought you were using me to find Gordon.'

'You were right.'

'Technically, maybe. I'm not sure I'd get any marks for my working though.'

Claiborne conceded that with a small nod. 'Sorry, Harper. A girl's got to look after number one.'

'Is that why you killed Frankie?'

'That was his own fault. He lost control and I wasn't going to suffer for that.' Claiborne made a dismissive gesture with the gun and stepped closer. 'Come on Harper, you know how this goes. Hands in the air, don't move a muscle, etcetera, etcetera.'

I lifted my hands half-heartedly. Claiborne didn't seem to care. She moved towards Gordon and stopped in front of him, looking down at him with naked hatred. 'Who else knows?' she asked him.

'Kno... knows what?' he stammered.

Claiborne looked over at me. 'You know, Harper, I asked him because I thought he'd be so scared he'd tell me right away. What do you know, eh?'

'Guess he's tougher than he looks.'

'You wouldn't tell me either, would you?' she said, almost sweetly.

'Nope.'

'I don't know what you want!' Gordon cried.

'Isn't it obvious, Gordon? She wants to know about Daniel.'

Tears started to leak from Gordon's eyes. 'I didn't know! I didn't know he was still alive. Ricky made me... he made... I thought he was dead.'

Claiborne's face had become an alabaster mask. Each word fell from her lips like a coin prised from a miser's grasp. 'Who. Else. Knows. About. Me?'

'I don't know what you mean!'

'If that's how you want to play it.' Claiborne reached under her baggy jumper and pulled out a small travel pillow, placed it on top of Gordon's plastered right leg, jammed the barrel of the gun into it and pulled the trigger.

Even with the improvised silencer the pop was loud enough to echo, though it was drowned out almost completely by Gordon's screech of pain. Claiborne cut him off by backhanding the gun across the unbroken side of his face. The chair tipped back with the blow and Claiborne helped it on its way with a kick, tipping Gordon onto the concrete floor.

She cast a quick glance at me to make sure I hadn't moved then stood over Gordon, the gun pointed at his face. 'Who else knows?' she said to me.

The situation had spiralled out of control more quickly than

I'd expected. Now Claiborne looked ready to kill Gordon and while he might have deserved it for the part he'd played in Daniel Dent's death, I couldn't just stand by and watch. Especially as I'd be next.

I spread my hands to my sides in a passive gesture, my voice calm as I tried to reason with her. 'This isn't the way to do it, Denise. You can get justice without killing anyone else.'

'You think you can talk me down, Harper? Do you? You think you can sweet talk me into giving you the gun and letting you take me in? Maybe you think I'll break down and confess, tell you everything.'

'You don't need to tell me anything. I see it all now.'

Claiborne barked a laugh. 'You don't have a clue.'

'This whole plan wasn't Frankie. If Frankie had his way he'd have beaten Gordon and Ricky to death with a rusty hammer. Same for anyone else who got in his way. He didn't care if he got caught, as long as Daniel's death was avenged. So someone must have persuaded him to play it cool. Someone who couldn't risk getting caught. Someone who couldn't risk Frankie getting caught either, in case the connection between them was found. I don't know what that connection was, but it was there.'

Claiborne raised her eyebrows, surprised that I hadn't figured out how she and Frankie and Daniel were connected. Then the surprise ebbed away and confidence grew in its place. 'If you're stalling for time I wouldn't bother. The cameras are off and the guy in the security room is having a nice wee lie down.' She gave me a sultry look that, a few days ago, would have left me feeling unsettled in an entirely different way. 'It's just us, baby.'

I smiled ruefully. 'I should have known when you killed Frankie. When he said a cop could fix a hit and run charge. I thought he was talking about you getting away with killing him, but he was trying to tell me it was you who got him such a light sentence for killing Steve Kelsey. But you were smart enough to put DS Rowe in charge of the case so your name wouldn't be anywhere near it.'

She gave me a wicked smile. 'Sergeant Rowe's a very loyal officer.'

'You mean he does what you tell him.'

'Depends how many shirt buttons I've got undone.' She laughed. 'He's even easier to manipulate than you.'

I let that fall on deaf ears. 'You couldn't get him off completely, not with all those witnesses, but you were happy for him to go to jail anyway, weren't you? Give him time to calm down while you worked out a plan to take revenge on the rest of them. And when he got out Frankie was happy enough to go along with the plan. A plan that got revenge and still kept your hands clean. Until Daniel Dent's body was dug up that is.'

Claiborne said nothing but her face coloured and her jawline tightened.

'Why didn't they identify him?' I asked. 'He had a record. His fingerprints should have been matched up in no time. Let me guess. A certain interested party in law enforcement had been buggering around with the records.'

'I couldn't possibly comment.'

She didn't need to. 'How did you discover it was Daniel?'

'Stewart circulated a description of the body, including photos of his tattoos.'

'And then you found out he was alive when they buried him.' In spite of everything that had happened it was impossible not to sympathise, to imagine the sickening horror felt on learning of such a terrible fate.

Claiborne looked down at Gordon, appearing to take some satisfaction in his pain. She looked angry still, but this time I sensed some of it was directed at herself. 'I never should have told Frankie that though. He lost control. Nearly ruined everything.'

'You knew you'd have to kill him, eventually, didn't you? You put this plan in motion to protect yourself and yet you still ended up killing him.'

Claiborne looked back up at me and there was real pain in her eyes. 'Hindsight's a wonderful thing, Harper. Now, quit stalling and tell me who knows about me.'

'It was you who went back to Gordon's house after Frankie had left Nicole there, wasn't it? Frankie was right: he *was* a man of his word. He'd been straight with me before, and if he said six a.m., then it would have been six a.m. But you couldn't take the risk that he'd let something slip to Nicole, could you? He told you where she was and you went there to kill her. No wonder Nicole thought Frankie was in a rage when he returned. It was you, and you could see your careful plan circling the drain.'

'And what if I did?' For the first time Claiborne raised her voice and the shout echoed round the car park. 'Who *fucking* knows about me?'

Again I carried on. 'You changed the timer. You couldn't kill Nicole right then and there in case Frankie had already been caught. Then it would be obvious someone else was involved. So you brought the timer forward to four o'clock, then you destroyed the control mechanism.'

'And if you'd kept your beak out she'd have been blown to bits. And you know what, Harper? You'd have been better off without her.' Claiborne gave Gordon a kick to check he was still conscious. He groaned and looked up at her from eyes glassy with pain, flinched when he saw her gun pointed at him. 'Anyway, so what if you know this shit now? It's a bit fucking obvious after I've put a gun to your head. Now, this really is your last chance. One of you is going to tell me who knows about me, or I'm going to shoot this prick in the face.'

Gordon sobbed in pain and fear as Claiborne kicked his wounded leg. He clutched the plaster cast and cried out. 'I don't... I don't even know what... please... I don't know what you want!'

Claiborne looked at me as she pressed the gun against Gordon's forehead.

I shrugged. 'Wouldn't be much of a loss, to be honest.'

'You bastard,' Gordon cried in horror.

'Fuck you, Gordon. You let a man be buried alive.'

'I didn't know he was still alive! There was blood everywhere. I was so drunk I couldn't see straight. How the hell was I supposed to give them an accurate verdict?'

Claiborne stood up and removed the gun from Gordon's forehead. She took a step back and swung a kick into his face like she was kicking through the goalposts at Murrayfield. His head snapped back and I saw blood and fragments of teeth break free of his jaw.

'How were you to know?' she screamed. 'You're a fucking doctor!'

Claiborne looked ready to lose control completely. I tried to reason with her. 'Denise, wait. Think about what you're doing. You won't get away with killing us.' Even to my ears the words sounded weak.

Claiborne looked back at me and scoffed. 'Of course I will. I'm one of them. They'll spend months looking for Frankie's accomplice then give up and stick your file in a cabinet somewhere. Maybe give it a once over every five years, if you're lucky. But rest assured, with me guiding the investigation you two will be in the unsolved pile for a long time.'

Neither Claiborne nor I realised the agonised howls had subsided until Gordon spoke. When he did he sounded as shocked as I'd expected. 'You're... you're a policewoman?' he said to Claiborne.

'Of course I'm a...' Claiborne stopped abruptly as she realised what Gordon had said. As the gears turned she spoke in measured tones. 'Don't you know who I am?'

'I've got no idea.' Gordon began to beg. 'Just let me go and that's the way it will stay. I've got no idea and I don't care. Just let me go, I won't even give a description. I'll give them a false description if you want – anyone you like – just let me go.'

I ignored Gordon's pleas for mercy and studied Claiborne as she turned to me in shock. I looked in her eyes and dropped the pretence.

'Do I look fucking stupid?' I said to her.

Chapter Forty-Four

'I told you,' I said. 'I know everything. Including why you helped Frankie get his revenge. Because it was your revenge too. Because you and Daniel Dent were lovers.'

My words were like a punch in the stomach. The gun wavered and Claiborne actually hunched over a little as though defending herself against their power. I watched her reaction and knew I'd been told the truth.

'Innes McKenzie told me. I couldn't understand why he helped me look for Frankie. But it was after he heard the name Dent that he got interested, and only because he hoped it would blow up in your face.'

'I wouldn't trust a word that old bastard says,' Claiborne snarled. 'He's been trying to burn me for years.'

'Maybe, but that's not his fault,' I said. 'After all, *we don't get to pick the things we got to do.*'

Claiborne's body jerked back at the shock of her own words being thrown back at her. The phrase Frankie Dent had attributed to his brother. Her jaw tightened as realisation dawned.

'You burned yourself with your big mouth. McKenzie only confirmed my suspicions. I wondered how Frankie found out his brother had been buried alive. It had to have come from someone in the police or in the mortuary. And Benny Buchan already told us the police were at the Blood Shed most nights, and that they knew Daniel Dent very well. Think Benny will identify you? And what do you think Rowe will say when they turn the screws on him? Think he'll take the hit for you? Or will he tell them you dragged him along there to take bribes from Ricky Bruises while you made out with your favourite illegal fighter?'

Claiborne's eyes darted around the car park before coming to rest on mine. 'Funny thing is, Harper, I don't see the cavalry swooping down on me. Did you think you could bring me in on your own? Did you think we had some kind of connection, that I'd be too smitten with you to kill you?'

'I was hoping my boyish charm might work in my favour.'

'No-one else knows, do they?' she said softly. 'If Stewart or any of the rest of them knew, they'd be here and I'd be in cuffs by now.' She shook her head in wonder. 'You really thought you could do this on your own.'

'I'm nothing on my own. You should know that by now.' I raised my hand and signalled.

There was a click and Claiborne turned to see the boot of the Synergie swinging up. Inside, sitting cross-legged in the boot with a video camera beside her on a tripod and a gun in her hand, was Jessica.

'How about you drop the gun, you skinny bitch?' Jessica called.

'Gosh,' I said. 'It's as if I knew you'd kill the cameras.'

Claiborne's head whirled between Jessica and I, the gun pointing from one to the other, as if unsure how best to make her escape.

'Jessica's got the video,' I said, 'and I've got the audio. So, to put it bluntly, you're fucked.'

Claiborne moved quickly. She ran to Gordon and grabbed him by the collar, pulled him as upright as she could and jammed the gun into his neck. 'Give me the camera,' she called to Jessica.

Jessica laughed. 'Eh, no.'

Claiborne knew better than to ask for Jessica's gun – the only way she was getting that would be one bullet at a time – but she needed that camera.

'Give it to me or I'll shoot them both.'

Unfortunately for Claiborne Jessica was as determined as I'd seen her in a long time. She climbed out of the boot and walked towards us, the gun held out at arm's length, her aim unerringly steady as she pointed it at the centre of Claiborne's chest.

'You can shoot Gordon if you want,' Jessica said. 'But I'll put a bunch of fucking holes right through you before I let you shoot Harper.'

I saw calculations run rapidly through Claiborne's head. She was intelligent enough to realise Jessica would never hand over either the camera or her gun. And that gave her two choices: try to kill all of us, or settle for Gordon, her original target. She began backing towards the far end of the level. She was heading for the presumably-stolen silver Octavia, the one Jessica had seen her arrive in and had identified in the text message she'd sent me.

Claiborne managed to get an arm under Gordon's chin and turned him in front of her. But she was too tall and his plastered legs were too cumbersome for him to be effective as a human shield. She could only drag him for several paces before he began to slide back down her body, almost pulling her to the concrete floor in her efforts to keep him upright.

'Come on, Denise,' I said. 'Give it up.'

'Fuck the pair of you. I am not letting this bastard get away with what he did to Daniel.'

Claiborne pulled her arm tighter against Gordon's throat, squeezing tears from his eyes, and dragged him back another few feet, edging ever closer to the car. She was struggling with the effort of dragging him while keeping us at bay with her gun, but still there was nothing we could do without risking Gordon's life or our own.

We followed, waiting for our chance. I felt the tension in my shoulders and a line of sweat running down my back. Jessica showed no sign of any such stress. Her concentration was unbroken, her eyes focused unblinkingly on Claiborne, while her arms showed no sign of toiling with the weight of the gun.

I prayed we could resolve this standoff without gunfire. I knew Jessica would have switched off the camera before moving her gun in front of its lens, but if she put a couple of bullets in Claiborne it was going to be difficult to deny we'd brought a firearm to the party.

We reached the Skoda and Claiborne leant Gordon against it while she dug a key from her pocket and pressed the fob. The lights flashed and the boot lock released. Claiborne popped it open and I saw Gordon's jaw tremble as he realised he was about to be bundled into another car boot.

Claiborne pressed the barrel of the gun into his forehead and pushed him back over the edge. With his legs in plaster he was unable to maintain his balance and toppled easily into the boot. It looked at first as though the plaster casts would be a problem, until Claiborne lifted her foot and stamped against Gordon's stomach forcing him deeper inside. She stamped again, for fun this time, and all the while the gun remained too close to Gordon's face for Jessica to risk taking a shot.

Claiborne slammed the boot lid closed and pointed the gun at me. 'Back off and neither of you needs to die.'

We didn't move.

'Harper, I never wanted to kill you and I still don't…'

'That's reassuring.'

'…but if you don't back the fuck up right now I'm going to shoot you in the face.'

'I'll have your brains parked all over this place before you even finish the thought,' Jessica said.

'Maybe, maybe not,' Claiborne said. 'But someone is going to die tonight. If you don't want it to be Harper I suggest you both give me some fucking room.'

I knew now we'd reached an impasse. Either we backed up or someone was going to pull the trigger. And that wasn't part of my plan.

We backed up.

Claiborne edged round to the driver's door, the gun pointing steadily at me. She opened the door, put the key in the ignition and started the engine. Somewhere below us I heard another engine start up, but Claiborne was too busy issuing one last warning to notice.

'You come near the car I shoot you and I empty the gun into the boot, okay?' she said. 'You can't save him now, so you might as well save yourselves.'

Claiborne jumped into the car and jammed it into reverse. The car shot back towards us and spun to face the nearest ramp, the one leading up from the floor below. The tyres squealed as she gunned the engine, and that's when the noise from below returned, suddenly much louder as it closed in on us. The Octavia leapt towards the ramp and Claiborne swung the wheel hard, aiming for the slope. At that moment the other engine noise became a deafening roar in the confined space and a huge blue SUV surged up the ramp and rammed the front of Claiborne's car, shunting it several feet backwards and crushing its front end with an almighty boom.

Mack slammed on the SUV's brakes, bringing it to a juddering halt beside the Octavia. Jessica and I darted towards the wreckage as Claiborne tried to fight her way past the airbag that had saved her from serious injury. Jessica reached the passenger door first and wrenched it open, dragging Claiborne from the driver's seat by her throat and slamming her against the side of the car.

Claiborne's face was bloodied from the airbag, but she was otherwise unharmed. She made a move for Jessica's gun. Jessica calmly pulled it out of reach, shoved it in the back of her jeans and smashed an elbow into the taller woman's face. Claiborne's arms dropped and her knees buckled at the force of the blow. Jessica took hold of the back of Claiborne's head with both hands and drove a knee deep into her stomach. As she bent double Jessica swept her legs from under her, knocking her to the ground in a crunch of broken glass.

Jessica knelt on top of Claiborne with her knee in the other woman's chest, pulled the gun from the back of her jeans and jammed it beneath Claiborne's chin. I wondered, in that split second, if Jessica even saw the face of the woman who lay beneath her. Did she see the features she was ready to destroy? Or did she see only the evil that had tried to kill us all once, the evil that had forced Jessica to kill to save us?

I watched, my breath held, waiting for the hammer to fall and Jessica to blow Claiborne's skull across the cold concrete floor. I had been there too, and I had seen the foul black thing that calls to us in that moment. I had heard the whispered guarantees of satisfaction and justice, and I knew how seductive its promises could sound. Somehow I had managed to resist.

Now I could only watch as Jessica wrestled with the same temptation. I knew how right and natural this moment could feel, how just, how true. And I prayed she would be as strong as I knew she could be. I prayed she would not fall, for I didn't know how she would rise again.

Only the pull of a trigger – the merest twitch of a finger – stood between Jessica and the destruction, not only of Claiborne, but of herself.

Claiborne too, seemed to sense her fate was in the balance. Her eyes were screwed shut, her mouth twisted in a grimace, her body tensed for the inevitable.

I saw the muscles in Jessica's arm tense and felt a twinge of pain run through my soul.

And then, suddenly, her finger was outside the trigger guard and the gun was pointing at the ceiling. Her fingers opened like a flower welcoming the sun and the gun clattered to the ground. Jessica's fingers slid under Claiborne's jaw and turned her face towards her own.

Claiborne's eyes were open now, bulging as they looked at the serenity on Jessica's face. 'You're lucky this isn't last week,' Jessica said calmly.

She stood up, leaving Claiborne lying on the floor, panting with relief. Mack stepped quickly in as Jessica came towards me. He flipped Claiborne onto her stomach and pulled her hands roughly behind her back, slipping a plastic tie over her wrists and binding them together.

Jessica stepped towards me and fell into my arms. I pulled her close and hugged her like I wanted to pull her deep within my body and protect her with my own flesh and blood.

In truth, I hugged her like I'd always wanted to.

And she hugged me back like I'd always wanted her to.

The spell was broken by Gordon hammering on the inside of the boot, his voice grating along every one of my nerve endings as he shouted for help. 'Could someone, *please*, get me some bloody help! Maybe none of you noticed, but I've been bloody SHOT!'

I took a deep breath and felt Jessica pull away, her fingertips trailing across mine until we were standing side by side, looking down at Claiborne, lying face down where Mack had left her.

Mack walked over to us, using a rag to wipe down the gun he'd lent Jessica. 'Keep an eye on her,' he said. 'I'll make this disappear.' A moment later he was heading back downstairs.

I popped the boot and looked down at Gordon's painfully folded body. He stared back up at me with a look on his face that said he'd only just realised what I was capable of. A trembling, accusing finger pointed at me. 'You told me you didn't know who the accomplice was. You did know, and you used me to get to her.'

'I lied to both of you, Gordon. Deal with it.'

I hauled Gordon out of the boot and dropped him on the ground ten feet away from the woman who wanted him dead. She glared at him across the scattered pieces of glass and a seething hatred tore across her face. 'One way or another,' she told him, 'I will fucking kill you. Whether it's me, or someone I've paid, or someone who owes me a favour – someone will cut your fucking nose off and feed it to you. And that's a fucking guarantee.'

Gordon looked up at me, his eyes moist with fear. 'Please tell me you got that on tape?'

I nodded. 'Every word.' Another lie. Neither Gordon nor Claiborne needed to know I'd turned off the recording when Jessica revealed her presence, ensuring no reference to her having a gun was caught on tape.

'Don't worry, Gordon,' Jessica said. 'The audio and video we've got will see the right people go to jail. No-one's going to dodge this.'

I smiled at Jessica's careful phrasing as I took my phone from my pocket and began to dial.

'Finally!' Gordon cried. 'I'm in bloody agony here!'

You will be in a minute.

'Stewart?' I said when the call was answered. 'It's Harper. It's time you heard the truth.'

'All of it?'

'All of it.'

'When are you coming in?'

'You need to come to me.' I gave him our location, then added, 'And bring some uniforms.'

'Why?'

'I've got two people for you to arrest.'

I hung up before Stewart could ask for an explanation and looked down at Gordon Dunbar with grim satisfaction. I'd watched his eyes throughout my conversation with Stewart and felt a deep sense of justice as they widened in shock and his mouth hung loosely open. He seemed to have forgotten about the pain in his leg.

'Two people?' Gordon asked in a soft voice.

'Did you think you were going to walk away from this?' I asked him.

'You told me you'd protect me if I helped you.'

'I was going to keep it quiet, Gordon. I really did consider it. But you should have realised by now – some things just won't stay buried.'

Epilogue

The sun shone brightly on the west end of Glasgow as I strolled into the outdoor seating area of Oran Mor, on the corner of Byres Road and Great Western Road. It was a popular venue on a warm summer day and, since this Sunday was looking set to be the finest day of the year so far, half of Glasgow seemed determined to find a beer garden and soak up drinks and sunshine in equal measure. This particular beer garden belonged to a converted church and its steeple loomed high above me as I removed my sunglasses and scanned the packed tables.

The small space was crammed full of people, but Nicole was easy to spot since hers was the only face that wasn't smiling. On the contrary, her eyes seemed determined to burn holes in me from the other side of the crowd. Several days had passed since her father had been arrested, but it looked like time had yet to heal that particular wound.

I pushed my way through the crowd and sank down into the seat opposite her. She looked at me for a couple of seconds, then tilted her glass of wine and asked in clipped tones, 'Would you like a drink?'

'No, thanks.'

Nicole took a long drink of wine and placed it very deliberately back on the table. She looked at me again. After a while I began to get bored.

'You wanted to meet?' I reminded her.

'I wanted to tell you that my father has been charged with murder,' she hissed.

'So I hear. Claiborne too. They haven't got the evidence on her yet, but Stewart will find…'

'I don't give a shit about her! I only care about my father. And you used him to get to her. He didn't even know she existed until you risked his life to catch her.'

'Has it occurred to you that it didn't matter if he knew about her or not? Claiborne knew your dad was involved in her lover's death and she was going to kill him for it. And she would have if I hadn't put her away. Nicole, whether you can see it or not, I saved your dad's life.'

'Saved his life? He's going to jail because of you. Because you lied to him. Because you manipulated him so you could get that policewoman on tape.'

'He's going to jail because a man died a horrible, slow death under a ton of earth, and he was involved.' I shook my head sadly as I saw Nicole had adopted her usual response. 'But if you need someone to blame, fine, blame me.'

'You're damn right I'll blame you. I hired you to protect him, not get him locked up.'

'And you chose *me* because you thought you could keep me quiet if he had done something. You thought I'd protect him to protect you.'

'And look what you've done to me!' More heads turned our way. 'You've taken my father away from me. How am I supposed to react to that? How am I supposed to live my life now?'

I rubbed my hand over my chin slowly, hearing the rasp of my stubble beneath my fingers. Nicole was upset at my actions, furious even, but not for how they affected her father, only for the impact they had on her. I looked at her and saw the true selfishness and ugliness of the person within, and this time there were no lingering feelings to cloud the issue.

'You know, Nicole,' I said. 'I did think about that. I thought about keeping quiet. But I knew I couldn't. And I wondered how it would affect you. I wondered what it would do to you, and how it would make you think of me. And you know what I realised?'

'What?'

'That I don't give a fuck what you think.'

I stood up and put my sunglasses back on. Then I turned my

back on Nicole, on the feelings I'd once held, on the years we'd spent together and all those times I'd foolishly longed for her. I walked away from all of that and pushed my way through the crowd. Somewhere behind me I was aware of a voice crying out in anger. A voice I no longer cared to hear.

I squeezed through the last of the crowd and out onto Byres Road. I crossed the road and walked up to the traffic lights where the green man awaited me. I crossed Great Western Road and passed through the gates into the Botanic Gardens.

As expected on a scorching Sunday afternoon, the park was just as busy, and I doubted there would be many takers for tours round the glasshouses. The pathways were heavily populated with kids on bikes and dogs on leads, while the grass lawn was a sea of sprawled figures enjoying the sun before returning to work the following day.

I found Jessica quickly, as though some instinct had guided me to her. She sat at one edge of the lawn, facing away from me, an ice-cream in each hand.

I sat down beside her and lay back on my elbows. She turned to me and smiled as she held out one of the ice-creams. 'You're just in time. Yours was getting all warm and eaten.'

I took what was left of the ice-cream and just carried on looking at her. Jessica turned away again and looked out across the grass, at the children playing, their watchful parents trying to enjoy a few minutes peace; at the couples engrossed in each other; the dog walkers, the baby buggies, at life as it flowed around us. She sat and ate her ice-cream, content simply to watch the world. And I lay beside her, propped up on an elbow, eating mine, content simply to watch her. We stayed like that for a while, I think, though time seemed less than important. Finally, the ice-creams were finished and I couldn't put it off any longer.

'So,' I asked, 'when do you start at Scotspy?'
'I don't. I turned it down.'
'Really? Why?'
'Someone else wanted to give me a job.'
I sat up. 'That's great. Who?'
'You.'

'Oh.'

Jessica turned back to me, took off her sunglasses so I could see her eyes, and she smiled. A real one. One that came from the heart, lit up her eyes and put a life in her cheeks that had been missing for some time. It was a smile that grabbed my heart and shook it.

'I haven't seen that smile in a long time,' I said.

Jessica nodded slowly a few times. Then she lay back on the grass and put her sunglasses back on. 'I was saving it for a special occasion.'

I lay down beside her and closed my eyes against the sun. 'Does this qualify?'

'Oh yeah. This qualifies.'

Then I felt Jessica's hand reach out and touch my own. Her fingers slid in between mine and I closed my hand around hers. She squeezed my hand and I knew I was where I belonged.

Yeah. This qualifies alright.

THE END